DEMON ON DECK

DEBORAH WILDE

te da media inc.
vancouver

ISBN: 978-1-998888-26-9 (paperback)

ISBN: 978-1-998888-25-2 (epub)

Chapter 1

Spa visits were fifty percent less relaxing with a murder in the building. Even spas as painstakingly detailed and chic as Thermae, where no expense had been spared to re-create ancient Roman baths.

The corpse had been fished out of the tepidarium, the largest of four caves at Thermae, each one designed to immerse visitors in an authentic experience.

I looked up at the ceiling arching over the warm pool. The knotted-up tension in my neck and shoulders had eased thanks to the hint of lavender in the air and the soothing instrumental music piped in through speakers hidden in the rough-hewn rocks forming the walls and ceiling. Both were highly appreciated to tone down my amped excitement and nerves on my first solo lead case, even though I was still a level two operative.

Gently glowing pot lights and pillar candles in heavy glass containers painted the ripples golden. It looked heavenly. However, as tempted as I was to book a treatment, a dead person's bathwater was not a selling point.

That said, this was far nicer than a normal crime scene.

Slipping on a pair of latex gloves, I crouched down next to

the victim, careful not to slide on the damp pool deck pavers made of sumptuous blue stone, and winced at the soreness in my muscles. My glutes resented split squats with a fiery passion.

Mason Trinh, my fellow Maccabee operative, swiped beneath the woman's thumbnail with a thin, moistened swab. "Three guesses as to cause of death and the first two don't count. Or does that fall under higher critical thinking and knock you out of the running?"

A heart attack or drowning would have been reasonable assumptions, were it not for the fat wooden stake jammed through the woman's heart.

"Oh, you're in fine form today, you cranky old stump," I said cheerfully.

His mouth kicked up in a half-smile, his bushy mustache twitching in amusement.

"Nice heft and girth, classic lines." I nodded in approval. "This stake is a beauty for killing vamps, but it's an odd choice of murder weapon for an Eishei Kodesh." I hadn't yet confirmed that our victim was a human with magic abilities, but it was a solid assumption. Had she been a vampire, all that would have been left of her was a clump of ashes, and stakes didn't work on demons.

Ask me how I knew.

Mason sealed up the swab as evidence. His careworn expression deepened, the bags under his eyes seeming to develop new bags. "Forty years as an operative, I thought I'd seen it all, but staking someone?" He gestured to a hank of his graying hair with a latex-gloved hand, shooting me an accusing glare. "I've aged before my time. Idiots. What is wrong with people?"

I stood up and smoothed out my navy pinstriped trousers. "Don't look at me. I'm neither stupid nor depraved."

"True. I've got six or seven different adjectives for your list."

"That's still fourteen shorter than my selection for you," I said sweetly. This was regular banter for us. Actually, I was one of the few people who looked forward to our interactions, and this was how he spoke to operatives he half respected and tolerated.

Come to think of it, I'd never met anyone who'd earned his outright admiration.

Other than Director Michael Fleischer, that is.

Mason was a legend in Maccabee circles for single-handedly solving several high-profile cases that had baffled the organization. However, the Vietnamese Canadian operative had moved from investigations to forensics about twenty years ago with a very public declaration that he'd rather spend the rest of his working days with corpses than the incompetent living.

Some days I didn't blame him.

I returned my attention to the dead woman, whom I judged to be in her early forties. The top of her navy bathing suit was soaked in blood, one of the straps hanging off a shoulder. Funny how being stabbed ruined perfectly good swimwear. Less expected was that although her hazel eyes were wide open and her lips were parted in a slight gasp of surprise, other than that, there were no signs of tension like clenched fists, or any indication that she'd struggled with her attacker at all.

"This feels personal," I said.

"Really?" Mason said scathingly enough to flay a person. "You don't think someone happened to be carrying a stake, looked in at reception, and thought, I could book a facial, but that's more of a Tuesday move."

"Aw, there's the tone of voice that makes newbs cry."

He chuckled. "Worked on you more than once."

"I'm older and deader inside now."

"That's the spirit."

"Are you done with the sarcasm?"

3

He shrugged. "Eh. But please. Continue."

"This wasn't random," I said, "and I'd also rule out a contract killing, unless the murderer had instructions to send a message. Off the top of my head, that narrows the possibilities to a vamp or demon compulsion to render her motionless."

"White flame magic is also a contender," he said.

Those Eishei Kodesh dealt in burning passions. They amped up people's emotions, and a powerful one could magically flood someone with calm to the point of remaining practically comatose if attacked. Handy for them, but a pain in the butt to deal with as the operative bringing them in. I hated having my emotions toyed with, for more than one reason.

"True," I said. "Still, an Eishei Kodesh would require a lot of upper-body strength to jam that stake through skin, muscle, and bone."

Say what you would about vampires, the same magic that enhanced their speed, hearing, smell, and strength made them vulnerable to a simple wooden stake. That still didn't make it easy to use one. I regularly did punishing weight training sessions and went on long runs to maintain my strength and stamina, and I didn't expect to fight many vampires in my line of work. I mostly policed Eishei Kodesh crimes.

All of which brought me back to how it would be much harder to use a stake on a human. Especially for the average person with a desk job and perilously little in the way of shoulder strength.

Ooh, this case was going to prove fun to puzzle out. Not that I wished death on anyone, but I'd spent the last two days helping out on an embezzlement case involving a fried chicken chain, where I'd combed through reams of mind-numbing files that reeked of grease.

"What else do you read from the body?" Mason liked to lob pop quizzes at operatives that had only two grades: begrudging pass or withering contempt.

The woman sported gel polish—intact and recently

touched up—on all her nails and her makeup was tastefully applied.

"She came here before work," I said. "A business owner, maybe a CEO?"

Her shoulder-length strawberry-blond hair fanned out on the deck around her head like a peacock's tail, though her cool undercut on one side was in need of a touch-up.

"Not any field that was too conservative," I added, "given her hairstyle."

"The spa owner said our vic ran a private consulting firm," Mason said. "She's been coming to Thermae every six months or so for a few years now."

An elaborate tattoo of vines and flowers peeked out the top of her bloody bathing suit. Sometimes tattoos had significance and sometimes they didn't. I made a note to get a photo from Mason and look into the design later.

"What else do we know about the vic?" I said.

Mason snapped a few photos of the body. "Only what she filled out when she booked the appointment. Emily Astor. Red Flame. There's a number and address in her file."

Businesses dealing with Eishei Kodesh in any hands-on manner were required to have them sign liability forms in case their magic was unexpectedly unleashed, but also so that practitioners knew which safeguards to have in place. Fire extinguishers, for example, if their client was a Red Flame. That magic devoured matter and burned things away—all it took was simple physical contact.

All Eishei Kodesh, translated from the Hebrew as Holy Fire People, had fire-based magic. The same flame that burned for eight days and nights in the Hanukkah miracle was used back around 150 BCE in a ritual, now lost in the fog of time, to create inherent magic ability. There was only one kind at first (the red flame ability), which, since it was the sole type of magic, didn't initially have a color classification.

The magic spread over the centuries through other races

and religions, and, like many a trait, changed and evolved. Maccabees catalogued the new powers using a system of colors seen from largest to smallest in a flame: red, orange, yellow, white, and blue. They coincided with the order of the most common power to the rarest.

I sidestepped a puddle. "There were easier ways to kill Ms. Astor. Easier places too." Whoever had done this hadn't taken her out in a parking garage, but in a place where Emily went to relax. Where she let down her guard. That was more evidence that her murderer had a serious beef with her.

Speaking of security, how did the perp get into the pool undetected by the owner? There was an emergency exit door in the short corridor outside the changing rooms, which led to the alley, but I'd verified that the crash bar was dead-bolted from the inside.

I made a note to ask the owner about other employees with keys.

The other way into Thermae was through the front door, and only the owner was currently working. Mason said she'd been up front until she locked that door to come give her client a massage and found her dead.

"Where's the owner now?" I blotted my forehead with the back of my hand. It was muggy as shit in here. Good thing my suit jacket hid pit stains. "What's her name?"

"Dawn Keller." Mason fished an evidence marker out of his bag and laid it next to the victim's chest as a size indicator of the stake. "Rachel offered to stay with Ms. Keller in her office." Rachel, another forensics tech, was a calming presence in the worst of crises. "Ms. Keller was understandably hysterical."

Or a good actor with a killer motive. Time would tell which it was.

However, if she was innocent, then she had my sympathies. It was bad enough finding a dead body, especially one she'd gotten to know as a regular customer, but if the media got hold of this, her business would suffer. A one-off murder didn't generally warrant Maccabee intervention with the press, but maybe I could petition the director to keep the spa's name out of any news reports in support of a local business.

"Did you sedate her at all?" I said, hoping Mason replied in the negative. It would counteract my magic ability to spot any weakness in Dawn when I questioned her.

I couldn't determine if someone was lying—that was a different Blue Flame talent—but most people showed signs of strain when concocting a story. I'd read those weaknesses and draw my own conclusions. My gut insisted that given the potential negative impact on Ms. Keller's spa, she wasn't involved, but I'd keep an open mind until that was definitively ruled out.

"No sedative," Mason said.

"I appreciate that." I made some notes on my phone, along with follow-up questions for our coroner, Dr. Malika Ayad, back at Vancouver Maccabee HQ.

It was best to interview Ms. Keller as quickly as possible, but first…

There was no reason to use the magic I'd inherited from my unknown demon daddy to check if Emily was a half shedim. Emily's death wasn't anything like that of the six infernals who were murdered in brutal ritualistic killings for their blood. However, it had been less than a week since wrapping up that investigation. I couldn't shake off the images of their tortured bodies, never mind the persistent inkling that they were part of a much bigger scheme, with more deaths certain to come.

I slid into my magic vision.

Each type of Eishei Kodesh magic involved one characteristic of fire. Blue Flames illuminated things. We shone light on that which was hidden, applying our powers to everything from mineral veins deep underground to flaws in existing physical structures or technology.

My specialty was people, and while my talent didn't work postmortem, my half-demon powers allowed me to identify other infernals. It was trickier when they were no longer breathing, but not impossible.

See, all Eishei Kodesh magic was synesthete, though it presented differently for the various types. We Blue Flames experienced our magic visually. I saw blue dots or streaks in people.

The main part of my demon magic had the same synesthetic quality, though I had no idea whether that was always the case or it was because it piggybacked on my Eishei Kodesh ability.

Regardless, there were shifting blue shadows in the backs of infernals' heads—in our primal brain. This was the section responsible for survival, drive, and instinct, and the place humans operated from during a loss of rationality, when we were overpowered by strong emotions. Generally, I saw them only on people who were alive.

But as I'd recently discovered, the shifting shadows in an infernal's brain swam down to harden into a fat blue double knot in the middle of the chest when under stress. Like when they were being murdered. All people felt shock and fear in their upper chests, but with infernals, it manifested as that double knot—and remained there postmortem.

I checked the victim's upper chest first, relieved it was knot-free. "Can I turn her head to the side?"

"There's no blunt trauma to the skull," Mason said.

"I want to examine it anyway, if that won't compromise anything."

He motioned his assent, no doubt thinking that I was a total idiot but liking me enough to let me be one.

I carefully maneuvered her skull. No shifting shadows here either. Not that I expected it. The two other half shedim I'd examined after their deaths hadn't shown those shadows, but best to double-check.

Emily Astor wasn't an infernal.

Sighing in relief that this wasn't a hate crime on top of being a terrible way to die, I pulled off my gloves with a sharp snap and thanked Mason.

He grunted, removed a pair of scissors from his bag, and cut open Emily's bathing suit. The stake had been jammed in with so much force that it was splintered at the entry point.

Her tattoo covered her torso. It was misshapen from the swelling and bruising on her chest, but once the design was revealed, an odd detail emerged.

A perfect two-inch circle of the tattoo was missing around the wound.

"You know," I heard myself saying, "somehow I don't think she got herself tattooed specifically with a big stake-me-here piece missing. That's…huh."

"Emily Astor," Mason said slowly, "said she was a Red Flame."

I gestured to the perfect circle. "This is not normal—"

Mason held up a hand. "Say she lied. Say she was a Yellow Flame, the kind with inherent healing magic." He sighed. "That would explain the tattoo removal, but it would have kicked in while her killer was staking her, and also fixed her ribs. Any guesses as to how many of those are still broken?"

I scowled. "I'm going to guess it's not the answer it should be for a Yellow Flame healer, which would be zero."

"Two."

"Then what's going on here?" I threw my hands up. "Is this another teachable moment?"

"No." His seriousness alarmed me. The most experienced forensics expert on Maccabee staff was honestly perplexed about something?

"The gap definitely isn't on purpose. It's not part of the design." I narrowed my eyes, comparing the ink-free area with the rest of the tattoo. "It's as if the stake broke the magic anchoring the ink in place and that much of her skin healed before she died. Except humans don't require magic to prevent automatic tattoo healing." A chill came over me. "Only vampires do."

Vamps' fast-acting healing abilities meant they couldn't keep a tattoo on their body without Eishei Kodesh magic pinning it to their skin. Without the assistance of this human magic, or in a case where that magic pinning was broken, say with a stake, a vamp's tattoo would start to disappear.

Except, there was one enormous problem with that line of thinking.

"Vamps don't leave a body behind when they're killed." Mason muttered under his breath about clusterfucks happening three months away from his retirement. Operatives died in our line of work, and while most survived to live out their golden years, that downtime was well-earned.

I barely registered his comment over my heartbeat thudding against my chest like a car careening into a concrete barrier. In a world where 99.99% of all vamps were turned humans, supernatural beings who thoughtfully vanished without a trace when staked, there existed a legendary rarity.

Born vampires, also known as Primes.

The odds were against Emily being one, given that even with all my Maccabee intel, I knew of only a single existing Prime. However, in the pro column was the tattoo disruption and how born vamps were the sole undead who could grow their hair. Our vic had that undercut in need of a trim, whereas for a made vamp they couldn't grow their hair unless they got extensions.

If my hypothesis was correct?

A breath shuddered out of me.

Say hello to Emily Astor, rare bloodsucker and giant liar. No Red Flame for her, oh no. She was a Prime, the one breaking the undead mold. I didn't know if Primes left a body when they were killed, because there were no records of Prime murders anywhere in the Maccabee archives.

Believe me, I'd checked after I broke up with my ex.

How had someone gotten a jump on a Prime? That should have been impossible.

I took a deep breath, but inhaling a field's worth of lavender wouldn't calm me down. Even other vampires or demons shouldn't have been able to compel Emily to meekly comply with her own death.

Vampires cared a lot about power. They were obsessed with presenting the image of being unkillable, untouched by the ravages of time. If word got out that a Prime, the flagship symbol of their immortality and unbeatable strength, was murdered, well, that very dangerous population was not going to be pleased.

They would, in fact, seek to restore that image of unassailable power at any cost. Knowing vampires as well as I did, that PR maneuver wasn't going to be pretty. It would, in fact, be antonyms of "pretty."

I raised my eyes to the ceiling. Bravo, universe, you just turned what should have been a fun murder puzzle into a terrifying mess.

Chapter 2

Mason, still grumbling, hadn't made that connection to Primes, and until I was certain I was one thousand percent correct, I didn't dare voice it. I didn't want to get him in trouble pursuing an unfounded theory—or spook him.

If Emily was a Prime, then the fact that those vampires didn't dissolve into ash was a well-kept secret. So well-kept that my organization founded thousands of years ago precisely to keep humans safe from vampires and demons wasn't aware of it, otherwise we'd have been taught something this important as novices.

I steeled my shoulders, a sick feeling in my gut, because there was only one way to quickly verify my theory.

How exactly did one ask an ex if you could stake him, then sit back and admire your handiwork? Should I lead with a joke or ask it like a scientific hypothetical? What would Ezra Cardoso, Crimson Prince and single known Prime in existence before today, prefer?

"I'm going to make a quick call," I said.

"Okay. I'm texting Rachel to help me pack up, so meet us at the transport van in the alley."

"Got it." I exited the cave into the central relaxation area of Thermae.

It boasted an elaborate mosaic on the floor and a frescoed ceiling of a forest complete with stags and birds hidden among the trees. Comfort was assured with padded sling chairs, a glass shower with six jets, and to further relax clients, a table with a hot water dispenser and a basket containing tins of loose tea. The more modern décor stood out against the ancient Roman aesthetic, but it was understandable that patrons would prefer a nice chair over a historically accurate stone bench.

I eyed the chilled lemon water sweating in the glass pitcher.

Pity it wasn't straight gin.

The four caves that created this immersive Roman bathing experience "worthiest of the noblest empress" flowed clockwise off this lounge area. Mason had given me a quick rundown on them. Each one had a fancy Latin name and a specific purpose.

The tepidarium, where Emily was found, was the first cave in a journey of pools and rooms with varying temperatures. Visitors kicked things off by relaxing in the body-temperature warmth of the water to strengthen the immune system without shocking the circulation system.

From there, they progressed to a small round cistern, where they alternated between a cold-water plunge pool and a dry-heat sauna. The third cave also had a cool-water pool, along with a steam room for sweating out toxins. The belief was that continually moving from a hot environment to a cold one stimulated blood flow, reduced tension, and improved breathing.

I wasn't some expert on Roman ablutions; there were handy plaques at the entrance of each cave detailing their purpose. I rubbed my neck, once more a hard wall of tension. Should my hypothesis be proved wrong—and they sanitized the bathing pool—I was totally treating myself to a session here, and not coming out until I was a puddle of blissed-out jelly. Could I expense it as a health benefit?

The final cave was divided into smaller treatment rooms for massages and facials.

I pulled out my phone. I'd have privacy to call Ezra in one of the treatment rooms, but cell reception was spotty enough in here, so I shouldered through the door and along the short hallway into the changing room.

The thick wood door shut with a quiet click, enveloping me in a tranquil hush. Even the changing room was designed to relax guests, with low lighting, subtle orange-scented diffusers, and calming sandstone colors. I washed my hands with the organic soap, closing my eyes and letting the warm water from the copper taps clean off the shock and horror of my revelation about Emily being a Prime, but no amount of lathering or inhaling the gentle scents in here would make my next task less stressful.

After a quick double-check to ensure I was alone, I sat down on the bench alongside the row of lockers, which were designed to resemble blocks of stone. Only one was locked.

I'd examine Emily's personal belongings later, but first I opened my text app. Although there was a strong cell signal here, I hesitated because this wasn't exactly the kind of topic one broached in a casual message. I could phone Ezra, but this would be a sensitive and uncomfortable topic for both of us, and I planned to use his initial reaction to determine how shocked he was by this information. That was only possible via a video call.

Unbeknownst to me, my ex had been working as a Maccabee operative for the past four years, gathering intel under the guise of being a jet-setting playboy. His mask game was strong, but I still knew him better than anyone, even though we'd broken up six years ago and I'd seen him again only recently.

Seen him. That was the understatement of the century. Try: I was once more familiar with the feel of his lips on mine. He no longer kissed me with a shy sweetness but an electric intensity bordering on a declaration of war. We'd done a stellar job of not discussing it, keeping our conversations since then strictly professional. Asking him about staking Primes ensured there'd be no repeats.

Exactly what I wanted.

Ezra had remained at the same hotel for the past few days since we wrapped up our last case, putting out discreet feelers on our next steps to track down the blood collected from the murdered half shedim on that investigation. However, we expected him to be reassigned to his next Maccabee gig anytime now.

He might have already checked out. Be completely unreachable. I wasn't sure whether to cross my fingers.

I stabbed the call button. Hopefully, I'd know if he lied to me when I asked my question. Not for the first time, I wished I could illuminate weaknesses in vampires, but that happened only when I was in a demon realm.

Ezra answered, wearing a towel wrapped around his waist. Water dripped from his jet-black curls onto his chiseled bare chest, glistening down his brown skin, and clouds of steam billowed in the air behind him.

I couldn't even objectively appreciate the sight because my mind conjured an image of his silvery-blue eyes dulled and lifeless, blood seeping down that immaculate torso, speared with a stake.

"Did you just moan?" he said in an amused voice, his smooth, low baritone hitting me like a shot of the finest whiskey.

I scrubbed a hand over my face, banishing the image of him impaled like Emily.

Ezra frowned and peered at the screen. "You look ill, and since it couldn't possibly be the sight of my—"

I swung a locker door open and shut with a loud clang, like I required the momentum of the action to voice my question. "Do Primes leave a body when staked?"

His expression didn't change, but his eyes darkened with the barest flash.

I white-knuckled the phone.

"Vampires don't leave bodies," he said.

I closed my eyes. Nice avoidance.

"Aviva?" he said sharply.

I blinked them open and began pacing alongside the long stone table under the mirrors, which held fluffy piles of folded robes and towels along with baskets of bath products. "Female, reddish-blond hair, hazel eyes, looks in her early forties. She was staked during a spa visit."

Ezra laughed, but it had a bladed edge. "I hope she didn't pay extra for a happy ending." He shifted the angle of the screen, allowing me to glimpse the tattooed line in Spanish on his left biceps. I grabbed a screenshot to examine it later because he hadn't been inked when we were together, and this was the first time I'd had a clear view of it.

The combination of Ezra having a more muscular physique than when we'd been together and this unfamiliar tattoo made me feel momentarily disoriented. The photos I'd seen of him over the past six years were impersonal snapshots. Seeing him bare chested, it hit me in a visceral way that this body was, in effect, a stranger's.

I was no longer the woman most familiar with the shape of him, and it took me aback that despite everything, some part of me had believed I was. Not that I was the person to unravel his intricate psychological layers, but that I still held the map to his body, and where other lovers might know the divot of his hips or the swell of his biceps, I alone had charted every inch.

A pang of betrayal twisted in my stomach. He'd gone and redeveloped himself like he wanted nothing of his past to remain. Yet, intertwined with this betrayal was a sense of curiosity and intrigue. Who was this new Ezra? What experiences had shaped him into the man before me? It was simultaneously thrilling and terrifying to think that there were parts of him I had yet to discover.

He slid on a knitted bathrobe in royal blue that resembled a boxer's wrap with an oversize hood that looked crazy comfy. Had he made that, sitting by a fire, letting the click of the needles and the feel of the yarn wash away his cares?

I wrenched my eyes—and my thoughts—away, and exhaled. This call was getting off track. "Any idea how someone could attack a Prime without them fighting back?" I injected a note of levity into my voice, hoping to make him amenable to giving me some useful information. "For reasons purely related to the case."

"They couldn't," he said flatly.

Yes, you are the baddest of the bad. I massaged my temples. *We all bow down before your prowess.* I gathered my shredded patience by my metaphoric fingertips and swallowed any snarky retort. "Our victim had a tattoo covering her torso, except on the broken skin surrounding the weapon."

Ezra went so still that I checked to make sure the screen hadn't frozen, but no, he'd grasped this damning piece of evidence. "Stop all forensics and lock the scene down immediately until I get there," he commanded.

My ex's first language was Spanish, and though he usually didn't have an accent when he spoke English, it peppered his harsh tone now.

His anger didn't bother me, but his high-handed directive sure did. He'd shown up on our previous investigation with special dispensation from the Maccabee Secretary of the Authority Council to lead it, though that wasn't the case now. This was plain old Prime paranoia and self-defense. And okay, maybe a heaping side of Ezra-knows-best.

However, in the end, this was my investigation and mine alone.

"If you have relevant information," I said, "then share it with me. As the lead operative on the scene, I'll take appropriate action."

Good thing Ezra didn't need to breathe because his cursing me out in Spanish went on for a long time. He curled his fingers in like claws, and I got the sense that he wished he could reach through the screen and throttle me. "Have you forgotten our last case so soon? Someone put a target on infernals' backs. Now you want to be front and center on a case involving a Prime that is going to attract unwanted attention? Do you want to be found out?"

I'd guarded the secret of my half-shedim nature ("shedim," the plural Hebrew term, was used conventionally for both singular and multiple demons, like the word "fish") from everyone except my mother and Ezra. However, another vampire and Maccabee operative called Roman Whittaker, who'd been one of the two killers in our last case, had known what I was.

I hadn't shared that bombshell with anyone; Ezra was simply extrapolating from the bigger picture.

He was also evading my order to report any relevant information.

"I'm a Maccabee with a job to do," I said with steely steadiness. "I took an oath, and I won't run away, regardless of who or what the victim is, or how dangerous this case is. I didn't do it when my kind was being killed and I won't do it when yours is."

"You're not equipped to deal with this," he said with forced patience. "Only I am."

Cherry Bomb, the Brimstone Baroness, as I fondly called my shedim side, opened her eyes from the dark pool deep inside me where she lived. She whispered several bloodthirsty, violent, and possibly anatomically impossible ways to show Ezra how wrong he was.

Yeah, she was me, and yeah, I referred to her in the third person. It was like how some people talked about their lizard brain or subconscious self as a separate being from their logical side. Granted, when other people said, "You don't want to meet the person I am before I've had my coffee—she'll destroy you!" they generally didn't mean it in a literal sense. But my Cherry Bomb was a bit more intense than your garden variety id.

"If me or my forensics team are in danger, then tell me. Right. Now." I practically growled into the phone.

"You're not. None of you are."

I searched his face, but my gut said he was telling the truth. Then what was with his reaction? Damn Ezra and his secrets.

"Do I have to secure the scene for any reason other than you keeping your cards close to your chest?" I said.

"Step away from this, Aviva."

"I'll add that to my to-do list. Now, if you have nothing to add...?"

"Don't you da—"

I hung up on him. Then I slammed two or three locker doors and let out a strangled scream.

For all I knew, he intended to not only steamroll this investigation but invoke some bullshit political reason and keep us from finding Emily's killer at all.

Well, tough shit. He wasn't going rogue to hunt that person down. The perp had to face justice, not vengeance.

Prime or not, Ezra had taken the same Maccabee vow that I had: tikkun olam.

The Hebrew phrase and our organization's motto referred to a mystical approach to all mitzvot, or good deeds. Broadly, it communicated the responsibility of Jews, now extended to all operatives, to fix the wrongs in the world.

Ezra could suck it up and play ball.

I shook off my irritation.

Mason would transport Emily's body to Malika at HQ any moment now. Our coroner would figure out that the victim was a Prime, and I had to speak to our director before that happened.

Oh joy. Perhaps if I spiked Michael's tea with a handful of Xanax before casually mentioning the murdered Prime in her territory she'd be chill about it? Hmm. Best to do a sweep of her office for projectiles, just to be safe.

I still had to speak to the spa owner, Dawn Keller, but I also needed to give Mason and Rachel a heads-up to stay alert for any trouble. I had nothing concrete to caution them about, but Emily being a Prime meant trouble on its own, even without Ezra's cagey warning. Sadly, I didn't dare tell them her status until I'd spoken to the director.

I entered the lounge area expecting the team to still be packing up. Mason's insistence on fitting things back in the van like he was playing *Tetris* with his life on the line made cleaning up a lengthy process.

But there was no sign of Mason, Rachel, the body, or any of Mason's gear. The candles in the tepidarium had all been snuffed out, and the music was off.

My poor heart had finally returned to a normal rhythm after the call with Ezra. Now either Mason had ditched his *Tetris* organizational ways for good (unlikely) or something had happened to my team. Bye-bye, calm.

A petite plump woman in her fifties, her trousers rolled up and her feet in flip-flops, hosed down the pool deck. She gave me a vaguely confused smile and tilted her head, making her dangling silver earrings swing. "Hello, dear. Do you have an appointment today or are you interested in more information about our services at Thermae?"

The skin between my shoulder blades prickled. This was

the woman who'd been freaking out because a client had been killed in her spa? "Ms. Keller?"

"Yes, of course." She smiled, a perfect customer service smile unmarred by unexpected corpses and panic. "I'm always so pleased whenever anyone's heard of my services. Word of mouth and trust is so crucial in my profession."

Luckily (or unluckily) for her, the strength to stake a vampire was also not crucial to her profession. This was also not a case of Rachel doing too good a job to calm Dawn down. Something was off.

I broke out my blue flame magic and scanned her for weakness. Her brain had deep navy swathes in it, indicating someone had messed with her mind. I tapped my fist against my forehead; a poor substitute for banging my head against the wall. "Were a man and a woman just here?"

"No." She twisted the copper tap shut. "I haven't had any clients yet today." She stumbled over the words, then frowned, her brows creased.

"Wait here. I'll be back." I bolted out of the spa area, down the corridor, and crashed through the emergency exit into the alley.

The transport van was gone.

Rain slanted down on me as I hit Mason's contact number, chanting "Pick up pick up" under my breath, but he didn't answer. Neither did Rachel.

I ran back into the spa on rubbery legs, but I couldn't let my anxiety for my colleagues' safety show and upset Dawn.

"My name is Aviva Fleischer and I'm a level two Maccabee operative. I need you to come with me, please." I showed Dawn the brushed gold pillbox ring on my right index finger, identifying me as a Maccabee.

We'd named ourselves after the heroes of the Hanukkah miracle—honoring them and their flame that formed the basis of our magic. Our ring reflected that heritage. The top of its round compartment featured an embossed flame circled by five tiny gems symbolizing each type of magic: red, orange, yellow, white, and blue.

All human Maccabees received their rings upon graduating from Maccababy novice to level one operative, and we never took them off. The part of our initiation ceremony that meant the most to me was the moment I slid the ring onto my finger and pledged the Maccabee motto. Finally, I was a part of something bigger than myself, changing the world for the better rather than trying to stop it from getting any worse.

"I can't leave." Dawn shook her head. "I have a client."

"They canceled." Rachel had phoned people booked in for today. "Please. Time is of the essence." When Dawn didn't comply, I prodded her to lock up and hustled her as nicely as possible to my car, skirting the bigger puddles. She'd grabbed a rain jacket; I got wet.

Dawn was understandably furious and upset, threatening to file a complaint against me. I sighed. It was better to have her alive and angry than another victim. More of a victim than she already was, I amended, given her current memory loss.

Regardless, I had to find Mason and Rachel, and I wasn't leaving Dawn alone.

I helped her into the car and ran around to the driver's side, phoning in a request to activate the tracker on the transport van. All official Maccabee vehicles had them. If I didn't justify the request with proper paperwork, I'd have a strip torn off me later, but that was a problem for future me. All that mattered now was that my request was granted by the time I cranked the ignition in my beat-up hatchback.

I squealed out of my parking spot, following the pulsing red line on my phone's screen toward Mason, Rachel—and Emily's corpse.

My wipers sped back and forth, a metronome to my panic level as I wove in and out of traffic, smashing down on my horn every few seconds.

Dawn screamed that I was a maniac and she'd see me arrested for kidnapping.

The gap to the transport van narrowed on the tracking screen, but the lump in my gut grew because they weren't headed to HQ.

I jammed my foot down harder on the gas pedal; too bad it was already floored.

Minutes later, I caught up to the van. It was parked in one of the two stalls around the back of a café.

"Stay!" I barked at Dawn.

Rachel sat in the passenger seat, scrolling on her phone. She jumped when I rapped on the window. "Aviva?"

I practically hopped up and down, flooded with anxiety. "Where's Mason? Where's the body?"

"What body? We stopped for coffee. You want one? I'll text him."

I sprinted around the back of the van and threw open the doors.

Mason's bag and laptop were gone. There was no evidence.

And no Emily.

I screamed out a swear so loud it scattered the birds from the trees.

Someone had killed a Prime and then stolen the corpse out from under the Maccabees. When this got out, there'd be a huge outcry, some very angry vampires, and who knew what response from the members of the Authority.

I braced a hand on the van door, my chest tight.

Someone would be blamed for this colossal mess, and I was the operative in charge on the scene. I'd spent less than two hours on my first case as a solo lead, and at this rate, they were likely to be my last. Heads were going to roll, mine probably among them. Hopefully not literally, but then again, we were working with vampires and the director, and with those two dangerous entities, nothing was off the table.

Chapter 3

One hundred and thirty-seven seconds was nothing in the grand scheme of life, not even a blip. However, I'd swear that in the one hundred and thirty-seven seconds that had passed between me delivering my status report and now, an entire ice age had manifested.

Maybe that glacial silence from Michael Fleischer, the director of the Vancouver chapter of the Maccabees, was actually shock, given she'd just learned I was the only person with any memory of the crime scene, and that we had no evidence and no body.

Or maybe the silence simply felt glacial because Michael —tapping her pen against the blotter on her desk at hummingbird speed—was also my mother. There was a chance I was oversensitive to her silences. Where others clocked a thoughtful pause, I saw a dangerous calculation.

Perhaps she was simply running through all the ramifications and implications of this crime, and the steely glint in her green eyes was not a visual cue that she was about to tear into me for this gong show.

Yeah, that was wishful thinking. With my luck, it'd be

Michael calculating *and* tearing me apart at the same time. My mother was nothing if not efficient.

It didn't matter that there was no way I could have foreseen any of this. Maccabees did not engage in excuses. We also did not assign blame, for example, on our exes for not being one hundred percent clear and precise that our victim's corpse was at risk of being body snatched.

I was the lead on-site, and I should have done more to secure the scene.

Don't lose the body. Procedure 101. My fellow operatives were going to have a field day when this got out.

I risked a glance at Darsh, the vampire Maccabee I'd brought with me to Michael's office. He was the first member of the Spook Squad that I'd found when I got back to HQ, and with a possible Prime as our victim, he needed to be in this meeting. He was also my good friend who I desperately wanted here for moral support.

Or, at almost six feet to my five-foot-five, to hide behind, if necessary.

Darsh looked from Michael to me, widened his large brownish-gold eyes, which were ringed in dark liner, cocked his head sideways, and mimed being caught in a hangman's noose.

I glared at him.

He winked and crossed one long leg over the other, the complicated buckles on his pants clinking softly. "Michael," he drawled, "could you put me in charge of this case before you stroke out?"

I sat up ramrod straight, internally cursing my still rain-damp suit. The fabric was bunched in the most unfortunate places. "No way. I'm the only one with any memory of the crime scene. We'll partner up."

Co-leading wouldn't earn me my coveted promotion to level three, but at this point, I wasn't sure what would.

Darsh ran a hand over his cropped black faux fur sweater

with a disarming casualness. "The victim wasn't simply a vampire, she was a Prime. This is Spook Squad jurisdiction." He pursed his lips into a mock pout. "Also, not to rub salt in an obviously fresh wound, but all of my bodies have an excellent track record of staying where I leave them."

I was going to kill him.

"Since it's all about you," Michael said without heat.

He knotted his shoulder-length silky brown hair into a messy bun. "Obviously."

I no longer braced myself when he snarked back at her. Mostly. I also no longer felt that sting of jealousy that he always got away with it.

Less mostly.

"How about some credit for figuring out Emily was a Prime and not a Red Flame?" I said. "Otherwise, this investigation would be headed down the wrong road and wasting valuable time." I crossed my arms. "Michael. Come on. I take full responsibility for what happened, but I'm the only one who has any firsthand knowledge of the crime scene. It's more expedient to allow me to at least co-lead."

"Director Fleischer, my apologies." Boyd Cranston, the level three operative who'd assigned me the case, poked his head in. He wasn't unusually tall or thin, but when he moved, he left the impression that he was part human, part wacky-waving-inflatable-car-lot-tube-man.

Inwardly, I groaned. I'd hoped he wouldn't catch wind of my return until after Michael verified I was still in charge.

Dawn Keller had called the Maccabees when she found Emily's body, instead of the Trad (self-labeled Traditionals, or people without magic) cops, since according to the victim's paperwork, she was Eishei Kodesh.

The level one operative who took the call passed it up the chain to a level three as per procedure, and Boyd was available. He'd reassigned the case to me, a level two. An atypical move.

Boyd loped across the office and grasped me by the upper arm. "Fleischer should have reported to me directly. I'm so sorry that she troubled you. I'll handle this." His fake concern over Michael's well-being combined with his ingratiating smile and weaselly voice turned my stomach.

I pulled free.

"There's nothing to handle, Boyd," the director said mildly. "I'm reassigning the case."

Darsh and I leaned forward, waiting for the object of the sentence, but Michael did not elaborate.

Boyd crossed his arms, an ungainly maneuver where one arm came up first and then the other flopped over it. "You can't. I'm the ranking operative who took the call."

Michael leaned back in her chair and steepled her fingers. "Everyone is so helpful today, reminding me how chain of command works." She broke out a smile reminiscent of one that Bruce, the shark in *Finding Nemo*, wore—before he went for blood.

I hastily looked over at the wall of living green bamboo reeds so as not to meet her eyes. Darsh, meantime, had gotten very interested in his sparkly blue nail polish.

Boyd, the idiot, continued sulking and looking directly at her. He could have only learned that Mason and Rachel had their memories wiped, but that was more than sufficient to make this case interesting enough that he wanted it back. "I figured the last time you let your daughter have a hand in running a case that it was a one-off, but if you continue to play favorites, I'll—"

Oh no, he didn't. I half rose out of my seat.

Darsh caught my arm and nodded at Michael.

Her expression right now would universally be described as predatory.

Boyd finally had the good sense to look abashed.

Michael gestured for him to continue. "Please describe what, exactly, you'll do."

"Nothing," he mumbled.

"That's right. And you know why? Not because I can assign a case to any operative of my choosing, but because you lost any rights to this investigation the second you sent Aviva to that spa to handle this on her own. You assumed it was some rich housewife who'd been murdered, and you couldn't be bothered to handle it personally. Did you make your tee off? So annoying how work gets in the way of a good golf game."

Glaring at me, Boyd opened his mouth, but Michael held up a hand.

"No," she said. "Operative Fleischer did not rat you out. I've worked with you long enough to know why she was sent alone. Understand this, Operative Cranston, if I want to make a goldfish the lead on this investigation over you, I will, and you won't say one word about it. Are we clear?"

Boyd bobbed his head, beads of sweat dotting his receding hairline. "Yes, Director."

"Go."

He bolted.

Michael stood up and followed him. "You two, stay put." She left her office, calling out for her assistant, Louis, before closing the door, leaving Darsh and me alone.

Darsh snickered. "Goldfish."

I grabbed a pen and chucked it at his chest. "You're an ass."

He caught it before impact and lightly tossed it back on Michael's desk. "I could say that there's no such thing as friendship when it comes to snagging lead, puiul meu, but I'm doing this precisely out of friendship."

He used a Romani term of endearment that roughly translated to "baby chick," which I normally thought was sweet, but I wasn't feeling the affection back for him right now.

"Your motives better be good or I'll tar and feather you," I said dryly.

"Promises, promises." He smirked, but then all the amused sparkle left his eyes. "Given what happened in the first hour of this investigation, it isn't going to lead anywhere good. You're not strong enough to handle any blowback." He cut off my protest. "Not from a lack of operative experience, but because you aren't a vampire. I'm a lot harder to kill than you are, Avi."

I twisted my hands in my lap. "Shit, Darsh, they're staking people out there. I don't want you to be a target either."

He stretched his jewelry-free hands out in front of him. Vamp magic interfered with the demon-killing magic cocktail stored in the rings, so undead operatives were exempt from wearing them. Besides, they could kill demons without an extra magic assist. "Despite my incredibly supple skin, I'm a lot tougher than I look."

I had no doubt. Darsh's age was unknown, but he was old, he was smart, and he was a survivor.

He was also one of the palest people I'd ever met. Vamps kept whatever skin tone they'd had in life, but Darsh hadn't liked going out in the sun when he was human. (Wrinkles and freckles? Ugh!) Vampires who'd been Eishei Kodesh had some measure of protection from the sun's rays and could stay awake during the day—unlike undead who'd been Trad—but Darsh still stuck to the shadows.

My hilarity died.

Darsh was staring out the window with a melancholic expression, like he was a bird who was supposed to fly south, except he'd lost his way and wasn't sure how to get back on the right path. He lapsed into this mood sometimes, but I hadn't seen it in a while and had hoped he'd mourned its cause and moved on.

The first time Ezra and Darsh met, my ex revealed that Darsh was the only vamp to escape punishment from the

Maccabees by striking a deal to become an operative. All details of that long-ago negotiation had been lost in an earthquake in a far-off city, and neither Sachie nor I had ever heard a whisper of that story before.

I wondered now if that was the reason for these moods he lapsed into. Part of me wanted to ask, to get him to talk to me, but it didn't feel fair, given the secrets I kept from him.

Since Michael hadn't returned yet, I kicked off my heels and flexed my feet against her plush light gray area rug, while I massaged one of the thousand knots out of my neck. If only I hadn't left the scene to phone Ezra.

I pressed my thumb into a large knot and winced. It wouldn't have made the situation any better. I would have lost my memory as well, and the body would still be missing.

I'd questioned Rachel, Mason, and Dawn while I waited for Maccabee healers to arrive. The operatives didn't remember being at Thermae, or how they got to the café. They'd seen the familiar mural on the side of the café's building and assumed they were there for a coffee run.

Dawn Keller didn't remember anything about her first client of the day and had to be sedated when she learned her spa was the site of a murder. I'd left right after one of our healers phoned Dawn's husband to come stay with her in the safe house she was being taken to. Until this was wrapped up, she'd remain under our protection.

I didn't mention the Prime angle or go into details of the crime, but Rachel was super pissed off when I told her about the memory loss. Her anger was healthy, compared to Mason's silence. Nothing I said, not even a self-deprecating comment, roused him to answer. He looked defeated, which broke my heart—and stiffened my resolve.

This man's illustrious career wasn't going to be stained in its final months by a perp getting one over on him. That wouldn't be the end of his story.

I drummed my fingers on the arm of my chair, waiting for

the director to return. Why hadn't whoever tampered with their memories affected mine? Had they been targeted while they were in the alley and the memory loss didn't extend as far as the changing room where I was?

Obsessing over everything was driving me crazy, so I pulled up my phone and flicked through my news feed. "Check it out. News of a robbery in our fair city has gone viral." I leaned over to share the screen, nudging my friend to look away from the window.

It took Darsh a second to come back from wherever his head had gone, but he read the breaking news banner. "Stolen artifacts = supernatural sticky fingers?" He rolled his eyes. "Catchy."

I played the video. The coverage started out less inflammatory than I expected. A number of allegedly powerful artifacts were stolen from a local gallery hosting an exhibit called *The Supernatural: Debunked*. This exhibit showed how magic was appropriated by profiteers—by debunking certain historical magic figures and revealing that they were Trad con artists.

"That actually sounds cool," I said. "I'd see that."

According to the curator who was interviewed in the clip, Eishei Kodesh experts certified that the artifacts didn't contain any magic, the items' reputations notwithstanding, so there was nothing for the general public to fear. Sadly, she went on to say that while these con artists were Trads, they ran these scams at the behest of more powerful Eishei Kodesh who wanted to push the lie of magic dominance.

I sighed.

"Aaaand there it is," Darsh said. "The anti-magic agenda. Saw it coming a mile away."

I frowned in his direction. "No, you didn't."

"Please." He closed his eyes as though resting them against the harsh strain of the, like, ten seconds of blue light he'd absorbed. "My people are storytellers. I know how to spot the tells."

An ominous feeling settled over me. What tells had he spotted during our friendship about the stories I'd told—the lies I'd told—to keep Cherry Bomb secret?

He blinked his eyes open and motioned at my phone. "Play the rest of the report. See how right I am."

I wasn't sure if I wanted that. Every time today I'd thought that it couldn't get worse, it had, and spectacularly. In spite of my better judgment, though, I pressed play. We'd see, Mr. Master Storyteller.

Chapter 4

The video continued innocuously enough. The gallery claimed that Eishei Kodesh were behind the theft because our kind couldn't bear to have the truth come out, then the report cut to a close-up of the most infamous artifact: Sire's Spark, a rough octagonal pinkish crystal about the size of a man's palm. According to legend, it had belonged to Abraham Ben Haim, a Yellow Flame and one of the world's most powerful healers, who lived in a shtetl in Poland in the late 1700s.

"Shtetl" was the Yiddish word for a small town with a predominantly Jewish Ashkenazi population. Abraham supposedly imbued the crystal with his magic and it became known as Abraham's Spark.

It was renamed Sire's Spark during the rise of the Nazis. Abraham meant "father of many" in Hebrew, and given Nazi interest in the occult, the owners were afraid that the Germans would not only take the artifact, but destroy it due to its Jewish roots.

The reporter listed the many great feats of healing attributed to the crystal: broken bones fixed, brain tumors dissolved, bullets expelling themselves.

"Act now and not only will you get this amazing healing

crystal," I said, "we'll throw in a free set of knives guaranteed to remove any organ simply by pressing the flat of the blade against the body."

Darsh chuckled wryly. "Regardless, Trads will get the case, not us."

None of the crystal's miraculous properties was anything more than urban legend, since the gallery's Eishei Kodesh experts hadn't detected any magic on it, so non-magic officers had jurisdiction over it.

"I hope whoever lands it isn't bigoted against magic," I said.

I was about to stop the video when the reporter said something that chilled me to the bone.

"It was widely believed that Abraham passed his magic into the crystal by infusing it with his blood, where his power lived. That gave the artifact both its alleged magic properties and its color," the reporter said. "According to the legend, the crystal's magic was based on that universal element of connection. As the sage himself said, 'blood calls to blood.'"

I'd never expected to hear that phrase in a news report, and I couldn't ignore it.

Dr. Athena Metaxas, the other perp in our last case, was an infernal. We suspected she'd found their half-shedim victims, but her partner offed her before we could find and question her.

Did the puppet master pulling Roman's strings expect Sire's Spark to be a foolproof infernal detector? Or was this crystal—and more half-demon blood—key to furthering their cause in a different way?

"Could someone intend to use infernal blood with this crystal to make vampires invincible?" I said. Whatever invincible meant. We hadn't been given an explanation, just a villainous hint. "You're the one who told us that blood could be used to amplify magic in some ritual. Could this artifact be used for it?"

Darsh tapped his fist against the armrest. "I only know that some power word was involved. By the time I learned about there being a ritual, the exact details were lost."

"Could this artifact be a substitute for the power word? Or a modification?"

"Neither should be the case," he said, "because this crystal heals. Healing doesn't use blood magic unless it involves a vampire. And our power isn't the same thing as a dark magic ritual. Besides, Sire's Spark was debunked."

"I get all that, but what if the experts didn't find its magic because it has to be unlocked? With blood?"

"Aviva," he said sharply. "The case with the murdered infernals is over, and like I said, the Trad cops will get this one. We have more pressing problems to solve."

"Right," I muttered. Infernals never made the priority list.

He glared at me.

"I agreed with you! It's not our case."

"But?"

But Ezra and I were still investigating. Admittedly, it had only been a few days since we'd wrapped the murder investigation up, so we hadn't made any headway into which high-level Maccabee we suspected was involved with finding half shedim to drain of their blood, but we weren't going to give up.

I'm not sure what prompted Ezra's interests, but mine were basic survival. Roman Whittaker had whispered that "they" would find me. How?

Because blood called to blood.

I had to find them before they found me.

However, I couldn't tell Darsh any of this because he didn't know I was a half demon. The world wasn't ready to embrace people like me, and I couldn't risk losing my friends —like I had with Ezra, my first love—when I shared my secret.

"But nothing." I scrubbed a hand over my face. "I can't get those poor people's desecration out of my head."

"I don't believe you. If you're up to something, tell me now, because I refuse to have you going lone wolf on a tangent during what will already be a fraught investigation."

"You're not the lead yet," I snapped.

"I will be," he said with maddening certainty. "And unless you want your role on this case to be a single written report of what you saw at the crime scene, you'll come clean about anything else."

"You can't—"

"I can and I will."

My eyes got a tingly pins and needles sensation that made my nose twitch. Fuck. Cherry Bomb would be bursting out onto the scene any second now if I didn't get myself under control. I quickly ducked my head, my fists clenched, and visualized punching Darsh until the sensation passed.

It took twenty-three imagined uppercuts and jabs, but when I faced Darsh, I was confident that my eyes had not turned from light brown to toxic green. "There's nothing to tell," I said evenly.

"There better not be." He crossed his arms.

The air between us turned bristly. Was I aware of the hypocrisy of acting like Ezra and keeping my secrets close? Yes, but I wasn't withholding information about our current case. It was an important distinction.

I wasn't jeopardizing anything.

Cherry snorted. *Whatever lets you sleep at night, babycakes.*

The door swung open, and my best friend, Sachie, waltzed in. She'd decided to grow out her pixie cut, but it was newly dyed her favorite fire engine red and matched the hoodie she'd paired with black jeans and Doc Martens. "The Three Musketeers are on the caaaa—" She stopped dead, looking between us with narrowed eyes. "Did I interrupt a pissing contest?" Her saccharine-sweet smile didn't reveal either of her dimples, and she'd already unearthed a small switchblade that she danced over her knuckles.

Ladies and gentlemen, Sachie Saito. Ready and willing to instigate peace via bloodshed. Thus far, I'd never incurred more than a menacing jab, but there was always that sliver of unease that my best friend would shiv me if necessary.

In her defense, she'd feel really bad about it after.

I think.

No worries this time, though, because Darsh disarmed her in the blink of an eye. He tossed the blade up in the air and caught it in his fist. "I'm keeping this."

Sach scowled at him. "Hey!"

"Sit." He pointed at the chair he'd vacated.

"Avi wasn't this bossy when she was lead," Sach said, sinking into the seat.

"Co-lead," Darsh corrected.

"Not that Darsh has been made lead now." I shoved my feet back into my heels.

That earned me twin looks of pity.

I threw up my hands.

Michael finally returned, closed the door, and sat down behind her desk. "We're all here. Good. Sachie, you and Aviva will report to Darsh."

Screw you, Darsh, for always being right when it came to Michael.

Sach gave a little fist pump. She'd worked toward being a part of the Spook Squad for a long time, and now she was on her first official case as a member of that team.

There weren't many vampire Maccabees in our global organization and zero full-demon ones. There weren't any other half ones in our supernatural police force either, but aye, there was the rub. If they did as good a job as me as hiding it, I'd never know.

There couldn't be many more, if any. The public loved

quoting the fact that very few infernals were carried to term. It helped people sleep at night.

Regardless, vamp operatives didn't have levels to achieve like their human colleagues. Once they graduated as novices, all undead operatives went into a general pool at their chapter called a Spook Squad. These squads were given cases to investigate, like any operative, but they focused on rogue vamps and shedim activity, not policing Eishei Kodesh.

Vancouver had three vamps in their squad: Darsh, Nasir, and the most senior operative, Cécile.

Sachie had been angling to become their first human teammate for a while. Her request was granted after our last investigation—the first time either of us had ever worked with vamp operatives on a case.

Unlike the rest of us, the Spook Squad got to combine all the fun challenges of solving crimes with more fighting and stabbing. Plus, there weren't the same strict protocols around arrests since their targets weren't human.

All of that appealed to my bloodthirsty bestie, and I smiled at her, happy she'd achieved her goal. It had cost her, both in a brutal training regime and certain friendships with other operatives.

I happened to catch Darsh's eye.

The fucker smirked at me.

My smile flickered, and I scratched my cheek with my middle finger.

Michael sent us both a sharp look.

In a rare show of solidarity, Darsh and I beamed innocently at her.

Michael sighed with great weariness of the soul. "Should we confirm without a sliver of a doubt that our missing victim, Emily Astor, was a Prime," she said, "this will be the most sensitive case we've ever had. I'll move Cécile and Nasir to other digs for the duration and give you run of the basement, but make sure not a single word of this leaks." She shook her head. "I spoke to our healers. They can't say whether Ms. Keller, Rachel, and Mason will get their memories of the events back."

Sachie frowned, not yet up to speed, but she saved her questions for our squad debrief.

"Did they just lose memories of the crime or of other parts of their lives as well?" I said. Their minds had been violated, but it would be horrible if they'd also lost precious personal memories.

"The crime," Michael said.

"That's worse." Darsh slouched lazily against the wall. "It means someone with incredible power focused the memory loss."

"Ms. Keller has been put under guard," Michael said, "but she's understandably upset and concerned about how long her business will be out of commission. I realize we're starting at worse than zero, since we don't have the victim or any evidence, but crack this as soon as possible." The director paused. "It's a given that you'll run into other vampires over the course of the investigation, and if our murdered woman was a Prime, they'll be powerful. Keep this under your hats and do not underestimate anyone you come in contact with or the potential threat to the investigation at any point." She looked directly at me.

"I won't," I said.

"We may cross paths with one of the vamp Mafias," Darsh said.

My mother pressed her lips into a thin line, and I wondered if she was thinking about Natán Cardoso, her former good friend and fellow Maccabee. He'd been turned and had risen to head up the Kosher Nostra, one of the most powerful vamp mobs.

He was also Ezra's father. I'd never met him, and I had no desire to. What kind of sick individual raised their only son to be a trained killer?

"I want updates in real time," she said. "Understood?"

Darsh nodded. "Got it."

A body thudded against the door.

I jumped.

"Yabai!" Sach said under her breath in Japanese.

The door opened.

"You can't go in there!" In all my years, I'd never heard Louis raise his voice. He may have been a supercilious, over-protective asshole, but he was generally unflappable, which made him the perfect assistant for Michael.

I bolted up, already halfway out of my seat to take arms against whatever misfortune was about to befall us.

Ezra strode in. Unlike his first visit to the director's office, he didn't deploy his legendary charm, and his easygoing grin was nowhere in sight. He wore all black, his expression grim. His silvery-blue eyes held turbulent darker swirls and his body was rigid.

Louis hovered anxiously behind him. The assistant's suit jacket was badly wrinkled on one side. "I tried to stop him."

"It's okay, Louis," Michael said. "Leave us."

He nodded and withdrew.

Sachie shot me an "oh shit" look, her eyebrows raised.

Darsh lounged against the wall, his relaxed pose belied by his gaze tracking each second of this encounter. I had no doubt he'd spring into action at the smallest provocation.

Ezra, at six feet, was a smidge taller than Darsh, with a good thirty pounds more muscle. He was a Prime and an assassin. However, my friend had the elegance and lethalness of a jungle cat and was older and more cunning. I couldn't say who'd win a physical altercation, and I didn't want to find out.

Michael looked at the framed parchment on the exposed brick wall certifying her appointment as director like she was checking her name was still on there and this wasn't someone else's mess to deal with.

Anyone else would have just seen a quick glance sideways,

but I'd spent a lifetime deciphering her every little twitch in case I'd fucked up and let my infernal side come out, even if only in front of her.

"To what do we owe the great pleasure of you still being here in my city when your investigation wrapped up three days ago?" she said.

"I stuck around to take in some of the attractions," he said flatly.

My mother glanced at me.

I clenched my jaw. Hard to say what was more insulting: that she lumped me in with the aquarium, or that she thought I'd lost my freaking mind and hooked up with him again.

"You're lucky I stayed," he continued seriously. "As the sole Prime Maccabee, I'm investigating this murder." He glared at me. "I told you to lock it down until I got there. This is on you."

Chapter 5

There was a moment of incredulous silence, then all hell broke loose.

"Did you just pull nonexistent rank instead of helping me in the first place?" I snarled. My fingers twitched, and I regretted not slipping one of the many lovely, sharp, throwable weapons Sachie kept around our condo under my suit jacket this morning.

Sadly, I was drowned out by the others who couldn't believe I'd phoned him at all.

Ezra didn't bother chiming in. He simply stood there, arms crossed and foot tapping, which only fired the rest of us up more.

"Enough!" Michael's voice sliced through the commotion, and we fell silent. She turned to me. "I'm not blaming you for your failure to secure the evidence, the body, or three people's lost memories."

How generous of you.

"But how could you share what, even you, Operative Fleischer, should have identified as classified details?"

Even me? I ground my teeth together. I was an exemplary

Maccabee. That wasn't ego. I'd worked insanely hard to be outstanding in my field.

My mother's gibe didn't stem from a lack of professionalism. It boiled down to the same thing: I was a half shedim.

Vampires hadn't been accepted without a lot of fear and bloodshed, and that was with the friendliest of them stepping out of the shadows in the 1960s to run a focused public relations campaign and allow them to walk openly among us. Some were good, others weren't, but either way, many were worshipped like celebrities.

Shedim, on the other hand, were feared and despised. As they should be. There was no such thing as a good demon. The shitty thing was that people were convinced that the pure evil inherited from a shedim overrode any possible humanity in their children.

I'd worked my ass off trying to become the youngest level three operative, the top rank before chapter director. A goal, by the way, that should have happened with the last case had Michael not gone back on her promise with a bullshit excuse. All I wanted was the chance to distinguish myself as a great Maccabee, both in regularly solving hard-hitting cases and mentoring those under me to help them achieve their own greatness to keep humanity safe.

I'd be such a force for good that when the day arrived that I came clean about my shedim side to my friends and colleagues, I'd be respected and embraced, parlaying that goodwill into a global change of thinking about my kind.

Except, how would that be possible when my own mother believed the worst of me? I was trying to adjust my plan and be such a model operative that Michael couldn't ignore promoting me, but damn, she was making it tough.

"I called the sole fellow operative who could verify my hypothesis that our victim was a Prime," I said. "As was absolutely my right." My words dripped off my lips like ice. "Ezra clearly had information that this operation was at risk and did not share it. Yell at him."

"I can yell at both of you," Michael said. "Don't underestimate my multitasking skills."

There was no danger of that. Still, I should have gotten a gold medal for the self-restraint I showed by not slow-clapping her for her mastery of shitting on me while dealing with other things.

However, that wasn't a fight to have in her office in front of her operatives—even ones who were my friends. I could separate out being a Maccabee and her kid. She might not be able to, but she held all the cards here.

Ezra, however, was totally fair game.

"You put being a Prime first," I said, "so don't you dare come in here now and throw me under the bus."

"Look." He spread his hands wide with a placating smile that I itched to smack off his face. "You can waste a lot of time trying to identify your victim or I can tell you who she is and why this is a larger problem than you realize."

"Someone's angling for a gold star," Darsh said.

Ezra ignored him. "Provided you put me in charge."

"This should be good," Sachie said.

"No deal," Darsh said. "You're emotionally compromised."

Ezra looked at me.

I wiped my sweaty palms on my trousers. Would he expose my half-shedim status to Darsh and Sachie as proof that I'd been emotionally compromised—that I'd kept pretty freaking huge secrets—on the last case and still been able to co-lead?

If Michael learned I'd told Ezra of all people what I was? Well, I wasn't sure what punishment would fit that crime, but my mother was nothing if not creative.

I shot Ezra a pleading look, though it killed me to do so.

He pressed his lips together but didn't say anything.

"You can't lead because you need someone with distance

to make smart, rational decisions that will solve this faster," Darsh said. "I understand your unease, since Primes are supposed to be near infallible, and I promise we'll do everything to find the killer. Help us or hinder us. It's your choice."

Ezra scratched a hand through the close-cropped black beard that lent him a piratical air, then nodded reluctantly. "Her name is Calista. She was the only other Prime, and while I don't know her exact age, speculation put her in her seven hundreds."

"That's pretty old," Sachie said. "Was Emily—I mean, Calista, compos mentis?"

Most vampires, once they hit the five to six hundred age range, tended to go insane from living so long.

"She was sharp as a tack," Ezra said. "I can't say for sure, but I don't think immortality affects us the same way. That said, she was a nasty piece of work. She owned the Copper Hell."

"That place." Darsh grimaced. "Yeah, that's a bigger problem."

Ezra's gaze darted away shiftily. It was just for a fraction of a second, but sadly, when it came to my ex, I was still far too attuned to his every reaction.

He was hiding something, but what? I tapped my foot against the rug.

"What's the Copper Hell?" Sachie said, drawing my attention to the other aspect of this reveal I wasn't clear on.

"It's what they called eighteenth-century gaming halls in London catering to the lower classes, but how is it relevant?" I returned their surprised stares with exasperation. "What? I can't watch documentaries? And why does it matter if Calista owned one of them back then?"

"This club is very much modern day, though it's been around for at least a couple hundred years." Michael massaged her temples with her index fingers. "And it's not just any gambling house. It caters to a magic clientele, and the stakes are far higher and deadlier than any run-of-the-mill casino."

"Suffice it to say," Ezra said, "we have to find the body immediately."

"Why the body and not the perp?" Sachie said. "I mean, we'll find Calista, but at this point, her killer is the priority, right?"

"Obviously the killer will have her body," Ezra said impatiently.

"That's not what you said."

"You're a sharp operative. You should have been able to figure that out."

Sachie reached for her blade that Darsh still held, but he tucked it into his pocket. She crossed her arms with a humph.

Ezra impatiently shook his head. "Where are we setting up shop?"

Darsh shifted sideways to block the door. "Answer Sachie's question."

"There's nothing to answer," Ezra said.

Darsh studied him for a long moment. "You're lying."

Ezra's fangs descended.

Nippers, as fresh converts to the life immortal were known, could barely control their fangs. One strong emotion, and bam! Fangs out. Older vampires, like Darsh, exercised the same level of control over them as an adult would with their own desires: there was a time and a place for such things. Ezra, being a Prime, had exceedingly good control of himself and his vampiric reflexes, rivalling that of many much older vampires.

I scanned the room, marking possible weapons. If something about Calista's death was making Ezra bug out this badly, then I wanted to get cracking on this case. I mean, I'd also happily arm myself, but that was secondary.

To me.

Sachie crossed her foot onto her knee for ready access to the thin stake she had stashed in her boot.

Michael tucked a strand of her silver hair behind her ear, letting things unfold, and mostly watching Darsh's reaction. He didn't look worried.

Humans and vampire operatives were trained to work together. I couldn't say that Ezra and Darsh would never come to blows, but neither of these vampires would hurt Sachie, Michael, or me.

Still, it was tough to reconcile that intellectual understanding with Ezra's puffed-out chest and the red haze that clouded his eyes.

My fight-or-flight response had definitely cast its vote.

Speaking of the workings of my primal brain, Cherry Bomb watched the situation between the pair unfold with the enthusiasm of a fan at Wimbledon.

"Careful what you accuse me of," Ezra said softly.

Darsh scratched his hair free of its bun. "Touchy, aren't you? Why? You lie on a regular basis gathering intel for our fine organization. I don't care that it's your go-to response, but I won't allow you to compromise my investigation by withholding information from me."

Ezra's fangs retracted, his eyes going back to their regular color, but he laughed coldly. "You think you could make me share anything I didn't want to?"

Darsh sashayed closer. "I have all sorts of tricks up my sleeve, but I don't need them." He poked Ezra in the chest. "My squad, my rules. You'll play by them or leave."

Ezra shifted his weight like he was going for door number two. That was crazy. He clearly wished to be part of this. Someone had murdered a Prime. There was no way he would sit back and wait for the outcome of our search.

I stood up and gently touched his shoulder. "Please stay. We need you. And you need to be here."

The look he flashed me before he wrestled his face into

that infuriating calm mask reminded me of a wounded animal who'd been freed from its trap but expected that they'd fallen into a worse fate.

"I started being challenged by grown vamps as a kid." Ezra flexed his hand then tightened it into a fist. No wonder Calista used an Eishei Kodesh alias if constant fights were the alternative. "My father impressed upon me that anyone who could defeat a Prime could destabilize vamp power structures in an ugly way. I don't know what our perp wants with Calista, but it's in our interests to retrieve her body and keep this entire thing secret. If we can't?" He spread his hands wide. "It's better that word gets out she killed herself than someone managed this unthinkable attack."

"That's a long-winded way of admitting you're feeling incredibly vulnerable right now." Darsh held out his arms. "Bring it in."

"I'd rather be staked," Ezra said dryly.

Darsh grinned. "If I find our perp, I'll ask for tips."

"Darsh, get keys to the elevator so that only you four can access the basement," Michael said.

"I'd like to sweep it for bugs, both magic and tech," Ezra said.

Surprisingly, Michael didn't argue that our chapter couldn't possibly be compromised. "Go ahead."

"How will you do that? Is Silas still in town?" Darsh said, too blandly.

Silas, a Southern vamp who was Ezra's best friend, got under Darsh's skin, but how much of that was his sweet old-fashioned charm grating on my cynical friend and how much of it was Darsh's attraction to the other vampire was anyone's guess.

"No," Ezra said. "He's back in Charleston, but I've learned to fend for myself on a few matters." He'd have to if others were constantly gunning for him.

"Silas is not to be brought on to this case or given any

details," Michael said. "Five of us is already four too many to keep Calista's death a secret." My mother was a big fan of secrets, that's for sure. She flicked her hand in dismissal, and we all headed for the door.

"Remember," she said, "updates in real time."

The second we were out in the hallway, Darsh slung an arm over my and Sachie's shoulders. "The band is back together."

"Did Silas go solo?" I joked.

"Yes. He'll release a thoroughly unmemorable album and fade away." Darsh did a two-step and neat little spin. "Us, on the other hand? We have choreography."

"Yeah, we do." Sachie did a hip shimmy.

I groaned.

I'd enjoyed many a night out dancing with Darsh and Sach, all of us hopped up on music and the sheer pleasure of cutting loose with good friends. The only downside was whatever song Darsh dubbed our choreo number for the evening. There wasn't any advance notice, he simply "felt it in his veins" when some random opening notes played.

He and Sach loved breaking out into synchronized dance movements, but I was always a half step and a quarter turn in the wrong direction. Don't get me wrong. I danced fine freestyle, but put me in a group number with staged moves and I was not a pretty sight.

That didn't account for all my unease, however. There'd been a forced note to his voice and movements, almost manic, and I was worried that his normal glittery persona was nothing more than a costume right now.

"No choreo," I protested.

Darsh raised an eyebrow. "Who's the boss here? There will be mandated dance breaks to keep our energy up and our spirits high."

Ezra lagged behind, his fists clenched, and his expression pinched tight.

Darsh turned back to him. "Cardoso? I may kid around, but I gave you my word. We'll get whoever did this to your friend." His expression was serious, but his eyes glittered intensely. Was this another part of Darsh's mysterious past?

"Oh, we're not friends," Ezra said. "The one time I met Calista, she tried to kill me. I'd planned to return the favor." He smirked but it was a shadow of his usual arrogance. "I hate when others crash my party."

My heart cracked at his lame attempt at levity. He could joke all he wanted, but when we were dating, he'd shared how hard it was being the only male Prime, being a Jewish vampire, being the son of a powerful mobster. With Calista dead, Ezra was the last known of his kind. It was bound to do a number on him emotionally.

I looped my arm through his. "Then let's crash theirs."

Chapter 6

Operatives were surprised when they first came into the basement where the vamps (and now Sachie) worked out of, expecting an overabundance of black leather or red velvet. Thankfully, when the rest of our building got its big reno a few years back, the squad down here got their own decorating budget.

Vancouver's HQ was located in a five-story building that occupied an entire city block on the border with Burnaby. It had started out as a garment factory in the late 1800s, but when that business went bankrupt in the Great Depression, the local Maccabees took it over.

There were no windows down here. (Thanks, former sweatshop!) The vamp operatives would have been fine with them because they were all former Eishei Kodesh and being born with fire magic in one form or another tempered the effects of sunlight once a person was turned. There was a strong correlation between the strength of their powers when human and their ability to survive sunshine.

Trad vamps, however, couldn't go out during daylight hours at all. They fell asleep at dawn and woke at dusk. Thus, the basement had been kept window-free so no Trad vamp suspects were fried while in a holding cell waiting to be inter-rogated.

Given this was my new workspace for a while, I was glad that all of the original perforated brown ceiling tiles were gone. As was the random clutter that had ended up down here over the decades in some kind of furniture graveyard.

Multicolored silk lanterns hand-painted in delicate flowers hung from the smooth white plaster ceiling. They cast bright pools of light over the large open space, with oversize couches and chairs in sumptuous colorful fabrics grouped together at one end. Sure, they were sturdy enough to bear the brunt of two vamps in full brawl, but the furniture's placement encouraged hanging out on breaks and provided a cheery vibe.

I tossed my jacket and laptop bag on a round plush chair next to an adjustable computer stand and gave Bentley, the squad's unofficial mascot, a chin nod. The large unicorn stuffie sat at his customary spot, riding a stumpy palm tree in a fancy Italian tile planter. "'Sup, dude."

Maccabee chapters were located across the globe, mostly in cities, since that's where the majority of Eishei Kodesh lived. Only Jews were recruited as operatives for the first several hundred years, though from the start, the positions were offered to both men and women. However, even once we welcomed non-Jews, the organization remained a secret until after the Salem witch trials in the late 1700s, when magic was now so pervasive that we stepped out of the shadows as a global police force.

The one big caveat to our reveal was that we kept demon and vamp hunting a secret.

Between Judaism forbidding the consumption of blood and the importance of light to Jews, my people historically protected ourselves from becoming vampires. It was a large part of why the Maccabees as an organization had been formed, but our secrecy about the existence of the undead changed in the 1960s when vamps made their first big public relations push.

Demons though? Most people still didn't know about them. That was good in terms of keeping a lid on mass panic, but bad because it was hard to root them out.

"Let's open up a couple offices and create a conference room," Darsh said.

Ezra was already underway using some app on his phone to sweep the basement, so Sachie and I helped Darsh.

The row of offices on the left boasted not only ergonomic chairs and modular workspaces, the walls could be reconfigured. We combined two of the offices, moving smaller tables together to form a long conference table next to a large whiteboard.

Darsh rummaged in the storage cabinet. "Meeting starts in five minutes."

"Enough time for coffee," Sach said. "I got a cappuccino maker installed down here," she said to me in a conspiratorial whisper.

We wouldn't have to commute up to the third-floor kitchen? I fist-bumped her. "You're a miracle worker."

The two of us headed past the reinforced iron door leading to the single holding cell, which nulled all magic, including vamps'. Apprehended shedim didn't live long enough to make the trip to HQ.

"I don't suppose you diverted any of the baked goods?" I said.

"I tried." Sachie entered the kitchen. "But even my bottomless charm couldn't swing that. We'll either have to swipe them from upstairs or make do with packaged snacks."

It took only a couple minutes to get our mugs of piping-hot caffeine joy and some cookies, but Darsh sniffed primly at us like we'd breached all laws of etiquette regarding timely behavior.

Sach had familiarized herself with the seating down here

long ago and didn't need to do her routine of walking around the table, checking each chair for maximum sturdiness before making her selection. She sat down by the notebook and pen she'd placed, while I took the seat beside her with my open laptop.

Ezra, sitting across from us, insisted on sweeping all our phones for bugs. When he was satisfied they were clean, he handed Darsh a blue dry-erase marker as indication to begin.

Our fearless leader passed it to me. "Your printing is more legible."

I couldn't say whether that was true since I hadn't seen his. Darsh texted, but those messages tended to be brief and factual. If he wanted a longer conversation, he'd speak to us face-to-face.

I got the impression he preferred to see us and read our body language, interpreting our communication through more than tone of voice. He certainly didn't seem to like inferring intent via written missives, because he'd broken Sach and me of long texts to him early in our friendship. Some of that may have come down to his native language Romani being a predominantly oral one, but I suspected it was also part of his nature, choosing to gather information based on all his senses. Like a predator determining a threat.

I uncapped the marker and stood at the board like a good student.

"What have we got?" Darsh said.

The details that went onto the murder board were depressingly sparse. Aside from Calista's name and approximate age, we had the fact that she checked in at the spa under the same alias as always (Emily Astor) and claimed to be a Red Flame.

She'd been the first client of the day. The spa was so exclusive that each patron had the place to themselves for the entirety of their booking. She'd been enjoying the different caves for approximately forty minutes before Dawn had gone to check on her and prepare the treatment room for Calista's massage.

Vampires weren't cold to the touch unless they were hungry, so Dawn wouldn't have noticed Calista was a vamp during her massages, unless the Prime needed to feed.

"Someone had Calista's schedule," I said.

"Any idea how often she left the Copper Hell?" Sachie was drawing a forest in her notebook. It was the only way she could sit still. Our teachers had berated her for not paying attention, but her perfect recall shut them up pretty quickly. "If she rarely did, then yes, someone knew her schedule, but if she was always coming and going, they could have been tailing her, waiting for the right opportunity."

"No clue," Ezra said.

I wrote it on the board on the list of questions to answer. Each new addition felt like a taunt.

"We need a timeline of her movements before she arrived," Darsh said.

"A list of enemies," Ezra said. His fingers twitched; it was too bad he hadn't brought his knitting to relax him because he'd gotten tenser and tenser with our lack of information.

"She owns a magic gambling house." I rubbed a smudge of marker off my skin. "I imagine it's a long one."

"Maybe, maybe not," he said. "She kept a pretty low profile. I doubt many of her patrons had met her."

Darsh nodded his chin at Ezra. "You did. How about your dad? Is Natán one of her enemies? Or a business partner?"

"Neither, as far as I'm aware."

Darsh leaned back in his chair. "Would you tell us if that wasn't the case?"

Ezra crossed his arms. "Are you going to question my loyalty at every turn?" His voice was bland, but his eyes darkened for a second—in hurt, not anger. He and Darsh had bonded on a side mission in our last investigation, and I guess Ezra hadn't expected to be met with this constant suspicion from Darsh. He'd thought that if they weren't exactly friends, he'd still earned some trust.

"You're the princeling heir to one of the most powerful vampire Mafias around," Darsh said. "You not only permit your Crimson Prince moniker to stand, you revel in the status of being Daddy's enforcer. Wouldn't you question it if our positions were reversed?"

"I'd remember that not everything is as it appears," Ezra said pointedly.

"I have a long and proven track record of my exemplary loyalty," Darsh said.

"Is it loyalty when the alternative is..." Ezra scrunched his brows together. "What was the alternative?"

Darsh gave a sharp smile. "Do you really want to find out?"

"No sign of a struggle," I said loudly. When Darsh didn't take my hint, still in a scowl-off with Ezra, I pointed at him. "You, lead by example." I pointed at Ezra. "You, be quiet unless you have something to add to the board."

A timer went off, followed by a rhythmic mélange of drums, accordion, and guitar coming out of Darsh's phone.

"What the hell is that?" Ezra said, genuinely alarmed.

"Dance break." Darsh was already up.

The singer's voice kicked in, a rich, throaty female singing in a foreign language. I recognized her a Macedonian Romani vocalist who Darsh was a big fan of.

When the rest of us stayed put, he motioned for us to stand, making the black beads on his black leather wrist cuff clack together. "Move your bodies. For the next three minutes, you're going to shake off the fog from sitting for the past half hour, and come back to this discussion with renewed energy and focus." He leaned forward. "Do it, or I will demand choreography."

Sachie shrugged, jumped to her feet, and started shimmying around the table.

Darsh was on his way over to me with an arm out like he'd pull me out of my seat, so I stood up. "All right already." Seeing Ezra still seated and scowling, I extended a hand. "Come on, Cardoso. Shake that undead booty."

I'd managed to get him onto a dance floor back in our dating days a grand total of once, and he hadn't done more than shuffle his way through the song. Being more muscular these days—and taking up more space—he might be even more self-conscious, but Darsh was doing full body rolls like an elegant seal and Sach was twerking at a chair, so it really was anything goes.

I raised my eyebrows.

Ezra gave an aggrieved sigh and stood up. Taking my hand, he twirled me into him and placed his other hand on the small of my back.

I smirked at the ridiculously formal waltz he led me into, expecting it to dissolve into chaos in seconds, but he controlled our moves with a surety and a smooth precision that I'd never seen in his dancing before. It was totally weird for this song, but still on rhythm, despite the thread of tension thrumming in his rigid stance.

I was so busy wondering how he knew these steps and why we were dancing this way that I missed my cue to turn and accidentally bonked his shoulder with my head. "Sorry," I mumbled.

"No problem," he murmured. "We're just finding our footing."

I was on the verge of making a quip about keeping things professional, but then Ezra shot me a grin, a kind of boyish excitement like he'd found the prettiest rock on the beach and had to show me.

"Relax your hold a sec," he said, eyes crinkling.

I did, and he spun me dizzyingly around the main room.

In all those period dramas I'd watched, I'd never grasped how the main characters could feel closer at formal balls, especially in their regimented dances and with all their niceties. But being this close to Ezra, feeling him guide me through space, his eyes my only anchor as the room spun around me, I understood.

I gripped his shoulder, steadying myself.

"I've learned a few things since last time," he said.

"Oh, no doubt," I fired back, disoriented and ready to annihilate him. "I bet the Prime Playboy had to have all the moves."

"I just thought it would be nice." His fingers on my lower back pressed gently against me with each spin, directing me out of the reach of couches and chairs. His hand enveloped mine, showing me where to go without dominating me or making this whole dance about how cool he was. It was about us being a team, and it *was* nice.

No. It was more than nice, and that had me worried.

And now, the thought of domination tugged me back to that kiss we'd recently shared that suddenly seemed to fill the narrow gap between our bodies. *Way to keep it professional, Fleischer.*

My eyes snapped to his heavy-lidded gaze.

He watched me intently, heat emanating off him, and electricity practically crackling between us.

I tensed up, overwhelmed.

Ezra's expression softened. He gave me a wry smile and twirled me out, setting me free.

As I spun away from him, I felt an emptiness in my chest. My blood pounded in my ears, and all I could think about was how badly I wanted to feel his hands on me again.

I stood there stupidly for a second, the music washing over us, then looked down at my feet like that would clue me in on what to do. When I looked back to Ezra, he was bouncing up and down in time to the music and bobbing his head with his lips pursed cartoonishly.

He gestured to the left and right like a flight attendant pointing out the exits on Disco Air.

I started laughing, and when the timer went off, I did in fact feel more energized and focused.

"Now." Darsh motioned us toward to the whiteboard. "Where were we?"

Sach started a new sketch in her notebook and just like that we were back. Business as usual.

"Who was responsible for the memory loss?" I said. "Vamp, demon, or Yellow Flame? Was that individual also the one who drove the stake in? Remember Dawn was up front, and the emergency door was bolted from the inside."

"Memory loss doesn't explain the actual staking," Ezra said. A vein throbbed in his forehead. "Calista would have smelled and heard anyone vaguely in her vicinity. It wouldn't matter if she recognized them and didn't believe them to be a threat, like the Trad spa owner, she wouldn't sit still and be murdered."

"She didn't look distressed," I said. "I don't believe she had any advance notice of this. Does that narrow it to a demon or could a vampire or a White Flame calm her enough to stay still before she was aware of them?"

"A powerful older vampire might be able to hide and pull that off," Darsh said, "but a White Flame is still human. They couldn't mask their breathing or heart rate from her."

The creature Sach was drawing was only partially outlined, but the horns and pointed tail made it already recognizable as a demon.

I pressed my lips together.

"Whoever it was didn't immediately remove Calista from the spa," Ezra said. "They waited, then took her to a secondary location. I'd bet it's here in town, because unless she was taken to the actual demon realm, anywhere else would be too difficult to get to, given her state and attract too much attention. Including Babel."

I frowned. "That means the perp was close at hand in the spa the entire time."

"You're all lucky you weren't killed," Sachie said to me.

"Yeah." My kingdom for some lavender diffuser, because my head throbbed at the realization of how narrow an escape I'd had.

Ezra had unearthed a tiny tangle of yellow yarn from his pocket, unraveling it with a tense jaw. "It was too close."

I shrugged. "Well, why bother to murder us when you can erase people's memories? But it doesn't explain why they stole her corpse."

"Could be they have their own timeline and place to announce her death," Sachie said. "A grand gesture to cement their power play. Any ideas, Ezra?"

Ezra was playing some long game with the Maccabees. He'd told me that he'd made sure they came to him and brought him into the fold. He never specified how or what he was up to, and few people knew that he played spy for us at all.

Fewer people still—i.e. his best friend, Silas, and me— were aware that the Crimson Prince was an empty title. Ezra wasn't his father's enforcer anymore, but the fiction stood because it benefitted them both.

"Nothing comes to mind," Ezra said. He'd made a single knot in the yarn and was looping it around his fingers in different patterns. "I'll make some inquiries."

"We'll check CCTV footage in the alley and around the café where Calista's body was stolen," Darsh said, "but I doubt we'll get any hits." Vancouver wasn't London. We didn't have cameras everywhere. "I want to chase down likely hiding spots starting in a five-kilometer radius from the point where Aviva found the van."

"Here's another thing for the board," Sachie said. "Does the name Emily Astor have any relevance? Are the number and address on file at the spa real or duds?" She shaded in the scales on her sketch of the ugly demon.

Something in my chest twisted, and I quickly looked away. If she saw my scales, would she find them equally grotesque? Like, sure, they were strange, but I also thought mine were kind of pretty. Like an iridescent shell you'd find glinting in the shallows of the ocean.

I wrote "intent" in all caps with a question mark and circled it for good measure. "A lot of questions and very few answers."

"I'll go to the Copper Hell," Ezra volunteered. "Listen to any gossip and try to get into Calista's office. Older vamps tend to distrust technology so there's a good chance she kept a paper calendar and accounting books. That might yield a clue."

"Why you?" Sach said.

"The Crimson Prince is the only one of us who can get an invitation." He bared his teeth at Darsh. I think it was supposed to be a smile. "Unless you have a problem with me using that nickname?"

"Only if you plan on going by yourself," Darsh said.

"I can bring one person. More than that might be construed as a show of force, given I'm going in under the auspices of the Kosher Nostra."

Sachie looked up from her notebook, gripping her pencil like it had transformed from a drawing implement to a knife. "Is this going to be like the Crypt where weak, puny humans are forbidden from going?"

"I'll take whoever Darsh feels is best suited to the task," Ezra said.

Darsh raised his eyebrows.

"I've accepted you're in charge, and I'll respect it. Contrary to what you think, I don't require an ego boost."

That was for damn sure.

"Oh, I'm aware your ego is plenty boosted," Darsh said. "Your ugly mug on the cover of this month's *Urban Swagger* mag is testament to that."

"Did you read the article or just look at the photos?" I teased.

"Neither." Darsh smirked. "Unlike you who knew there was an article to be read."

Ezra quirked his lips, self-satisfied.

"Get over yourselves," I snapped, my cheeks flushing. "It was a reasonable guess."

"As to who is going," Darsh said, "it'll have to be a weak, puny human. I'm staying here to get this investigation up and running. Though, whoever stays behind with me can pore through the CCTV footage because I hate staring at a screen for long." It's true. He wasn't addicted to his phone like so many of us, and I'd never seen him binge endless hours of TV either. "I'll get started on a timeline and the fake name Calista provided," he added.

I raised my hand. "I'll stay with you."

I'd prevented Sach from going to the black market in the vampire megacity of Babel. There'd been good reasons, but it was only fair she visit the cool-sounding gambling house now.

"You'll have to wear a glamor," Ezra told her.

"Oh, then hell no." Sachie flipped her notebook shut and mimed gagging. "They hurt. It's like a flu body ache on steroids. Plus, I did it once and had a bad allergic reaction."

I tried to hold it in. I really did. But laughter burst out of me at the memory. "Oh my God, and the whole time it looked like your body was trying to swallow your eye. I had night-mares about you for weeks!"

Sachie scowled, but then closed one eye and adopted a moaning monster pose. It set me right off again into helpless laughter.

"The glamor is not up for debate," Ezra said, shooting me a dark look as I wiped tears from my eyes. "I would never bring a Maccabee operative with me as a guest, and it's a good bet that they'll log your appearance."

"In that case, I volunteer Aviva as tribute. This is my first official Spook Squad assignment. I'll stay and back Darsh up."

"Rock, paper, scissors?" I asked hopefully, holding a fist out to Sachie.

"Nope," she said cheerfully. "You took Babel, you can take this assignment and suck it up."

I groaned.

"I'll get it approved," Darsh said. "Aviva, go upstairs and talk to Sharnaz about a glamor. They'll fix you up."

"A *suitable* one," Ezra corrected quickly.

"Have Sharnaz give you a little black dress as part of it," Darsh said, already sending the text to our resident master of glamors.

"I don't need a magic outfit." The more complicated I made the glamor, the more painful it would be to get and maintain.

"I've seen your wardrobe," Darsh said. "Yeah, you do. Also ask Sharnaz to layer up some thin gold necklaces and give you stacking rings. Maybe go blonde too. With bigger—"

I winged a marker at him. "Finish that sentence and die."

Ezra snickered, quickly turning it into a cough.

"Avery Francis, trust fund baby." Sachie mugged at me, knowing I hated every single thing about this.

"There are other suitable disguises," I said. Ones that didn't force me to play vacuous arm candy for my ex.

"Not ones we have time to prep," Ezra said.

We'd see about that. I gathered my belongings. "Do I come back here after? Or are we going straight there?" I put my laptop in the bag and zipped it up. "Where is there anyway? The Copper Hell isn't in Vancouver. Exclusive or not, I'd have heard of it if it was." I slung the bag over my shoulder and smoothed out my suit jacket. "It's not in Babel, is it?"

Was that the real reason Ezra insisted that I glamor up? The moment I stepped into Babel, all of Cherry's distinguishing features would appear and I'd be powerless to stop them. I gripped the bag's strap. Part of me yearned to feel the freedom of her physical form again, but I'd been identified as a Maccabee, albeit a full-demon one, when we were in the Crypt. Having that same demon arrive with Ezra when he was supposed to be Mr. Hotshot Assassin enjoying his playtime would raise too many questions.

Would a glamor even hide Cherry there?

"It's not in vamp territory," Ezra said. "The Copper Hell isn't just the name of the gambling house, it's the name of the enormous yacht it's located on. The ship moves around in international waters, but no one can pinpoint its location. It's not caught on radar or satellite imagery."

"Quite the magic trick," Sachie said.

"Quite the paranoid Prime," I said.

"True on both counts." Ezra pulled out his phone. "There are doors all over the world that enter directly onto it. We'll meet at the portal here in town." He sent me a text with the location.

"Gee." I fluttered my lashes. "I hope I don't get distracted by shopping or taking selfies and forget."

"I believe in you, Avery." He held up a fist.

I shut my laptop. This place was on a ship, huh? Good, because if Ezra made a single crack about my disguise not being "suitable" enough, I'd push him overboard.

Chapter 7

The left head on the cartoon Cerberus adorning the sign for the Jolly Hellhound Pub was a dopey-looking fucker with its tongue lolling out. The dog's head on the right was asleep while the one in the middle stared directly out at the viewer with evil red eyes.

I was going to be so pissed off if there was an actual hellhound we had to get past, because my entire body hurt. The bulk of the glamor magic was concentrated in my stomach and thighs because those were solid body parts able to handle the strain of pinning the glamor to me. I had greater muscle mass in my core and legs, typical of most women, and it would be too much to, say, anchor the glamor to only my arms, though it still had to be affixed across my entire body.

However, I disagreed with Sachie about the disguise feeling like a flu achiness. In my opinion, it was the same as the dull, heavy pain I got halfway through my menstrual cycles sometimes.

Plus, I was still sore from my workout this morning, so this new layer of suck made me downright cranky. I had no energy to tangle with some demon dog and no brimstone-flavored Milk-Bone to make friends with one.

At least the discomfort would only last six hours, because like Cinderella, my glamor had an expiration date. Unless I ended up with an allergic reaction to it. The list of possible side effects that Sharnaz had rattled off sounded like they were straight out of a comedy skit: *may cause pruny fingers, facial gout, and an exploding liver.* I kept waiting for Sharnaz's laughter and a "just kidding."

I was still waiting.

According to the timer on my burner phone, I had five hours and thirty-seven minutes to poke around the Copper Hell and then get free and clear before turning into a pumpkin. Probably not literally, but one of the side effects *was* orange puckered skin, so I couldn't discount it.

To take my mind off the pain while Sharnaz was torturing —I mean glamoring me, I'd scrolled through some of the online Maccabee resources for information on the Copper Hell.

I'd found a footnote about an operative who'd gone undercover there sometime in the 1920s. Glamor magic was still pretty crude back then, so he'd relied on a physical transformation. The disguise held; his cover story didn't.

He was mailed back in pieces to his Mumbai HQ. It took eight weeks.

Reassuring myself that wouldn't happen to me—if nothing else, global shipping times had improved—I cracked my knuckles and opened the pub door, hit with a wash of warm beer-scented air. It was unnerving seeing large, callused man hands instead of my perfect French manicure, but at least I wasn't hairy.

Sharnaz had been a bit too keen to try that detail out and their pout when I'd kiboshed it was Oscar-worthy.

They'd done a fantastic job of magically disguising me as a dark-skinned South Asian man in a beautifully tailored suit. I'd opted to keep my regular height of five foot five so that I didn't have to worry about eyelines, but we made my undercover persona, Arjun, stockier than me. If someone touched me, they'd feel Arjun's build.

The pub's interior was generic with a lot of wood paneling, a couple of dart boards, and a dinner clientele in a mix of suits and jeans. Once past the entryway, the pub smelled like spiced grilled meat. A server presented a table with their orders ranging from burgers to steak, and a delicious-looking lobster mac and cheese. The Jolly Hellhound might look like a dive bar, but the food had a high-end appeal.

Ezra hadn't arrived yet, so I took a seat at the bar where I could see the door, and ordered a pint of whatever lager they had on tap, pitching my voice low.

The bartender barely glanced at me before grabbing a glass and dispensing the golden liquid with the barest of foamy heads on top.

I munched my way through some surprisingly fresh and salty pretzels from the bowl in front of me.

A couple of women at the end of the bar cast interested looks my way. *Yes, I am a fine-looking gentleman, thanks.*

"Been working here long?" I asked the bartender.

"About five years." He slid my drink over. Good. He'd know where the portal in this place was and wouldn't ask questions.

I nursed my beer, waiting for Ezra to arrive and grateful I'd stopped and grabbed dinner on the way. It had already been a long day and I had hours more on that boat.

Thanks to Sharnaz being as gossipy as most operatives, I'd managed to learn a bit more about the artifacts stolen from the Trad gallery, including Sire's Spark. The gallery owners were adamant that Trad cops investigate, and since they weren't really magic objects—allegedly—Michael had no reason to pull jurisdiction over what amounted to paperweights with great PR.

Maybe she hadn't heard about the "blood calls to blood" aspect of Sire's Spark, which it had in common with the infernal murders. Yeah right. Like she hadn't gone over every detail of our reports with a fine-toothed comb. She either didn't believe Sire's Spark was relevant to the last case or, more likely, didn't care.

My mother had been clear about her lack of concern for any more dead infernals. It wasn't worth my energy to be upset about it. Sadly, knowing that didn't prevent it from happening.

Yet my gut insisted this artifact was pertinent to these deaths. It would be tricky to investigate without gaining the attention of the Trad cops, but I intended to try, and since Ezra was my partner in this hunt, I needed a moment to fill him in.

The door opened and a murmur ran through the pub, like the entire bar had been half-asleep and suddenly jolted back to full awareness. I didn't have to look over to know who had entered.

Ezra had that effect on people.

Chairs were hurriedly scraped back, half the room moving tables out of his wake. The two women at the end of the bar fled, while the bartender overpoured a beer, the liquid flowing over his hand. He'd gone pale, his eyes wide.

This guy must have seen all types going through the portal to the Copper Hell. Ezra being a vampire wouldn't faze him, this was all the Crimson Prince.

I rubbed my legs from the glamor discomfort. Awesome. A pinched throbbing was developing at the back of my neck, running up into my head.

To make things worse, Cherry bobbed up and down in my mind, excited for all the trouble we'd find.

Not trouble. Fact finding only. No fights.

Her presence withdrew to sulk.

I didn't bother looking up; there was no need. Each of Ezra's steps closer rippled through me as though he was trans-mitting an electromagnetic field, energizing me.

I slugged back some beer, trying to focus on something other than his nearing presence—and failed. His solid, sure steps were like a warrior's, which put me in mind of the other thing I'd researched while I was being glamored: Ezra's tattoo.

The angle of the photo made the first few words impossible to decipher, but the rest of the Spanish was clear: soñaba con conquistar el mundo. Plugged into a translator, it came out as "I dreamed of conquering the world." Gag. I kept my to-do list on my phone. But hey, you do you, Ezra. He was powerful, charismatic, handsome, friends with celebrities and heads of state, and had fans who called themselves Ezracurriculars. What was next? Renaming a continent after himself?

Señor Conquistador—I snickered, he'd always be Count von Cardoso, supervillain, to me—took the barstool one down from me, and I fought not to inhale his familiar cologne with its notes of cardamom, cloves, and bergamot, that spicy orange. It tangled with the fresh, cool aroma of a windswept summer breeze that was his natural scent.

I tapped my thumb against the pint glass, covertly studying him through half-slitted lids.

He'd foregone the suit I expected in favor of black jeans paired with a black vest and a soft-looking white shirt with the first few buttons undone, exposing brown skin with a light dusting of hair. Over top, he wore this incredible brown leather jacket with black patches on the shoulders. Cut like a Victorian gothic frock, it fell past his hips.

On anyone else it would have looked like a steampunk costume, but Ezra elevated it to a timeless "death-bringer about town" look. I coveted it hard.

I'm not sure if he'd inherited his broad shoulders and height from his Venezuelan Sephardic father, but his darker Middle Eastern coloring was all courtesy of his Mizrahi Jewish mom. He'd loosened his jet-black curls into soft waves raked off his forehead, his dark brows strong slashes over eyes whose silvery-blue swirls reflected the turbulent danger of a stormy sea.

There might come a day when he didn't take my breath away; it would be nice if I could pencil it in for tomorrow.

Ezra pushed away the mostly empty bowl of pretzels that sat between us. "One Bitter Abyss."

"Ri-right away." The bartender snapped into action.

A woman at a nearby table watched him with a feline smile flitting at the corners of her lips. She toyed with the stem of her wineglass.

I snapped a pretzel into shards, wishing I could chide Ezra, because what was the point of striding in here in full mobster assassin mode if you weren't going to terrify everyone? I'm sure if I didn't know that ginger ale made him hiccup uncontrollably, I, too, would be cowering right now.

Ginger ale, huh? Cherry Bomb smirked. *Not how raking your teeth along his inner thigh made him shiver?*

Yo, demon self. Save your evil for others.

I munched on the rest of the salty snacks, watching the bartender assemble bitters and cognac in a heavy cut-crystal glass.

He fired in a squirt of simple syrup then dripped absinthe in from a dark green bottle before garnishing it with a twist of lemon, and placed the drink before Ezra. "The back room is open for you to drink in privacy."

Ezra nodded and slid off the stool. Almost casually, he nodded at me and said, "Get him the same."

I quickly checked my glamor, but it was intact, and Sharnaz had assured me that my natural scent was muffled by the musky cologne magically woven into the disguise.

I wasn't the only man who sat alone or the only one in a nice suit. The second I had my own Bitter Abyss, I headed through the door with a "Private" sign on it and into the back room, joining Ezra.

The small space was pretty basic. The four tables each had

a beat-up lampshade over them, casting weak white light. There was a metal door at the back of the room, a clackety hum from the baseboard heater, and that was about it.

Ezra had barely touched his Bitter Abyss. "Following orders like a pro, I see."

"Those weren't orders, just a misguided suggestion." I used my man voice to get in the habit. "Arjun is a much better choice. He won't attract as much attention."

"What if the plan was precisely for you to attract attention so I could snoop undetected?"

I laughed and flapped a hand at his outfit. "And here you are, the picture of subtlety. My bad."

"Well, you won me five bucks off Darsh for not showing up as Avery." He held out his fist for me to bump.

I left him hanging. "I like the two of you better when you don't bond."

Ezra nodded at my glass. "Try it."

Why? Was this some hilariously disgusting beverage that he wanted me to choke down? I took a sip and made a face because it was too intense for my tastes. "Do I need these ingredients to go through the portal? Is it not the same as going through the rift?"

A liminal wasteland called the Brink lay between earth and the vampire megacity Babel, which was built in an abandoned demon realm. Entry to the Brink was via a portal known as a rift. No one knew how or why they'd sprung up.

There were about a dozen rifts worldwide; Vancouver's had been the last to be discovered about a hundred and fifty years ago, back when we were a fledgling city. They weren't painful to traverse, more like getting a tight hug from a clingy relative who you couldn't wait to get away from. Happily, it only took a couple of seconds to get free of its embrace.

"I don't know how the portals into the Copper Hell are made," Ezra said, "but it feels no different than walking through any door."

71

I rubbed my sore legs. "Then why the drink?"

He traced a finger around the rim of the glass. "Most people going into the Copper Hell are either nervous or amped up. The alcohol relaxes them, and the Bitter Abyss order is the code for the bartender to unlock the metal door."

"Like with a speakeasy. Cool." I sniffed myself. "How'd you know it was me? Didn't my scent change?"

"It did." He licked a drop of booze off his finger.

"Then what? There were other men here by themselves and I sat like a dude, legs wide, chest puffed out." I wasn't angry, just curious about which of my undercover skills required more work.

"I'd know you anywhere, Avi." He said it with a wink, an unexpected lightness settling over his Crimson Prince, hunter-mode demeanor, but there was a hidden charge, a depth to his words. If I still knew him better than anyone, saw him more clearly, well, the reverse also held true.

"That's not stalkerish or anything," I said, aiming for deadpan and not flustered. "And as I've repeatedly told you, you no longer have use of my nickname." We were the only ones in the back room so revealing my name didn't place me in danger, but it was still a jerk move.

He grinned. "We never fought when we were together."

I hadn't thought there was anything to fight about. Not until the end, but when I tried to pick a fight then—God, how I tried, because his anger would have been better than the cold wall he gave me—he wouldn't participate.

"You were sweeter back then too," he added.

"Bet you miss that." I took a healthy slug and set my glass on the table, instantly regretting the alcoholic burn down my throat.

"Not in the least."

Whatever, you weirdo.

He stood up with a firm tug on his leather jacket. "There'll be others watching the gambling. Blend in with them. See if you pick up any gossip about Calista or where her office might be. It's a big yacht. People love to show off that they know the ones in charge, or that they know things they're not supposed to. If you're going to be an unmemorable presence, use that to your advantage. Overhear things. We'll need to access the guests with useful information, but without having to play and place any bets."

"Better keep remind me how to job thing because walk and talk use all think thing." I tapped the side of my head.

"You done?"

"I don't know. Are you? I assumed that if I went in looking like someone with a dick, you wouldn't treat me like an idiot. Apparently not, and now you've ruined any calming effect from that gross drink."

"I don't want you calm. I never have." Ezra opened the metal door, revealing a mesh net woven of magic light strung across it. I couldn't see through it or hear anything from the other side. His lips curled up into a smile with sharp edges and no warmth, his fangs peeking through. "I want you dangerous."

Ezra stepped into the doorway and vanished.

Chapter 8

As I walked through the door, Cherry chiding me about being turned on by Ezra's last words, magic bit into me from all sides. It was kind of like all three heads of the cartoon dog on the pub's sign had decided I was their new favorite chew toy. I felt simultaneously snagged in that mesh net and like I was tumbling through a void, being pulled apart.

My body changed and morphed with a sudden violence that knocked the air from my lungs. The pins and needles sensation in my eyes was overwhelming, almost blinding, while the briny smell rushing up cold and fast off my skin was so strong that I had to swallow down the taste of bile.

There was an entity, an awareness, in this portal, and it planned to break me down for its inspection.

Cold sweat beaded my skin, and I couldn't drag enough air into my lungs for a single normal breath. This thing hadn't just seen past my glamor, it had seized upon my deepest secret and wanted it exposed.

Claws sprung out of my left hand and scales bloomed across my body. I fought to suppress the change and hold on to my glamor, but Sharnaz's disguise tore painfully away from my skin in ribbons like thin wrapping paper, dissolving into the void.

The unseen presence dove deeper inside me, and I screamed, the sound echoing and swirling to batter against me.

A low, familiar hum like a million thrumming locusts vibrated through my veins. Crimson strands of hair whipped against the frosted green scales armoring my face, and my shoulders bulked up, turning my runner's body to a boxer's physique.

Two needle-sharp horns pierced the top of my head.

Laughter vibrated against my skin, like whatever was drawing out my shedim side was pleased with the results.

My fear that I was about to be tossed into the Copper Hell in this aggressive-looking—and highly top-secret—form was a distant second to my inability to sense Cherry Bomb.

It was like she was sealed behind some soundproof barrier. She still existed, but I couldn't feel or even hear her. It was like my gut instincts had suddenly been severed, and I felt as vulnerable as a toddler in a rioting crowd.

Time seemed to stand still as I battled against the force within this portal. I was positive that if I was cast out of here without reclaiming myself, I'd lose Cherry forever. She'd be sealed out of my consciousness, wrapped in eternal bubble packaging I couldn't pop. I couldn't let that happen.

I visualized each part of my human body, clawing piece by piece through the blazing pain and forcing myself back to my regular form. Sweat ran down my neck, while my back and shoulders were tight from exertion by the time my claws returned to fingers.

With that last part of the transformation, Cherry roared back into my head. Her screams of fury were deafening.

Adrenaline coursed through me, giving me the necessary push to tear myself free.

Doubled over and gasping for air, I stumbled out into a

foyer barely bigger than a broom closet. A rush of wind at my back signaled the portal closing behind me. I continued through the open door ahead, but I was so discombobulated that I was unable to appreciate the rippling brushed steel walls wrapping around the huge circular room, the narrow windows spaced in even rows peering into the night sky and inky waters, or the honey-colored lights spread across the ceiling that cast soft glows through swirling clouds of smoke.

Balls clanking in a pachinko machine, the riffle of chips, the clackety-clack of a roulette wheel—the sounds mingled with the rumble of a dozen languages to create a dull roar that vibrated through my head. It was peppered with the metallic clang of engines that shivered up through my feet, though there was no choppiness on board this yacht.

A few hundred people milled about. Some were clad in jewel-toned saris, others in black tie. There were embroidered cheongsams, kilts, racing leathers, one bushy blond Viking-looking dude in fur and metal, and some wearing barely anything at all, like the person clad simply in a swathe of green feathers. However, all of them were as showy as peacocks.

The patrons hunched around the tables like vultures, eagerly awaiting their turns. Varying degrees of despair and hope emanated off the patrons, but greed fogged the air more than any perfume.

Ezra, only a few steps ahead of me, turned around, his eyes widening a fraction before his expression tightened.

I looked down at myself. My own legs, my own arms, and my own preposterously underdressed clothes greeted me.

And here I was, in front of the most dangerous people in this reality.

Happily, there was no physical trace of Cherry. I stood there, not a South Asian man, but as me, wearing only the unbleached tunic and pants I'd changed into before being glamored. I didn't have makeup on either, because Sharnaz insisted on a blank canvas.

All that time and pain acquiring this disguise for nothing.

To add insult to injury, my body still felt dull and heavy. My thick, dark brown waves were plastered to my skull in a messy tangle, my clothes were comprehensively wrinkled, and worst of all, my Maccabee ring glinted like a beacon.

"Abandon hope all ye who enter" wasn't the official slogan of this magic gambling house, but right now, it might as well have been.

I curled my bare toes into the moss-colored carpet, trying to anchor myself to a firm reality. The rug was sharp and prickly, grating against the soles of my feet.

Suddenly, excitement spiked through me hard enough to make my legs shake. Cherry had sensed full demons present.

Or had she? I looked around. Everyone had a human body. Some patrons were Eishei Kodesh, others were vampires, like the employees who made no effort to hide their fangs.

Could shedim be disguised here when my glamor had been stripped away? That didn't feel fair. That aside, were there demons present or was this simply Cherry's reaction to an especially dangerous place?

I narrowed my eyes at an exceedingly generic white guy speaking to the vamp employee at his table in a harsh guttural language that sounded like Klingon punctuated by clicks.

That was a demon language for sure. The client was either a regular or the employee had some kind of translation device, because the vamp dealt them another blackjack card.

It made sense for demons to glamor since some wouldn't have opposable thumbs in their natural form, but I wish I knew how they'd kept their disguise, because it didn't bode well for me.

I ducked at a loud pop, but it was a champagne bottle being uncorked. My heart wouldn't stop racing because everyone here was an enemy, and too many of them were staring at me.

The chatter in the room died off slowly, and even the furious clack of mah-jongg tiles at one table stopped. The dip in sound was like the swoop of a rollercoaster plummeting from the top of the track.

Two staff members—one male, one female—headed toward us. Their fitted gunmetal-gray trousers and collared button-down shirts were accessorized by flat, assessing eyes. The Copper Hell's logo was embroidered above their hearts: a fat flame bound diagonally by a thin copper band.

Training and self-preservation kicked in. I couldn't believe I had to do this, but my life was on the line and I was quite fond of it.

I wrung my hands together, a sniveling expression on my face, and turned to my companion. "Please no. I don't want to be here. I can get you the money I owe, I swear."

Unholy amusement lit Ezra's eyes for a split second. Awesome. Well, I had no one to blame but myself. And whatever was in the portal. Lots of blame for that.

My partner's cold laugh sent shivers down my spine. "You think your debt can be paid off that easily, Maccabee?" He roughly gripped my shoulder.

I winced, hissing in pain. It wasn't all Ezra; the damn lingering glamor ache was truly a bitch.

He relaxed the pressure, keeping his fingers stiffly bent so no one could tell otherwise.

The employees shifted closer, and patrons stared with calculating shrewdness as if formulating how to take me off Ezra's hands. A desperate, in-debt Maccabee would be quite the prize.

"I told you when I bought your marker that I didn't care about the money." Ezra stroked a finger against my cheek. "You'll prove your worth in other ways."

I wrapped my arms around myself because the purr in his

voice had turned my nipples into mini spears under my paper-thin tunic, and I couldn't stop myself from remembering that ill-advised kiss.

Ezra's eyes darted briefly to my lips, but he quickly turned and scanned the room. "Which table's hot tonight?"

The female vamp employee touched her sleek black bracelet and a hologram popped up with six squares. Each one displayed the faces of two to five players.

Ezra studied it for a moment, then pointed at a square with three players. "Them."

"Wait," I said. "Who are they?"

"Did I give you permission to speak?" His sneer sliced through me.

Glad as I was that he was running with my plan, I almost rolled my eyes. *You aren't treading the boards at Stratford, dude. Tone it down a notch.*

I shook my head in answer to his question, regretting the motion immediately since it kicked off a pounding in my temples.

The thing was, no one else looked surprised that Ezra was acting a breath away from twirling a nonexistent mustachio and tying me to a railroad track. Some appeared scared, others wore sly expressions like they were setting him in their sights as well (good luck with that), while most took his attitude as matter-of-fact, but still avoided him.

No one stepped forward to call him friend.

Ezra embraced this role, but I didn't believe he enjoyed it. My ex was a social creature and the Crimson Prince was strangely isolated. Maybe he'd created the Prime Playboy as much to belong as to play spy, because it was hard to remain an island of one for extended periods of time. But even then, Ezra was an outsider. Any relationships he formed in that guise were built on a lie, an illusion.

I dug my nails into my palms to drive away the wistful sting in my chest.

"What are they playing?" Ezra pointed at the players in his chosen hologram.

"Hazard," the female employee said.

Who wouldn't want to play a game with that name, given the circumstances? Sign me right up.

"That'll do," Ezra said. "Set her up there."

That documentary I'd watched about the history of gambling mentioned that hazard was a dice game. One that I had no freaking clue how to play.

"What are the rules?" I said.

"Roll the dice and make sure you win," Ezra said.

My vamp escorts hauled me away.

Elaborate chandeliers boasted cascading tiers of crystals that seemed to swivel as we walked underneath them, as though each one was a magic eye tracking all that happened. Who's to say they weren't in a place like this?

My car key in my pocket thudded against my thigh with each step like a drumbeat leading to the gallows—or to the shore of a deep, cold lake of fear. *This is my plan*, I reminded myself. *I am not helpless in this situation. And I am not alone.*

To boost my spirits, I dubbed the employees Li'l Hellions in my head because envisioning these bloodsuckers as a motley group of Depression-era rascals with newsie caps ratcheted down my spiraling emotions by several notches.

Other Li'l Hellions manned the tables, which were set out at spacious intervals. One dispensed cards in a blur, another calmly snapped the wrist of a much larger man who played his domino tile too soon. The man cried out as the Hellion calmly and efficiently reran the round.

There was gambling from all over the world represented here, and not just the obvious choices. I spied heated tournaments of popular board games.

Over to my right, a man roared in triumph, flinging his winning cards down on an oval poker table. He thumped a fist on a padded leather bumper, and his opponent, a woman in a Chanel suit, cried out, begging for another chance.

"Banker calls the forfeit," the Li'l Hellion at their table said with no emotion whatsoever.

The female opponent ran but got only a handful of steps because manacles made of purple and orange magic captured her wrists and ankles. A fat collar jerked tight around her neck, and her lips were magically sewn together in garish stitches.

More purple and orange magic swirled around the bound woman. Her skin grew pallid and her body shook harder and harder, her head thrashing so violently I braced myself for the snap of her neck.

A magic stream of light poured out of her. It split into two, half going into a slot in the table next to the banker and the other half swirling into the winner. His cheeks lost their jowly, ruddy appearance, and while he didn't look younger, he looked healthier.

The female player grew gaunt, and when the manacles released her, she slumped forward like a rag doll.

How had some life force or vitality been taken from her? There wasn't Eishei Kodesh magic that could extract life, much less transfer it.

Demons, Cherry answered in a giddy voice. The magic that rendered this yacht invisible, the portal, the mechanism for betting and collecting bets, it was all demon magic. It had to be, though we were here on earth.

Regardless, the fact that this megayacht wasn't built in a demon realm like Babel meant I had control over my physical form. Sadly, that wasn't much of a consolation considering my own emotions made me vulnerable to exposure.

One of my escorts prodded me to walk faster.

Even if I stayed calm and locked Cherry down tight, the bets themselves were deadly. I stumbled. What would I be forced to risk?

Ezra touched the small of my back, not for comfort but to get me moving.

I ground my teeth together, keeping my eyes on the carpet, because the prickling that preceded the toxic green eyes of my stage-one shedim form was so strong, it made my teeth throb.

Ezra didn't want me calm? Mazel tov. He'd gotten his wish.

Cherry cackled in my head.

He'd said it was no big deal to go through the portal into this gaming hell, yet I'd been broken down and stripped bare. If he'd known from the beginning that I'd end up exposed and left with no choice but to play the only card in my hand—being in his debt—he'd also find out how dangerous I could be.

Now that was a future worth surviving for.

Chapter 9

The Hellions stopped before a spiral staircase blocked off from the rest of the hall with a velvet rope and a surly vamp standing guard. He unhooked the rope, and I was forced up the stairs through another door into a central atrium.

It was a breathtaking space with a soaring glass dome providing a mesmerizing view of the starlit sky. Multiple glass doors were thrown open to the night. Directly ahead through one of them, I spied the sleek jut of the prow. I breathed in the salty sea breeze. This yacht was more streamlined than I expected for a ship this size, but it allowed for a hell of a smooth ride.

There were far fewer people up here. Most milled about an enormous buffet table and nearby bar, while others conversed at smaller lounges within the atrium. One lounge overflowed with a lush garden, another glistened with multiple water features. They should have warmed up the large space, made it more personal, but look closer and you'd see the plants had a spiky, almost carnivorous quality, and the water in the small fountains thrust jets up in an aggressive rush instead of a soothing patter.

The closest lounge on my left—stern? port?—grouped hard-edged furniture around fire pits that didn't emit any heat.

The back wall was two stories high, lined with rows of black doors that spanned the width of the ship.

Ezra stalked behind us. I didn't hear his footsteps, but I sensed his brooding gaze trained on my back.

Outside, a flicker of silver scales reflected off the moonlight before disappearing under the waves with a quiet splash. I'd have rubbed my eyes, wondering if I'd really seen a giant serpent's tail, but my arms were firmly held by the Hellions.

The vamps steered me up another smaller spiral staircase to the second floor and along the walkway to the fourth door. My female handler rapped twice.

I'd rather floss with a cactus than be confined with dangerous players while fumbling through an unfamiliar game with high stakes, but as there were no handy desert plants available, I'd have to see my plan through.

I steeled my shoulders and stepped inside.

"Ezra, pet. It's been a minute." One of the players from the hologram, the woman was of Chinese heritage, with a huge afro, a colorful kaftan, and killer jade-green heels. Some of the consonants in her melodic British accent were tempered like other Cantonese speakers I'd met in Vancouver's Hong Kong community. She rose gracefully from a highly polished round table, but at his stony expression, she hesitated to approach him. "Alas," she murmured. "Nary a trace of the Prime Playboy today."

"Maud." He gave her the briefest nod, then narrowed his eyes, tracking every detail in our surroundings.

The room rocked a "big game hunter on acid" vibe. All the chairs were upholstered in a zebra skin fabric. At least I hoped it was fabric. The gold ceiling held complicated glass fixtures resembling UFOs. No doubt they contained security cameras, but they also provided a diffused light that bounced off wallpaper featuring a colorful jungle scene, and along the leopard print carpet.

If the point was to induce nausea then good job, room.

One chair at the table was missing, allowing space for a female Hellion with pale green eyes and white-blond hair shaved down to a half inch to stand. The far end of the room was dominated by a fully stocked bar. A large flat-screen television displayed Monet's waterlilies.

The two other players didn't bother greeting us. A serious Black man in a pressed tuxedo held a pair of small white dice, looking impatient. The other guy hooked his thumbs into his red suspenders, fangs peeking out of his happy smile.

Since my blue flame magic didn't work on vamps, I used it to illuminate any weaknesses on what I assumed were the two humans. Sadly, nothing showed up in my synesthete vision, not even the tiniest dot denoting a bead of sweat at their temples or rapid pulsing signaling their increased heartbeat.

Weird, since the Black man had clearly recognized the Crimson Prince. His eyes had narrowed with a slight wariness. He'd almost immediately gone back to an inscrutable expression, but I should have detected some lingering internal aftereffect of that emotion.

There were three possible reasons why I couldn't read Maud or the man with the dice, none of them good. The first was because they were also vampires. If any or all of them were old enough to compel me, that would really suck. A compulsion wouldn't affect rolling dice, but they could make me bet that I'd reveal my deepest, darkest secret or cluck like a chicken.

I shot Ezra a sideways glance. I'd rather tell the world I was an infernal than play chicken in front of him.

The second possibility as to why I couldn't read them was if the serious dude and Maud wore shielding devices. These rare and expensive instruments wouldn't do squat if a Red Flame decided to touch and torch them, but they blocked all psychological attacks on their person from Eishei Kodesh or vamps.

The final reason was if the pair were psychopaths who didn't experience fear, guilt, or remorse. That didn't exclude the other two reasons, though.

Look at that, a veritable "I'm screwed" buffet of possibility.

I had no shielding device, and not only was I battling my own emotions, I had to fight to keep Cherry's in check because the danger of this place had juiced her up.

The Li'l Hellions shoved me into the chair between the Black man and Maud.

"A newbie and you already have two fine specimens manhandling you?" She batted her lashes at the two employees, flicking a gold lighter on and off. "It took me a whole month to earn that."

Heh. I liked Maud. I mean, if she'd slept with, or worse, been romantically involved with the Prime Playboy, I'd still want to toss her out a fourth-story window, and she'd be out for blood in this game, but the woman had a great sense of humor. Too bad I couldn't make my usual snarky retort friendship opener, because right now I was the destitute, thoroughly cowed operative in Ezra's debt.

Full disclosure: it grated to be seated next to this stunning woman. It grated more that my discomfort stemmed from Ezra's ability to compare and contrast us.

Fuck it. I embraced my strung-out, sweaty appearance. I excelled when other people underestimated me.

Ezra hovered behind my chair. Had he been human, he'd be breathing down my neck.

I was tempted to elbow him and get him to back off, but the Hellion stationed at our table, our banker, stared him down with her eerie pale eyes until he dropped into a club chair slightly off to the side, looking bored.

"Get me a drink." He shrugged out of his Victorian-style

leather jacket, leaving him in his vest and soft white shirt. Somehow that didn't lessen his menace factor. "Rh-null. Chilled."

Suspender Vamp laughed. "Not even the Copper Hell carries Golden Blood. Less than one in six million have that phenotype."

"Would you like your entire bottle from the cellar, sir?" my female handler said.

"A glass will do," Ezra replied.

The two Li'l Hellions who'd accompanied me bowed and withdrew.

I may have been gaping at Ezra keeping a bottle here at the Hell of incredibly rare blood that I didn't know existed, but Suspender Vamp's eyes bugged out like a cartoon character.

Ezra laughed unkindly. "That's not a good look, Clyde."

The other vampire flushed angrily, mottling his already ruddy complexion. Not an attractive addition.

Our vampire banker rapped on the table to return our attention to the game. "Caster, roll your Main," she said.

The Black player rubbed his thumb over the dice, then balled them into his fist, shook fast, and released them in the shallow depression in the center of the table.

The dice clattered against the wood in an oddly soothing sound. I didn't trust it for a second.

"My Main is eight," he said in a French accent.

"Caster, place your forfeit."

He unstrapped a gold watch from his wrist. Its face was cloudy, and as the player set it on the table, a chorus of whispers emanated from it.

I averted my eyes and tried not to listen.

"I'll Nick," he said.

All this was new terminology to me, so I repeated the words in my head, sussing out the meanings as best I could according to context. Unless Nick referred to a certain dice combination, it meant win, since the guy wouldn't bet against himself.

"Players may bet," the banker said.

Maud shook her head, flicking her finger back and forth through the lighter flame. I used to do that with candles when I was a kid.

"He'll Out," Clyde said. "I'll forfeit my sense of smell for one hour."

You could bet senses? What. The. Fuck.

The pale-eyed banker looked at me, but I shook my head. I wasn't betting anything until I understood the rules. "Caster may roll," she said.

He rolled a ten.

"The Chance is ten," the banker said.

French guy rolled again and got a six. He rolled a third time and got an eight, which was his Main.

His face fell.

"Caster is Out."

Clyde chuckled and snapped his suspenders.

Okay, apparently the Caster had to roll his Chance in order to Nick or win, but if he rolled his Main, he lost. He was Out. Did other numbers come into play? The six hadn't.

A tiny magic whirlwind scooped up the watch that had been wagered, spinning it faster and faster until it cracked in a jagged line across the face.

The banker flicked the whirlwind away and handed half the watch to the vampire. The other half went into the slot in the table next to the banker.

The whispers grew louder and more agitated, the watch face now roiling with smoke.

Satisfied, Clyde grunted and stuffed his half in his pocket.

The male Hellion, now wearing white gloves, returned with a champagne flute of blood on a silver tray. He placed the glass on the side table next to Ezra, bowed again, and left.

Ignoring Clyde's greedy stare, Ezra took a sip, rolling that first taste around in his mouth like a true connoisseur. *Delighted that rare vintage pleases you, Conquistador.*

"Play passes," the banker said.

The Frenchman, sitting on my left, held the dice out to me.

I blinked.

After a few expectant seconds, he took my palm and placed the dice in it, as though I was a very slow and idiot child.

Ezra growled. "Hands off my property." He didn't compel the man. He was too young, even as a Prime, for that vampire ability to work on a person, but his command landed like a gavel.

The man dropped his hold so fast that my knuckles hit the table.

My achiness from the glamor and crossing through the portal was finally dying down, and now this? I shook out my stinging hand and shot Ezra a defiant glare.

Maud regarded me thoughtfully.

Whoops. Forgot to play meek and scared. Oh well, it wasn't necessarily a bad thing for them to see I had some fire.

Clyde jerked his thumb at me. "Haven't broken this one yet?"

Ezra took another sip of Golden Blood, not deigning to respond. A power play in hemoglobin form.

"Caster, roll your Main," the banker said.

I rolled a two.

Silence.

A two was no good, but an eight was okay? All right, there were parameters as to which numbers could be a Main. I rolled again and got a ten.

More silence.

Above two, less than ten.

I rolled a five.

The Banker looked at me expectantly.

"My Main is five," I said.

"Caster, place your forfeit."

I glanced at Ezra for some direction, but he simply watched me dispassionately.

Money was no good, and I didn't have a magic artifact to wager, nor did I want to bet any of my senses or a body part. Talk about problems I never thought I'd face.

I squeezed the dice. Say that Maud and Frenchie were human and something happened that allowed me to illuminate their weaknesses, hazard wasn't like poker, where I could read tells to get ahead. This was strictly a game of chance, so maybe my magic was the safest thing to bet. If I could bet a sense, I could bet my powers, couldn't I?

"I bet—"

"Forfeit," Maud murmured.

My cheeks flamed. My newb status here at the Copper Hell was perfect for our plan, but I hated presenting myself as anything other than totally competent. "I'll forfeit ten minutes of my blue flame magic."

"This isn't the kiddie table," Clyde scoffed.

"Minimum one hour forfeit," the banker said.

"I'll forfeit one hour of my blue flame magic," I said with forced patience. How on earth would they measure an hour's worth? Should I lose, I'd be at the banker's mercy to properly claim the wager. I had to trust that Hellion not to break me, mind, body, or spirit. I rolled the dice around in my clammy palm. "I'll Nick."

The French player spread his hands wide. "I'll forfeit an hour of my life. She'll Out."

"Out," Maud agreed. "I'll forfeit an hour of my magic."

She hadn't specified what her magic was. I mentally slapped myself upside the head for announcing mine.

My annoyance must have been obvious because she smiled at me with no trace of malice. "Rookie mistake, pet."

"She'll Out for sure." Clyde stroked his chin. "I'll forfeit one hour of strength."

Look at me, bonding the others in their conviction of my failure. I shook the dice vigorously and slammed them onto the table.

The first one stopped on three. The second die teetered. It looked like I might land the two and get my Main of five, which I hoped was a good thing on the first roll.

There was the faintest wisp of warm air and the die tumbled over onto the four.

"The Chance is seven," the banker said.

I swallowed my incredulous laugh. Either Maud or the Frenchman had used orange flame magic to fuck with my dice, which made one of them human.

Orange Flames radiated heat into or out of things: people, a log, the air, anything really. They could force my body heat out of me to the point of giving me a lethal case of hypothermia, so I was lucky this one hadn't attacked me directly.

Whoever it was hadn't manipulated the dice when I rolled to determine my Main. Was that not allowed, or did it not matter what I declared, since cheating helped only once that first number was set?

I rolled again, hoping for lucky number seven, my Chance, but I got a four.

Expectant silence. All right, four was a neutral number.

Another roll landed me a three.

Clyde snickered. "She's Out."

Why? What the hell were the rules?

"Banker calls the forfeit."

Before I could wrap my head around the fact that I'd lost, a slicing pain burned its way through my body, bringing tears to my eyes. Blue magic smoked off my skin, and I couldn't catch my breath, unable to do anything more than bob along helplessly in the wake of the agony tearing through me.

The magic split into four streams. Two went into the other

players, one went into the slot in the table next to the banker, and the final one went into a tiny dented brass box that the vampire had pulled out and opened.

The pain dissipated so suddenly that I practically flopped over face-first.

"How disappointing," Ezra murmured and had another swallow of Golden Blood.

I couldn't find an iota of concern in his icy expression. Sure, that would have given our subterfuge away, but... *But what?* I chided myself. *Buck up and get your head in the game.*

Ezra hadn't chosen this table without a good reason. He was trusting me to use this angle somehow and further our investigation. He wasn't making small talk with the others to gain information, so it had to come down to the forfeits.

I took a moment to catch my breath, spinning my Maccabee ring around, and letting my consternation show. Neither of us had any way of influencing the dice. The only thing we could use were forfeits and only if I won.

Clyde patted the box before placing it back in his pocket. "This'll come in handy."

I filed away the information that there were artifacts that allowed vampires to collect and use Eishei Kodesh magic.

The banker nodded at me. "Caster, roll your Main."

I said a prayer and rolled the dice.

Chapter 10

"My Main is nine."

"Caster, place your forfeit."

"I'll Nick..." I clenched my fists in my lap, still feeling shaky from losing the last round. Obviously, I bet that I'd win, but what wager would cause the least damage to me in case I didn't? No, that didn't matter. What would be the best wager to ensure we left this room with a solid clue? "If I Out, I'll forfeit a memory."

That barely roused any interest in the others.

Losing one hour of my magic had been agony, and I couldn't imagine how bad a memory might be. Would I remember it if I lost? I shook off my fears. This made the most sense as a forfeit, because if they did the same, I might learn something.

Except, this only worked if I won *and* could demand specific memories from them.

"Her memory will involve a topic of your choosing," Ezra said. "Vice versa should she Nick."

Points for being in sync with me and reframing it better, but damn. I'd have to be very creative with what I shared to fulfill the terms of the wager.

The silence went from vague curiosity to as loaded at Ezra's statement as if he'd pulled a pin out of a grenade.

Maud set her lighter down on the table.

I twisted around with a snarl, intending to tear a strip off Ezra, because my undercover persona would never agree to that, when a needle thin probe invaded my mind, a command to accept the wager as stated.

This wasn't Eishei Kodesh magic. That would have been either a blanketing of calm along with the certainty that this was the right thing to do, or an amped-up blaze of competition making me want to take any risk to win.

No, this focused, almost surgical directive was a vamp compulsion.

Cherry scoffed at it, which was interesting. I'd had a vamp compel me before, and I wasn't able to block them. The demon magic was working in my favor. Finally, something on this stupid boat was going my way. Halle-freaking-lujah!

Ezra didn't have compulsion magic, nor did he need to force me in this situation to agree.

So by process of elimination, that meant Clyde was behind the compulsion. Why? Did he want to show me something in particular or, more plausibly, did he want to learn something specific from me? About Maccabees? About Ezra?

My bet was on the latter.

"Does the Caster agree to the forfeit?" the banker asked.

"I agree," I said placidly.

Maccabees received some defensive training in shielding our thoughts, provided we had time to prepare. No one would think to ask if I was an infernal. Regardless of whether they wanted dirt on Maccabees or Ezra, I could give them something that wasn't too damning, but still satisfied the bet.

"Who's willing to match the forfeit?" Ezra said. "Henri? Care to find out if she has information on Maccabee security protocols? That would come in handy in your line of work."

"Bien sûr, if she does, but that's a big if."

"Her mother is a chapter director," Ezra said.

Ice slid down my spine.

"We'd each get any memory we want?" Clyde said eagerly. "That's three memories. Four if you include the house."

"No." I white-knuckled the dice. I couldn't defend myself against that many memories being exposed. The odds that I didn't hand over important Maccabee information, or out myself as a half shedim, were not in my favor. Plus, paying one forfeit had been excruciating. Four might kill me. "I don't agree to that. You still need my agreement, right?"

"Yes," the banker said, but she glanced at Ezra.

Seriously?

Ezra didn't look perturbed by my outburst. Nor did he disagree. "You always were a greedy little fuck, Clyde. No wonder my father would have nothing to do with you."

Clyde's fangs descended.

Ezra raised an eyebrow.

The other vamp hissed, but when Ezra broke out a smile that would make the Grim Reaper ask for pointers, Clyde backed down with a grumble.

"The winners will agree upon a single memory," Ezra said. "Should she Out, they'll all get the same one."

I let out a relieved sigh.

"Chances are good she'll lose," Maud said. *Why, pet? Because you'll mess with the dice and make sure I do?* She was back to flicking her lighter on and off.

I winced because using a lighter too often hurt my fingertips. That woman must have mad calluses or a better class of lighter than the gas station cheapies I ended up with. Oh. Hang on. I clutched the dice tightly, their edges biting into my palms.

Sachie was an Orange Flame. She could light a candle with her magic but that required a ridiculous amount of energy. It was far easier to use matches. However, she didn't like lighters either, because her magic made her fingertips even more sensitive than mine.

None of that told me what power Maud had, but it meant Henri was the Orange Flame.

The Frenchman leaned forward. "What are you playing at, Ezra? Why would you allow her to place this wager? How does it benefit you?"

"I have more important things to attend to." Ezra put his jacket back on, the leather rustling softly. He'd armored up, though his strategy wouldn't involve charging across the battlefield with a war cry. He'd hunt his prey patiently, in the shadows. "The sooner her debt is repaid and I wrap this up, the better."

Good. Set the clock ticking and get them to agree.

"I don't believe you," Clyde said. "Why forfeit a piece that still has value?"

A piece? I ground my teeth together.

Ezra crossed his arms, his muscular biceps flexing. "Perhaps this will convince you that I wish to be done with her. Should she Out, *she'll* be the forfeit in the next round. One month's servitude."

I gasped, genuine fear slicing through me, raising goose bumps on my arms. Would Ezra sacrifice me to find Calista's killers? They'd stolen his chance at revenge, so now he'd take his fury out on them and damn whoever got in the way? "You can't do that."

"I can and I will." He met my eyes with a flat stare that bore no trace of humanity.

For the life of me, I couldn't tell if he was acting anymore. Desperate, I looked at the banker.

She stared back impassively.

I bowed my head and dug my nails into my thighs. The facts I had to draw conclusions from weren't reassuring.

My ex possessed patience, stealth, and cunning, and he

went to extremes to achieve his goals. Who's to say I wasn't acceptable collateral damage?

I certainly couldn't.

I wasn't surprised that the rest of them spoke about me like I was some object to possess, but how could Ezra behave this way? There was keeping up appearances and then there was cruelty. If I lost this round, not only would I have to share a memory, but he'd promised my servitude—or worse—as the wager in the next round. There was no rescinding that.

"Her debt is not as amusing as I anticipated," Ezra said. "Either way, I want to be done with this." He eyed Maud, a wicked grin breaking free. "There are much more entertaining things to occupy myself with later."

"The Prime Playboy returns at last," she said. "How delightful."

I was numb, struggling to convince myself this was all an act and Ezra had my back.

The three players consulted among themselves then announced my forfeit would be my memory of transport procedures for taking dangerous Eishei Kodesh criminals to the magic maximum security prison in the Canadian prairies.

I felt ill as I agreed, but at least I didn't know where the rest of the prisons in the world were. It was now my turn to state their forfeit. It was small consolation that it was my choice, not Ezra's.

I could ask for their last memory of Calista. I surmised that some, if not all of them knew her or Ezra wouldn't have picked this table to park me at. That was too obvious, though, given I was a Maccabee. It smacked of an investigation.

"You'll each provide the detailed memory of your time today at the Copper Hell," I said.

Henri frowned. "I've only been here an hour. That's not much of a forfeit."

"I'll still get your valuable impressions on other players. I have a debt to discharge." I didn't bother to hide my sneer at Ezra. "The sooner I'm done with this, the better."

He shrugged. "We're on the same page."

The other players agreed as well.

"Roll." The command came from Ezra, not the banker. She didn't chastise or correct him.

I grabbed the dice, digging deep into my self-control to keep my hand from shaking. It occurred to me that Ezra hadn't used my name this entire time. Did it help him dehumanize me and forget we were supposed to be on the same team?

If I was truly on my own, then I had to save myself. Chance and luck would determine my roll, provided I neutralized Henri's orange flame magic. I pointed at the carafe of ice water on the bar. "Can I get a drink first?"

The banker nodded, and I poured myself a glass.

I took a long swallow, then returned to the table, making a show of wiping my sweaty palms off on my loose pants. I was pretty sure that if I rolled my Main of nine that I'd win, but I didn't know what the other numbers signified.

"Come on, nine." I picked up the dice, shook them, and rolled, jostling the water glass in the process.

It spilled all over Henri, who jumped up, cursing. One Frenchman: officially neutralized.

Maud chuckled.

The dice came to a stop. Six and three.

Ultimately, if you didn't have luck, you didn't have anything, but tonight, the Lady was with me big-time.

I gasped and laughed out loud. "I Nicked. I won, right?"

"Caster wins," the vamp banker agreed.

Clyde blurred out of his seat to lean over Ezra. "You did something to affect the dice. Bystanders can't get involved."

Ezra flicked him in the chest with his middle finger to make him move back. He didn't have to do it hard, which was more insulting. "Like what, exactly? I don't have orange flame magic to influence the roll, and no matter how fast I am, I couldn't grab the dice and set them on nine without you noticing something stuttery about the dice's movement. Did you? Did any of you?"

Maud and Henri blanched at Ezra's menacing tone, but Clyde got sulky. "No, but she couldn't have been that lucky given the memory she stood to lose. Arrest him."

"The house senses no interference," the banker said. "Banker calls forfeits."

Maud, Henri, and Clyde looked vaguely ill. This was going to hurt.

Good, Cherry thought. True, I shouldn't be the only one suffering. Too bad Ezra was getting off scot-free.

None of the three made a fuss. This wasn't the lower level where players had to be bound and forced to comply.

The house collected all the forfeits at once. So long as I lived, I'd never forget their animalistic cries, or the blood streaming from their tear ducts and ears.

I parted my lips on a soft sigh and my blood pumped harder as I rode the high of collecting their wagers—their knowledge—the rush made sweeter by the losers' misery and pain.

Information crashed over me: images of a dozen different games in sharp smooth colors flooded my mind, conversations played simultaneously like a six-track audio board in my ears, and the sour sweat of Maud's last opponent clogged my nostrils.

The air took on an electric charge, while the carpet felt thin and hard like a chessboard.

The taste of blood filled my mouth.

Everything was a surreal swirl of emotion and past fragments, save for Ezra's solid, unwavering image.

My body grew taut, strung like a wire up to the snapping point. A twang ran through me, then all of us were released.

Maud, Henri, and Clyde were pale and quiet.

Even Cherry was overwhelmed.

I couldn't sift through all the information, nor was I allowed to leave until I played a third round of hazard. No one bet, so it was me against the house. I wagered losing my scent for an hour, but I won.

As soon as my third turn was over, I passed the dice to Maud, stood up, and saluted the others. "A pleasure," I said snidely.

Ezra shot out of his seat and was gripping my elbow before I registered that he'd moved. "Time for you to discharge your debt."

My stomach tightened with a peculiar mix of anticipation and dread. This was all part of the role he was playing, part of the plan I'd set in motion, but the intensity in his eyes made me question how much of it was an act.

Chapter 11

Ezra deemed our debrief happen in the men's room at the end of the walkway, muttering "no cameras" before he shoved me inside.

The guy taking a piss at the urinal swore and told me to get lost, but when Ezra pulled the hand dryer off the wall and crumpled it like it was paper, he hurriedly tucked his dick away and bolted.

"What did you lear—ouf!" Ezra flinched.

I shook out my fist. He hadn't actually doubled over, but my bruised knuckles were totally worth it. "Forfeit that, asshole."

Kick him in the groin. Punch him in the head. I swear Cherry was shaking pom-poms.

I eyed Ezra.

He stomped over to the restroom door and locked it, trapping the two of us together. "You think I'd have let it get that far? Thanks for the trust, partner."

"Oh no." I poked Ezra in the chest. Hard. "Only one of us gets to be outraged, and it's not you."

He slapped my hand away. "It would never have come to you being the forfeit."

"You couldn't guarantee that." I hopped up to sit on the clean counter. It was better than standing barefoot on the tiles of a public restroom, despite them looking meticulously clean and glossy. "You said it yourself. You couldn't influence the dice."

He rubbed the back of his neck and, for an incredibly powerful vampire, suddenly looked sheepish.

I picked up the crumpled hand dryer, ready and willing to brain him with it. "Explain yourself."

"Okay. See…" He exhaled, then did a double take. "Your eyes have gone green."

I swiped the dryer a couple times in his direction, blinking to get my shedim self under control. "You're trying my patience."

Ezra flinched at my growled words. "Vamp compulsion gets stronger the older we are, right?"

"Vamps can't compel inanimate objects. Not even Primes."

"No, but Primes have a mild twist on compulsion magic. At least I do." He paused. "Telekinesis."

"Bullshit."

He held out his hand for the dryer.

Was Ezra about to show me one of those cards he kept so close to his chest? A thrill surged through me, and the air was thick with anticipation. This covert rendezvous transformed the familiar space into a sanctuary of shared secrets.

I slapped the dryer into his palm. Or into an arena where blood might still be spilled with no one the wiser. That didn't lessen the excitement.

"If you're done bruising me," he muttered.

"Not even close."

Sighing, he placed the dryer on the counter and stepped back a few feet. A second later, it did a somersault and slid jerkily over to him. There was no wisp of warm air like when Henri had manipulated the dice with his orange flame magic.

"Even this sized item tests the limits of my ability," he said. "It's mild. A party trick, though no one else knows about it."

"You fucker. You didn't think to mention this ace up your sleeve before we came here?" It was much better for my mental well-being to hang on to my anger than imagine a young Ezra with long stretches of time by himself practicing this little trick, knowing he had no one to impress with it.

"Could you fake a racing heart and accelerated pulse when I did it?"

I blinked. "Uh, well, no."

"Exactly. I knew there'd be vampires here. Demons too." He narrowed his eyes. "Which begs the question of why they're walking around glamored and you aren't."

"This is not my fault! I have no idea why this happened, and if you're accusing me of deliberately blowing—"

"What? No." He raked a hand through his curls. "That's not what I meant. Look." He reached for me.

I crossed my arms. I still felt as raw as if I'd been flayed, and I wasn't ready for non-violent physical contact with him.

"I wouldn't have harmed you, Aviva. I swear it."

I laughed bitterly. I hadn't been in any danger, fine, but it would take time getting over my feelings of betrayal and the fear I'd end up in debt to one of the other players. "Bit late for that."

"I did the least damage I could," he said quietly.

I frowned, suddenly unsure whether we were still talking about the dice game. However, my anger dissipated. I checked in the mirror and found that my eyes had returned to their light brown color. "It's a fair question," I admitted. "About why my cover was blown."

I told him what I experienced stepping through the portal.

Ezra picked up the hand dryer, manipulating the metal in different directions to re-form it. The dryer roughly assumed its original shape, but it was never going to once more become smooth and shiny and unmarred. Same, dryer. Same. "I don't love that something knows you're a half shedim," he said, "even if it's just a supernatural security system. Though it might have worked out in our favor. You lost the glamor, but this story played out better."

"And since my human form is my natural state, I wasn't exposed to all and sundry. I guess that's a silver lining." Still sitting on the counter, I turned on the tap and wet my hands, using my fingers as a comb to detangle and fix my hair as much as possible. "Let's run through the memories I got."

"That was an excellent call, by the way," he said.

"You'd think I'd exceled at making critical assessments for years or something."

He tossed the still-dented dryer onto the counter. "I wasn't being patronizing. Look, we got through a tough situation together. Either this is a fight about something else, or you can move on like the professional I know you are."

"Let's move on," I said tightly. Guilt sat in my stomach like a heavy stone, but I didn't have it in me to apologize for being overly sensitive.

I launched into the memories I'd gotten from Maud. She was super chatty and Ezra stopped me multiple times to clarify a point of conversation. The only useful information from her time at the Copper Hell tonight was when she ordered some rare vintage of wine at the bar in the atrium, was told the shipment had been delayed, and that Calista was looking into it. Maud had gotten sulky and flirted with the bartender to let her speak to Calista.

He'd refused, saying Calista was busy and would get to it in due course.

A bouncer showed up and told Maud to let the bartender do his job. Maud hadn't liked that, but she'd dropped the issue. Neither the bouncer or bartender acted cagey about Calista.

"They don't know she's missing." Ezra paced the restroom.

"Someone has to be running this place, though. What did Henri get us?"

"Some useful tells if I planned to gamble against some other players, but nothing in terms of this investigation. Clyde had an interesting memory, though. There are staff corridors throughout the yacht."

"I know that already." Ezra pulled a key card out of his coat pocket with a cocky grin. "I thought it might be useful, so I liberated it from the guy who served my drink."

I high-fived him. "You weren't wrong. One of the doors in the hallway up here was of great interest to Clyde. He didn't know the security code and a wrong try ends in…" I sucked my bottom lip into my mouth, sorting through more memories. "I don't know the specifics, but Clyde really didn't want to get it wrong, and a key card wouldn't unlock the door. I think I can find where it is, though the code is anyone's guess."

"One thing at a time," Ezra said. He unlocked the bathroom door.

With a grimace, I slid onto the floor. I was going to bathe in a vat of disinfectant when I got home.

I followed him back to the spiral staircase, staying close as we descended. There were entrances to the staff corridor here in the atrium, but we'd be too exposed. Ezra was pretty sure he knew of another one outside, so we left.

The night wind whipped my hair into my face. I was barefoot, in a thin tunic and pants, and I was freezing. I'd have sprinted to our next destination because my toes were going numb, but there were other gamblers out here and we had to play our roles, so I shuffled miserably after Ezra.

A grizzled man in his late sixties leaned against the railing, idly watching us approach. He sucked on his cigarette, not caring about the ash that fell onto his wool fisherman's sweater. From his gray eyes that caught the moonlight to his windswept salt-and-pepper hair, this older man was handsome in a rugged way.

However, he appeared out of place among the menacing vampires and glittering humans. Was this the captain? His bulky muscled arms looked capable of hoisting masts or steering jibs.

Did one steer a jib? Maybe I should have read more pirate books. Watched a documentary or two.

He flicked his unfinished cigarette into the ocean. "Having fun?" His voice was gravelly and conjured up the rough swell of a stormy sea, but it wasn't unpleasant. There was something mellifluous about it, something that hinted at freedom swimming in the wild waves.

Ezra brushed past him without a second look. The Crimson Prince didn't deign to notice most people. It was generally better for them that way.

I gave the older man one last curious look over my shoulder.

He leaned out on the railing, his face to the water, but, as if sensing my gaze, turned. He was too far away, and it was too dark to see his eyes, but I shivered, positive that he was seeing into me. I picked up the pace, glad when we turned a corner and he was lost to view.

The key card worked perfectly on the scanner, and Ezra and I slipped inside the corridor without being seen. It was empty, but we had no idea how long it would stay that way, so I guided us as quickly as my legs—and Clyde's memory—allowed. We eventually came to a narrow stairwell. "Up here." We hurried onto a tiny landing.

"Voilà." I motioned at the heavy wooden door with a numeric keypad mounted next to it. Best-case scenario, it'd set off an alarm. "How are we going to get past—"

Ezra punched in the final number of a six-digit sequence, and the light on the keypad turned green.

I planted my hands on my hips. "Maybe warn me next time! Also, how did you possibly know the passcode?"

"Lucky guess." He grasped the polished brass doorknob, and I flinched, but he opened it without incident.

The rich scent of aged leather and mahogany was the best thing so far in this damnable place. It reminded me of the resource library at Maccabee HQ, where I'd spent many happy hours. I smiled, flicked on a green-shaded standing lamp, and whistled softly.

Dark wood paneling similar to the one in the Jolly Hellhound extended halfway up the walls, giving the room a warm and inviting feel. This was amplified by the small sofa and steamer trunk on wide, worn floorboards, which provided the perfect spot for gazing out at the panoramic view of the sea through the large window, framed by the heavy velvet curtains that were drawn back to the night. Directly under the window was an imposing antique oak desk, its surface worn smooth by years of use.

Ezra locked the door.

Behind the desk was an old high-backed leather chair with brass rivets and wooden armrests. I sat down, swiveling slightly, and opened the single drawer searching for a laptop, but there wasn't one.

Ezra combed through the topmost shelf of one of the two bookshelves bolted to the walls, whose glass doors kept the manuscripts and leather journals from falling out.

I opened one of the Moleskine journals on the desk. "Back to that lucky guess."

"It really was a guess," he said. "Calista is an ancient Prime. She prides herself on her cleverness, so her numeric password wouldn't be something obvious, but it would still be easy for her to remember. Like the birthday of a loved one."

The journal was written in some kind of coded shorthand. I flipped it shut. "How could you possibly know that? I thought you weren't friends."

"We weren't." Ezra's smile was acidic enough to dissolve

bodies. "I told you she wanted to kill me. She just also wanted to meet the only other Prime before she had her henchmen take me out."

I put down the journal with a jerky slap. "But you're clearly still here."

"Disappointed?"

I smirked, and I guess Ezra decided not to wait and hear my answer because he pressed on.

"Calista was big on hierarchies," he said, "and in her mind, my existence threatened her power. It didn't matter that I had no interest in challenging her."

I was about to retort that Ezra was perfectly happy to play top of the food chain when it suited him, but I didn't because it was exactly that. An act. He had accepted Darsh leading an investigation that Ezra was deeply invested in without much protest.

Yes, he'd pulled rank on our previous case and steamrolled over Michael's authority, but how much of that had been Ezra armoring up to enter the lion's den? It was bad enough he'd be crossing paths with Michael, he had to suspect he'd see me as well. At the time I believed that didn't matter to him.

I stood corrected.

Plus, he'd not only accepted me as a true co-leader, he'd valued the input of the rest of the team.

"Calista sounds like she was quite the special unicorn," I said.

"The night I was presented to her, she was sitting at a banquet table like some queen." He snorted and unrolled a parchment scroll, his eyes scanning the thin paper. "She drank a toast, saying that her lucky day had become more fortuitous with our meeting. I made it my duty to find out what made the day special. It was her lover's birthday. Giacomo Girolama Casanova de Seingalt. April 2, 1725."

I gasped. "*The* Casanova?"

Ezra nodded. "Infamous womanizer and equally infamous gambler."

"Bet you didn't know Casanova was obsessed with magic," a new man's voice said.

I yelped because the grizzled old guy from the deck had stepped out of the solid wall next to me, filling the room with the scent of salt and night air. *Not a man.*

He snapped his fingers at me to move.

It took a second for my brain and legs to coordinate, but I hastily vacated the seat.

The demon sat down in the sturdy chair and swung his rubber boots onto the desk, still talking. "Alchemy, kabbalah, you name it, Casanova practiced it."

Ezra edged closer to me, but the shedim stopped him with a wagged finger. "One more step and you'll be sleeping with the fishes."

"Spare us the mob movie quotes," I said.

He furrowed his brow, then shook his head. "Let's cut to the chase, Operative Fleischer. Did you find my partner yet or are you fucking around with your thumb up your ass?"

I opened my mouth. Closed it. Opened it again. "Ho-how did—"

"Ho-how did I know?" he mocked with a sneer.

Demon-killing time. Wheeeee! Cherry sounded like a sugared-up toddler. We routinely hunted demons since the energy expended in the fight helped sate my shedim self. This asswipe would be a joy to take out, but I'd twigged on something he said. It was important, I was certain of it, but I wasn't sure what it specifically was.

"If you've got relevant information," Ezra said, "then tell us." The silky menace behind his words would have sent most people scrambling to do his bidding.

"Shut up, Cardoso. I'm not talking to you."

Ezra's gobsmacked look would have been priceless under

any other circumstance than the one where a demon moved through walls and didn't bother to glance at the Crimson Prince when he insulted him.

That said, I'd hit my limit of cowering and simpering for today, and I was frustrated that I couldn't puzzle out what was important about the demon's words. I arched an eyebrow. "Have you got an alibi for Calista's disappearance?"

"I could make you both disappear right now. Make it so you never existed. No one would come for you. No one would remember you. Still think I need an alibi, missy?" The amused glint in the shedim's eyes suggested he was enjoying himself.

Like vamps, demons were exempt from my illumination abilities, but according to my synesthete magic, *I* was a pulsing ball of blue. No kidding, given the danger.

Or the rush.

"Missy?" I pressed my hands to my chest. "Ow. I'm so wounded. Shouldn't a demonic douchebag have better comebacks?"

Blue dots spiked throughout my chest. A distant part of my brain cautioned me about mouthing off to this particular demon, but I couldn't help it. I'd been accused of taking people's weaknesses too far, and I'd certainly illuminated my own in certain situations.

But for the first time ever, I was actively exploiting my weaknesses, like a scab I couldn't stop picking at. I'd been warned during training against turning my magic vision into self-harm. I'd always scoffed, believing myself free from those impulses.

This demon pushed my buttons, and childishly—or suicidally—I wanted to push them back. Unfortunately, the only way I'd see his weaknesses was if I deployed the magic in my ring. My own blue flame abilities didn't include that talent. Not that I was against his death, but I'd have to tenderize the shedim first for that magic to expose his kill spot and take hold, and there was no way I'd get the chance.

Ezra started forward, his mouth open, but the demon flicked a hand at him. A surge of water slapped against the window, slipped through the glass as a liquid tendril, and swam up Ezra's body to imprison him. He shot the shedim an annoyed look and broke free. "Answer my question."

The demon blinked and the water cascaded to the floor.

I would have done my own double take, because Ezra had shrugged off a demon binding like he was swatting a mosquito, but I was busy jumping out of the puddle. My bare feet were already cold. Wet was not an upgrade.

The shedim narrowed his eyes. "No one likes a show-off."

Water rose from the boards to once more trap Ezra in an anaconda's embrace. He tried to get free, but the tip of the plume smacked him across the face hard enough to jolt the vamp's head sideways.

Fury rolled off Ezra in waves.

I took an uneasy step back.

"You——" he snarled at the demon.

The fiend slapped a water gag over Ezra's mouth.

The entire imprisonment took less than three heartbeats.

The demon waggled his fingers at me. "Now, can we have a civilized conversation, or do I feed you to a kraken?"

I was eighty percent sure kraken did not exist. "You set the tone when you asked if I was 'fucking around with my thumb up my ass.'" I made the air quotes.

He chuckled. "I did, didn't I?"

I ground my teeth together. "What do you want?"

"Your stellar conversation skills." He sat up, his rubber boots thwacking onto the floor. "To solve this, you useless twit. Calista and I have been partners from the beginning, and I'd hate to have to break in a new one. I'll do it if I have to, but what a waste of my time."

"What a prince," I sneered.

One of the bookshelf doors popped open. A slim notebook flew off a shelf and hit me in the gut. I grabbed it before it fell to the floor.

The cover flipped open and dogeared looseleaf spilled out. I grabbed the papers. Smudged calligraphy ink, ballpoint pen, even charcoal and blood, the items were written with all kinds of implements, but the thin slanted printing never changed. Most of the lines were crossed out, but there were still plenty of things written in that shorthand code.

"I can't under——"

The demon brought his fingers and thumb together in a "shut it" motion.

A muscle ticked in my jaw.

He gave a rusty laugh.

The coded words gleamed gold then audibly and visually cracked, the letters on the page rearranging themselves into lines of names.

"Cali's shit list," he said. "People banned from the Copper Hell."

There were a lot of names on it, and it didn't mean that any of them were responsible for her disappearance, but still, it was something. I clutched the book to my chest. "Thanks, uh…Beelzebub? Steve?"

"You should have stuck with demonic douchebag. At least it was alliterative. You can call me Delacroix, but don't make a habit of calling me at all." The demon scratched his head with his nicotine-stained fingers. He pulled a tiny shell out of his hair, threw it on the ground, and crushed it underfoot. "You have three days to get Calista back."

That was it! Both Ezra and this demon spoke about retrieving the body, not finding her killer. The timeline always seemed important to them. "This isn't about vamp power dynamics," I said. "What's actually going on? Why is three days such a hard limit?"

Ezra tensed in his watery prison, but Delacroix smirked.

"Isn't that the timeline for famous resurrections?" he asked.

"Vampires can't rise from the dead when they're undead to begin with."

"I'm taking poetic license. Sue me." He narrowed his eyes. "You don't know, do you? Great. The C Team is on this case."

I made that same "shut it" motion back at Delacroix. He clenched his jaw.

Cherry chortled. I didn't—audibly—though I relished the hit, but only because Ezra's brown skin had gone unnaturally pale, his eyes wide above the magic gag.

Vampires don't leave bodies when staked. It was one of the first things operatives learned about the undead. Calista was a Prime. I ran through all the conversations we'd had about her and came to a chilling conclusion.

This case had been fraught with disturbing twists from the start, but this new one cast a long eerie shadow over the entire investigation.

"Calista's not dead, is she?" I shivered. "If she was, we wouldn't have a body, like all vampires. Our suspect staked her to subdue her and abduct her. The perp needs her for something. What?"

"I have no idea," Delacroix said tightly, "but I have an active imagination. You better pray that whoever has her is more limited in their thinking."

I straightened the loose pages into a ruler-straight bundle like I could put my world back into order. This had huge ramifications on the case. It changed everything, made it so much more dire. Michael was going to lose her mind. "I have to tell my team."

Ezra made a strangled sound from behind his gag.

"Oooh." Delacroix pulled a cigarette out from behind his ear. He patted himself down, as if looking for a lighter, then sighed. "Someone doesn't like that idea. I can't blame him. I wouldn't want it getting out that I could be staked and imprisoned in my own body. Alive. Aware. Helpless." He dropped the words like each one was more delicious than the last.

Ezra flushed angrily, his eyes darkening. He struggled so hard in his bindings that he was going to hurt himself.

My hand flew to my mouth. Is that what had happened when Calista captured him?

It was bad enough to imagine the excruciating agony of a stake tearing through my flesh, breaking ribs and piercing my heart, but then to be trapped, unable to scream or move? Had he felt that horrific pain or had he mercifully blacked out?

I instinctively reached out for him.

Ezra snarled at me, and I jumped.

"I have to tell them. You know I do." I stood by the decision, but I hated the plaintive note in my voice.

Delacroix winged me on the side of my head with the unlit cigarette. "Don't even think about having second thoughts. I have eyes and ears everywhere, so save us both the trouble and assume that I'll know every move you make." He leaned forward. "You'll do *whatever* it takes to find Calista. Earn your girl detective badge and find Calista or I'll find you."

His eyes bored into mine, their color blotted out by a darkness so pure it made obsidian look like gray with delusions of grandeur. An ancient cunning studied me, promising untold cruelty should I fail.

I sucked in a swift breath. No, I'd beg for cruelty. Delacroix would upend my life with a chaos that was fearsome and violent beyond belief, and for an encore, he'd erase my very existence.

I nodded my understanding, since my vocal cords were jammed up.

The office door opened, revealing not the hall, but another portal strung with magic mesh. Fearful of where it led, I grabbed on to the sofa, but I was torn away like scrap newspaper. I tumbled into the abyss with a scream, reaching out for Ezra, who was still trapped.

His silvery-blue eyes were dull with anguish. He remained gagged, but he didn't need to speak, because when he slowly and deliberately looked away from me—like in making my choice to tell the team, in leaving him behind, no matter that it wasn't my choice, he no longer wanted anything to do with me—it said everything.

Chapter 12

The portal didn't harm me; it didn't need to. Delacroix had already done all his damage. I was deposited in the driver's seat of my car, which I'd parked a few blocks from the Jolly Hellhound pub.

I cranked the heat, then rested my head against the wheel, waiting for Ezra to appear in the passenger seat. Charging back into the Copper Hell—assuming I got through the portal —would make things worse. As would calling for backup. Besides, Delacroix's grudge wasn't with Ezra. The shedim only bound and gagged my partner to threaten me without any interference.

Well, if Delacroix wanted me scared that he could find me anytime, anywhere, then mazel tov, demon.

The rumble of tires, a quiet conversation between friends, every little noise outside my window made me jump and check the seat next to me. But it stayed empty. After twenty minutes, I reluctantly conceded that Ezra wasn't coming. At least not here. That made sense. He wouldn't be released into my car. He'd either been sent back to the pub, which I couldn't see from here, or he was back at his hotel.

I texted him, but Ezra didn't reply. Okay, that didn't mean anything. He was angry and upset. But he was fine.

I pressed my phone to my chest, then placed it carefully on the console, wrenched the key in the ignition, turned up the music, and peeled out. I pressed down on the gas so hard that the lines on the pedal imprinted into the sole of my bare foot.

Neither Chrissie Hynde's ferocious vocals nor the driving guitars and frenetic drums on the Pretenders' early tracks cleared my snarl of thoughts. I didn't have a choice about telling my team that Calista was alive. Yes, they'd figure out what she'd done to Ezra, but I couldn't risk the investigation.

And beyond the horror of what Calista was suffering, Delacroix had made my priorities—and his retribution—clear.

I gunned it through a yellow light.

We should have destroyed him when we had the chance, Cherry whispered in disgust.

Yeah, well, we wouldn't have gotten close enough to weaken him.

Delacroix wasn't low level like the other demons we'd killed. He was far more vicious, self-serving, and flat-out evil.

I rolled down the window, the wind a mean slap to my skin that I welcomed. I'd always believed that shedim didn't unearth any desire that a person didn't have inside them to begin with. For some, these urges were already close to the surface, and for others, they were deeply buried within their subconscious, but they didn't spring out of nowhere.

Demons spotted those desires and tapped into them no problem. Take my mother, for example. I didn't develop my love of those 1970s punk goddesses like Blondie and Joan Jett because I was on some retro musical kick.

My rule-abiding mother wore out the grooves playing her favorite songs like "Bad Reputation" and "One Way or Another" on repeat and teaching me the lyrics to the adrenaline-fueled, female-driven, transgressive anthems.

I often wondered if shedim chose their victims because

they sensed which people would be most receptive to their particular persuasion. After all, the demon who'd trysted with Mom hadn't incited her to violence or into conning other people, and I doubted one could. He'd simply coaxed her bad-girl side out for the first and only time in her life.

So, what did it say about me and my game of taunt the demon? I didn't have a death wish. Did I crave violence so much that I'd take it wherever I could get it to the point of endangering myself?

I'd been badly injured fighting other demons to sate my Brimstone Baroness, but I'd seen those injuries as necessary to my survival. Tonight was different. I hadn't mouthed off to Delacroix to feed Cherry. I could have kept my mouth shut.

Had Delacroix worked his demon magic to amp me up, or was that all me?

Was he still plying his magic on— I glanced at my phone's still-dark screen, then smacked my hand against the wheel.

Ezra, who was absolutely safe and sound now, should have been upfront with us from the start. I wouldn't be in this position if he had. Not that there was a position to be in. I had to tell Darsh and Sachie, full stop.

Ezra kept my secret. I shook my head. No. It didn't work that way.

I used the fob to open the security gate at my condo tower and pulled into the underground parking. Luck was with me as I took the elevator to the ninth floor, and I didn't run into any neighbors in my disheveled state. I crept inside the apartment I shared with Sachie, feeling awful at my relief that she wasn't awake, but telling myself that it was simply because I should update her and Darsh at the same time, and not that I was wavering or feeling guilty.

The living room curtains were open, and the moonlight filtering in was bright enough to steer myself safely past our textured sectional couch. I picked up a whetstone that had slid onto our short-pile area rug and tossed it next to the short dagger on the reclaimed oak coffee table.

Ooh, Sach had bought a dirk. I wonder where she'd stash this one? Hopefully not in the tampon box. Dealing with my period sucked enough without gouging a finger because there was a screwdriver hidden inside the carton. It was worse when I actually required a screwdriver and had to go through all her hidey-holes to find one because our tool kit had been raided.

My bestie owned the place, decorating it with cool artisanal furniture. I was her mortgage helper. Real estate in Vancouver was insanely expensive and, more importantly, we enjoyed living together. We could decompress in comfortable silence after a hard day, or hang out making each other laugh so hard we couldn't breathe. I might not have made it through the dark headspace I'd been in after Ezra and I broke up if she hadn't been by my side.

I tiptoed down the short corridor lined with framed photos of the friendship that had started in grade one when we jointly held the championship titles of blowing the biggest bubbles with our gum.

It wasn't a friendly rivalry at first. I practiced for weeks to beat her, but after I accidentally spat my gum into my long hair, Sachie was the only one who didn't laugh. She threatened to pummel anyone who called me Gummilocks. In return, I shared my ketchup chips with her and that was that. We shared everything over the years—clothes, foods, good times and bad, and all our secrets.

Other than the one I was too scared to tell her in case she walked away. Like Ezra had.

I checked my phone. No new text notifications.

I shut my bedroom door with a quiet click and flicked on the light. Growing up, my mother had impressed upon me that my ability to keep my person tidy (i.e. hide Cherry) extended to a tidy room. More remarkable multitasking from my mother: teach my young self that demons = dirty *and* get me to clean my room. The woman hated messes.

I was still excessively tidy, thanks to lots of drawers that I shoved things into. My walls were a soft dreamy blue that matched the tumble of wildflowers on my duvet cover, while the high-gloss white furniture was softened with pieces like my tufted bench that served as a foot board, a plush carpet, and fairy lights cascading down my curtains.

It was my refuge and safe haven, but tonight it failed spectacularly at both.

My phone buzzed, and I practically launched myself over my bed to grab it off the bedside table.

It was spam. I pried my clenched fingers off my phone and headed into my bathroom, hell-bent on calming down.

Sadly, a long, hot shower involving half a bottle of my fanciest bath wash to scour myself failed to relax me enough to fall asleep.

I tossed and turned all night, going back and forth on my decision of whether to tell Sachie and Darsh or keep Ezra's secret like he'd kept mine. I refused to obsess about whether Ezra was okay, because it was preposterous to think otherwise. Yes, his texts showed only delivered and not read, but I'm sure he saw them pop up as notifications. He just didn't feel like opening them.

The only reason I checked my phone screen a half dozen times was to make sure I still had a cell signal because Vancouver had a city-wide outage recently, and as Maccabee HQ had been unable to get hold of anyone, protocols had been put into place for checking in.

Thursday morning, I slipped out for an early run to clear my head. After I'd showered, dressed, and eaten, I still had an hour until our meeting with *all* my team members, so I dolled up in a dark green pantsuit that made me look both fine and super badass and drove to the central Trad precinct in downtown Vancouver.

Never had I appreciated shoes as much as I did today. I rarely wore these sensible black pumps, but after being barefoot at the Copper Hell, they were as precious to me as Cinderella's glass slippers.

The hulking building that housed the Trad precinct was painted an aggressive yellow, and whenever I visited, I fought the urge to bounce inside with my dukes up. Today was no exception.

I asked to speak with Detective Olivier Desmond, then was left to cool my heels in a bright, airy reception area filled with plants. There was even a small aquarium with colorful tropical fish. I sniffed. Must be nice to be so flush with cash.

"Aviva." Olivier's warm smile was a balm of sunshine. His suit showed his lean, chiseled frame off to perfection, the navy fabric hugging his solid hips and strong thighs. "Sorry to keep you waiting." He'd tempered his Nova Scotian accent in the two years he'd lived out west, but it still had notes of that combo that sounded like New York and an Irish twang. He tilted his head, his green eyes twinkling against his black skin. "Is this a hug occasion or business?"

"Can't it be both?" I said flirtatiously.

"I like how you think." He pulled me into his strong embrace. His close-cropped, afro-textured hair tickled my cheek.

I inhaled his crisp cologne, my chin resting on his broad shoulder, enjoying this moment with a handsome man before pulling away. "This is business though."

He laughed. "Can we speak here or do you need privacy?"

"We're good here." I sat down and crossed one leg over the other. "Did you hear about the theft at the *Supernatural: Debunked* exhibit?"

Olivier sat down next to me, notching his chin up with a mock stern look. "Have you come to poach our case?" he teased.

"No. You can do all the heavy lifting. I just want the details."

"Oh, if that's all. Can I give you any other sensitive information? A list of undercover officers perhaps?"

I laughed. "Details on one artifact in particular. I have reason to believe that Sire's Spark may actually be magic."

"No shit?" He scratched the dark stubble along his jaw. "Well, that would put it in your purview. I'm not on the investigation myself, but I can get you the information and you can try the city's best burger at my favorite pub. Nine PM?"

"Is this business or pleasure?" I said.

"Can't it be both?"

I shot him a wry smile. "Given our track record, I have to ask: do you hate this place that much that you'd inflict our bad luck on it?"

"They did take the wonton nachos off the menu, which should land them a special place in hell. But no. This is me being an eternal optimist. Third time's the charm, right?"

I'd had high hopes for my first date with this hot, smart cop. We'd met shortly after he transferred here from Nova Scotia, one of the Maritime Provinces on the east side of the country. Sadly, those hopes were dashed pretty quickly when part of the ceiling in the kitchen at our restaurant caved in due to a recent snowfall. No one was hurt, but it certainly killed the mood when the chef came out to apologize and say that, unfortunately, our appetizers (and entire dinner) would not be coming out on time. Or at all.

On our second date, the play we'd gone to had barely begun before a fire broke out. Luckily, we helped evacuate the theatergoers quickly because the building was engulfed in no time. We'd stuck around to give our reports and help comfort traumatized patrons. Points for playing good Samaritan, but zero sexy vibe.

Not once had he lost his cool. Olivier was a surfer; his chill nature was in his bones. Being with him would be so easy.

You thought that about the other one too, Cherry scoffed in my head.

I resisted the urge to check my phone in case Ezra had touched base.

Olivier cocked an eyebrow. "Think you can pencil me into your busy social calendar, Fleischer?"

"Provided nothing work oriented comes up, I'll be there, but the burger better be on point. What's the name of the place?"

"The Jolly Hellhound."

I turned my noise of surprise into a light cough.

Olivier was a Trad, but he was also a cop. He might know about the portal in the back room, but if he didn't, I wasn't about to bring it to his attention. It required a code drink to access after all, and Delacroix already didn't like me. I kept my eyes on my phone. "Found the address. I'll see you at nine."

"Text me if you can't make it. I'll still get you the file."

I stood up. "Detective Olivier Desmond, you're a mensch."

"That's what my mom always says." He winked at me. "Stay safe out there, Fleischer."

"You too."

Seeing Olivier had drastically improved my mood. I sailed into the basement at HQ at 10:50AM to find Darsh, Sachie, and Ezra sitting in the main room.

My sigh of relief was tempered by a flare of anger. He could have let me know he'd gotten away from the scary demon, especially when he was always going on to me about how I didn't have to do things alone.

Failing that, he could have simply made eye contact. Perhaps a brief head nod of acknowledgment. But I got nothing.

I dumped my laptop bag on the floor and sat down next to Sachie.

While Darsh's sartorial choice was to go monochrome in a

red T-shirt and jeans, and Sachie wore cargo pants and a crop top, Ezra was armored up in a black suit, a bored look on his face as he spoke.

He drummed his fingers on the armrest. "Primes can't be killed with stakes. Calista is alive and aware, just incapacitated. She's trapped in her own body."

"Damn," Sachie said, munching her way through an apple Danish.

My eyebrows shot up. All that agonizing and Ezra had taken things into his own hands. It was surprising he'd speak so easily about the suffering Primes could experience, though I should have expected he'd control the narrative. He was as much a master of spin and keeping secrets as my mother.

"Do Primes require beheading to be truly killed?" Darsh said. "Or fire?"

A muscle ticked in Ezra's jaw. "Both work."

"Interesting," Darsh murmured.

I shot him a "Seriously?" look.

"The more you know," he said unrepentantly. "You learned this yesterday, did you, Cardoso? Since you'd never hold back anything this important and be kicked off the investigation, right?" His eyes glinted dangerously, including me in their feline assessment. "Let's hear what you have to say on the subject, Avi."

My stomach sank. I hadn't foreseen this reaction, and I didn't want to be responsible for Ezra being booted. He'd go rogue. *He'd never forgive me.* I twisted my gold Maccabee ring around my finger, darting a glance at my ex, but he studied his nails with a frown. "I learned this yesterday."

"I see," Darsh said.

"Cut him a break," I said.

"I don't need you to speak on my behalf." Ezra finally looked at me, and I wished with all my heart that he hadn't, because he'd excised any shred of feeling for me. He'd gazed at Delacroix with more warmth. "Calista abducted me six years ago."

I went very still.

"How?" Darsh said.

"After a chaotic and dangerous job."

"You failed to spot her trap?" Darsh said. He mouthed "Oops."

Ezra scowled at him. "I was preoccupied. And yes, my knowledge of being incapacitated when staked is firsthand. Before that, I believed a stake would kill me."

He recited this with impartiality, as though he was reading a grocery list, but he might as well have been firing darts into me. Ezra could imply that his preoccupation was due to the job he'd been on—one for his father, not the Maccabees, since he wasn't working for us yet—but I knew better.

His preoccupation was our breakup.

Chapter 13

As the person who'd consoled me through the darkest timeline, Sach instantly grasped the full picture and shot me a sympathetic smile.

"If you only know about the effect of staking on Primes because it happened to you, it's hardly wide-spread knowledge," Darsh said. "Could one of the individuals involved in that trap have done this?"

"No." Ezra smiled thinly, the darkness in his voice making me shiver.

"Well, someone was privy to that info." Sachie finished her Danish.

"Delacroix, the demon co-owner of the Copper Hell, believes it's someone on this list." I dug into my bag for the journal of names.

"How altruistic," she said.

"Not really," I said. "Fail and he'll make my life a living hell. Plus, she'll wake up, and hell hath no fury like a woman staked." I handed Darsh the book, deliberately knocking against Ezra's leg, since he was once again refusing to look at me. "You said my team wasn't in danger when I phoned you from the spa. What if the body had made it back to HQ?

Malika would have removed the stake during her autopsy. Calista would have killed our coroner before rampaging through the building."

"You don't snap to full consciousness and strength," Ezra growled. He schooled his expression. "I would have arrived here long before there was any danger to any operatives."

"You lied to me."

"I omitted some facts. Everything I said was true."

"What else was omitted?" Darsh didn't bother asking Ezra.

"In three days, her healing magic will expel the stake and she'll wake up. Two days now," I amended.

"First off, it's not an exact timeline, and I'm sure the perp is smart enough to make sure that doesn't happen," Ezra said. "Preventative measures can be taken." He mimed slowly pushing a stake back into a body.

I flinched. Was he also speaking from personal experience?

Sachie reached for her coffee cup. "The Maccabees failed to prevent the body snatching. If we don't find Calista before she gets free, she'll come for us too."

It wasn't Maccabees plural who'd messed up; it was me. But that wouldn't matter. If the Prime went on the warpath, no operative would be safe.

I groaned and buried my head in my hands. What was seven billion steps up from losing one's shit? Because that would be Michael when she found out. Maybe I could get into a witness protection program?

Sachie patted my back, but I wasn't reassured. "That was the worse problem you referred to yesterday, wasn't it?" she said. "Not any vampire power plays."

"Guilty as charged," Ezra said. "If you thought Michael was unhappy about you losing the body?" He narrowed his eyes at me and whistled. "She'll hate these optics." He leaned into his drawl on "hate."

The vitriol in his eyes made me feel sick. Did he blame me

that much for making him vulnerable? Did he hate me for leaving him behind? My own anger rose up hot and fast. That was so unfair. *He* withheld important information. It wasn't my fault I saw him trapped by Delacroix—that I'd seen him at less than optimal power.

I wasn't Ezra's emotional punching bag.

Shooting pain stabbed through my left hand. My fingers were shriveling and warping into claws. I hastily clasped my hands behind my back.

My eyes hadn't turned green. There wasn't any telltale prickling that presaged that nor had anyone let out a gasp of surprise and horror, but I'd never had my demon features appear out of order either.

Darsh shot me a curious look at my spiked heartbeat, but hopefully he assumed it was because of my concern over how angry Michael would be.

Once again, his phone sounded with a timer. This time, we were treated to some Flamenco music.

"Not *now*, Darsh," Ezra said tightly.

Sach froze, already halfway out of her seat.

Darsh swept an assessing glance over all of us, ending with me. "Avi?"

"Everyone up!" I cried.

Ezra shot me a confused look at my enthusiasm when he clearly and deservedly expected me to lash into him for his asshole comment about optics, but I couldn't do words right now. I could do claws, and possibly homicide, but words, not so much.

Keeping my demon hand hidden from view, I danced my way over to Bentley, the unicorn stuffie, in the main room, clutching him tightly until the three minutes had elapsed and I was one hundred percent human-looking again.

"Are we ready to be civil?" Darsh asked when we once more resumed. The question was pointed at Ezra.

He ignored it. He'd produced knitting needles that were

attached with a skinny flexible cable, along with some mint-green yarn, and was starting some new item. This delicate-looking project was incongruous with his black suit and aura of power, but he handled the needles so naturally, without any trace of self-consciousness, that it was endearing.

I wasn't ready to think fondly of him yet. I turned to my other two teammates. "What did you learn yesterday?"

"It was a bust on the CCTV footage," Sachie said. "Same with the address and number on the spa files. I spoke to Dawn though. She still remembered that while Calista, or rather Emily as she knows her, had appointments roughly every six months, she only ever made them the day before. She paid extra to ensure a booking."

"Our perp had her schedule then or had a rough idea of it," I said. "This wasn't a crime of opportunity. Any leads on where they're hiding her?"

"The best commercial possibilities nearby are a small warehouse that was formerly a printing company and a doggie day care that went under," Sachie said. "The warehouse has a private loading bay, and the staff parking for the doggie day care is behind a high fence."

"We can't get warrants to enter without probable cause," Darsh said, "so I did a quick recon and I'm ninety-eight percent positive we can rule them out. The day care is for lease, which means showings, and there's a large construction site next to the warehouse. Too much traffic. That said, if our perp has her stashed in a house, that'll be a lot harder to determine."

"We can't track her through local blood suppliers," Ezra said. "Our perp could have procured blood anywhere—a store, a vamp café, or brought it with them if they aren't from here."

"You're assuming they're feeding her while they've got her paralyzed," Sachie said. "Can't a Prime go longer without blood?"

"Yes, but if she's not nourished at some point," Ezra said, "then they may as well have killed her to begin with."

Thanks to his incredible speed, his craft project was a third done. I narrowed my eyes. A baby's hat? Who did Ezra have in his life to gift this to? I steered clear of visualizing him cradling a black-haired, blue-eyed baby of his own. I hadn't imagined that six years ago, and I certainly wasn't going to start now.

"Depending on what they want Calista for, her energy needs could be high." Ezra set the needles down, pulled a folded paper out of his pocket, and tossed it on the table. "I wrote down everything I could think of that they'd want her body for. Some are more likely than others." He resumed knitting, the gentle clicking almost hypnotic.

Sachie, Darsh, and I peered over the sharp, precise printing written on thick stationery. Ezra's list included: cutting off a finger as proof for ransom, using eyeballs to pass retinal security scans, using Calista's fingerprints to access bank records, and livestreaming her beheading. The black-market possibilities at the Crypt got their own section: selling her skin, selling her organs, and forcing her to breed with human males to create dhampirs—human-vampire halfies.

"That's dark, Cardoso," Darsh said.

"It's disgusting," I said. "Forced breeding?"

"I don't condone rape," Ezra said, straightening out stitches. "Ever. However, a Prime can mate with a person to create a supercharged human. We have to consider it as motive."

"A lot of practical applications if you create a race of people like that," Sachie said. "Mercenaries sold to the highest bidder, wiping out the vamp mobs and putting power back in the hands of human criminals, toppling governments. Meanwhile, we can take Calista's fake name off the board as having relevance. There's no Emily Astor who's a Red Flame living here in Vancouver. No record of one anywhere in Canada, but I searched the archives. There was a Red Flame serial killer with that name back in the 1800s in Cornwall."

I made a moue of distaste. "Cute."

Darsh swore under his breath in Romani. He'd been flipping through the book, his expression becoming grimmer and grimmer. "I've decided to let you stay, Cardoso, but only because we'll need all hands on deck to get through these names with the clock ticking. You and I will identify any vamps in Calista's journal that the records can't and head into Babel for follow-up. Sachie, you and Aviva tackle any Eishei Kodesh. Between us, we'll narrow down the suspect list."

"Got it," I said.

"Ezra?" Sach said. "Did you find any upcoming events where our perp might declare open season on existing vamp power structures?"

"Nothing in the foreseeable future. That doesn't exclude our perp planning a secret attack on a single vamp or group, or the Copper Hell itself, but the suggestions I offered for motive take our search beyond a mob power play."

Darsh held up the book. "No blood suppliers, no hiding spots. This list is our best bet. We'll spread out in the conference room and break it down." He paused. "In case it isn't perfectly clear, our job is to rescue Calista. That means no unfortunate accidents." He shot Ezra a hard look.

"Scouts' honor." Ezra held up two fingers in pledge. "For the duration of the investigation."

"That's all I care about."

I headed for the kitchen because if I didn't get my first coffee after a meeting like that, I was going to kill someone.

The espresso machine on the counter made up for any shortcomings in the mostly empty cupboards. There were only some mismatched glasses and mugs, and a few snacks on a lonely shelf.

I loaded the pod and hit the button, inhaling the rich aroma, when a less desired scent tangled with the coffee.

"I didn't leave you behind on purpose," I said. "I would never do that. But yes, I would have told them about Calista if you hadn't." I didn't turn around to look at Ezra. He didn't bother with that courtesy, why should I? "We're on an active investigation. Calista being paralyzed and, you know, *not dead* was way too relevant and important to hold back."

He snapped his fingers. "Funny how certain details were neither relevant nor important when infernals were being killed."

I whipped around. "Darsh," I hissed.

Ezra glanced at the knife I'd grabbed. "Planning on using it?"

"Keeping my options open."

He gave me a snarky smile. "Darsh left to update Michael, and Sachie is in the conference room. She can't hear us."

"Regardless, I never kept any secret that could compromise our case."

"No, you got very creative with how you framed new information."

"Information which I always shared. You're the one who brought up Calista trying to kill you." I exchanged the knife for the lone carton of milk amid packages of blood in the bar fridge and poured it into a small metallic pitcher.

Since only blood sustained vamps, any food was purely for taste or because they missed the ritual of eating. It was a divisive topic in the vamp world, and some purists killed over their belief in an all-blood diet. Ezra and Darsh didn't eat, but they both drank non-blood beverages.

"You could have told us about the paralysis without mentioning the other part and we'd have assumed you knew because you're a Prime," I said. "Not because it happened to you. I'm not going to let you kill me with a thousand mean little cuts because you weren't creative." I shoved the pitcher under the steaming spout and turned it on in a blast of noise, hoping Ezra took the hint.

He propped a hip against the counter next to me. "When you couldn't get creative on our last case with the murdered infernals, I covered for you, so you wouldn't be exposed. Or have you forgotten that?"

My cheeks flushed and I cast my eyes downward, my gaze rooted on the floor at the tips of my toes. Right. Screw that. This situation wasn't the same thing at all. I poured the espresso and warm milk into a mug. "I appreciate what you did, but it's not like you contacted me last night to come up with a plan."

He crossed his arms, his chin notched up. "Back at you, sweetheart. I was a little busy getting free, what was your excuse?"

I sipped my coffee calmly, despite the sour knot in my stomach. I was dying to ask him what happened after I left, how badly Delacroix hurt him, if he was unable to let me know when he left there because he had to heal, but the words sat like ashes on my tongue because only one of my many questions right now mattered.

Did Ezra feel like I was killing him with a thousand little cuts right back?

"I thought that you of all people would understand wanting someone who knew your secrets, to be there for you without having to ask," he said softly.

I bit my bottom lip.

Our silence lasted three precise, sharp heartbeats. Long enough to wind the cycle of hurt between us tighter, far too short for me to know how to resolve it.

His eyes bore into mine, the same weary resignation that I felt reflected back at me. "I don't want us to be like this," he said, his voice low and gruff. "And I'm sorry. I was completely out of line lashing out at you."

"I'm sorry too." I tilted my face to the ceiling and shook my head. "I wish…"

That I hadn't met him? That he hadn't come back? That

our whirlwind romance had been allowed to grow and bloom into a deep, steady love?

"What are you thinking?" There was a heavy weight to his words.

I shrugged helplessly. "Let's soldier on as professionally as we can. Which reminds me, I may have a magic artifact tied to the missing blood."

Ezra blinked at my abrupt change in topic. "I spoke to Burning Eddie. He doesn't know anything about the missing infernal blood."

Eddie was a demon who hated vamps and humans, but also trafficked in human blood. He'd have heard if demons or vamps had it. I guess that was a good thing, but if that brought us back to a highly placed Maccabee's involvement, why would a human want to amplify vamp magic? Why would an operative who was supposed to fight evil want to make vampires invincible?

Stompy footsteps grew close.

"Conference room," Darsh called out. He never sounded this terse and he certainly didn't stomp. Oh, dear. "Now."

"Duty calls." Ezra gave me a wry smile, then left.

Sighing, I dumped my coffee down the drain. Well, I was awake now.

One good thing about hiding Cherry my entire life was that I was a hell of a compartmentalizer. I strode through the main area, locking the entire interaction with Ezra away to be examined at a more convenient time.

Or never.

A flash of mint green caught my eye.

I stopped and blinked.

Bentley was sporting a new cap.

That was the hat that Ezra was knitting earlier? I peered at it suspiciously, but this wasn't some ironic, mocking gift. Not given how he'd perched it precisely to stay on Bentley's head while avoiding his unicorn horn, or in the careful interweaving pattern of ribbed and straight stitches. The design even kind of complemented the miniature palm tree that Bentley was riding.

I stormed into the meeting room and took my seat at the table with a muttered "Quit being cute, Cardoso."

He shot me a baffled look, but I didn't elaborate, more concerned about Darsh.

His lips were pressed in a tight line and his usual shininess and snark were wiped away in favor of a worn-down somberness.

"How angry is Michael?" I said.

Darsh shook his head and gave a quiet "Let's get to it," and that was it, despite the many, many searching glances I gave him.

The knot in my stomach grew. Who would come for me first? Michael or Delacroix? She held my career—my dream —in her hands; he held my life. I wasn't sure which was worse.

For the next several hours, we powered through the list, using global Maccabee databases to separate names into vampires, Eishei Kodesh, and unknown. The last group only had a handful of names on it, which was good, since it certainly included demons.

We kept up the dance breaks. Sach and Darsh were developing a partner dance with choreography, and while sometimes Ezra and I just jogged around the basement, it did feel good to move. It kept us alert and helped us feel like we were going forward.

I missed our waltz though.

Darsh and Ezra took their shortlist of vamps and unknowns to Babel. Either they'd confront them directly or use informants to determine whether the name should be crossed off.

I didn't envy them the job. Asking questions in the vampire megacity put a target on your back, and any vampires or demons who frequented the Copper Hell were powerful and lethal. Like Ezra, they wouldn't be happy about the humiliation that got them banished had come to light.

Sachie and I had an easier time whittling down our list, mostly because humans aged and died, and these names had been accrued over a couple centuries.

We settled on three Eishei Kodesh as our final group: Simone La Clerc, José Ferreira, and Quentin Baker.

La Clerc and Ferreira were Yellow Flames. That magic was predicated upon the idea that fire cleanses. It applied to concepts, complicated ideas, and systems like the body, brain, or an alloy. Not all Yellow Flames could cleanse memories; we'd have to narrow down their particular talents.

La Clerc, an elegant woman with sleek blond hair and hawkish features who'd amassed a fortune as a hedge fund manager back in her thirties, was suspected of masterminding a pyramid scheme in France that set off an economic collapse. I had my doubts that she'd staked Calista, but she could have worked with a stronger vamp or demon who did.

"Elegant," however, was not in the top thousand adjectives for Ferreira. With his prominent brow, stocky tattooed body, and broken nose, even his photo looked like it'd cut you given half a chance. The man had served time for human trafficking, but sadly, while Canadian offenders could receive a life sentence for that charge, in Brazil, Ferreira's home country, they served an average of four and a half years. He'd done three.

Quentin Baker, a lobbyist for Canadian arms manufacturers, was a handsome man in his late thirties with a charming grin and steel in his eyes. He was a White Flame, which eliminated him as our memory loss specialist but would have let him keep Calista calm enough to stake her.

His physique was indicative of a man devoted to working out, so combine both those things with him being the only one in the book who lived here in the Lower Mainland, and it earned him a spot on our suspect list. Regardless of how unlikely it was that a human got the jump on a Prime.

"A grifter, a straight up piece of shit, and a warmonger. We meet the best people." I gathered up the chip bags and sandwich wrappers littering the conference table.

Sachie cracked her lower back. "We need to confront them in person. Without any heads-up."

"Yup." I took the trash to the kitchen, feeling high off the four double espressos I'd drunk. I had enough caffeine in me to run a marathon leaving cartoon puffs of smoke in my wake, and I practically skipped back to the conference room. "Baker is easy, provided he's here in town and not in Ottawa, since Parliament's in session right now. The other two are in Paris and Rio."

"Flying is going to take time we don't have." Sachie snagged the final Oreo. "The Copper Hell has doors to lots of places. Could you get us in?"

"Highly unlikely." I straightened up the pens and notes scattered across the table. "I didn't get the impression I was allowed back, but even if Delacroix allowed it, they wouldn't let a second Maccabee in, and my glamor was torn off when I stepped through the portal."

"Right."

Would the same thing happen if Sachie entered in a magic disguise or had my shedim magic triggered the demon magic in that portal? I didn't know and I wasn't risking my friend. I was also under no illusions that without Ezra there, both for my fake cover story and my protection, I'd have been screwed. Okay, he wasn't much help when faced with Delacroix, but I'd never have made it that far without him.

Sachie licked the cream out of her chocolate cookie sandwich. "Too bad the Brink is a gong show. It would be nice if we could cut through Babel."

"It would," I said blandly, grateful for the first time ever that the Brink was a nightmare to cross and I wouldn't have to expose Cherry to my team.

That liminal wasteland between earth and the bloodsucker megacity was pure chaos. Distances were unpredictable; a journey that took mere minutes one day could take hours or days the next. Sadly, we didn't have the superspeed that allowed vamps to cross it quickly, and motorized vehicles tended to crash into trees that suddenly appeared or go over a cliff that hadn't been there a moment ago. Bicycles got flat tires within seconds.

The Brink was a cruel mistress, and that was before we factored in the meteorological disasters, be it Death Valley temperatures, arctic snowstorms, or a hail of frogs. She was nothing if not creative.

However, we *would* face any or all of that, which would add precious time and certainly deplete our energy before facing these suspects. Since going through the Brink here in Vancouver and into Babel to get to another city wasn't an option, I'd gotten a lucky break. See, the second I stepped foot in Babel, the foundational magic of that former demon realm would snap me into shedim form. I found that one out the hard way.

My accusations to Ezra about keeping relevant secrets played in my head on a loop, so I was thrilled I didn't have to decide whether or not to out myself today to my best friend. *Hypocrite, thy name is Aviva.*

"Rock, paper, scissors for who tells Michael we need a plane on standby?" I rested my fist against my palm. I didn't want to miss my date with Olivier, but I'd text him later if we were flying out tonight.

"Coward," Sach said.

"Says the woman who faked stomach flu to get out of dinner with her parents two nights ago. Throw."

"Fine."

We played. I won and Sachie texted Michael.

138

La Clerc's information was on my laptop screen. I clicked on the trackpad to close that window and revisit the profile we'd built for Quentin Baker, but an important detail jumped out at me. "Rukhsana! Brilliant."

"Sorry?" Sach looked up from her phone.

"La Clerc lives in Paris now, but she's from Lyon."

"Ah. You think your informant will know her?"

"I think it's a relatively short detour that's worth taking." I put my laptop in my messenger bag.

"Sure. It'll only take ten minutes to get there."

No, my darling friend, most people required double that to get from Maccabee HQ to Rukhsana's chop shop during rush hour. Considering the "oh shit" handle in Sachie's car had my fingers etched into it, the Brink might be the better option, but I knew better than to fight Sachie for driving privileges when her keys were already in her hand.

I pasted on a smile. "Away we go."

Chapter 14

Sachie almost sideswiped two cyclists and a moving van in the short drive to Rukhsana's base of operations in Strathcona, Vancouver's oldest neighborhood, where she worked out of the back of a former brothel.

I exited the car on a thrum of adrenaline, tempted to crack the expensive bottle of Glenfiddich single malt whiskey to calm my nerves after the breakneck pace of the drive. I'd picked up the liquor in addition to my usual offering of donuts for the guys in Rukhsana's chop shop.

The corrugated loading bay door accessed by the alley was raised slightly, yet no one guarded it, which was strange.

Sachie and I had a whispered exchange. She'd check the chop shop while I'd take the stairs to Rukhsana's office. We ducked under the door to find the usually orderly illegal business trashed.

Stacks of tires were scattered around the floor, their rubber slashed, while metal shelving units were toppled—the car parts usually stacked in their cubbies not only flung across the concrete but bashed against the walls. The pieces lay battered next to black marks on the white paint. This wasn't a random burglary; the desecration was vengeful.

We didn't see any employees, but Sachie leapt a torched motorcycle carcass to check the closest car for employees while I took the stairs two at a time, brandishing the Glenfiddich bottle, my messenger bag thumping against my hips.

I burst into Rukhsana's office, but at first glance, nothing was amiss. Her leopard-print wingback chairs and settee were intact, the chandelier shone with twinkly good cheer, and her laptop sat untouched on her desk.

The woman herself, however, was an entirely different story.

Slumped against a love seat, Rukhsana looked like she'd come out of a sandstorm, exhausted, battered, and utterly spent all but for a glimmer of that feral rebellious grit that had gotten her this far.

I placed the bottle and donut bag on the ground and moved to help her, but she grunted and pulled away. I winced at the blood pouring down over her shaved head, despite the bunched cloth she held to her brown skin. "Who did this to you?"

"Bah. It is nothing. Someone believed I meddled where I did not. I'll handle it." Her melodic French-accented voice was wavery. The woman's skull was tattooed with a coiled snake, she had multiple piercings, had never met a car she couldn't hotwire, and was plugged into social circles at every level in Vancouver. All this at twenty-six.

Rukhsana Gill didn't do wavery.

I pulled out my phone to call an ambulance, but she grabbed my arm.

Her head shake made her sway slightly. "Non. It looks worse than it is."

"You might have a concussion."

Sachie's footsteps clattered up the stairs.

I relaxed at her easy gait. She'd have run if there was a problem. I glanced at Rukhsana. A worse problem. "You must have a healer who won't ask questions. Let me phone them."

"She's on her way."

Sachie poked her head into the office. "Clear."

"Where's your crew?" I said. It was only mid-afternoon, but Rukhsana was never without protection.

"Unharmed and elsewhere." Her reticence was frustrating, but at least her staff was safe. Though the fact she'd sent the guys away was baffling. She hadn't met with someone one-on-one because she trusted them; the woman didn't trust anyone outside her inner circle. So who did she think she could handle on her own?

Sachie nodded at Rukhsana. "You need to lie down with your head and shoulders elevated."

Rukhsana allowed us to help her into that position though she refused to discuss what had happened. She was too busy berating me for bringing another Maccabee to her establishment, especially when I could have brought the Prime Playboy back for a follow-up visit. If I could have exposed Ezra's status as an operative, I would have, just to see the look on her face.

"I'll bring him when you're in a better condition to drool over him," I said. Or better yet, I'd hand over his number and she could text him directly, sparing me the flirtatious exchange.

She blinked up at me, her gaze still foggy. "Why are you here, chère? You brought donuts and top-shelf liquor. Out with it."

"Did you ever cross paths with Simone La Clerc back in Lyon?"

Rukhsana readjusted the towel she used to apply pressure. "That old goat? Who'd she fleece now?"

"The Copper Hell," Sachie said. She perched on a spindly chair with gold legs, shifting her weight every few seconds like she was ready to jump when it inevitably buckled under her. The seat had not been her choice; she'd been directed to sit there and not touch anything by Rukhsana.

"Their buffet is magnifique."

"I didn't get a chance to try it," I said.

She slitted her eyes at me. "They let you in? How disappointing. As are your investigation abilities. You're about eight years too late with your information. Simone was banned years ago."

The sum total of my surprise that Rukhsana had visited the Copper Hell? Zero. I'd never managed to unearth what type of magic she possessed, but this confirmed she was Eishei Kodesh.

"Did La Clerc have any hard feelings over it?" I said.

"Bien sûr. She got over it pretty quickly, though, and capitalized on her notoriety by running high-stakes poker games for Trads." Rukhsana shrugged. "Smart, since it was as close as any of them would get to the Copper Hell themselves. She did it for years, made a fortune." She tucked one of the velvet pillows beneath her shoulders. "I heard she married some count and went straight, but who knows?"

I raised my eyebrows at Sachie, and she shook her head. I agreed. This didn't sound like our perp. Three suspects whittled down to two.

"Can you tell us anything about José Ferreira or Quentin Baker?" Sachie said.

"Information on three people?" Rukhsana pressed a fingertip to her gash and winced. "You take advantage of me when I am weak. This will cost you more than a bottle of booze and some pastry."

Those were goodwill gifts to keep her crew happy so they'd give me continued access to her. I compensated Rukhsana financially for intel, via a wire transfer to a shell company. It wasn't much—Maccabees didn't officially pay bribes and it came out of my pocket, but she was worth the cost. I nodded. "Deal."

"I've never heard of Ferreira." She traced her fingertip over the top of a scar poking out of the collar of her blouse. "Baker hasn't been seen for a few months. Not here and not in Ottawa. If you find him, send him my way. We'll call it even for this visit." Her voice was casual; her expression was not.

"You had previous dealings with him. Did he trash your place today?" Sachie said, echoing the direction of my thoughts.

Rukhsana snorted. "That's far too obvious for him. He's merely unfinished business."

I recognized the edge in her voice; it was the same one I had for a long time when Ezra was brought up. The lobbyist had charmed more than Canadian politicians.

I glanced at Rukhsana's collarbone. At least my scars were on the inside.

"I have no clue of his whereabouts," I said, careful to keep any sympathy out of my voice, "but if I find him, I'll be keeping him."

She pouted at me. "Cardoso, Baker, you get to have all the fun."

"Rukhsana?" A petite blonde with bead bracelets halfway up her arm poked her head into the room.

"That's our cue." Sachie stood up.

The healer sat down next to her patient.

I slung my bag across my torso, and gestured at Rukhsana's wound. "If you ever want my help with this, I'm here."

"I won't," she said automatically.

I rattled the donut bag that was now on her desk. "Tell Jordy they didn't have cinnamon old-fashioned, so I got him apple fritters."

"I will." She waved a hand at me. "À bientôt."

Sachie and I were halfway down the stairs when a soft "Merci, Aviva" floated down.

My partner and I returned to her car in silence, but the second we were inside, Sachie texted Darsh that Baker was now our prime suspect. She dropped a pin in Baker's address

144

in case they came back from Babel early and wanted to join us, but we didn't expect that to happen.

We weren't worried that Darsh didn't reply to her text. He and Ezra were more than capable of taking care of themselves. Then again, they weren't tracking down the junior league of the criminal set. While not everyone who frequented the Copper Hell was automatically a criminal, they did have a certain status and cunning, and anyone on Calista's shit list was immoral and ruthless.

I'd received my own text. It was from Dr. Malika Ayad, my friend and the Maccabee coroner, asking me if I'd heard Mason was taking medical leave until his retirement. I swore and showed Sachie the message. "If Baker is complicit, then I'm going to nail him. Mason deserved to go out on a high after his career, not a whimper."

"Totally." She started the engine.

Baker's house was roughly forty minutes away in normal people drive time—more if there was an accident on the bridge to West Vancouver—but if we wrapped this up quickly, I'd make my date with Olivier.

Getting any information that he had on Sire's Spark would be good, but more than that, I was looking forward to spending time with him. He was a genuinely nice guy. He wasn't a pushover, and being a cop, he'd seen his share of dark shit, so he wasn't naïve either. He was chill and solid and managed to keep an optimistic outlook on humanity that I found refreshing. Plus, he was incredibly sexy. There was every reason to look forward to this date and no reason to feel guilty for wanting to go out and enjoy myself with him.

I repeated that sentiment a few times.

Sachie noticed I was distracted and let me pick the music. She claimed it was so I didn't remain a stressed-out bunny, but given we did the ride in a vertigo-inducing nineteen minutes, the playlist of hard rocking 1970s female singers also helped her drive faster.

Baker's West Vancouver residential neighborhood was comprised of multimillion-dollar homes, where people were either admitted onto the individual gated properties or they drove on. Sach's car would stick out like a sore thumb.

There wasn't a commercial district within walking distance where we could unobtrusively park, so we pulled into the mostly empty lot at a primary school.

I staggered out of the car.

"Looking a little green there, Avi." Sachie opened her trunk.

I shot her the finger, too busy gulping deep breaths of fresh air to verbally reply.

"You have no one to blame but yourself." She stashed a couple of knives and a thin stake on her person. "If you hadn't hounded me to play endless rounds of *Mario Kart* in grade six, I would never have discovered my talent for racing."

"Sure, blame the victim." I pocketed a lighter that was doctored to shoot flames but frowned at the small tool with a bulbed handle and steel spike that Sachie held out. "An ice pick?"

"An awl. It's a woodworking tool."

I stuffed it up my sleeve. "Your ability to find new stabby things is…"

"Inspiring? Impressive?"

I kicked off my pumps, tossed them in the trunk, and pulled out a pair of slip-on runners. "Terrifying."

Sachie patted my head. At five-eight to my five-five, this was annoyingly easy for her. "Remember that the next time you pilfer my stash of ketchup chips." She gave a wicked cackle, slammed her trunk, and headed for the street.

I hopped into my sneakers and hurried after her.

Our five-minute walk took us along quiet streets nestled in among huge trees. Most of the time we couldn't see the properties—sorry, estates—for how wooded this neighborhood was. It was like being in the country; even the hum of nearby highway traffic was muted.

Baker's address was stamped on the metal gate in a narrow driveway. Trees pressed in from both sides. On the left stood an unclimbable fir, but the one on our right was perfect.

Sachie shook a branch, discharging a gentle flurry of red and yellow leaves. "Conveniently sturdy." She spun in a circle, assessing the other driveways on the street. "Most people have trimmed the lower branches along the perimeter of their property, but these haven't been touched in a while."

"Rukhsana did say he hadn't been heard from in a few months."

"True." Sachie pressed the intercom a few times, but no one answered. She did one last check to ensure nobody was around, then used the branches to scramble over the fence, dropping stealthily to the ground inside Baker's property.

Here's to answers, I thought, and followed her.

Chapter 15

I landed in an overgrown lawn choked with weeds, which was odd since this posh neighborhood did not tolerate second-class plant life.

A tingle of alarm tripped up my spine.

There were too many trees to see the house, so we crept forward, keeping sight of the driveway to our right as a guide.

The blue spruce, wild patches of fragrant heather, and Japanese maples ablaze in color were beautiful. Fall sun kissed our cheeks, an eagle soared high overhead, and still I checked over my shoulder every two seconds.

Sachie was equally jumpy, but we made our way through the woods without incident. We crouched in the long grass, surveying the stunning modern mansion.

"It looks totally normal from the outside," Sachie said. "Then again, it wouldn't fall into disrepair in a few months like the grounds have."

"I don't like any of this." It didn't help that Cherry vibrated with excited anticipation. "You think we'll find Calista in there? She had to be taken somewhere secure, but this is some distance from where the transport van was parked."

"Hard to say."

We crept around the back, keeping under the windowsills and out of sight.

Sachie whistled softly at the mansion's red cedar accents, large windows, and multiple balconies to enjoy the view up here on the cliff.

A light breeze off the water blew a lock of hair into my face. I tucked it behind my ear and turned my back to the wind, studying the property.

The pool had an infinity edge overlooking cruise ships in Burrard Inlet, but it also had leaves and pine needles floating in the water, and there was moss growing between the flag-stones. The artificial turf on the small putting green was matted and damaged.

Baker spent a lot of time in Ottawa to lobby the government, but people like him kept up appearances.

I nudged Sachie, keeping my voice low. We were hidden from the neighbors by all the trees, but I didn't know who or what might be inside listening. "He has the money to employ a gardener on a regular basis to take care of the property, so why hasn't he? If he was mixed up in this abduction, wouldn't he want things to seem as normal as possible?"

"Yeah." She angled her face to one of the upper balconies, shielding her eyes from the direct sunlight with one hand. "The door up there is cracked open, so the alarm isn't on."

Cherry sat up sharply like she was rubbing her hands together in glee. *Game time.*

We crept up the deck stairs to the sliding glass door on this level, but the fabric blinds were closed, and we couldn't see in. Sachie used her heat magic to twist the lock, then slid the glass door open. I stepped onto the cream carpet in the living room and threw my arm over my nose and mouth, the reek of garbage making me rock back on my heels.

It was made worse by the heat that was cranked up to

slightly less than inside a volcano temperature. The ceiling dripped with condensation.

The room itself was ostentatious with white furniture, a baby grand piano, and an enormous gold marble fireplace as a focal point, but once my eyes stopped watering from the stench and I could get a better look, I noticed scuff marks on the paint and a layer of grime over everything.

Sachie leaned over the sofa, grimaced, and pointed. There were bloodstains on the fabric. She tapped her forearm, right above her wrist, and I did the same. It triggered a subcutaneous electric signal that could be paired to any partner. This was the best communication solution Maccabees had found for whenever we had to go into the Brink. It didn't have cell reception and the chaotic magic reduced walkie-talkies to a staticky nightmare.

Sach was the last person I'd been in the Brink with, and we hadn't reconfigured the signal to work with anyone else yet.

We split up, Sachie hugging left, while I went right. I kept my back to the wall in the hallway, but the only assault was to good taste thanks to the textured wood paneling that probably cost a fortune but looked like it had been torn off the sides of old station wagons.

I stepped into the kitchen and gasped in horror. Bad idea. The hot garbage juice stench was unbearable in here and I gagged, dry heaving. I tapped the signal to change it from a single steady pulse to a double pulse followed by a pause to let Sachie know I'd found trouble.

And it wasn't the lack of waste disposal.

All the glass in the cabinet doors was smashed and the words "AM I ALIVE" were scrawled in dark paint across the white quartz countertop.

I cautiously scraped a nail through a couple of the letters, flaking them. As I examined the chips under my nail more closely, I swallowed. This wasn't paint. It was dried blood.

My skin prickled like a full-body warning system and even Cherry muted her excitement in favor of a wary caution.

I crouched down to examine a series of crooked gouges in the bamboo floorboards.

A cast iron pan whistled overhead. It smashed against the fridge, denting the stainless steel and breaking the door off its top hinge.

I jumped up and spun around, my heart fluttering in my throat like a moth trying to escape a jar, but I was alone.

Look again, Cherry said, calm but insistent. Most of the time, she was off the walls or excited for bloodlust, but now and again, she got like this, like a cat staring intently at something invisible. *Don't you see it?*

I tsked. I was clearly alone. Maybe the pan had just fallen.

At an angle like that? she pressed. *Really?*

The smell of rot and decay made me unable to focus. I looked directly in front of me, but that hurt my head, and my gaze jumped elsewhere—

An invisible body slammed me backward against the counter, ice-cold hands choking me.

I fought to break free from my unseen assailant, but the longer I scrabbled at the hands cutting off my air—or stared directly ahead—the more my vision blurred and my head throbbed.

Black dots danced in front of my eyes and my lungs burned. Two voices warred in my head. One was calm, assuring me there was nothing to see, and the other was Cherry screaming at me to fight.

I fumbled for the lighter in my pocket, flicked it on, and shoved the flame at the crushing weight on top of me.

The smell of burning flesh mingled with the garbage. For a split second I swore I saw an arm, but it was gone in an instant, along with the flame, which winked out.

"Am I alive?" The whisper was followed by a crazed cackle, but I was no longer pinned down.

My lighter was also gone, but I'd take that over being choked by an invisible assailant. I stood up on shaky legs, the mere act of inhaling scorching my bruised throat, and scanned the room. The calm voice no longer uttered reassurances, and I didn't have any weird lurches in vision, but Cherry was growling.

Who attacked me? Was it the owner of this place? I searched for a name, but it eluded me, which was odd since I remembered everything else: Calista, visiting Rukhsana, coming here with Sachie.

Shit! I sprinted through the house, bellowing my partner's name and the word "Invisible!" My brain wouldn't function any more clearly than that.

Sachie was in the master bedroom, wrestling with nothing. I tried to see it out of the corner of my eye like I could sneak up on its true form, but all I saw was a blurred screen like a person on television who needed their identity protected.

She flung out a hand and a patch of skin flared for a second like a mirage shimmering out of the desert air.

If I hadn't thrown myself sideways, the searing heat she'd pitched at her target would have burned out my eyeballs. Instead, it sizzled past my ear.

Sachie gestured with her hand like she was dabbing paint on a canvas. She was sucking the heat out of this room and throwing it around, but she didn't hit anything because we didn't see any more flashes of our attacker.

I slid into my blue flame synesthete magic, and pivoted in a slow circle.

The human form jumping around frenetically was awash in blue with darker pulsing dots all over its head and torso. It was nauseating to look at, even when seen only through my magic sight.

I pointed. "There!"

Sach scored a couple more hits on our assailant, but it wasn't enough. When she looked directly where I pointed, she swayed woozily and had to look elsewhere, and the revealed slivers of our opponent remained visible for only a second.

I focused harder. Blood seeped out of my tear ducts and nostrils.

At least the temperature in here dropped, with Sachie using up the hot air for her projectiles.

"Am I alive? Am I alive?" The whisper resumed in an eerie chant, whipping around us.

Sachie gritted her teeth and slowly curled one hand into a fist.

The whisper cut off abruptly and the form in my synesthete vision stuttered.

"Again!" I cried, wiping blood from my eyes.

She'd switched tactics, pulling heat from our opponent instead of pushing it into them. Sachie made tugging motion and ice crackled over every surface.

I hugged my arms around myself, my teeth chattering, and my skin turning blue, but our attacker was barely able to move. This was a good start, but I couldn't keep staring at them in my synesthete vision and they hadn't become visible.

Heat had worked, albeit in brief flashes. What about sustained pain?

Yeeeeees, Cherry crowed.

I yanked the awl from my sleeve and stabbed it through our assailant's foot.

The scream was definitely male, but I couldn't tell if he was visible because a wave of bright blue light flooded over me like a tsunami. Blinded, I stumbled backward and crashed against the bed.

The man cried out again in agony.

I'd braced myself for the next wave of blue, but while Quentin Baker's feet blazed in my magic sight, the blue across the rest of his body dialed way down, which was weird. I hastily wiped my eyes and nose on my sleeve, feeling like a fog had lifted from my brain.

"Quentin Baker!" Sach sounded as relieved as I felt to have remembered his name, though her jaw was bruised and she was moving slowly.

I'd stabbed his left bare foot and she'd shoved the dirk through the right one. He was stuck fast, pinned to the floor and bleeding. The brutality of what we'd done was shocking, and I was tempted to pull out the implements of this torture, but Quentin wasn't screaming anymore.

He was swaying, staring at his corporeal feet, and smiling.

It was almost impossible to see any trace of the handsome, confident man from our photo in this ruin of a human being. His cheeks were hollow, and his ribs stuck out from his sunken chest like the masts of a ghostly vessel—and those were his best features. His bare chest was covered with a grotesque patchwork of nicks and burns.

I shook my head as if that would drop understanding on me.

Sachie gently grasped Quentin's shoulders. "Who did this to you?"

Quentin widened his eyes. He looked down at where she held him, and his pain-glazed eyes lit up with a cautious hope. "Am I alive?" He spoke above a whisper for the first time, his voice rusty.

"Yes," she said, "and you need medical attention."

"Alive! I. AM. ALIIIIIVE!"

"Quentin," I said firmly. "Did Calista do this to you? Where is she?"

He recoiled and dropped his gaze back down to his feet.

I thought his fear was confirmation that she was responsible for his condition, but when he didn't speak, I shot Sachie a confused glance.

She shrugged, as lost as I was.

"Calista." His voice was ugly with hate, and spittle flew from his lips. "LIAAAARRRRRR!"

Sachie leaned forward. "Did you stake her because she

154

lied?"

"ALIVE! ALIVE! ALIVE!"

Quentin Baker was most definitely alive. He was also completely insane, and if he had Calista, we might never find her before her healing magic expelled the stake and she went on the rampage. I sat down hard on the mattress. Fuck.

Sachie pulled her phone out of her pocket. "We have to phone Michael. We're not allowed to call a healer without her clearance."

"Do it." I crouched down by Quentin, trying not to shudder at his mangled, bleeding feet and the manic laughter bouncing around the room. "If we pull these out, will he disappear again?"

"We can't leave them in," Sachie said. She'd put her phone on speaker, and the shrill rings while we waited for Michael to pick up did not add to the ambience. "We've crucified the poor guy to the floor."

Suddenly, Quentin bellowed in anguished rage.

My heart sank because the edges of his solid form were once more flickering and blurring. Once again, a mild throbbing danced through my temples when I tried to look at him.

We were losing him.

He rocked back and forth, repeating "Alive" in a plaintive cry.

"Quentin, hang on," I said helplessly. "We'll fix you."

"Hello?" Michael's crisp voice punctuated the despair blanketing the room.

"We have a suspect," Sachie said. "But we need a healer to—"

Quentin's arms had blurred into invisibility.

"To what?" Michael prompted.

Quentin glanced between Sachie and me, his red-rimmed eyes utterly and heartbreakingly lucid. "I got her good, right? She's gone."

I didn't have the heart to tell him that Calista was still

alive, so I nodded. "Yeah. You did."

He gave a satisfied smile, then with a lightning-fast motion, he ripped the awl from his foot and speared it through his jugular.

Blood sprayed over both of us in an arc.

Sachie's phone clattered to the ground. She tried to staunch the bleeding while I held Quentin, who struggled to get away, forgetting he was still pinned to the ground with the dirk.

Everything is okay. I didn't hear the words, I simply accepted the suggestion to relax and let things be, like a blanket cocooning my mind.

Sachie loosened her pressure on the wound, but a moment later, she blinked, frowned, and pressed down again.

The suggestion had dissipated as fast as it came on. Quentin had used his white flame magic on us, like he must have with Calista to keep her calm enough to stake her, but he was broken and dying, and it didn't take.

"Operative Saito," the director snapped. "What is going on?"

Quentin collapsed in a limp heap in my arms. He smiled and met my gaze, gripping my hand. "Thank you." He shuddered once, and the light faded from his eyes.

"Quentin!" My voice was a plaintive plea.

"Aviva?" my mother said. "Are you both all right? One of you answer me."

We were covered in blood, no closer to finding Calista, and I held a dead man whose body was so gaunt and battered as to be insubstantial. Yet I trembled under the weight of all he'd suffered.

His blood would wash off my hands, but it would never be gone. I opened my mouth, but nothing came out.

Sachie managed a shadow of a bitter laugh.

Suddenly, Darsh was there, picking the phone off the carpet. "Michael," he said firmly, "we'll call you back."

Chapter 16

Darsh's frown grew deeper and deeper the more he surveyed the room. "Okay. We need to debrief then consult with Michael about how she wants this place secured."

"How are you even here?" Sachie shuddered. "Like, yeah, agree, but let's not debrief in this room."

"Absolutely not," Darsh said. "And we're here because we're your super smart, super stealthy vampire teammates." At her blank stare he added, "You sent us the location, puiul meu. Can you help Aviva?"

This last was to Ezra, while Darsh placed an arm on Sachie's shoulder, turning her gently toward the door.

"Yes," Ezra said. "The rest of the house is clear. No sign that Calista was ever here."

Darsh nodded and escorted Sachie out of the bedroom.

"Let me take him." Ezra stared down at me, worry clouding his eyes, but when he tried to pry my hands off Quentin, I jerked away. "Aviva, please. You can't do anything else for him."

Sachie's footsteps changed from a heavy tread down the stairs to a clomp in a distant part of the house.

"I know. I just…" I carefully lowered Quentin's corpse to

the carpet, pulling the dirk out of his foot so I could lay him down.

He remained corporeal.

I sighed and closed his lids.

A door downstairs opened and closed. Sachie and Darsh had left the house.

"Was Calista involved in whatever this was?" Ezra's voice was exceedingly neutral.

"Oh yes." I stood up and pressed my palms against my eyes. "Vampires and demons, the humanitarians of the super-natural world."

"You're half-demon," he said quietly.

I snapped my eyes open. "Is that your way of pointing out that I hurt Quentin as well? Thanks, I was there."

Cherry huffed, annoyed at my boring human guilt.

"No. I—" Ezra raked a hand roughly through his curls. "I meant that you were trying to help. As are Darsh and I." He'd lost his suit jacket somewhere and his eyes looked tired.

I touched Quentin's shoulder. "It's hard to see this as doing good."

"He's out of his misery," Ezra said. "Take comfort in that."

"It's not enough." I rubbed the back of my neck.

Ezra held out his arms.

I hesitated.

"Thirty-second hug," he said. "You can pretend I'm anyone. You look like you need it."

I let myself be folded in his gentle embrace, laying my cheek against his chest, feeling the familiar heat of his body against mine and his arms sheltering me from the world. But as his hug tightened and he rested his chin on my head, murmuring that he was here if I needed him and that I'd get through this, I braced myself against the relief that surged through me.

It made me want to pull the awl out of Quentin and stab

Ezra with it. Okay, not in the heart, seeing as I didn't want to paralyze him, but his biceps were a viable target. Maybe a calf?

Heart is best, Cherry encouraged.

Yes, this was an extreme and unusual reaction to a person caring about me, but I didn't want my ex's feelings for me to be complicated, and I definitely didn't want to feel that way back.

Why wouldn't he just let me hate him? I had done it brilliantly for the past six years. I'd earned gold, not as a medal, but as hot molten threads gluing my pieces back together into a new, beautiful, stronger me.

Hate was easy, but this new dynamic was sending hair-thin cracks through my walls. Sure, we kept hurting each other, but I hadn't exactly let go of him yet. What was I doing? How many times could I be re-fused before, like Quentin, I could no longer recognize myself?

Ezra couldn't be my safe harbor—the one who made the bad stuff fade away. He couldn't be my sanctuary because there would come a time when he wasn't. It's who we were.

We're a lot more than that.

I banished the unwanted thought and stepped away.

My phone pinged. *Looking forward to tonight.* I sighed at Olivier's message, debating whether I should bail, but he had that file on Sire's Spark.

"Problem?" Ezra said, his brow furrowed. "Anything I can help with?"

I glanced down at the screen, which now bore my bloody fingerprints. "Nope." I typed *Same* back to Olivier. "I'm seeing my contact about that artifact."

"You want me to come?"

Sure. We'll all grab a beer. I almost laughed. "No. I'll handle it and fill you in."

I forced one last look at Quentin's feet to burn the memory

of what we'd done into my brain, then walked out of the room to clean my hands, if not my conscience.

I found Sachie and Darsh afterward on the deck outside the living room. It was only early evening, but it was already dark, and I bundled deeper into my gross, dirty jacket against the chill blowing off the water. Being cold and breathing fresh air beat staying inside that horror show.

Sach rested against Darsh on a sofa, her eyes closed, and her hands pressed between her thighs. She'd washed the blood off but that hadn't eased the tension in her slender frame at all.

"We should have worn all black like Darsh to hide the stains," I joked weakly, sitting down in a chair on the other side of the vamp. Luckily, I had an excellent dry cleaner who'd turned her Yellow Flame expertise into cleansing stains and who no longer asked questions, because I liked this suit.

"I don't know," he mugged. "I think it really jazzes up your look." He gentled his expression. "You two up to walking us through this?"

Ezra braced his hip against the deck railing.

Sachie and I kept the recap brief and dry.

"Quentin must have lost a forfeit," I said. "He admitted to attacking Calista."

"This wasn't invisibility." Sachie opened her eyes but didn't move her head from Darsh's shoulder. "It was like he was doomed to live in the cracks of reality." She paused. "Joke was on Calista. She did such a good job that she didn't sense him coming."

"Quentin's anger was at her, not Delacroix, even though it had to be demon magic that made him that way," I said, "but you're right. This wasn't simple invisibility. When we were at the Copper Hell, Delacroix threatened to make it so Ezra and I didn't exist." I shivered. "I didn't realize the literal horror of that threat." I drew my legs into my chest and wrapped my arms around them. "But the terms of this forfeit work with

Quentin's obsession of whether or not he was alive. All those cuts and burns on his body were attempts to verify his existence."

"What's odd is that we couldn't remember him when we tried to look at him." Sachie frowned. "Was that something Calista added on to his lost wager?"

"No, it was a side effect of standing at ground zero of the demon magic," Ezra said. "Primes could compel you directly to forget him, but we couldn't place that as a general condition on someone, if that makes sense. The compulsion is directed at the person who has to forget, not at the one to be forgotten."

"I bet Quentin's condition wasn't some personal payback," I said, "because Delacroix would have pointed us to him."

"Or taken care of Baker himself," Ezra said.

I picked up a leaf that had fallen onto the seat next to me and systematically shredded it. "This was just another forfeit to the shedim. Motherfucker instigates so many of them that he doesn't keep track."

"The patrons believe Calista is responsible for them," Sachie said.

Darsh frowned. "If Quentin lost, why ban him as well? Did he get violent? It feels like overkill. You said he called someone a liar. Do you think it was Calista?"

Sach gazed off into the distance. "No, it was whomever told Quentin that if Calista was dead, he'd be normal again. That's how he was enticed to work with them."

"Yeah, because her death would never have restored Quentin, or any patron suffering from a lost wager, back to normal," Darsh said. "I'm not certain killing Delacroix would do it either."

"I volunteer to try and find out," I said brightly.

"Hey, pushy," Ezra said. "Get in line."

I was amazed he'd openly joke about it.

"Quentin was lied to, but that lie was the only thing that

would keep his focus long enough to stake Calista, because his mind was broken," I said.

"Let's go through what we've got," Darsh said. "Baker believed he killed Calista, but he was deceived. Did whoever fed him that BS know the truth that staking a Prime wouldn't end them?"

"And who'd know about Quentin's condition to use him like that?" I said.

"Whoever Baker lost to and any onlookers." Darsh nudged Sachie off his shoulder and stretched out his neck.

"Then that's who we need to find," Ezra said.

"How'd it go with your inquiries in Babel?" Sachie asked.

"We ran into a very helpful shedim who was one of our unknowns," Ezra said in a wry voice.

That got a smirk from Darsh. "He was so happy to service the Crimson Prince."

"You mean be of service," Ezra corrected, but the other vamp just batted his lashes innocently.

"That too."

Ezra shot him the finger and Darsh laughed.

Nice to see I wasn't the only one who swung hot and cold with Ezra. "What did that shedim say?" I tore off a ragged cuticle. "Why was he on the banned list?"

"He tried to poison a rival in one of the lounges," Ezra said. "Cheating in games is fine but the social spaces are neutral zones."

"That rule is utter horseshit," I muttered. "Did he tell you about the other suspects on your list? Have you whittled it down?"

"Some he crossed off for us," Darsh said. "Others we spoke to. There are a couple more vamps to find, but none of them feel right as the one who played Quentin. Between Ezra and me, we know their reputations. They're thugs, sheep who follow orders."

"I talked to a few vamps in other Mafias," Ezra said.

"Still nothing about any power plays or any enmity with Calista. She stayed out of vamp politics and had enough wealth and power to stay safe from any mob looking to take over."

"Obviously she didn't," I said, "given what happened." I scratched at some dried blood on my cheek that I'd missed cleaning off. "I really, really want a shower, so what are our next steps?"

"First, take a moment to appreciate that we caught a break," Darsh said. "We can say with ninety-five percent certainty that Baker stabbed Calista, then handed her over to a Yellow Flame, not a vamp or demon. We'd have heard something in Babel if either were involved."

"Great. Who and to do what though?" I clenched my fists.

"Our moment of appreciation isn't over," Darsh chided. "This generation only savors achievements for like three seconds before immediately wanting more."

"I'll tell Delacroix that when he comes for me because I didn't find Calista fast enough and whoever's kidnapped her has killed her. For real this time." I exhaled slowly, but my stomach remained in knots. "Sorry, Darsh."

"No," he said, "you're right. I'm going to the Copper Hell to find out who saw Baker lose." He smirked at Ezra again, but it was faint. "Alone. I'm all for being tied up, but I like my restraints less watery and demony. Less tentacle porn with an evil dom, more good old-fashioned rope play."

My eyebrows shot up. Not at the rope play comment. That wasn't news. But Ezra told him that Delacroix overpowered him?

"Darsh is lead on this case," Ezra said, "and he deserved to know that if we returned to the Copper Hell, I might be more of a hindrance than a help."

I crossed my arms. "Did I ask?"

"Not out loud." He leaned back against the railing with a small smile.

163

Sach shot me a look that said I'd be sharing that story with her.

"How will you get in without me?" Ezra asked Darsh.

"I told you." He ran a hand under his arm. "Tricks. Sleeve."

"Yeah? Pretty interesting tricks if they allow you entry as a Maccabee," Ezra said. "What's your story, Darsh? Since you know so much of mine. Do you have some nicknames you haven't shared with the class? I'm sure you had a rich and varied life before making a deal to become an operative."

Sach nudged my leg and I shrugged, both of us dying to know what Ezra might have found out. Did Darsh have the equivalent of the Prime Playboy in his past? The Crimson Prince? What could he possibly have done to be sentenced by the Maccabees? Vamp criminals didn't serve jail time. They were staked. How did he talk them out of that and into letting him be an operative instead?

"Whatever you think you know," Darsh said mildly, "you don't." He smiled at Ezra. "And curiosity killed the cat. It would be prudent to remember that."

Speaking of cats, Darsh reminded me of one who lived deep in the jungle. He was slinky lethal elegance, from the way he stretched out his legs—lulling you into believing he didn't have a care in the world and certainly wasn't attuned to your tiniest movement, definitely wouldn't pounce in a blink—to the purr in his voice that never quite went away.

The Roma weren't accepted, even today. I couldn't imagine what kind of horrible discrimination Darsh had faced back when he was still human. Had he adopted these characteristics then, or had he formed and perfected this lazy insouciance after he'd turned?

Ezra pursed his lips, studying Darsh, but he didn't push it.

"Now I'm rethinking my plan to go to the Copper Hell," Darsh said, "because the more time passes, the greater the danger Aviva is in from Delacroix. I was focused on the investigation and not your safety."

"Okay, hang on," I backpedaled. "Yeah, I got whiny, but that was mostly because I just watched a guy die horribly and I was nervous about the same happening to me, courtesy of demon Davy Jones. That doesn't mean I want a bodyguard, especially if it compromises our search. Darsh, you're the best candidate to go to the Copper Hell. We still have a day and a half before Calista's stake organically comes out, longer if it keeps being jammed in. I doubt whoever has her will kill her before they use her to achieve their goal, and we'll know when that happens. We can talk more about keeping me safe then, but meantime, accept that I'm tired and sorry."

"No apology necessary." Darsh stood up. "Sach, Avi, go home and get some rest so that bright and early tomorrow you can comb Quentin's accounts for any unusual deposits."

"I doubt he needed to be paid to go after Calista," I said.

"Me too, but we can hope. As for you, Ezra?" My friend's smile widened. "Phone Michael back and coordinate the cleanup."

Ezra's sour look was a thing of beauty.

Sachie was subdued enough on the drive home that I wasn't grabbing for the handle every five seconds. That in itself was all kinds of wrong, but I didn't have time to dwell because I'd already texted Olivier that I was going to be a half hour late and I didn't want to keep him waiting longer.

I raced into the condo, took the world's fastest shower where I still managed to use up the rest of my fancy bath wash, changed into jeans and a sweater, and hurried into the living room.

"Where are you going?" Sach stared up at me with bleary eyes, scrolling on her phone. Her hair was wet, she had her favorite pj's and thick sleep socks on, and her forearms were pinkish from having scrubbed them religiously to cleanse herself of that entire awful Quentin situation. She let out a huge yawn. "I'm ordering pizza. Or sushi. Maybe Indian. What do you feel like?"

"I'm meeting Olivier." I zipped up my boots.

"Ooh. Poké, good suggestion." She waggled her eyebrows. "You're up for a date with Point Break?"

"I show you one video of him surfing…" I muttered.

"That man can curl my wave anytime. Bump my lip. We could get pitted together. Shorepound—"

"I'm putting the parental controls back on your Google searches," I said drolly.

"That's okay. I saved an entire PDF of terms to annoy you."

"You're a source of endless joy." I transferred my wallet, keys, and phone into a smaller purse. I could have left it on that joking note, but after all that had happened today, did I really want to? Quentin had been so desperate to be seen that he'd gone mad wondering if he was still alive, burning and cutting himself to find proof of his existence. But when he finally was seen, he killed himself rather than be lost to that invisibility again.

Keeping Cherry invisible was exhausting. I wasn't ready to come out before I was completely convinced that Sachie could handle my truth, but maybe I could share a bit of it.

"It's not a date," I said. "I'm looking into where the blood that was drained out of those infernal murder victims ended up. I think there may be a connection with a robbery the Trad cops are investigating."

Sachie blinked, then laughed and gave a fist pump. "Darsh owes me ten bucks," she crowed.

"Yo-you can't have known I was going to do this." I gripped the top of the sofa, able to taste my heartbeat.

"Riiiiight," she scoffed. "Because I haven't been your best friend for a gazillion years and lived with you and stuff."

"What does that mean?" *She knows* played on a loop in my head. I mentally assembled lists of items for a hasty move.

Sach did a double take at my sharp tone. "Jeez, chill. You beat the shit out of Roman Whittaker, trying to learn why he and the doctor murdered those people, and when he only spouted that vampire invincibility bullshit, you ripped his tongue out. You are so committed to attaining justice, and those victims were denied it. Even if they were infernals, most of them were good people."

Even if. My best friend, one of the most open-minded and inclusive people around, couldn't escape the global rhetoric and lose the conditional praise of those half shedim. I didn't want her to accept me because she knew me as good people. I wanted acceptance. Full stop. I mustered up a faint smile.

Sachie tapped her screen. "I want Thai."

"Okay, well, I'm heading out."

She flung a pillow at me and hit me in the chest. "Ask for help if you need it. I'm your person, dummy."

I hugged the pillow to my chest, knowing it was true with ninety-nine percent of my heart and mind. I consoled myself that one day, we'd get all the way there. It was a bittersweet feeling, but like so much in my life, I put the emotions into a neat little box, tucked it away, and focused on what I had to do.

This was a baby step in terms of coming clean to my best friend, but it was still a step. Or maybe it was the outline of a gate in the walls I'd erected as a stronghold for my entire life. Either way, there was the start of a path that I hoped would one day take me to her side with no secrets between us.

"I know," I said, "and I will."

"Good." She paused, and something dark passed over her. "I don't know if you've noticed it, but Darsh is getting worse. I see him staring at the sky sometimes, at night. I don't know what he sees, but he always looks so sad."

I shrugged helplessly. "You think he'll talk to us?"

"Not until he's good and ready." She sighed. "Go away

and let me order my pad Thai." She waggled her fingers at me in a wave. "Don't burn anything down."

"Not a date." I grabbed my coat and purse, and left, feeling better than I had all day. Granted, it was a shit day, but if I wasn't yet ready and able to be an open book, at least I'd revealed there was a story to tell.

Chapter 17

My determination to keep things positive propelled me through the taxi ride to the Jolly Hellhound. The cab smoothly navigated the streets while city lights flashed by in a dance of colors that resonated with my newfound optimism.

The buzz of lively conversation greeted me inside the pub. A few people played darts or shot pool, and a drunk couple danced next to their table, but most enjoyed their meals.

Olivier, tucked comfortably in a booth, shot me a friendly wave. It was a simple, yet heartfelt acknowledgment that banished any residual unease at returning here.

We made lighthearted small talk until my drink arrived, and I eagerly took the first sip of deliciously cold cider.

This was so much better than a Bitter Abyss. I sighed deeply in satisfaction.

Olivier chuckled. "That bad of a day, huh?"

"Big-time. But that was then, and this is now." I clinked my glass to Olivier's. "L'chaim. Third time's the charm. Here's to good company, good conversation, and no disasters."

"I'll drink to that," he said.

I smiled.

Then Ezra walked in, saw me with Olivier, and every happy feeling fled.

Of all the dive bars in all the towns, in all the world, he walks into mine? Get a grip, Fleischer. I wasn't Humphrey Bogart, Ezra wasn't Ingrid Bergman, and more to the point, I didn't have—or need—a full bottle of gin to drown my sorrows in. Even if this was a date, which it wasn't, well, not entirely, it was none of Ezra's business.

I chugged back half my cider, returning my focus to Olivier.

His dark green sweater was rolled up, showing nicely muscled forearms. He was a great cop and a great guy, not just for his high clearance rate on cases, but because of the promise in his strong shoulders, his shrewd intelligence, and his kind, sunny smile. It took a certain strength of character to keep genuinely smiling and seeing the good in life when the world has shown you some pretty awful stuff.

I darted a sideways glance at my ex ordering a drink at the bar. Ezra was about as sunny as an existential crisis.

"Ready for one of those burgers?" Olivier said.

"They better live up to the hype."

He made a "yikes" face. "Noted." He looked around for a server.

A group of boisterous vampires cheered at the arrival of their pitcher of blood. Since it was night and any vamps who'd been Trads in life were now awake, I couldn't tell if they'd had Eishei Kodesh abilities when alive. Not that it mattered; they all had the same magic now and most of the patrons didn't look perturbed by their presence.

Olivier caught the eye of a waiter who was using his red flame magic to light tea candles on tables.

The man came over, and Olivier ordered two burgers, checking in with me on how I wanted it grilled and whether I'd have fries or salad.

I stared at him until he nodded.

"Right," he said. "Dumb question. Fries."

I didn't think I'd have any appetite earlier, but after my chat with Sachie, it had come roaring back. My stomach rumbled now in punctuation of that fact, and the server smiled, promising it wouldn't take long.

I asked Olivier about his last trip to Tofino on the west coast of Vancouver Island for his latest surfing adventure. He was partway through a crazy tale of surfing during one of the storms that Tofino was famous for when I heard my name.

"Small world running into you here," said the worst disaster of my life. Ezra sauntered to our table with a bemused yet haughty smile. "When we last spoke, I figured you'd be tucked in for the night."

"I had to work the adrenaline out of my system after a shitty work day." I fished some of those yummy pretzels out of the small silver bowl on the table. "Ezra Cardoso, Detective Olivier Desmond. The man keeping me out past bedtime."

Olivier extended a hand. "You didn't mention you had famous friends, Aviva," he teased. He leaned into me, an excited look on his face. "You wouldn't know Astriid by any chance, would you?"

The raspy-voiced vampire singer with one name and two songs currently on the Billboard Top Ten reminded me of Blondie. I was a fan. Olivier had good taste.

I laughed. "Sorry, no."

"I do." Ezra hovered at our table like an old pal determined to catch up. "She's a delight, just like my *friend* Aviva here."

The pretzels turned to dust in my mouth. "Ezra and I have known each other for a while. He happened to be in town, and we ran into each other earlier." Since his employment with the Maccabees was on the down-low, I kept his status as my team member under wraps. "But what a coincidence running into you now," I said evenly.

Dealing with Michael and the cleanup at Quentin's would

have taken a while, so Ezra hadn't followed me—that wasn't his style. Then why was he here? Was he going back into the Copper Hell?

His phone buzzed repeatedly. He glanced at the screen, quickly typing something before feigning a look of regret at Olivier and me. "I'd love to catch up further, but I have plans to meet a friend. Nocturnal adventures of my own. You two enjoy your evening."

Oh, really? Who was this little rendezvous with? I narrowed my eyes, clocking half the women in the pub, before I caught myself with a snort of disgust.

"Great meeting you, Olivier. Bye." Ezra, having noticed me looking around, flashed me a smirk and left.

"I guess he was in Prime Playboy mode tonight," Olivier mused, reaching for the pretzels. "But I can see how he'd terrify anyone he was hunting."

Not if you were naked, Cherry chimed in silently. She provided a supporting argument of graphic memories in case I'd missed her point.

I finished my cider and signaled for another one.

"There was an interesting development on the gallery theft you asked about," Olivier said.

Mercifully, the server deposited our burgers and fries, along with my second cider.

I thanked him and popped a fry into my mouth, salivating at the salty crispy pillowy perfection. Then I promptly shoveled in four more.

Olivier swallowed his food, wiped his hand on a napkin, and placed the thin beige file that had been on the seat next to him onto the table. "We got an anonymous tip on where to find all the artifacts. Well, all but one."

I stilled, my burger halfway to my mouth. Excitement curled through me, mostly for this news, but I'm not going to lie, a fair bit was for the meat in my hand.

Cherry snorted at my phrasing, but I stood by the sentiment.

"Sire's Spark?" I took my first bite. The burger did not disappoint.

Olivier touched his nose and pointed to me.

I leaned forward and lowered my voice. "You think the upstanding caller still has it or was it gone before they phoned in the anonymous tip?"

"That's the million-dollar question."

"Who stole them from the gallery in the first place? Did you catch that thief?" The burger and fries were both so outstanding that it was a shame to have to choose which to eat next. So I didn't. I stuffed some fries under the top bun and took a bite. Oh, baby. Creative problem-solving for the win.

"Say now." Olivier did the same with his fries. "How come I never thought of that?"

"I excel in outside-the-box thinking."

He slitted his eyes. "Do you?"

I blushed and took another bite, tapping the folder with my free hand.

"I wouldn't say they caught them exactly." Olivier added more ketchup to his burger. "We got a partial match on a print on one of the exhibit cases in the gallery."

"The thief didn't wear gloves?" I tsked that rookie move.

"We suspect he did, but he couldn't get this one clasp open with gloves on. To be fair, he wiped it off, but not well enough. We ran it through the system and got a match to a Trad called George Green."

The name sounded vaguely familiar. Since I'd polished off half my burger, I stuffed fries into the other half. "What was on his rap sheet?"

"There was no B&E on his record, but he did have a previous conviction for carjacking."

I choked on my fantastic burger. *That* George Green.

Olivier pressed a glass of water into my hand.

I sucked it back until the coughing fit had passed. "Sorry. Took too big a bite and it went down the wrong way."

George had been rechristened Jordy, the French variation of his name, by his boss, Rukhsana, after he complained about how boring his name was. It had taken me three donut bribes to learn that.

I drank some more water to cover my confusion. I couldn't see Jordy freelancing, yet I couldn't see Rukhsana sending him in to steal the artifacts either. Or masterminding it in the first place. She had her chop shop and her network of spies and was happy with her net worth and her fingers in all the pies.

This had to be the incident she referred to when I found her after the attack. The one that someone mistakenly believed she was mixed up in.

"Is Green in custody?" I said.

"No." Olivier pulled out another photo but hesitated before handing it over. "You might not want to see this. It's pretty gruesome and we're eating."

I wiped my hands, a pit of dread opening in my gut. I'd seen some peak gruesome today. It couldn't be worse than Quentin Baker, could it? "Gruesome how?"

"Officers went to Green's house, but they were too late. He'd been murdered."

I snatched the photo away from him.

Rukhsana had assured me that her guys were safe. Had she lied, did she not know, or had this murder occurred after I'd seen her? She loved her crew, and Jordy was a particular favorite. Of everyone's.

I tried to see any trace of the donut-loving, good-natured man with the ZZ Top beard in this face with lifeless eyes and the blood pooled behind his head from his bashed-in skull. But I couldn't.

Mainly because it wasn't him. This man was clean-shaven, and Jordy didn't have earrings. If he did get piercings, it'd be round ear plugs, not small gold hoops.

Did I have an obligation to the Trad police to report this mistaken identity? To Olivier? To this victim? To Rukhsana, my informant who was clearly up to her eyeballs in something shady—like homicide?

Jordy was a sweet if misguided young man. I didn't like that he'd been fake murdered, or that there was a body count connected to the theft of Sire's Spark. I had to untangle this.

"Explain something to me, Aviva."

I jerked my head up. "Sure."

"Why are you looking at the photo with relief?" Olivier dropped his napkin next to his half-eaten food. "Because I can only think of two reasons. Either George knew something about you that died with him, which doesn't look good for you, or that's not who we think it is. Which is it?"

As a lifelong surfer (they had them in Nova Scotia, go figure) there was a fluid elegance to Olivier's movements like the smooth curl of a wave. Being around him usually gave me the same easy happiness as bobbing in the ocean on a beautiful summer's day.

Facing him now, though, was like being caught in the whip of a stormy sea, all dangerous swells and an undertow you didn't see coming until it was too late.

I crossed my arms. "That sounds suspiciously like the start of an interrogation, Olivier. Care to modify your tone?"

"I haven't decided."

"Take your time." I riffled through the report in the file. He didn't stop me, but he didn't apologize either. I had no idea whether the address was actually Jordy's, but unlike the Trad cops who didn't mention Rukhsana Gill anywhere in this file, I had someone to interrogate. "Thoughts on who has Sire's Spark?"

"No." It was hard to read whether he really didn't have an answer or just didn't want to share. He plucked the file away and placed it on the bench next to him.

That was a dismissal if I ever saw one. I grabbed my jacket

and purse. "Thanks for all this. Dinner tonight is on me. If I'm free to go, of course."

"I wouldn't advise leaving the city, but sure. Knock yourself out."

"See you around, Olivier."

"Count on it." He turned back to his meal, dismissing me.

Sighing, I headed to the bar to pay the bill. Excellent burger, too bad about the guy. No, that wasn't fair either. Olivier was doing his job. Still, it was disappointing that we'd crashed and burned before we ever had a chance to get started.

Speaking of crashing and burning, there was no sign of Ezra, but I'd had eyes on the door. He hadn't left.

Hopefully he was in the back portal room, because getting Rukhsana to spill about her involvement in this was going to take more than cold hard cash. I was going to pimp my ex out to charm Rukhsana for information, and I had zero qualms about doing so. *Spruce up, pretty baby, because mama has a job for you.*

I did a circuit of the bar to make sure I hadn't missed him in some quiet corner, but Ezra was nowhere to be found. He wasn't in the back room, and I doubted he'd gone out a staff entrance, which meant he'd gone into the Copper Hell. On Darsh's orders? Was Darsh in trouble and that's why Ezra had gotten a text?

I fired off messages to both of them, but by the time my Uber had arrived, I hadn't heard back. I wasn't going to Rukhsana without Ezra, so I phoned her, leaving a message when it went straight to voice mail.

"It's Fleischer. I got the tragic news of Jordy's death and I'd like to pay my condolences in person." I dropped the faux sympathy from my voice. "It's not optional. Call me back."

Chapter 18

Shockingly, Rukhsana did not call me back.

That night I dreamed that I found fake Jordy's body, but Olivier caught me standing over him with blood on my hands and tried to arrest me. We fought and I escaped, running in circles through unfamiliar streets until Ezra cruised up in a limo and swept me inside. As we sped off, in this car with fuzzy dice hanging and bobbing from the "oh shit" handles, I leaned against Ezra, exhausted and relieved, and picked up a shot of copper-colored booze that awaited me on the popup table.

Ezra laughed and tucked a lock of hair behind my ear and said, "I've got you."

I woke up with gritty eyes, a kink in my shoulders, and a vague horniness that I refused to satisfy, though there was plenty of time before we had to go to HQ. I stormed into my bathroom and slathered on a face mask to zhuzh (Darsh and I had a bet on whether the origin of this word was Yiddish or Romani) up my day with glowing skin, instead of with a mind-blowing orgasm fueled by thoughts of my ex hugging me.

Not even naked hugging.

This was not good. I stuck my tongue out at my reflection with my fetching combination of pink clay cheeks and a foamy toothpaste mouth.

The glass in the mirror melted like one of Dalí's clocks, and I jerked back. My toothbrush splatted into the sink, spraying me with minty-fresh froth.

A red and purple portal pulsed behind the runny glass.

I darted a glance at the bathroom door, but the mezuzah was still affixed to the frame.

These prayer scrolls, wrapped in a decorative case with a seemingly gibberish word engraved on the back, were actually powerful prayer spells to keep the forces of evil at bay. Jews hung them on the doorways of their homes.

The ones in our condo were the super-protective variety used by all Maccabee chapters as wards, notably against demon attacks. Operatives could bring demons across those wards—though it hurt the fiends—but they couldn't get in of their own volition.

Half shedim had no problem crossing. A point in our favor that our humanity trumped any inherent evil.

While mezuzahs didn't keep out vampires, the myth about them needing to be invited into homes was true. Once they were in, it was impossible to keep them out—like any invasive species. Though it wasn't the same for public buildings, hence why Ezra could come and go at will at Maccabee HQ, much to the director's dismay.

Given the portal now doubling in size, this mezuzah ward was clearly faulty. Did paying top dollar not mean anything anymore?

Cautiously, I poked the mirror. The glass was springy to the touch, but it still existed.

I nodded, taking back my earlier ire. I'd been wrong: the ward was still functioning, which meant the portal couldn't open up directly into my home.

I poked it again, a bit harder. My fingertip went through. I immediately yanked it back. No burn or injury.

The portal doubled in size. Tripled. Quadrupled, until it encompassed my entire bathroom wall. It pulsed behind the glass and the drywall, and I couldn't see what lay beyond it, but the swirling colors darkened as if in displeasure.

Colors, not mesh. This wasn't a portal to the Copper Hell.

"This is me asking nicely," Delacroix's disembodied voice said. "Don't be rude."

Did he simply want an update or was there more to this? Delacroix was responsible for the demon magic at the Copper Hell, and I assumed that included whatever presence was inside the portal that had sussed Cherry out. Was this tête-à-tête so he could blackmail me about being a half shedim?

Sadly, refusing wouldn't make the situation any better. I was going to have to leave the safety of my nice warded-up bathroom.

I eyed the portal, then my bare feet and pajamas. I didn't know where my slippers were, and getting dressed or wasting more time would only piss the shedim off more. The only weapon that would reliably kill a demon was my Maccabee ring, which I never took off, but I didn't like my odds of getting close enough to Delacroix for it to be effective.

Fan-freaking-tastic. I took a deep breath. Here went nothing.

Feeling as nervous as a first-year witch standing on Platform 9¾, I ran at the wall, using my hand to protect my nose, but I sailed through.

"Fuck! Fuck! Fuck!" I hopped up and down on the hot concrete, trying to acclimate to the arid wind blasting me in the face while my brain made sense of what I was seeing.

Nestled against jagged, obsidian cliffs, under an apocalyptic sky, stood a pancake house. It had large, curved windows showcasing an inviting glow, touches of chrome, and a pastel green awning shading the entrance.

A neon sign, complete with a dancing pancake wearing a chef's hat, proudly announced the restaurant's name: Flaming Flapjacks. The "S" flickered with a hissed sizzling sound.

I pinched myself, but the pancake house of the damned remained annoyingly real. Where was I? I glanced up, hoping I was in Babel, but the bone-white octagonal moon quashed that.

I was in the demon realm. To the best of our knowledge (since it's not like we could gather census information, though operatives had been taken there before), there was only one. Babel had originally been a part of it, but it had been abandoned before being claimed by vampires. For some reason, I had no choice there about appearing in my shedim form.

This part of the realm was different. It was definitely demon, but the urge to comply and let Cherry out was a muted siren's song, not a demand I was unable to refuse. I remained human.

Delacroix might not have any idea I had demon blood. He could have brought me here instead of back to the Copper Hell as an intimidation technique. Were that the case, I wasn't handing my secret over to him.

I expected my Brimstone Baroness to be yelling at me to take her off her leash, but she thoughtfully regarded our surroundings, sharing my opinion that she'd be best used for a surprise attack.

Anger smoldered alongside my icy fear. I didn't sign up for this crap. I was an operative investigating a case, not Delacroix's minion who he could threaten and beckon at will. I clomped inside, steeling myself to be greeted by a variety of musical options: "Highway to Hell," "Sympathy for the Devil," or an endless loop of dental chair Muzak. Instead, I was treated to the old '50s hit "Great Balls of Fire." Still on brand and catchy in a nostalgic way.

The hostess, in a beribboned red and ebony minidress, was

pretty cute for a giant fly with human hands, though her bristly, stick-thin legs were a bit unnerving. She greeted me with an unintelligible buzzing, narrowing her large bulbous eyes, which she'd dolled up with glittery green mascara.

"Delacroix is expecting me."

Her buzzed reply sounded a lot like muttered swearing, but she grabbed a plastic laminate menu and set off through the busy restaurant, flying a few feet above the ground.

The place smelled like maple syrup, but also sulfur.

I locked eyes with a shedim who was all hands and mouths, shoveling some sort of pulled meat product into at least six gaping maws, and had a sudden desire to go vegetarian. At the sight of me, he dropped his food, shot to his feet, and lurched in my direction.

Before I could react, the hostess broke apart into a swarm of flies, the plastic menu fluttering to the floor. The flies enveloped the other demon with a furious buzzing.

I stood there, frozen.

Her attack only lasted seconds, at which point the swarm calmly reformed into the hostess.

There was no sign of the other shedim. *The (waffle) house always wins.*

She picked up the fallen menu and with a weirdly clear expression of exasperation for a giant fly, jabbed her index finger at a large sign on the wall in jaunty script that read, "Bring your appetite; leave your grudges!"

Any remaining demons still eyeing me turned hastily back to their food.

Maybe Delacroix hadn't brought me here to blackmail me?

Thrilled as I was that no one gave me a second glance despite being the lone human in the place, part of me wanted to give in to my Cherry Bomb form and blend in while forced to spend time in this dangerous space.

I was about halfway across the restaurant now and it was taking all my acting abilities to keep my expression neutral, because holy shit. Some of the patrons had human glamors—more or less—but one booth was occupied by a sea slug demon oozing dark liquid onto his short stack of blueberry pancakes, while another table held a party of shadows with eerie glowing eyes, cutting their eggs Benedict in silent tandem movements.

I made the mistake of peering closer at their meals and almost vomited because what I'd taken for poached eggs was a pockmarked puck thing dotted with teeth. I did not care to educate myself about the sauce.

Thankfully, the floor wasn't sticky, and I didn't have to worry about stepping in acid, molten lava—or worse.

The hostess led me out a door onto a screened veranda where the fans spinning lazily overhead did little to dispel the four hundred percent humidity. She gave me the menu and left.

There was only one group out here, eight shedim seated around a long table. Their ability or desire to look human varied wildly. One had an old man's face, but the rest of him was a person-sized bat. He ate directly off his plate.

Actually, the human glamors all involved looking like old men, some pudgy, one with Popeye biceps, and one with a gaunt face and bugged-out eyes.

A few hadn't bothered. One demon was basically a goat in an oversize sweatshirt. There were holes cut into his top hat to accommodate his curved horns.

I frowned.

There was a Kangol on a demon with a pompadour, and a floppy hat adorned with sharp metal lures worn by a blue demon with one eye and four tusks. I doubted the hooks were used for fishing.

Okay, what was up with the hats? Awww. Perhaps a shared love of headgear and evil had brought them together.

The other shedim went with baseball caps bearing fun sayings like "Flame-Grilled for Flavor," "I went to Hell and all I got was this lousy cap," and "Demon Tested, Hellfire Approved."

One cap boasted the dancing pancake logo from the restaurant's sign with "Devilishly Good Eats!" on it. I had to hand it to the business, their branding was perfection.

"Welcome to Brimstone Breakfast Club." Delacroix beckoned to me from the head of the table.

Okay, boomer.

A half-eaten plate of waffles piled high with whipped cream and strawberries was in front of him, and I grimaced because waffles were one of my most favorite foods and I didn't want anything in common with this demon.

He eyed me, his lip curling in a sneer. "Pink pajamas. What are you, five?" He'd traded his heavy fisherman's sweater for a shirt in a shimmering fabric with an iridescent quality. It shifted from deep sapphire blues to emerald greens as it caught the filtered, hazy light, its buttons tiny gold anchors. He'd tucked his hair under a black baseball cap with "Hotter than Hades, Cooler than You" in jaunty white script.

I smoothed down the front of my pj top. "We can't all be the fashionista you are."

He put his cigarette out on the cheek of the demon next to him. The gloomy-looking creature had a donkey's face and a mane attached to a sunburst of short hooved legs that sprouted from his neck.

Delacroix was picking on Eeyore demon. What a dick.

Except Eeyore demon perked up at the literal burn, nudged Delacroix's head affectionately with a hoof, then used his disconcertingly long tongue to extinguish the smoldering hair. *Whatever floats your boat, buddy.*

A chair shot out of the main part of the restaurant, hitting me in the backs of the knees, and knocking me onto it. It slid into place between Delacroix and the donkey.

"Try the Hellfire Hash." Delacroix tapped a photo on my menu of a greasy lump. "Evander swears by it, right?"

Bat demon looked up from his plate, fluttering his leathery wings enthusiastically. A noxious orange sauce dripped off his chin. He didn't close his mouth when he chewed, and the eyeball he bit down on squirted viscous fluid.

"I'll pass, thanks," I said weakly.

"Your loss." Delacroix's eyes danced with amusement. "But if you aren't going to eat, then you can get right to the part where you tell me you've found Calista."

This would have been the perfect opportunity for him to trot out my secret, but he cut into his waffles without uttering any threats.

A modicum of tension drained from my shoulders. Like ten percent of cautious optimism's worth.

"Miss her that much, do you?" I said sarcastically. Unwise? Yes. But he was a demon, not a grieving family member. He didn't want her back for sentimental reasons.

"I miss her running the business. Dealing with mundane bullshit in her absence was not part of our agreement. I gave her the magic tools, I kept up my end. I've got a sweet setup. No more working hard, no more looking over my shoulder for backstabbing shedim and irritating do-gooders. Just sit back and enjoy the delicious flow of misery and greed in peace."

Called it.

One of the demons said something in a language I didn't understand.

Delacroix laughed. "Right. And hang out with old friends. Now." The air grew cold and damp. "Where is she?"

Every single demon stopped eating and swiveled their heads toward me expectantly, transforming in a blink from a bunch of—admittedly weird and monstrous—old people at their favorite diner to a panel of judges eager to pronounce a death sentence.

I flashed on Quentin's agonized madness, haunting his

house while agonizing over whether he was still alive, and revised my opinion of what they'd do to me. Death would be too easy. I swallowed and crossed my arms so no one would see my trembling hands. "We found the man who attacked her and are very close to finding whoever ordered—"

A wave crashed through the veranda. The shedim who could grab their plates did so, but everything else was swept into the far wall.

Including me.

I tumbled off my chair, fighting to swim my way out while holding my breath, but my lungs were burning, and my brain insisted that breathing was better than not breathing. I opened my mouth—and choked. Water went down my throat with the force of a fist and I panicked, flailing hard.

An invisible hook pulled me up to the surface. I sucked down a huge breath through my coughing fit and then a plume of water slapped me back under the localized waves.

I couldn't let Cherry out to see if that gave us a fighting chance because I was too busy not drowning and grabbing precious gulps of air before being forced under once more.

My arms and legs no longer worked properly, and I had about as much energy to fight back as a newborn kitten, but I refused to give that bastard the satisfaction of giving up.

At long last, the water disappeared and I bashed my nose on the damp floorboards, numb.

Delacroix stood over me, his hands on his hips. "The next time we meet, you better have earned your girl detective badge."

I'll kill you someday. I unclenched my fists and shakily pushed to my knees. "How long until next time? I'd like to set up a countdown to that happy day."

The shedim pulled a cigarette out from behind his ear. "Whenever I decide." He flapped a hand at me and another stream of water washed me away.

I didn't have time to freak out because almost immediately

I was back in my bathroom, sprawled in my tub, soaking wet, and unable to calm my racing heart or the shivers racking my body. I couldn't make myself move, scared that time didn't pass in the demon realm in the same way, and that if I left this room, I'd find myself twenty years in the future.

It didn't matter that my robe hung on the back of my door, or that my glass soap dispenser sat next to my bottle of hand cream. The lights in here couldn't banish the watery darkness that still permeated every pore of my body.

I tried to take a deep breath through my tight rib cage. Humans didn't want me because I was a monster, and the monsters dismissed and toyed with me. Any sense of safety, of empowerment, all my hard-won agency in becoming a Maccabee and working toward my dream, all of it had been ripped away with that first splash of water.

I gritted my teeth, determined to sit up, but it proved a Herculean task. At first, I managed only to raise my chin off my chest, then I gripped the sides of the tub, but little by little I was upright, my spine straight.

Beaten but not broken.

I'd speak with a Maccabee trauma counselor at some point —those rare operatives who entered the demon realm didn't exactly leave unscathed, and the situation was treated very seriously. However, if I did it now, Michael would remove me from the case.

I pushed my anxiety away, leaving me with a hot, tight anger making my skin itchy, so I threw on my gear and went for a run in the woods at Stanley Park where I pounded out— and screamed out—my frustration and fury.

I didn't come across any demons to vent my murderous rage on, but when I emerged from the trail onto the beach, sweaty and hoarse, to a muted sunrise with dark clouds and frothy waves tumbling against the shore, I laughed.

I was Aviva fucking Fleischer. I'd survived hiding my true nature, heartbreak, driving with Sach on the regular, and the demon realm. I was here, I was alive, and I had big plans for my future. No one, not even a crotchety evil hellspawn, was going to ruin them.

But one day? I made my vow on the darkest storm cloud. Delacroix would pay.

Chapter 19

I returned to the condo with freshly baked croissants from the bakery downstairs, and hopped in the shower—sadly reduced to using regular bar soap. If I was going to be taking seventy percent more disinfecting showers, I'd have to start buying bath wash in bulk. While the soap didn't have the ooh là là luxury of the product that I only splurged on for my birthday, the hot water was certainly a balm for my sore body and exhausted spirit.

Once I was presentable, I joined Sachie for lattes in our kitchen, filling her in on the Brimstone Breakfast Club while rain slanted against the windows. The oppressive fall weather was tempered by our buttery-yellow walls, wooden cabinets with a rich honeyed finish, and a cozy breakfast nook with a cheery sunflower fabric on the bench. It made the room feel like a sunny haven on the gloomiest days.

All of it gave me a much-needed semblance of normality and comfort, but my calm came from more than that. The fact was I couldn't dance to Delacroix's tune because I'd been doing all I could and he still put me through— My brain skidded away from the memory.

Delacroix was literally the house at a casino, where every

game was rigged in his favor. There was no point trying to win at his table.

Besides, this wasn't a game, it was my life. I had to chart my own course, and right now, that meant gently bobbing in a decades-long haven of a friendship to get into the right mindset for the work ahead.

"That shedim is worse than drug-resistant gonorrhea," Sachie said when my tale was finished.

She squeezed my hand, and if we held tight to each other for a few seconds longer than was normal, well, that was okay.

Sachie dug in the bag for a second croissant. "What happened with Point Break last night?"

She agreed with my call to withhold the information from Olivier that Jordy wasn't the murder victim in the photos. "Be careful. Detective Desmond has you in his sights now." She lathered raspberry jam on the pastry. "Wow. A demon and a cop both taking an interest in you. Your popularity is on the rise. I was worried you wouldn't ever bounce back from that unfortunate bathing suit incident in our sixth-grade camping trip that lost you most of your friends other than moi, of course, but look at you."

I threw a napkin at her. "Too soon, you shit." I licked my finger to gather the crumbs on my plate. "So much for any romantic prospects with Olivier."

"It could become an enemies-to-lovers situation."

Not another one. Though, I guess Ezra and I were more lovers to enemies. "Mmm," I said noncommittally.

She narrowed her eyes, her mug halfway to her lips. "Oh no. No. No. No. What did you do with Ezra?"

"We were talking about Olivier."

"And that's an Ezra look."

"I haven't done anything." I sipped my latte with a deliberate and hopefully not forced nonchalance.

"Liar." She whipped an ice pick out of her shirt.

189

"Jesus." I sloshed coffee onto my hand and quickly blotted it off with a napkin. "Where were you hiding that?"

"Special side holster on my bra."

"Nice. But how do you keep from stabbing yourself?"

She pulled off the clear plastic safety tip. "Now stop deflecting. Did you sleep with Ezra?"

"No. But…" I dropped my gaze to my mug, running my finger around the rim. "We kissed."

"At the Copper Hell?"

"No. When we were at the safehouse in London. Before you and Darsh showed up."

The ice pick clattered to the table. "That was days ago!" she sputtered. "You kept your lack of impulse control and insanely poor judgment from me all this time?"

I leveled a flat stare at her. "And here I thought you'd disapprove."

Muttering under her breath, Sachie hit some keys on her phone.

I braced myself for the familiar strains of "Gaston" from Disney's *Beauty and the Beast* to drown out the hum of the dishwasher. She'd forced me into endless rounds of karaoke on her Disney villains playlist after Ezra and I broke up. It had been a lifesaver, but if I heard that song one more time, I might strangle myself and undo all her good work.

She slid the phone over to me. "Here, check this app out. Sarah and Parminder both raved about the guys they've met."

I frowned at the dating site home page. "I'm not interested. Work is my priority right now."

"Work is the problem because it keeps you in Ezra's orbit."

"We had one kiss, born of adrenaline, and now firmly in the past." Because I've crossed over into hug fetishes now. *Like an idiot.*

"Ezra aside," Sach said, "you've been so focused on achieving level three operative that you've neglected your personal life. You're sure you can't repair things with Point Break? I had high hopes for him."

I shook my head. The truth was that even if I could, I no longer wished to. When I met someone I clicked with, I'd be keeping a major secret from him. I was already worried about how Sachie and Darsh would react to Cherry, I wouldn't want to throw someone else I cared about into the mix.

But damn, I missed the feeling of someone's hands on my body and that delicious moment after they slid inside me, when they consumed my senses. No thinking, no feeling *anything* except these physical sensations. It was way better than meditation.

I narrowed my eyes. Sexual attraction to Ezra didn't scare me, but our hug did. It shook me up. No, it *swept* me up, making me feel at the mercy of my emotions for him, and I refused to feel that way again.

Was the answer to getting past these unwanted feels to fuck Ezra out of my system? Redirect us back onto safer ground because this would only be sex—and sex on my terms?

Hit it and quit it?

"Are you thinking about your dating profile?" Sachie said hopefully. "Because I volunteer to weed out guys for you so you only see the winners. No work on your end, just a fun decision of choosing between only good options on the menu."

"Ezra and I are still attracted to each other."

"Thanks, I have eyes." She hastily swiped through the app store. "What about the Happily-Ever-After app? That sounds like a nice place to start, and I have tons of great photos of you we could use."

I winced. She was going off the deep end. "Do I get a twittering bird or a prancing deer avatar for meeting Prince Charming? Should I provide my shoe size? Does it come with a playlist?"

Sachie narrowed her eyes, visions of ice picks and dirks no doubt dancing in her mind.

Right. Provoking the predator bad. I made calming motions with my hands, and went for a little levity. "Seeing as I've already parted my lips for Ezra, perhaps my legs should not be far behind. I could be as the Red Sea with a wet parting."

A muscle ticked in Sachie's jaw.

"Better that than a burning bush?" I joked. Her muscle ticked two more times. "I'm not going to fall for Ezra or try to work things out. I'm talking one night of mind-blowing sex to get him out of my system. That was part of the problem the last time. Things didn't end on my terms, so this is me rectifying that. Plus, I don't have to be scared of him walking away."

"Because been there, done that?" Sachie said. "I'm not sure it works that way."

"Because I'll walk away first."

There was a strange sense of happiness in that sentiment, an odd relief that I'd finally hold the upper hand in this intricate dance we'd been locked in. He'd be reassigned soon enough, so technically, he'd be leaving, but symbolically, it was my turn to decide when to step onto the floor and when to gracefully bow out. I'd control the narrative this time.

"You've lost your mind." Sachie picked up the weapon, fingering its tip. "I see I've been going about this all wrong. I intended to stab Ezra if he broke your heart again. I've made lots of 'just in case' notes during this investigation, but apparently, I need to root out the problem at its source." She pointed the ice pick at me.

I brushed it carefully aside. "I can fuck people without falling in love or wanting more."

"And hopefully you will again, grasshopper. But on the Happily-Ever-After app. Or the deviant sex app. Or any of a thousand million other options. Not your ex. You and Ezra are a car crash, Avi. Why can't you see that?"

"I'm suggesting this plan precisely because this collision is inevitable. We're both Maccabees. We can't refuse to work together because of past history. I'm trying to make this collision a hit-a-patch-of-black-ice-skid-together-in-slow-motion, versus the sudden T-boned-by-a-semi that happened to me last time."

"You're full of metaphors today, aren't you?"

I shrugged. "I'm on a roll. But like I said, it's happening in slo-mo. I can engage defensive safety measures and walk away unscathed. Use a firm hand on the wheel, employ good rubber tires, don't pump the brakes." I made the motion with my fist, hoping to earn a smile.

Sachie replaced the cap on the ice pick and stashed it in her boob holder. "I love you," she said quietly, "but I can't go through that again."

I dropped my gaze to the table.

My friend recently had a big fight with her parents when she told them of her transfer to the Spook Squad. This had been the main point of contention for years in an otherwise close relationship. She didn't want to talk about it, but their estrangement was eating her up, and I didn't blame her for not being capable of dealing with my situation. Especially since she'd already shepherded me safely through the darkness once before.

"You won't have to," I said, meeting her gaze. "I promise. I'm a big girl, and *if* I do this, I do it with my eyes wide open. Trust me? Please?"

She nodded reluctantly.

"Speaking of a certain Prime, however." I applied the red lipstick that I'd left on the table a few days ago. It went perfectly with my red tailored pantsuit and was required to help fortify me today. "Ezra might have gone back to the

Copper Hell last night. I haven't heard from him. Darsh either. How about you?"

"Nothing."

"I don't love that, but let's go with no news is good news." I put my dishes in the sink. "Do you want to come with me to visit Rukhsana on our way into work? I want to get to the bottom of this before Olivier does."

Sachie patted the ice pick stashed by her boob. "I got you covered. Even when you make bad decisions, but especially when you don't."

I laughed. Sachie truly was the best.

It's not like I'd forgotten the watery blade at my neck if I didn't find Calista, but I didn't think that combing through Quentin's laptop would yield a magic bullet. Putting it off for an hour wouldn't matter, especially when there was a better chance of Darsh and Ezra returning with something useful.

Besides, I was worried about Rukhsana and Jordy and still determined to learn whether Sire's Spark was connected to the slain half shedim on our previous case.

Sadly, we showed up to the chop shop to find Rukhsana had cleaned it out—both the business and her office. Worse, when we exited the loading bay, Olivier lounged against the brick alley wall.

At least it had stopped raining.

"Come here often?" He snorted at my blink of surprise. "Yeah, us dumb Trad cops figured out who George Green works for."

"I've never thought you were stupid, Olivier." Those officers hadn't yet discovered the true identity of the dead man, but if Jordy and I hadn't once discussed piercings and tattoos, I wouldn't have realized he wasn't the vic either since I'd never seen him without his beard.

Rather than Olivier appearing mollified by my honest statement, his frown deepened.

"I also didn't think you were on this case," I said.

"I've taken a special interest. Tell me what's going on."

"No can do," Sachie said. "Confidentiality and all that."

"Sachie Saito, right? I've heard about you." He crossed his arms.

My friend burst out a happy, two-dimple smile and jammed her hands in the pockets of her leather jacket. "I love when my reputation precedes me. A pleasure to meet you, Point Break."

Olivier narrowed his eyes.

I stepped in between them. "I don't know what's going on and that's the truth. I told you I suspected that Sire's Spark is magic. While I can't prove it yet, Rukhsana didn't steal those artifacts from the gallery. Technically, she doesn't steal cars either."

"Splitting hairs, Fleischer. Word on the street is that she jacked the exhibit, yet you're pretty quick to defend her."

Her name was being tossed around in conjunction with the theft? To the point that the cops heard the rumor? Rukhsana had said more than once that her reputation was everything. She was also ruthless. What if the murdered man's name really was George Green, a different George Green than Jordy, and that unfortunate coincidence was what brought all this trouble to her door?

How far would she go to deal with it?

"I'm not defending her because of an emotional connection," I said. "I'm using logic based on years of knowing how she runs her business."

"Yeah? So how are you tangled up with her?" He raked a hard "break the witness" gaze over me.

Like I hadn't used that move on the regular myself. I almost rolled my eyes.

Sach showed no such restraint, snorting loudly.

Olivier glared at her. "Got something to say, Rambolette?"

A sinister glimmer danced in Sachie's eyes.

"Back to Rukhsana," I said. There was no way I was

outing my prime informant right now. Nothing about this felt right as a Rukhsana-sanctioned job, but why did someone want to frame her for it and why had she closed up shop? Was she in danger? More danger than being bashed in the head?

"Your mom signed off on Trads handling this," Olivier said.

"My *mom*?" I clenched my fists, well and truly pissed off now. "That's Director Fleischer to you."

He held up his hands. "Sorry. That was unprofessional. Still, until I get official word that something has changed, I'll have to regard any investigation on your end as interference. Can you trust me to unravel this?"

"I trust that you're a great officer and committed to justice, Olivier. I really do."

"But Rukhsana is your informant, and you want to protect her." He sighed.

"Smarter than the average bear, aren't you?" Sachie said.

"Armed to the teeth, aren't you?" he replied.

Her smile this time was almost as sharp as her ice pick.

The charged air between them was delightfully amusing. I made a note to try to get them to have dinner together. While I was in the restaurant creeping on them, of course. They'd either hit it off, or kill each other, and either way, it would be a great night of entertainment for me.

However, now was not the time. I pointedly cleared my throat.

Olivier blinked like he'd forgotten I was there.

I shot Sachie a wicked grin; she scratched her cheek with her middle finger in reply.

"Will you at least give me a heads-up if you're getting in over your head? One person's dead already." The concern in his voice was clear.

I forgave him my earlier frustration. Olivier honestly meant to do the right thing, both for the case and for me.

"I'll do my best. And I'll try to stay out of your way. I truly don't want to compromise your investigation."

"Guess that's the most I can hope for." He peeled off the wall and, with a small salute, walked out of the alley.

Sachie and I tracked him—okay, we tracked his tight ass—until he'd turned the corner and was lost to view.

"What was it you said?" I looped my arm through hers as we returned to the car. "He could curl your wave? Maybe he'll humpback you. Or rail bang you."

"I think that means getting hit by a surfboard between the legs."

"Don't bring reality into euphemisms, Sach."

"My bad. But no, there will be no rail banging." She sounded pretty firm about that, but I hadn't been best friends with her for most of my life to know the reason.

"Anything I hoped would happen between us didn't and won't. It's all clear if you're interested."

"I'm not." She sniffed primly. "He called me Rambolette."

I grinned. "Yeah, he did."

We got back to my car (I couldn't handle Sachie driving twice in two days), and she immediately agreed to one more quick stop.

Mason Trinh refused to let us into his neat ranch-style home. He stood behind his screen door in a sweater and jeans, looking tired. "If you're here to guilt me into going back to work, do it from the porch." He motioned us back. "On the step. In the puddle."

"Fine." Sachie kicked water at his door with her Doc Martens. "We'll come here every day and annoy you until you go back to work, you stubborn old bat."

"Please come back," I said. "You've had this brilliant career, Mason. The spa should not be the case that you end on."

"I lost a body, kiddo."

"No, you were fucked with. And I'm as much to blame as

you are. More. I was lead at the scene." Ezra told me to lock it down until he got there, but I'd been so determined to be in control. I should have hung up the damn phone and raced out to ensure my team's safety.

I couldn't tell Mason that, however, because then I'd have to disclose that Calista was a Prime.

"You failed to psychically foresee the one-in-a-million possibility of someone cleansing our memories." Mason opened the door, stepped onto the tiny landing, and made the sign of the cross. "I absolve you of your guilt."

"I'm Jewish."

He made a Star of David.

"I'm not looking for absolution," I said.

"Yeah, well, you get it anyway." He gentled his cranky tone. "I'm not coming back."

"What are you going to do at home?" Sachie challenged. "You look tired. Come back to work and you'll be energized."

"Gee, thanks, Saito. I'm gutted my skin care regime isn't doing more for me. I'm tired because my wife has signed us up for every activity under the sun. She's got us curling. Sweeping a ball on ice. It's preposterous." He shot a fond look inside.

I frowned. "You're taking medical leave until your retirement because you're…happy?"

"I'm taking medical leave because I can cash out all those sweet, sweet paid sick days I'm owed and take my honey on the Alaskan cruise we never had time for. The happy is a side perk." He gazed off into the distance. "Almost every retired Maccabee I know has that one case that made them walk away. This was mine." He snapped his gaze back to ours. "It was a good run and now it's time to leave. I have no regrets."

"Mason!" a woman called from inside. "Ten minutes until book club."

"Yeah. Yeah." He turned back to us and gave a resigned sigh. "Tell anyone I did this, and I'll deny it, but…" He held out his arms.

We did a group hug—for all of five seconds. Then he stepped inside the house and closed the screen door. "Now get lost. I've got nine minutes to make up some bullshit about *The Old Man and the Sea*. An old guy takes eighty-five days to catch a fish and I'm supposed to be profound about it."

"We're going," I said, "but don't be a stranger. I'm not sure what I'll do if you're not around to heckle me on a semi-regular basis. I might get some self-esteem or something."

"Can't have that happening."

We were halfway down the front walk to the car when he called out, "You two are two of the best and brightest I've ever seen. Don't let anyone tell you otherwise."

Sach and I spun around, but he'd already slammed the door closed.

I wiped the moisture out of one eye. "Well, damn."

"He had to get the last word in," Sachie grumbled. She nudged me. "You ever worry when you get a new case that it might be the one that breaks you?"

"Yes. All the time." But I didn't mean it like she thought. I didn't worry about walking away from my career, I worried that Cherry would be revealed, and I wouldn't have a choice.

Chapter 20

A nice, shiny gift had been left on the basement conference table back at HQ: Quentin's laptop, along with a sticky note containing the passwords to his main screen, his email, and his banking info. Although Michael had ordered this case locked down, it was okay to have IT get us into the computer that Ezra had procured at Quentin's house. They fulfilled so many of these requests that it wouldn't raise questions, but we couldn't trust anyone outside the team with our specific searches.

"Oooh." Sachie dropped into a chair and pulled the high-end laptop toward her. "Pretty."

"Yeah," I murmured, studying the murder board. Something on it twigged at a distant thought. It wasn't the CCTV, the blood, or Calista's shit list. I paused on the timeline itself.

Dawn Keller, the spa owner, had said that the Prime visited every six months, booking one day in advance and paying handsomely for the last-minute privilege. That tracked for security reasons, so what about this was nagging at me?

The clack of typing pulled me out of my musings. "Want to start with emails or with banking info to find a connection between Quentin and the mastermind?" Sachie said.

I did a double take. "That's it. The connection."

"I just said that."

"No." I pointed at the board. "Of all the spa joints in all the world, how did a Prime who spent most of her time running a magic gambling club on a megayacht cloaked by demon magic stumble upon a place here in Vancouver? Thermae is nice, but come on."

The typing stopped. "I asked Dawn when I interviewed her and she said she didn't know." Sachie's eyes had a dangerous gleam. "Methinks I should press her a little harder."

"Or," I said, "you stay here and comb through the laptop, and the operative who isn't reaching for the hidden weapon in her boobs can take a crack at Dawn."

Sachie dropped her hand with a huff. "If you think that's best," she said sulkily.

"I really do."

She turned back to the screen. "Bring me back a turkey sub from Knuckle Sandwich and I probably won't stab you."

"I'll even get extra cranberry sauce."

She inclined her head regally. "In that case, you shall live to see another day."

I bowed and left, driving over to the safe house where the Maccabees had stashed Dawn and her husband until the case was wrapped up. She'd already suffered memory loss; we didn't want our Yellow Flame perp hurting her more.

Maccabees operated two safe houses in the Metro Vancouver area. They'd installed Dawn in a corner ground floor townhouse in a quiet complex. The neighborhood skewed to a demographic in their forties and fifties. No young children running around, yet not filled with nosy retirees either. It had a private entrance and good visibility to monitor anyone coming or going. There'd be multiple surveillance devices and motion sensors but those wouldn't be visible.

I parked my car across the street in a small strip mall with a nail salon, a dry cleaner, and a supermarket. I chose a spot away from most of the other cars since it was harder to grab a person when you had nowhere to hide. Not that I expected trouble on this visit, it was simply training and habit.

As I was paying for parking at the machine at the edge of the lot, my phone buzzed with a text from Darsh telling me to come back. I frowned. I was already here, and I really wanted to speak with Dawn, but he was in charge, and I'd return if his decision was final. I asked if I could have twenty minutes with her and was granted that, though he said that he didn't want me alone in the field right now. He'd send Ezra to meet me.

I sent back a thumbs-up along with a pin for where my car was, though I was worried about his phrasing. He didn't want me alone right now? Neither he nor Ezra had answered their phones for the last several hours. What happened at the Copper Hell last night?

Instead of crossing the street directly to the townhouse complex, I did a quick circuit of the strip mall, and only once I was positive that I hadn't been followed and there weren't any immediate threats in the vicinity did I head over.

I identified myself to the Maccabee who peered through the peephole, requesting privacy to speak to Dawn. He let me inside to a clean yet hopelessly out-of-date kitchen and promised to keep Dawn's husband in the den.

The heavy curtains were drawn against prying eyes, and even though the lights were on, it was still gloomy and sad in here.

To no one's shock, Dawn was about as thrilled to see me as a teenager at a family reunion. The fiftysomething woman could hold her own against any adolescent in an eye-rolling competition, though her dark bags weren't quite as effective as a teen's emo raccoon eye look in the disdain department.

"If you're not here to tell me I can open my spa, you can leave." She glanced back to the game show playing on the small television sitting on the counter. It was so ancient that it was barely one step up from having bunny ears for an antenna.

"That depends on you." I sat down in the chair at the pitted kitchen table. A thin stream of smoke that smelled like jasmine on a cool night streamed off incense sticks jammed into a blue glass bottle on the counter. It was pleasantly subtle, calming, and totally out of place with the cheap laminate cabinets and yellow appliances. Dawn must have brought the scent diffuser from the spa.

It worked though, because under its spell, some of the leftover stress from Quentin's house melted out of my body. "I have one question. It could break everything open and get you back to business."

"I've answered a million questions already," she said frostily. "I don't know anything else. It's bad enough that I can't remember what happened, I'm losing money and clients by staying closed. I need to make a living."

"Of course you do," I said gently. "None of this is fair. You're as much a victim as Emily Astor." I used the alias that Calista used for her spa visits. "You've undergone a horrible, violating experience. Did you make an appointment with the psychiatrist that our healer recommended?"

She turned the volume down with the remote control. "Not yet."

"Please do. Sarah is kind and patient. I know from personal experience." Maccabees were required to undergo psych assessments after difficult cases or bad injuries to be cleared to return to work.

Dawn gave me a startled look. "Aren't Maccabees too tough for that?"

"We can be tough." I smiled. "But internalizing trauma isn't being strong. Getting help is. That's the brave call and I hope you'll do so."

She toyed with the remote for a long moment before nodding. "What do you want to know?"

"How did Emily know about your spa?"

Dawn shrugged. "I have no idea."

She sounded completely truthful. She didn't make overt eye contact, nor did she look away, or show any sign of tension.

I examined her with my blue flame synesthete vision. There was no pulsing blue dot over her heart or pulse spots indicating a rapid beat, nor were there any dots showing sweat or swathes of tension. A layperson might take that as indication that she really didn't know, but I was highly trained and highly experienced.

She was lying.

Dawn was a Trad civilian; she didn't have access to one of those devices that Maud and Henri did, which blocked psychological attacks and prevented me from reading her, and there was no indication she was a psychopath and free from empathy or guilt.

Owning a spa didn't make her a Zen master, and innocent people had some kind of physiological reaction to being questioned by authority. I should have seen some discernable reaction via my magic vision.

Break her, Cherry coaxed.

Calm your tits, Baroness.

"Okay, well, it was worth asking." I stood up, then tilted my head. "There haven't been any adverse effects to your business, have there? Any mention of it on social media? We've done our damnedest to ensure no word of the incident got out."

"Not a peep. I really appreciate that."

"Good. Obviously, we had to notify Emily's family, but other than that, you're good."

A giant blue dot flared up over Dawn's heart, pulsing at warp speed. "Fa-family?"

And awaaaay we go, Cherry squealed in excitement.

"Did you not know?" I snapped my fingers. "That's

204

right. The only info you had on file for Emily was her magic type and contact info. She had a partner." Not that Delacroix was particularly familial, but he was technically Calista's partner.

"Really? Oh." Dawn hurried over to the sink, got herself a drink of water, and shot it back like a teen with their first Jägerbomb.

"They don't blame you."

She let out a yelp and almost dropped the glass; I'd snuck up on her. "N-no. Of course not. Why would he? It's not my fault."

"I never said it was a he."

"Sorry," she said quietly. "I should know better than to make assumptions." She placed the glass on the counter and tried to ease around me.

I stepped sideways to keep her trapped. "You're right though. Her partner is male. Oh! I bet he'll know how Emily found your spa. I didn't need to bug you after all. Thanks so much for your time."

Dawn grabbed my sleeve as I turned to leave. "Don't bother him."

I glanced back, my eyebrows raised.

She let go of me. "I mean, does it matter one way or the other how Emily found Thermae? It could have been anything. A friend, an online search."

"Dawn." I frowned. "Are you scared of Emily's partner? Do you know him?"

"No," she said, staring directly into my eyes. Her voice was steady, but she was one massive blue dot.

"Well, good. And for the record, I was only testing you," I said. "We didn't tell anyone about Emily."

A huge swathe of blue in her body immediately disappeared. Yeah, right, she didn't know about Delacroix.

Finish her, Cherry ordered.

"But she does have a partner, and you know perfectly well

who it is, don't you? You know Emily Astor is an alias and who your client really was."

She darted a nervous glance into the hallway.

"Your husband is in the den. He can't hear us, but it's interesting you're hiding this conversation from him. You've got a choice, Dawn. Answer my question or I'll go and never come back again. I'll make sure you leave the safehouse and return to your normal life."

She leaned back against the counter. "How is that a bad thing?"

"Because the reason we didn't tell Emily's partner about her is that we didn't have to. Delacroix is not a happy demon right now."

I caught Dawn right after her eyes rolled back but before she hit the ground in a dead faint. Once I'd slapped her cheeks a few times to rouse her, her entire story changed.

And what a story it was.

Dawn not only knew exactly who and what Calista was, the Prime had funded her spa. See, Dawn came from a long line of people who'd worked for the vampire over hundreds of years. None of them were ever employed at the Copper Hell —those were always vampires—but Calista wanted non-magic humans to see to any earthly needs, like lawyers, bankers, and yes, spa owners.

They had no magic to pose a threat, and Calista paid them very well to ensure their loyalty. Obviously, there were always the stupid ones who were convinced they could fuck over a Prime and get away with it. Dawn wouldn't say what had happened to the few examples she knew of who had tried, but she almost fainted again bringing it up. She hadn't betrayed Calista.

"My mistress trusted me and I let her down." Dawn buried her head in her hands. "She's gone and it's my fault."

I refrained from telling her that Calista was still alive because I was scared news of her exceedingly displeased mistress waking up would give the poor human a fatal heart attack.

"Why every six months?" I said.

She fiddled with the hem of her sweater. "I can't tell you. I'm sworn to secrecy, and I won't break that promise, even if Calista is dead."

I leaned in so we were practically nose to nose. "Either you tell me exactly why she came to see you like clockwork, or I will bring you to the Copper Hell right now and deliver you to Delacroix myself." My growled statement was decidedly demonic sounding.

Cherry Bomb approved.

Dawn trembled, her eyes pooling with tears.

What was I doing? I softened my voice, taking pity on her —and taking a giant step out of her personal space. "Help me. Please. Do it for Calista."

"The—the Copper Hell is protected by demon magic." She paused.

"I know. Go on." It took all my restraint not to shake the information out of the woman.

"Delacroix set it up, but Calista controlled it."

I crossed my arms. "Controlled it as in she decided who's allowed to enter?"

Dawn nodded. "That and the glamors. Only demons were allowed to have them. Calista would rather no one did, but Delacroix was adamant otherwise. He insisted that all shedim be able to enjoy the club, and if they had to glamor to do that, then so be it."

How kind of him. Well, it explained why my Arjun glamor didn't stick, and, if Dawn was correct, meant Calista controlled the presence in the portal that unearthed Cherry. Sure, Delacroix created that magic, but he wasn't monitoring it. She was.

Had Calista been there during my visit, she probably would have learned I was a half shedim. With Delacroix's rule in place about demons looking human, she may not have forced my hand, but she would have had a dangerous Maccabee secret.

Not that I'd have been there in the first place, but still. She had bigger problems, and I doubted she was aware of who was crossing into the Copper Hell anymore.

The important part was that Delacroix truly didn't know about me.

A knot I'd been carrying in my gut unwound.

"Okay, Calista ran the portal," I said. "How was that tied to her spa visits?"

"It took its toll on her. The treatment I provided was specifically taught to me by her to allow her to rejuvenate and carry the magic load."

I grabbed her shoulders. "Had you done that treatment already?"

"I—I don't remember for sure, but if she was in the bathing pool, then not yet."

Son of a bitch. Calista was keyed to the shedim magic and her strength had been waning before she'd been abducted. Who knew how low her strength was now—if it existed at all? Anyone could get through the portal.

"If someone wanted to change the settings, how would they do it?" I said.

"I don't know, I swear. But part of the treatment involved eye drops she'd bring with her."

It involved a retinal scan at the bare minimum. Our perp had captured Calista to change the portal settings and allow them to go in glamored. As for whom and to what end, I didn't know yet, but I was revved up to find out.

I sprinted back to my car, firing a text reading *BREAK-THROUGH* to Sachie, Darsh, and Ezra. I wasn't paying attention when I dug my keys out of my pocket and ran across the street, and I bumped into some dude with the hood of his sweatshirt up. "Sorry."

He shrugged it off with a "No problem," and hurried on his way.

I stopped. I'd caught only a brief flash of his face, but there was something familiar about him. "Hey!"

He broke into a run.

I sprinted after him.

A thunderous *BOOM* tore through the air. I was blown off my feet, the shock wave sending me sailing. The explosion punched into my back and head like I'd been whacked with a shovel, and reverberated through my body, which had gone numb and tingly.

I hit the concrete with my left hip, and the lash of pain radiating out stole the breath from my lungs. Heat from the blast had seared a strip down my spine, and pops of hot metal shards from my fireball of a hatchback burned through my clothing.

My car insurance is not going to cover that.

The acrid taste of oil and burning rubber made my throat ache, a high-pitched ringing in my ears blocked out all sound, and stars danced in my vision. I was hypnotized by the sight of flames and paralyzed by the blazing bonfire of pain inside me.

"Help," I whispered, then the world went black.

Chapter 21

I woke up groggy and disoriented, surrounded by so much white it hurt my eyes, though whatever I rested on, lying on my side, was as soft as a cloud. *Jewish afterlife is Hollywood Heaven? I didn't see that coming.*

People were arguing, so that tracked. My people enjoyed a vigorous discourse, and it made sense that would become a main activity when we had literally all the time in the world on our hands. *Does this mean endless bagels?*

Ezra's face appeared above me. His forehead was crinkly from worry lines and his brows were so furrowed, he practically had a unibrow like Bert from *Sesame Street*.

I snickered and poked him between the eyes.

"Aviva." He caught my hand, keeping it loosely in his grip, though the rest of him was as taut as a drawn bowstring. "How do you feel?"

I giggled and waved my hand through the air. Colors trailed in its wake, so I did it again. "Great," I slurred.

Ezra's dark expression wasn't befitting of the heavenly version of angels—more their wayward brethren. I supposed they were allowed to visit. The same as relatives you didn't like but couldn't exactly hide from when they knocked.

"Do vampires go to heaven too? Because that is so going to fuck up people's belief systems." I moved my jaw up and down a few more times without speaking because it felt funny.

"This is bullshit." Sachie's frowny face floated somewhere around my feet.

Aw. My friends opted to die rather than spend their lives without me. Was there a thank-you card for that?

"We've got a unique opportunity here." Darsh moved into view, wearing a dark purple knitted toque shot through with sparkly thread. Were angels allowed to accessorize? "Aviva is an adult and I say she decides."

"She's in no condition to decide," Sachie shot back. "Not that of all things." She shook her head at Ezra before glaring at Darsh. "We don't need this. You're not thinking straight because—"

"My judgment is fine," Darsh said. The cold expression he leveled at Sachie was weird, like the stress of today had caused the glittery mask he wore to slip and reveal a glimmer of the ancient being he was.

I sighed. I wasn't dead; I was in the middle of a team argument. Correction: I was the reason for it. My stomach twisted and I winced.

"Upset Aviva further and you're both out," Ezra said in a hard voice. He tightened his grip on my hand, stroking his thumb over my palm. "It's okay," he assured me.

I relaxed a bit, my muddied brain clearing enough to take in some important details. I wasn't floating under clouds but a white canopy, the bed linens and closed drapes also white, and I was hooked to an IV. Ah. I was in a hotel room. Probably Ezra's. In his—nope. No energy to think that.

"Why are you all fighting? And why are you looking at me like that? I was okay being dead, but now I feel like I'm actually dying and that kind of sucks." My speech wasn't crystal clear, but I was understandable enough. My shedim magic allowed me to burn intoxicants out of my system, and I

cleared away some of my fog. Just enough for a basic comprehension, not enough to affect stopping my pain or making my
friends suspicious about how I was suddenly completely lucid.

"Someone blew up your car," Darsh said bluntly.

It all came rushing back.

"The safe house." I bolted up with a cry, but the wave of
pain knocked me back against the bank of pillows. "My hip.
Ow. Oh, fuck."

Ezra was already turning me on my side, smoothing out
what was not a light blue, basic-issue angel robe that I wore
over my underwear, but a sterile burn blanket. "Everyone is
fine," he said. "There wasn't any damage at the strip mall
either. You'd parked far enough away from the businesses and
other vehicles. We think someone put a tracker on your car."

My poor car. I groaned. She was crap, but she'd
performed her duties to the best of her ability. *Thank you for
your service.*

He rested his hand on my left shoulder. "You've got to stay
on your right side, okay? Your left hip is broken, and you
suffered third-degree burns on your back."

"Nerve damage?" I didn't feel anything there, not even a
distant throb. The IV was obviously dispensing quality pain
meds, but that degree of burn destroyed nerve endings. I swallowed down the taste of bile. "Why aren't I with a healer?"

"Excellent question." Sachie glared at Darsh.

"Ezra procured an extensive first aid kit and you're stable
for now." Darsh sat on the bed next to me, ignoring Sachie's
angry growl. He fixed his knit cap, which had slid low on his
forehead.

That was Ezra's handiwork. Why did Darsh get a gift and
not me? I was the one who had been blown up. I glared at
Ezra, who frowned.

"Was it Delacroix?" Sachie said.

"It's not his style," Ezra said.

I nodded. "He favors a more hands-on approach. Plus, he

wouldn't do anything to impede progress on getting Calista back."

"Fantastic," Sachie snarked. "Our suspect list is anyone other than that one shedim."

"Actually," I said, remembering that guy in the hoodie, "I saw who—"

Darsh flapped a hand in dismissal at Sachie and turned to me. "Whoever did this believes you're dead."

That stopped me in my tracks. "Wait. Why?"

"Because when I found you," Ezra said tightly, "you weren't breathing."

I was missing something. I glanced at the IV, annoyed because the painkillers were making it challenging to sort through events. My car was tracked. Someone planted an explosive while I was in the safe house. They must have been watching and seen Ezra's reaction.

My brain ground to an infuriatingly slow conclusion. I narrowed my eyes. "What did you break?"

"He ripped the payment machine out of the ground and flung it into a pickup," Sachie said.

"He sold the story," Darsh said approvingly.

"It wasn't a story," Ezra ground out. "I thought she was dead."

"Still." Darsh rubbed his rib cage.

Ezra crossed his arms. "It's still bothering you?"

"Not at all." Darsh dropped his hand. "It means Aviva is now an ace up our sleeves. If our perp thinks you're dead, they won't see you coming."

"They won't see me coming if I'm dead of an infection." I clutched the burn blanket like Linus in the Charlie Brown cartoons. It was warm, but hardly comforting. And what was up with Darsh?

"That's the catch. No one can know you're alive." Darsh paused. "Not even a healer."

"Catch?" Sachie spat. "This is your friend we're talking

about. The operative under your leadership. You're putting her at risk."

"I'm doing what's necessary," he said, steel in his voice. "That's what a leader does. Makes the tough calls to keep worse things from happening."

I frowned. Were we still speaking about my healing? "Did something happen at the Copper Hell last night?"

"Something always happens there," Darsh said. "That's not relevant. Say we brought in a healer, it would take hours or days to heal you, and you might be left with permanent scars."

Healing sessions were often more painful than the original injury. And scars? I moaned and closed my eyes.

Ezra stroked a hand over my hair.

"You can't let Michael think I'm dead." I couldn't put my mother through that kind of grief. For long.

"She's the only one outside this room who knows the truth," Darsh said. "She agreed to keep your status under wraps and has taken a few days of personal leave."

An ugly spurt of bitterness twisted through me. I couldn't remember a real event in my life that had her taking time off, but hey, good she could sell my fake death, I guess.

"Michael was less thrilled about my solution," Darsh continued, "but when I convinced her that it ensured Aviva's immediate good health, she signed off on it."

Immediate good health? Yes, please. I liked the sound of—

I snapped my eyes open, realization slamming into me like a sledgehammer hitting a brick wall. There was only one way to immediately heal me that my mother would hate.

My pulse quickened. Darsh wouldn't ask this of me. The very idea was preposterous. Except Ezra wouldn't meet my questioning gaze, and Sachie looked furious.

"What's your solution?" I gripped the blanket.

"Ezra heals you. He's a Prime." Darsh said it without a trace of remorse, knowing my history with Ezra and that I'd have to drink from him, an intimate gesture even when based in healing, not sex. "I'd offer, though his magic is stronger than mine for this, but I'm a tad run-down after visiting the Hell." His hand crept back to his side again protectively, but his expression warned me off asking.

I'd never drunk from Ezra. He'd never bitten me or given me his blood when we were together. Rumor said both were an incomparable rush, and I'd been tempted. So tempted at times that my fear of how his Prime blood might interact with my shedim nature barely kept me from begging for it.

Please. That was exactly why you wanted it, Cherry said. She'd been hovering under the surface of my consciousness.

He'd offered to heal me with his blood once before. On our last case. I hadn't been injured nearly as badly, and there was a Trad civilian present. It had been a no-brainer to refuse him.

I had to refuse now as well. Plus, as novices, we studied cases, admittedly rare, where human operatives who fed off vamp Maccabees to heal them resulted in obsessive behavior on the part of the Eishei Kodesh.

Ezra wasn't merely some vamp; he was the former love of my life, and a Prime. Sure, I'd come out physically intact, but what about psychologically?

I didn't want to undergo a painful healing session with a Yellow Flame and risk scarring, but drinking from my ex would leave an entirely different scar.

Complicating our current emotional connection violated every intention I had for the two of us.

"Aviva is not in a lucid state to consent to this," Ezra said.

"At least I'm giving her a chance to decide," Darsh said.

"Big words, Darsh," Sachie said. "You aren't allowed to compel an operative." While undead Maccabees mostly dealt with vamp and demon criminals, that policy was in place for all operatives, so that witness statements stood up in court. No one wanted a case thrown out because the witness had been coerced.

"I'm the lead. I could order it." Darsh ran a thumb under his black leather wrist cuff. "But thanks for thinking I'd force her."

"Sorry," Sach muttered and raked a hand through her rumpled hair.

"I won't order it either," he said, "but time is of the essence. Aviva, you won't be in any state to choose if we take you off the painkillers and you black out or go into shock." He clenched his fists. "We've been chasing our tails, and this could finally be the break we need. Isn't it enough I—? Could you just—" His hand drifted to his rib cage again. "Fuck!"

I blinked because Darsh's fangs had descended, and he never lost control.

"Put those away." Ezra shoved the other vamp halfway across the bedroom. "Or you won't be around much longer."

Darsh puffed up like a cobra, and then suddenly Sachie was between the two of them, a blade at both their throats.

"Out," she ordered. "Both of you."

"I'm not leaving her," Ezra said.

Sachie dropped the weapon she had trained on him with a sympathetic shake of her head. "You're not her bodyguard, Ezra," she said, not unkindly. "And you're in no condition to talk her through this."

"Why do I still get the knife on me?" Darsh said.

"Because you're an asshole and I love you sixty percent less right now," Sachie said. "Are you going to talk to us about whatever is going on with you?"

"I'm perfection incarnate," Darsh said.

She gave him a sad smile. "You're really not. Either way, this behavior is not going to fly." She jerked her head at the bedroom door. "Give us ten minutes and wait in the hallway outside the suite. Aviva and I need to speak without vamp eavesdroppers."

Darsh rolled his eyes, and Ezra pulled himself away from my side with the slowness of untangling from a web of sticky toffee, but incredibly, they both obeyed.

There was a soft click.

Sachie poked her head out the bedroom door to check they'd really gone. "Okay." She sighed and pulled a chair up next to me. "Bet this wasn't how you saw yourself ending up in Ezra's bed again, huh?"

"Ha ha, you're hilarious." I pulled the blanket up to my chin. "I'm scared, Sach." Whatever little adrenaline I'd been coasting on fled. "What am I supposed to do?"

"I can't tell you that, but you do need to make a decision and fast, because one way or the other, you have to get some healing magic into you."

"I look that bad?" I joked weakly.

"You're always gorgeous to me, babe, but it's not one of your top-ten looks." She ran her fingers through her hair in a stuttery motion, strain etched into the tight corners of her eyes and mouth.

I must have looked as lost as I felt, because Sachie patted my hand. "Let me tell you what Darsh learned at the Copper Hell so you have more facts to make your decision."

Since the Hell had precautions in place to keep vamps from compelling their bankers and no one was willing to offer up the information, even for a substantial amount of money, Darsh had to play the house in a game of Two Truths and a Lie.

The forfeits had been so brutal that Ezra had to come get him. I remembered Darsh rubbing his rib cage and winced. Part of his payment must have included prolonged pain, or he'd have healed already.

"That's awful, but it's not what's been upsetting him lately," I said.

"No," Sachie said. "But Darsh doesn't leave his self-preservation to chance. He knows what kind of place the Copper

Hell is and that the odds weren't in his favor of walking away unscathed. Why play?"

"He's taking being leader very seriously."

"Too seriously. I think that something in this case is tied to the reason he's a Maccabee. Either Calista or the Copper Hell itself."

"Or being in charge? Maybe he failed someone once?"

"I didn't want to go there, but yeah," she said.

Pain snaked through my hip, and I hissed. "We can't help him unless he opens up. For now, tell me what he learned."

"Sorry. Of course."

This business with Quentin started a year ago. The arms lobbyist had been angling to get his opponent, a notorious cybercriminal, to agree to a wager to settle their longtime heated rivalry about whether physical weapons or technical ones were more destructive.

Quentin challenged the other man to a game of dodgeball to see who was right. Who needed a gym when they set the playing court as the entire world? And the ball? Bombs versus data.

My disgust grew exponentially when I learned that the two players weren't in danger of being killed themselves during the game. Oh no, nothing so pedestrian. They signed a binding magic contract at the gambling hall with their forfeits and off they went. The point was to take out the other player's resources. Civilians, governments, everyone and everything was acceptable collateral damage.

I searched my memory for world events that fit that time-line. "You mean that bomb strike in Northern Africa and the rapid inflation of the Romanian leu were part of some game?" I balled my hands into fists. "I'm glad that scum Baker is dead, because if he wasn't…"

"Yeah, my sympathy drained pretty fast for Quentin after hearing that," Sachie said. "There's more though. The forfeit itself."

Since this particular game of dodgeball was rooted in destruction, Calista suggested that the forfeit reflect that, and that the loser should be destroyed. Not die; that wouldn't ensure the same degree of suffering they were inflicting on others. No, they would be turned into shadows of themselves, existing in the cracks of the world and forgotten by all. She didn't usually interfere in forfeits, but dodgeball was played so infrequently that this was a special occasion demanding a grand wager.

Both players were arrogant enough to agree.

"It took Quentin three months to win," Sachie said.

"What? He won?" I said. "Then why did we find him like that?"

"Quentin's collateral damage included a vamp that Calista had turned. The first one in centuries."

"Kill and ruin thousands of humans, no problem, but don't harm a specific vampire," I sneered. "I'm almost glad he staked her. It would be bad enough if he'd lost and become that way, but Calista robbed him of his humanity and turned him into a literal and metaphoric shadow, doomed never to be touched, spoken to, or seen." All in the name of revenge.

I was still committed to rescuing Calista, but I longed to raze that fucking gaming hell to the ground. Preferably with both owners in it, since none of this would be possible without demon magic.

"Who knew the final outcome?" I asked. "Other than Calista?"

"Only the two players and the banker, which is who Darsh played against."

"Who's our perp? The banker or the cybercriminal?" I said, confused.

"Neither. The cybercriminal took his own life, and the banker is fanatically loyal to Calista. Her job at the Copper Hell means the world to her. We've got Quentin's motive, but we still don't have any lead on who he was working for, and don't forget, anyone could have learned about the game since then. Darsh was really hoping that the breakthrough you mentioned would break the case open."

"It might, and if we launch a sneak attack based on that information, we wrap this up before it gets any worse." I'd get Delacroix off my back and out of my life. "No wonder Darsh wants me to stay dead."

"It's understandable for our case, but I don't think it's the best thing for you, personally. Sex with Ezra would be bad enough, but drinking from him?" She set her lips into a compressed line and squeezed my hand. "This sucks."

"Yeah," I said softly. For the first time ever, I wasn't sure if I could do what was best as an operative, but time had run out for me to choose. The IV was dry, the effects of the meds were fading, and the fiery pain inside me was a maelstrom making each breath and tiny gesture a nightmare.

Ezra healing me would take minutes. A healer could take hours or days, which would also impact the case, and I was already on thin ice with both Michael and Delacroix.

My heart, my career, or my life? I didn't get to have all three.

I bit down on my lip, trying to still the butterflies in my stomach. "I've made my decision."

Chapter 22

"Are you sure about this?" Ezra's voice cut through the silence. He'd dimmed the lights, leaving the room shrouded in shadows and uneasy tension.

Cherry vibrated with anticipation, but I was suddenly very conscious of how alone we were. At my request, Sachie and Darsh had left the hotel, promising to return in half an hour.

I lay stiffly on my side. I'd peeked under the burn blanket while I was waiting for Ezra. If I was a canvas, I'd be lauded for the glory of dark purples, blues, and reds blooming over my skin like wildflowers in a night garden. But I was human, so I looked like a crash test dummy after a weekend of questionable decisions.

Ezra glanced down at my hands, which were so tightly clenched that they'd gone white, then back to my face. His eyes possessed more shades of silver and blue than the giant Crayola box I'd coveted as a child. They bore into my soul, revealing a mixture of concern and something more dangerous.

He guarded facts like a dragon with treasure. What was he withholding?

My heartbeat sped up. "Is there any way this might bond us or pose a risk you haven't told me about yet?"

"A blood bond is only possible if we drink from each other in a specific ritual. It would allow our magic to strengthen each other's when we're in close proximity."

That could be useful in certain situations.

"But we'd be weakened if we spent too much time apart," he added.

Thank you, next. The vise around my chest eased somewhat that we wouldn't end up bonded. I also wouldn't be turned since he'd have to bite me and drain my blood before offering his own. "Good thing it's a one-way street this time," I said, "and we don't have to worry about being weak since we'll be off in different directions once this job is over. Any other possible unwanted side effects of drinking from you?"

"No? My blood should heal you. That's it."

I picked at nonexistent lint on the blanket. "The question in your voice is really reassuring."

"I haven't done this with anyone before. Shoot me for not knowing the fine print on the offer." He made uncharacteristic, short jerky movements with his hands while he spoke.

Perversely, his annoyance eased my anxiety. On that point, at least. "Will your blood taste good? Some fine vintage like Golden Blood is for you?"

"Don't believe the marketing. Most human blood tastes the same." His eyes dipped to the pulse thudding in my throat. "There are exceptions, I expect."

I licked my bottom lip, feeling dangerously drunk.

"Okay. Let's heal you." Ezra's fingers shook as he lifted his wrist to his mouth.

I frowned. He was nervous?

He took a totally pointless deep breath, let his teeth elongate to sharp fangs, and bit down on the fragile skin at his wrist.

The swift brutality of the gesture reminded me of a cobra's strike.

I flinched, yet I leaned toward his extended wrist and the nourishment on offer like a flower to the sun.

Our gazes locked.

Ezra's lips curved into a knowing smile. "You always did have a taste for danger."

I pressed my lips to his warm, inviting skin, tentatively tasting that first drop. There was no hint of hot copper. The complex flavor was peppermint candy and cool raindrops on a hot day with deeper earthy notes, but for a moment, I hovered between the fear of the unknown and the desperate need for healing.

The rush that kicked in a second later was insane, like mainlining an energy drink while riding a roller coaster during an earthquake.

More, Cherry demanded greedily.

In utter agreement, I gripped Ezra's forearm and sucked on his wound.

Ezra let out a rough moan, and I couldn't help the involuntary shiver that ran down my spine at that sound.

It was like a switch was flipped on my pain. A shock wave of relief rippled through my body, starting at the point of contact and spreading like wildfire to every injured part inside me. The elixir of life, that crimson nectar, worked its magic, weaving its way through my bloodstream like liquid lightning.

The world around us faded into insignificance, reality reduced to a mere backdrop. I was connected to something ancient and primal, as if tapping into a force that transcended time and space.

My wounds became distant memories, my body awake with a renewed and profound vitality.

Ezra fisted his hand in my hair, angling my head so I didn't lose a drop, his breathing ragged. His fingers brushed against my horns and a jolt of pure desire shot through me.

Horns?!

Sitting up, I jerked away from his wrist, feeling the needle-sharp boney protrusions with one hand, and clutching the burn blanket to my chest with the other.

My hair and skin were normal, and I didn't feel any prickling to indicate my eye color had changed. Great, just my cranial erogenous zones had made an appearance. I hadn't realized that was possible—or how good it felt to have them stroked. Lucky, lucky me learning new facts about my body.

I flushed in humiliation. "Sorry," I mumbled. "Thank you."

Ezra notched my chin up with one finger. "You can have more. As much as you need." There was no judgment in his eyes, only a hunger he didn't bother to hide.

There it was. The unwanted side effect. Ezra wanting me right now was a hollow victory. His rush came from being fed off, not anything personal.

"I'm totally good now." My voice was barely audible. "Thanks for saving me."

Ezra traced his thumb over my lips, wiping off the last drop of blood. "You were always worth saving, Aviva." His voice was dark with something that mirrored the tumultuous whirlpool of emotions churning within me.

I shivered again, already missing the intimacy and exhilaration.

Our faces were mere inches apart, and our eye contact had a gravitational pull, a magnetic force drawing me in. Uncertainty hung in the air like a heavy curtain while the atmosphere crackled with unspoken words and unsaid confessions.

Ezra brushed his knuckles along my jaw, barely a touch, and my breath caught in anticipation.

The boundaries of our past and present blurred, leaving us with a thirst that couldn't be quenched by blood alone.

Desire flowed between us like a live current, urging our surrender.

I scrubbed a hand over my face. I wanted him, but I also felt like a suspect desperately trying to look away from an interrogation light, while too blinded to see anything other than that one white-hot spot.

Well, I wasn't going to surrender. Nothing so passive. When the time came, I'd set the rules.

I cleared my throat. "I should get dressed."

Physically, I was better than ever, free of any aches or pains and ready to share my breakthrough with the team. The entire healing had taken less than ten minutes, and now we'd close in on our perp. We'd rescue Calista before she Hulked out on the world, I'd get Delacroix off my back, and Michael would be delighted that this case was put to bed.

But when Ezra left, telling me that Sachie had brought me clothes, and that I should come out when I was ready, the only taste left on my lips was regret.

I dressed in the soft, comfy purple sweats, blessing Sachie for bringing me new underwear and socks, and checked my reflection six times to make sure I appeared entirely human.

Ezra had invited Sachie and Darsh back to the suite, and I joined them at the expansive dark wood dining table, talking around mouthfuls of turkey subs that Sachie had ordered for both of us from Knuckle Sandwich.

Large picture windows wrapped around the hotel suite, showcasing a panoramic view of Vancouver that flowed across the open-concept living room/dining room/kitchen, to the spacious bedroom, and into the bathroom with its soaker tub and the sleek black control panel in the shower with more buttons than a cockpit.

I'd obviously taken a moment to suss the place out, same as I would any new environment. There was a single door exiting from the suite into the hotel corridor, the living room led out onto a narrow balcony, and none of the windows opened.

The best weapons in a pinch were the crystal wine decanter on the bar cart and the heavy white porcelain bedside lamps, while the biggest threat was the cardamom, cloves, and bergamot of Ezra's cologne mingled with the fresh, cool scent of a windswept summer breeze that lingered on his designer clothing.

Darsh listened to my debrief on my visit with Dawn, sipping from a mug of blood, but Ezra had foregone sustenance for knitting, his fingers flying as he made a yellow jumper for his cousin Orly's "ridiculous dachshund, Schnitzel." He sounded cranky as fuck about having to do this, but the finger grooves he was carving into the needles didn't come from him being upset about a dog's sweater.

Having me feed from him had done a number on him as well. That wasn't a shock, but it hit me that Ezra really hadn't been given a choice. Okay, yes, he could have technically refused, but he wouldn't have. Not for anyone on our team who required him to heal them. How much regret did he feel now, having experienced that intimacy with me? Was he angry at Darsh? At me?

I couldn't tell by his manner, so I focused on what I could do, laying out everything Dawn had told me about working for Calista and the settings on the portal.

"I agree that our perp is taking control of the portal to go in glamored," Darsh said. "That's a good breakthrough, but it still doesn't tell us who's masterminding this or the timeline."

I licked a drop of cranberry sauce off my thumb. "It doesn't, but I saw the vamp who bombed my car."

"What?" Ezra snarled. The knitting needles snapped into dust, loose yellow yarn pooling into his lap.

I wagged a finger at him. "Any payback will be mine. That said, chasing him down saved my life, because I was far enough away to survive the explosion. He works at the Copper

Hell, but there's more to why I recognized him." I rubbed my head. "Sach, could you do a sketch based on my description? Ezra, Darsh, and I have all been in the Copper Hell now. Maybe you guys can put a name to the face?"

"Sure," she said, "but before I get my notebook, I have something to add. I didn't find any suspicious deposits in Quentin's account, but I did find dozens of emails he'd sent to an address that kept bouncing back. I tracked the IP and it's in Hong Kong."

"That's it!" I dropped the sandwich onto my plate. "The vamp. He's a bouncer at the Hell and was in the memory of Maud's that I won. They spoke after she flirted with a bartender about speaking with Calista. Maud's from Hong Kong, right?"

"Yes." Ezra threw the half-finished doggie sweater across the room with a curse. He immediately got up and retrieved it, carefully rolling up the loosened yarn, and placing it on the counter.

"Maud who?" Darsh demanded. He grabbed Calista's notebook off the glass coffee table and flipped it open.

"Liu," Ezra said.

Darsh nodded, his eyes rapidly scanning the entries.

Sachie swallowed her last bite of turkey sub. "If Maud's a Yellow Flame, she assumed she erased your memories, same as the others, but when you showed up at the Copper Hell, she got suspicious."

"She didn't believe my story." I toyed with my Maccabee ring. "I wonder if she thought I was using Ezra to gain entry to the Copper Hell?"

"We can hope," Ezra said. "Then she won't have reason to believe I'm part of the investigation."

"She wouldn't think that anyway," I said. "Not of the Prime Playboy or the Crimson Prince."

"She was suspicious enough to try and kill you," Sachie said.

The timer went off on Darsh's phone, and the disco classic "We Are Family" kicked in. Darsh paused the music with one hand, Calista's notebook in the other. "We don't have to dance if you're not up to it," he told me.

"I can't believe I'm saying this, but I kind of look forward to it now," I said.

"Yeah, you do!" Sach pulled me up and spun me around.

Today had been categorically awful so far, and it should have been nice to blow off steam in a silly group, but it felt awkward. Sachie and I twirled each other around, but we kept shooting glances at our teammates. Ezra did push-ups in the other room, while Darsh kept falling still and zoning out.

Sach and I finally gave up and sat back down before the timer went off. Darsh didn't even protest. He turned the music off and called Ezra back.

I'd slipped up. It was always fun dancing with Sachie, but I'd danced with the person who needed me least right now. I sighed. It's not like I could go back and fix it. The moment had passed, and now all we could do was press on.

Chapter 23

Darsh showed us a name in the notebook. "Changying Liu. Her name is crossed out."

"Because she's dead," Sachie said. "That's one of the Eishei Kodesh I checked. We never investigated the children of people in the book. Is she Maud's mother?"

"She is," Ezra said. "But why is she on Calista's banned list? Did Maud have questions that Calista wouldn't answer?" He frowned. "Questions she couldn't get close enough to the Prime to ask?"

"Did she kidnap Calista for answers or to get into the Copper Hell glamored?" Sachie said. "Because Maud obviously has access to the place on her own."

"Why not both?" Darsh said.

"It is both," I said slowly.

Ezra nodded, clearly thinking the same thing.

"Maud wanted answers," I said, "but if she believes Calista is responsible for her mother's death, that wouldn't be enough. The Prime doesn't have family, but—"

"She has the Copper Hell," Sachie said.

"Exactly," I said. "She's going to disguise herself as Calista and burn the place down. The only question is when."

This changed everything.

Darsh sent Ezra back into the Copper Hell to question the vamp bouncer who tried to blow me up. If he wasn't there, Ezra would track him down in Babel. I modified the order to have him deliver the vamp to me. Both Darsh and Ezra were good with that.

Sunset came early in Vancouver in October, so while it was only 7:30PM, it was already dark, creating the perfect conditions for Darsh to break into the doggie day care and former printing shop in the warehouse that he'd first identified as possible hiding places near where Calista had been abducted from the transport van. He'd had good reasons to eliminate them, and he didn't hold out much hope now, but we were desperate.

Darsh kept his knitted hat on when he left.

Sachie left to meet with Sharnaz, our Maccabee expert on glamoring, to learn all she could about taking on a magic disguise solid enough to fool demon magic, like who could do this and how long it might take. Anything to narrow down the timeline of when Maud would go back to the Copper Hell, since if we couldn't find her with Calista, that would be the best place to apprehend her.

I was given the task of compiling a detailed profile of Maud and her mother, using Darsh's laptop and his logins to all Maccabee resources, since as a member of the dearly departed, I couldn't use my own.

His username? BitingWit.

Damn. That was way better than springtimebutcher22, the meanings of my first and last name plus my age when I created that login.

Unfortunately, any hope that I'd strike paydirt and find skeletons in Changying Liu's closet was dashed pretty quickly.

The Red Flame had been a professor at the University of Hong Kong. There were pages of links to her scholarly publi-cations, a few mentions of tennis tournaments she participated in, and the obituary of her death ten months ago at age fifty-five, from pneumonia. She hadn't been on social media, but Maud was, and there were plenty of photos with her mother in her various accounts, showing the two foodies having a great time at restaurants around the world.

Nothing indicated a gambling problem or any behavior that would have gotten Changying banned from the Copper Hell. I stood up and stretched out my back.

Changying's name on Calista's list was also not accompanied by a helpful date. She could have been banned at any point during her life, though I doubted it was near the end. Her pneumonia happened suddenly, and she'd been teaching and publishing up to her death. There was a press release from the university about how shocked and grief-stricken her faculty was to lose such a celebrated and respected physicist.

I drummed the slender stake that Sachie had thoughtfully and a little pointedly left for me on the table. Why was the professor banned from the Hell? The only thing that made sense was that she'd lost a forfeit that cost her too much and caused an outburst Calista refused to ignore.

If Maud had drunk the Kool-Aid of her mother's hatred toward Calista, then this was a revenge crime.

Had Maud been planning this ever since her mother died? Had the plan been put into place by Changying while she was still alive? Or was it only when Maud learned of Quentin's situation that she saw her opportunity to get back at Calista?

Speaking of mothers, mine texted me. I stared at the screen, my face scrunched up in confusion. The last message I'd received from her on our personal text chain—two months ago—was simply the directions to the seafood restaurant we were having dinner at. Now she'd sent a heart emoji.

When a friend of ours from university passed away, Sachie and I had called her phone to hear her voice, and left messages on her birthday every year until the number was no longer in service.

It was a smart move on Michael's part to have this record of grief over her dearly departed daughter. The explosion would have been reported back immediately to Maccabee HQ, not because it was me, but because these things were monitored. Combine it with Ezra's outburst and there would have been a moment my mother believed I was dead.

I hoped it hurt. Was that mean-spirited? Absolutely, but since my deepest fear was she'd mostly be relieved, I wanted her, even for a second, to feel my loss on a visceral level.

She didn't send a follow-up message, and I wasn't going to divine any insights to my mother's emotional state from this single emoji, so I put my phone away. It wasn't like I could text her back. I was dead.

Moving on. The timer that I'd set on my phone buzzed— yes, I'd decided to keep up the dance breaks. I started up Blondie's "Sunday Girl," singing and grooving around the hotel suite for the requisite three minutes before I dove back into the puzzle that was Maud Liu.

The more I learned about the twenty-seven-year-old, the more I wished we'd met under different circumstances. I confirmed she was our Yellow Flame, but she was also a freaking professional poker player who held multiple world titles. She'd won her first tournament at the tender age of twenty-one. How cool was that? She was smart and well trained in deception and bluffing.

While I couldn't wait to face her, this meant that she was careful about her curated image. Sure, her love of travel, food, and fashion was evident in all her photos plastered on social media. She was a jetsetter and probably crossed paths with Ezra on a regular basis. However, I couldn't find anything that explained why she'd kidnapped Calista or what her end game was.

I shook my head. It had to involve her mother.

I yawned and stretched my cramped-up shoulders, ready

for a caffeine fix, when the door to the suite banged open. I yelped, jumping a foot in the air.

Ezra strode in with his fangs out and his hands bloodied, carrying a human-shaped lump of bruised flesh. He tossed them down on the floor, where the person hit with a groan. Kicking the door shut, my ex wiped blood off his cheek with an oddly elegant movement, and unfurled a sly smile. "Don't say I never gave you anything nice."

I studied the doubled-over heap of vamp bouncer. "I'd call this more of a regift. Not even that. Recycled? Previously used for sure."

The bouncer attempted to sit up, but Ezra kicked him in the head with zero effort or emotion, and the other vamp fell back to the floorboards. He curled into the fetal position, whimpering.

"Gently used," Ezra protested, crossing over to the kitchen.

"You have some schmutz of his skin and hair on the toe of your shoe." I wandered closer to the bouncer. "So, agree to disagree. What's his name?"

Ezra grimaced and wiped his shoe clean with a paper towel. "Constantine."

Had the bouncer renamed himself after the Roman emperor? Points for knowing his history, but talk about delusions of grandeur. He was muscle at a gaming hell, not ruler of an empire.

"Did you speed him here all the way from the portal at the Jolly Hellhound?" I said. That was a not-inconsiderable distance to blur here without being seen, and Ezra didn't look winded.

He tossed the paper towel in the trash then washed his hands at the kitchen sink. "We had to stop a few times while I reissued my invitation to accompany me back for questioning, but essentially yes."

I crouched down next to the bouncer, gratified at how his

eyes widened at the sight of me. "You should have killed me properly, but since you didn't, you owe me answers."

He looked away.

I grabbed him by the hair and yanked his face back to mine. "I'll say when we're done. Where did you take Calista?"

"Cali's been kidnapped?"

Maud was a slender woman. She wouldn't have the physical strength to carry Calista from the transport van to wherever she'd stashed her. Especially without being seen by someone *and* after expending all the energy necessary to wipe three people's memories. Constantine, on the other hand, could easily have accomplished that. I still believed Maud was in charge, but the vamp was part of this.

"Where's Maud holding your boss, Constantine?"

His mouth fell open in shock at my knowing that Maud was involved, then he clamped his lips shut with a defiant glare.

"Awwww, look at you protecting your…girlfriend?" I laughed, letting go of him to sit back on my calves. "You poor, deluded idiot. She's a professional poker player. A regular patron of the Copper Hell. Did she tell you how much she cared about you? Did she let you kiss her? Fuck her?" I leaned closer. "Bite her?"

A muscle ticked in his jaw. Gotcha.

I feigned a sympathetic smile. "You really think the two of you connected? It meant nothing. Have you seen her since? I bet you haven't. I bet she hasn't spared you a second thought. Why would she? She got what she needed from you."

The water snapped off, and I glanced over at Ezra to warn him off interfering. He was tight-lipped, his mouth downturned.

Constantine lunged at me, knocking me to the ground and pinning me with my hands trapped in his grip along either side of my head.

For a second, I panicked, but it had been beaten into me

over years of training that fear was the mind-killer. The brain was the most important weapon for self-defense. I tore all panic away, planted my feet on the ground, and snapped my hips up, simultaneously tucking my elbows in.

The vamp fell forward onto all fours, unbalanced. He moved to correct his position immediately, but I'd freed one of my wrists, and delivered three rapid-fire, hard strikes. The third one hit his throat, and he lurched back, freeing my other hand.

Getting out from under him now was easy. I swung my arms around him in a wide circle, latched on to the small of his back, and tucked my head against his stomach.

My opponent struggled to regain dominance, but I clung to him like a baby monkey, shimmying myself up his body until I could trap one of his arms against his side. I again planted my feet on the floor, snapped my hips again, and rolled him underneath me.

Keeping his arm locked down, I struck under his chin with the palm of my free hand, then I elbowed him in the gut and punched him in the groin.

Constantine deflated with a pained moan.

I jumped to my feet and flung a sweaty lock of hair out of my face. It had taken only seconds to free myself, but I breathed heavily.

Ezra lounged against the kitchen counter with a tea towel swung over one shoulder. "Nice moves, Fight Club." His tone was teasing, but even from this distance I saw a barrier lock into place behind his eyes, making him impossible to read.

I cracked my neck from side to side, backing out of lunging range from Constantine, who was still curled up. "One more chance. Where's Calista?"

"Fuck you, cunt."

I mock shuddered. "Ooh. Hit with the most unoriginal burn ever. You suck at insults as badly as you do at killing people, buddy, but I don't have the time or inclination to teach

235

you manners. Ezra?" I motioned for him to have at the other vamp.

"You putting me in, Coach?"

"Yup. Don't let the team down."

"Oh, I won't." His expression turned coldly sinister. He grabbed the front of Constantine's shirt with one hand and hauled him to his feet like the two-hundred-pound vamp was as light as air. "Answer her."

Constantine shook his head.

Ezra's fangs descended. He slammed the vamp against him, biting down on his neck so savagely that a tendon crunched.

Constantine screamed and started sobbing. A dark stain spread over his pantlegs.

I wrinkled my nose. Gross. However, I was fascinated by how Ezra could make a bite either deeply pleasurable, like he had when he healed me, or deeply painful, for Constantine.

Ezra released him, and the bouncer fell to his knees, babbling an address in Vancouver where he'd picked up the explosives for my car from Maud.

I bounced on my toes in anticipation of going another round with the woman. The forfeit she'd lost during our game of hazard would be a fond memory in comparison.

My ex swiped his tongue over his fangs, then spat Constantine's blood on the floor in front of the other vamp, who flinched so viscerally, it seemed that of all the injuries he'd sustained today, Ezra rejecting his blood was the worst cut of all.

Ezra glanced over at me. "Anything you want to add?"

I raked a gaze over the miserable shit who'd tried to kill me, reduced to blood, piss, and sobbing. He was nothing. Less than nothing.

But he'd tried to kill me.

Sachie's stake was in my hand before I consciously registered it.

"Please," Constantine begged. "Spare my life. You can arrest me. You're a Maccabee."

"True, but…" I reached Constantine in four quick strides and grabbed him by the shoulder. I let my eyes turn toxic green and my claws come out. "I'm also so much more."

I drove in the stake.

His gasp was cut off. Well, falling apart into puzzle pieces of ash had that effect.

I wiped off the stake and slid it into my sweats against the small of my back. "Let's go get Calista." I bounced on my toes again, expecting Ezra to fight back, to protest that I was supposed to play dead and that I had to stay here.

Instead, he grabbed his cool gothic leather hunter's jacket from the hall closet and draped it over my shoulders. "After you."

Chapter 24

Ezra didn't bother to change or cover his bloodstained clothing. Deliberate choice or time constraint? Likely a bit of both.

I had to piggyback him while he sped us down sixteen flights from his penthouse hotel suite, but I made him put me down a couple blocks away in a parking garage. "I've ridden you enough." Ezra's lips twitched, and I rolled my eyes. "You know what I mean."

It was around nine on a weeknight. There were plenty of cars parked, but no one was around. I bashed in the window of an older sedan.

"Careful of my jacket," Ezra said, on the alert for anyone approaching.

I checked the elbow. "It's fine." I brushed glass off the driver's seat, then popped the lock for Ezra to climb in.

"I assumed your new car would be purchased, not hotwired," he said. "That it might come with sensible options like heated seats and functioning glass in all its windows."

"Consider this a rental." I couldn't loosen the screws in the kick panel of the steering column using the stake as a makeshift screwdriver, so I tapped the plastic cover. "Tear this off so I can get at the wires."

"I'm not sure I appreciate being used like this," he grumbled, but did as I asked.

"No one is as good a tool as you."

He snorted, but despite his amusement, there remained a distance between us that I couldn't quite explain. We hadn't blood bonded, but that healing session was insanely intimate. I'd expected to feel closer to him for a while, and it was strange that there was a wall between us.

I found the battery voltage wires and identified the three I needed: the one for the electronic control module for the engine, the one for the body control module, and the signal starter wire. I tore the plastic connector off the wires and attached the ones necessary to make the lights appear on the dash. It had been a while, and it took me a couple of reconfigures to get it right, but once I did, it was a simple process to add in the starter wire.

The engine purred to life.

"Heh." I patted the steering wheel. "I haven't lost my touch."

Ezra placed his hand on his chest with a gasp. "Aviva Jacqueline Fleischer, did you break the law?"

I released the parking brake and threw the car into drive. "I like to think of it as situational ethics in pursuit of a higher good. But if you don't want to be an accessory, feel free to run."

Ezra stretched his legs out as much as possible and propped his hands behind his head. "Feel free to ride me through town." He snickered.

"That's not—shut up." I tore out of the lot, my face flushed.

"So," Ezra said conversationally, as I careened along back streets to the address, "when did you hone this criminal skill set?"

"There was this boy," I said.

"Please don't tell me you learned to impress some horny sixteen-year-old that you thought was a bad boy."

"First of all." We flew over railroad tracks, the car bouncing hard as we landed. "I was fourteen."

"That makes it worse."

"And he wasn't a bad boy. Give me some credit for not being a total cliché."

"My apologies." Ezra's voice went tight as I careened around a corner and down a stretch of industrial road like I was drag racing.

"Winston was the smartest kid in school. He'd beaten me to become president of the debate team and always edged me out for the top spot on the honor roll. He was insufferable, always lording it over me."

"So, you hotwired a car and stuffed his body in the trunk to take out the competition." Ezra nodded sagely.

"How'd you know?" He did a double take and I laughed. "My plan was to show Winston that he could keep his book smarts because I had street smarts. Sachie got one of her cousins, a mechanic who was amenable to cash bribes, to show us how to hotwire a car."

"I should have known she'd be involved."

"She didn't want to be left out of the fun," I said loyally.

"Did you show Winston smarty-pants up?"

"Kind of." I shook my head with a rueful smile. "I hotwired the car, but Winston didn't bow down and cede that hotwiring beat running club meetings, so I decided to drive him around until he professed my superior coolness."

"You held him hostage."

"Hey. We were fourteen. Anyone who could drive was cool, and he was supposed to acknowledge that." I screwed up my face. "It didn't go as planned."

"You killed him?"

"As far as I know, Winston remains alive and well."

Ezra smirked. "You didn't know how to drive, did you?"

"Nope. Sadly, all my *Mario Kart* wins didn't translate to real life. I hit reverse instead of drive, shot backward into a stop sign, denting the bumper, and fled the scene of the crime."

"A positively Shakespearean tale of hubris."

"Luckily, I was never caught, and I put the fear into Winston about how being an accessory to grand theft auto would kill any university applications."

"Ah. The real lesson was in intimidating one's opponent."

"More like knowing which information was most relevant to a person." I cut across a main street that was littered with speed cameras.

"And you never committed another illegal act until tonight."

"What do you think?" I said sweetly.

"That you've been such a good girl all your life, even with Cherry Bomb."

I pulled up to the curb at the address Constantine had given us—a neat Craftsman bungalow popular in Vancouver in the early twentieth century. "Not everything is as it appears." I was reaching for the wires to turn off the engine when a massive realization hit me. "Son of a bitch!"

I gunned it around the back of the house. The home wasn't simply close to the café, it shared the back lane with the business, and in fact, the car port was directly across from the parking stalls.

I turned into the covered car port.

Ezra was out of the car before I'd turned the engine off.

I jogged into the backyard. A broad magnolia tree planted by the high fence cut off any line of sight from the neighbor to the east, and with the house situated on a corner lot, there was no neighbor to the west. Clocking the motion sensors, I followed Ezra's trail through the shadows and down the back stairs to the basement door.

He waited for me to catch up, then broke the knob off. The door swung open.

It was dark, musty, and eerily silent.

Be very, very qwuiet, Cherry enthused. *We're going Prime hunting.* She added a deranged Elmer Fudd laugh for good measure.

Ezra listened for other sounds in the house. He pointed upward and shook his head, but some noise beyond my hearing range caught his attention, and he strode directly to a door at the far end of the basement corridor.

Heavy blackout curtains covered the window, and the light switch didn't work. Ezra didn't need it to see, but I turned my phone on and whistled.

The room was empty save for a single showpiece: Calista in a dirty shapeless brown dress, gagged and bound with fat iron chains to a freakishly thick wooden chair. A regular chair wouldn't hold her, I got that, but this was like something a zealous child had built using oversize beams instead of blocks.

The Prime's strawberry-blond hair was lank and tangled, and her eyes were propped open with eye clamps straight out of *A Clockwork Orange*. Wires ran from the clamps to a slick computer tower, with a monitor displaying 3D scans of her eyeballs.

Add in a heavy metal lever whose entire purpose was to keep the stake jammed in Calista's heart and the utter stillness of the vampire, frozen in this torture yet still possessing a barely leashed sense of power that punched into me, and I had to hand it to Maud. She'd really gotten one over on a Prime.

I glanced at Ezra.

"Don't think of this as a how-to guide," he said.

"I mean, I do love adding to my skill set, and it's so nicely laid out."

He shook his head and turned to the captive vampire. "It's so good to see you again, Calista." Ezra practically hummed

242

the greeting. I'm amazed he didn't skip over to her. "No, that's okay. Don't get up."

I rolled my eyes but didn't say anything. It couldn't be easy for Ezra having his tormentor gift wrapped in front of him and not being allowed to kill her. I moved closer, shining my phone's flashlight slowly over Calista.

Her fingertips had been burned off. A needle was taped into the top of her hand, the tube leading to an IV stand mostly hidden by the chair. The empty bag on the stand had a smear of blood inside it.

"How do we keep her subdued but able to answer questions?" I pointed to the monitor. "The scan confirms our theory about Maud using Calista to take control of the magic portal settings at the Copper Hell, but we need to know when she's going in."

"What do you say, Calista? Ready to play nice in exchange for your life?" Ezra twisted the metal lever away and pulled the stake halfway out.

She sagged forward and would have fallen off the chair had the chains not been holding her.

He freed her eyes from the clamps, dropping them to the ground with a clang, and laughed. "It must grate having me be your rescuer. Seeing you debased and powerless like this."

She growled at him, blinking rapidly like she was trying to get moisture back into her eyes, but she still didn't possess the strength to keep herself upright on her own, so she was a long way from recovered.

"That's enough," I said mildly. "We don't need her riled up more than she already is." The thing is, there was no way a Prime was going to meekly comply and answer questions. I wouldn't hold my breath for a tearful thank-you either.

"Calista isn't close to riled up. She's infamous for keeping her cool. She can flay a person raw without batting a lash." Ezra tipped her chin up. "Can't you?"

The female Prime flinched in slow motion and her eyes spat hate.

"Ezra, stop." I didn't care that he was taunting her, I just couldn't bear learning anything else about what he'd suffered at her hands, or I'd be tempted to kill her myself.

He didn't even glance at me. "I believed all your pretty lies. How I'd consigned myself to live in the shadows once I formally accepted my father's offer of enforcer. How, as the only other Prime, you understood that life better than anyone and you'd be there for me." He laughed harshly. "I've got to hand it to you, Cali. Your physical torture never held a candle to the pain of realizing that was all a story to make me lower my guard. I never saw you coming."

I closed my eyes, wishing he'd go back to details of being flayed, because this was killing me. If Ezra had never met me, never rushed from the smoking embers of our relationship into assassinating people for Natán, totally at odds with who he was and his dreams for himself, he would never have been alone and an easy mark for Calista's physical and psychological torture.

Ezra didn't create the Prime Playboy out of a desire to connect—or not entirely. He did it for the same reason he publicly flaunted his role as Crimson Prince: it was the ultimate offensive play. If you were always in the spotlight, someone would notice if you went missing.

They might even care enough to help.

I swept an assessing gaze over my ex. That's why he wanted me to go public with Cherry. Except we weren't in the same boat. I kept her a secret precisely because the people I trusted to keep me safe weren't ready to deal with her. I frowned. Did Ezra really not believe he had anyone in his corner when he was growing up? What about now? He had to know Silas was there for him. Was one person not enough? Did everyone he charmed into his orbit act as another brick keeping him from being swallowed by the dark and his fears?

"There was no other Prime to mentor me. I wanted to gift you my loyalty." Ezra's voice startled me out of my thoughts. "But all you wanted was my blood."

I flinched.

"That's all in the past though," he said in a matter-of-fact voice.

Relief surged through me and I stepped forward to catch his attention. "How long will the stake hold her now that you've pulled it partway out?" I said.

"At least a day."

"Good. I'll stand guard in case Maud shows up. You go to the Copper Hell and tell Delacroix to get his ass here now."

Calista narrowed her eyes at Ezra.

"No," he said, "I'm not going to torture you. I made a promise recently, and I intend to honor it."

I pressed a hand to the warmth spreading through my chest. Ezra was putting the vow he'd made to the team over his need for revenge. I'd hoped he would, but it could have gone either way in the last few minutes. After all, Calista had wreaked vengeance on Quentin for far less.

Calista scoffed dismissively behind her gag.

Ezra swung his gaze to me for a split second, and in it, I read profound regret. "I'm disappointed about it too," he said to her. "I really did want to break you." His fangs dropped, and he slammed his hands to either side of her head.

"Ezra! No! Don't." I lunged for him.

He broke her neck with a loud snap, then with a snarl, he tore her head clean off.

The shock on Calista's disembodied face would have been funny if it weren't so dire. Her life didn't ebb away all at once. It took seconds or millennia, a haunting sight that unfolded in stages. The first involved a profound stillness, not like when the stake was fully jammed in, but as if time itself had calmed. The fire in her eyes receded, and the hazel color darkened, shadows creeping over the vibrant hue. Her eyes turned glassy, taking on an almost metallic sheen, which was finally replaced by an emptiness that looked like it stretched into eternity.

Look at that. Primes do leave a body.

She deserved it, Cherry said in a smug voice.

I mentally hissed at her to shut up because that so was not the point. Gaping at Ezra, I shook my head like that would reattach Calista's head to her throat. Or turn back time to the glory days of when Delacroix wasn't going to destroy me.

Ezra held Calista's skull aloft in a gruesome parody of the statue of Perseus with Medusa's head. Her blood dripped down his arm and onto the floor in fat plops.

"You promised," I said in a shaky voice.

"I did." His voice was oddly flat.

"I'm fucked." I spun away, shaking. "Delacroix is going to come for me and—"

"Aviva."

I whipped around. He'd flung Calista's head into the corner like a discarded soccer ball. "What?"

"I did what I had to." His features were cloaked in shadow, but apparently that explanation was sufficient, because he turned his back on me and methodically broke Calista's chains apart one by one.

"You did what you wanted to."

"This was never what I wanted."

Right. Because he'd planned to torture her first. Was I supposed to be grateful that he'd spared me seeing that?

I'd stupidly taken Ezra at his word that he'd do what was best for the investigation. We all had. This betrayal would have been bad enough yesterday or this morning, but for Ezra to so cavalierly put me in Delacroix's sights now?

I removed his jacket and flung it at him. "You let me drink from you. You healed me. How could you turn around and doom me now?" Ezra wasn't that good of an actor; the intimacy we'd shared in that moment had gone both ways, yet he'd irrevocably destroyed it. "Make this make sense." My

246

voice cracked. I wasn't that stupid. I couldn't be. Not again. "Was this payback for what I said to Constantine about him being an idiot about Maud letting him bite her? You know I was talking about them and not us, right?"

"It was 'deluded idiot' actually," Ezra said, "but no. Not everything is about you."

I stomped my foot in frustration, my fists clenched at my sides. "This isn't you breaking my heart, Ezra, and it's more than you screwing me over. Delacroix is going to kill me. You don't want that, I know you don't, so why?"

He put on his hunter's jacket. "Stop being so melodramatic." His tone was so harsh it physically knocked me back a couple of steps.

Had Ezra's nervousness and reluctance to have me drink from him been nothing more than a fake out so I'd lower my guard and he could wreak his revenge? I stepped back from Calista's headless body slumped at our feet. He'd learned from the best, right?

My face crumpled, and with a half sob, half laugh, I fled.

I could escape the house, but it was only a matter of time before Delacroix learned what had happened and then? There'd be nowhere to run.

Chapter 25

Stomping along the sidewalk past the café, getting soaked, because of course it was raining, wasn't nearly as satisfying as revving into the night. I couldn't get in my car and run because it had been *blown up*, and I was too messed up to try to steal another one. To add insult to injury, every drop of rain was an icy reminder of all the ways Delacroix could hurt me.

I'd just gotten home and taken a hot shower when Sachie banged on my door. "Ezra really killed Calista?" she said, her voice tight.

I flung the door open, pajamas on and my towel wrapped around my wet hair. "He told you?" I gaped at the chunky green scarf wrapped around her neck. "More importantly, he knit you something?"

Sachie patted it. "It's warm and soft as petting a bunny rabbit."

"And you accepted it? From the man you warned me off?"

"I warned you off the man, not his knitwear. Those are of impeccable quality. And to answer your other question, Ezra showed up at HQ, calmly dropped that bombshell about Calista, and refused to elaborate, beyond insisting you had nothing to do with it. That's when he gave me the scarf."

Holy shit. Calista's murder wasn't something he could hide, but I didn't expect him to march directly to HQ, do not pass Go, do not collect $200, and confess either.

"What part of 'rescue mission' wasn't clear?" Darsh growled from our living room.

I sighed, and followed Sachie down the hall.

Darsh was coiled on the edge of our sofa, his expression grim and a beer bottle–sized blood beverage cracked open in front of him. The popular brand was magically infused with a high alcohol content, allowing vamps to get drunk. Darsh's serving was half gone.

He still wore his toque.

How come they got gifts and I didn't? I had Ezra's literal blood running through my stupid veins. Surely that was worth a pair of socks.

I took the chair farthest from Darsh, impressed at Sach's utter nonchalance in throwing herself down next to our murderous-looking friend.

"I tried to stop Ezra from killing her," I said. "It happened too fast."

Darsh nodded, and a knot unwound in my chest now that I knew he wasn't mad at me. "Calista had to die," he said, "but not until after we'd caught our suspect."

"Wait." I crossed my arms. "You condoned her murder?"

"She was a Prime," he said. "She wasn't going to forgive and forget. Whether today or years from now, she'd have her revenge."

"On Maud," Sachie said.

He shook his head. "On anyone who witnessed her humiliation. Memory loss wouldn't matter."

"Then why wait to kill her?" Sachie said.

"Why did the Crimson Prince work so hard to become a Maccabee spy?" Darsh said.

I shrugged. "No clue."

"Me neither, but he did." Darsh scraped at the corner of

the label on his bottle. "A revenge kill during an active investigation case is enough to get him booted out of the entire organization. I told him as much, and you know what he said?"

I shook my head.

"It saved him a resignation letter."

I flinched. "That's not right. Darsh, we need to speak to him."

"No," he said firmly. "We do not. That's an order." Darsh hadn't given many direct orders on this investigation, but this was categorically one with no room for interpretation. "Not until this is all over," he added. "Ezra will be lucky if the Maccabees only kick him out and don't decide to treat him as a liability."

"Like they meant to with you?" Sachie said.

I eeped and darted a fearful glance at Darsh.

"That's what they do, Sach." He sounded resigned. "Our overlords are only benevolent up to a point. And in Ezra's case? The Crimson Prince, holder of secret intel, going off into the wild? I don't want any of us near that shitshow until we have the leverage of this closed case on our side."

"They could kill him?" I choked out.

"I don't know."

Sachie went into the kitchen.

"Tell them it was self-defense," I insisted.

"After he confessed otherwise to me and Sachie?" Darsh arched an eyebrow. "How many people would you like to implicate in lying for him? Besides, he seemed pretty set on leaving."

Sachie returned with the good bottle of vodka we kept in the freezer and poured us both shots.

"The asshole was growing on me." Darsh took a healthy swallow of alcoholic blood. "I tried to protect him."

A dull, heavy silence descended on the room.

Sach and I half-heartedly clinked shot glasses. The cold

booze had a sharp kick going down, but when it hit my stomach, a warmth blossomed through my system.

Sadly, it wasn't enough to overcome my fears about Ezra. I understood a world where he'd hurt me. It was dark and painful and lonely, but eventually, color and laughter would return.

I couldn't fathom a world where he no longer existed at all.

I didn't want to.

"Please tell me something good," I said.

"Delacroix will be out of your life soon," Sachie said.

"Right," I muttered. "So long as I stay alive until then and we have a precise timeline of when Maud is going to attack in order to stop her, I'll be peachy."

Sachie refilled my shot glass. "Good thing we have exactly that."

A tendril of hope snaked through me. "We do?"

"Delacroix probably thinks you're dead anyway," Darsh said.

"Thanks, sunshine, but I'm not counting on that as an absolute. I'm safe so long as I stay here behind wards, but I can't do that indefinitely, and sadly, wearing a mezuzah around my neck won't help."

"Seeing as you're not a door," Sachie said.

"An aspiration I never before had." I fired back my second vodka shot. "The thing is, getting from here to the portal at the pub will be risky for me."

"It's a risk we'll have to take." Sachie shuddered, making a face at the vodka she'd swallowed. "Sharnaz was very helpful. There are only a handful of Eishei Kodesh in the world capable of attaching a glamor using digital scans of a real person's fingerprints and retinas. Fewer still who could make them fool demon magic and take control of the portal. The closest person is in Los Angeles, and guess who flew down there this morning?"

I closed my eyes briefly against the surge of relief. And possibly because the vodka was making me feel nicely blurry. "Any idea how long it'll take to glamor Maud?"

"Sharnaz assured me we're looking at a twenty-four-hour minimum. Even without factoring in travel time from the LA airport to the Eishei Kodesh glamorer and then Maud getting to a portal to the yacht, she won't show up at the Hell before tomorrow morning."

Darsh propped one of our decorative pillows behind his head and slid the fuzzy blanket that was folded over the back of the couch over his body. He had an open invitation to crash here, and honestly, I'd feel better with him around. "We'll head for the Jolly Hellhound around 8AM," he said, "which will still get us there before her. For now, get a good night's rest."

Sachie held up the vodka bottle, her eyebrows raised.

I nodded and held out the shot glass. "Purely for medicinal purposes so I don't lie awake brooding." Or shaking, after this bitch of a day.

"I'll drink to that," Sachie said. We fired back the vodka.

"Maybe Delacroix will take his anger out on Ezra," Darsh said, his eyes already closed.

"Maybe." Except I didn't want that either.

Happily, I swaddled myself in my blankets and slept like a baby until my phone woke me. It pulled me out of such a deep sleep that I felt nauseous and disoriented. "Hello?"

"Aviva?"

"Huh? Who's this?"

"It's Jordy. Rukhsana is laying low for a while, but if you want to meet, I'll bring the donuts."

Did I? Not really, but if my last act was to ensure he was safe and sound, that wouldn't be so bad. Delacroix hadn't sent his "no can refuse" invitation portal the second Calista died, so he wasn't keyed to her in some way. Hopefully, news of her demise would take time to make its way back to him.

Damn, I did not want to be the messenger when we got to the yacht. It would suck to get the jump on Maud only to have Delacroix kill me. Especially since I intended to kill him first.

I agreed to meet Jordy, throwing on a warm black hoodie, black jeans, and a pair of flat ankle boots in the dark. Today's mission did not call for a nice pantsuit and heels. It required something that would hide demon blood.

It was only 6AM, but I woke Darsh when I tiptoed into the living room. I told him I was going to see an informant on some other business and that I'd be back before we had to go to the portal.

Fifteen minutes later, my Uber pulled up to the address I'd been given—an older apartment building in the West End. I'd spent the ride twitchy, convinced I'd be sucked through a portal to face Delacroix's wrath since I wasn't behind mezuzah wards, but I arrived in one piece.

Jordy buzzed me into a gloomy lobby that smelled like dryer sheets and popcorn, with a carpet that was a 1970s vision in faded paisley. He waited for me halfway down the hall on the second floor, his hands jammed into his pockets. His ZZ Top beard was gone, revealing a baby face cuteness and a weak chin.

"Looking pretty good for a corpse," I said.

"Yeah," he mumbled. "Sorry about that."

I was relieved, pissed off, and tired, all in equal measure. "You better have ponied up for the good donuts and not some supermarket shit."

"I did." He glanced around once, then ushered me inside before turning two dead bolts on the door.

The studio apartment had a futon in one corner across from a flat-screen TV on a steamer trunk, a cheap wooden table, and a heap of boxes.

"Are you coming or going?" I sat down on one of the two chairs.

"Camping out temporarily?" He took the seat across from

me and cracked open the bright yellow donut box from my favorite bakery.

"Should I still call you Jordy or do you have a new name?"

"George Green is dead. Long live Jordy Gill." He'd taken Rukhsana's surname in his new alias? Why not. The young woman played mom to her crew. A mother lion, but still.

I helped myself to a jelly donut. "Why's Rukhsana being framed for stealing the exhibit artifacts when we both know that's not her style?"

Jordy blinked at me. "You believe she's innocent?"

I swallowed my mouthful of pastry. "Well, I did. Of theft, at least. Am I wrong?"

"No, but…"

"But why am I convinced? She does very well for herself in terms of money and power with her current operation. Why would she risk that for a bunch of mostly worthless non-magical artifacts when she's never engaged in B&E before? Plus, she claimed her attacker was misguided. I concluded she was framed. How am I doing?"

"Pretty well." His general good humor had been restored, and he bit into a cinnamon old-fashioned with a smile.

"And the murdered man? The other George Green?"

Jordy's smile faded. "That wasn't Rukhsana either. Green was behind the gallery job, but his fence ratted him out to a powerful client."

"Who got the wrong idea because of his name. This client killed Green and assaulted Rukhsana?"

Jordy nodded and took another bite.

"Why'd Green steal them in the first place?"

"I can't talk to the dead, Avi," Jordy said with a laugh, "but my money is on the money. It doesn't matter if the artifacts were debunked of magic, there are still collectors who'll pay a tidy sum for them."

I sat back on a rush of disappointment. I'd been positive that Sire's Spark was stolen because of some tie to the missing infernal blood, and that someone high up in my organization had ordered the theft, just like they'd ordered those people's murders.

This wasn't some nefarious plot to help vamps become invincible, but the one artifact that mattered was still out there, in play somewhere.

"I doubt the fence left an anonymous tip for the cops to come and get them," I said.

"Nope. He was so mad."

"Who has Sire's Spark now?"

He shrugged.

I didn't buy it. I took a deep, steadying breath. "Are you still in danger? Is Rukhsana?"

He grinned. "I told her you cared."

"I do. So let me help you both. Tell me who attacked her." That person might know something useful about Sire's Spark.

"They don't matter anymore," Jordy said. "She dealt with them."

I sighed. However, as he hadn't explicitly said the person was dead, I could still plead plausible deniability if Olivier demanded answers. Ah, damn. Olivier. "The Trad cops are investigating," I said.

"We know. They won't find any loose ends."

"That's great for you, Jordy, but honestly, I feel I'm owed more than an admittedly delicious donut and some cryptic small talk."

Jordy wiped sugar crystals off his mouth with the back of his hand. "Why? About what?"

Sire's Spark. But how could I tell Jordy that I wanted to see the healing crystal for myself? Hold it in the palm of my hand in case...

In case what? Cherry scoffed. *Your shedim blood activates it? Then what? Would you help with the vampires' quest for invincibility?*

Most people with a devil on their shoulder have an angel balancing it out, I fired back.

255

My head rang with laughter.

Jordy peered at me, munching on his second doughnut. "You okay there? Your face is twitching weird."

"I'm fine. Look, the Trad cops know I'm connected to Rukhsana, and I've gotten some heat on that score. I kept my mouth shut that you weren't the dead man."

In a blink, the burly man's affable good nature was replaced by something darker. "Is that a threat?"

"It's a request. If Rukhsana has any leads on the missing artifact, I'd appreciate them so I can restore some good will with my fellow officers."

He didn't answer, suddenly very busy brushing crumbs off his shirt.

I narrowed my eyes. "Not a lead. She knows where it actually is."

"Not exactly."

My already hair-thin patience snapped. "Where's the fucking artifact, Jordy?"

He hesitated but caved under my glower. "Rukhsana believes a Maccabee took it."

"Why the hell didn't you lead with that?"

He shrugged. "I had to make sure she could trust you."

I blinked. "Rukhsana thought it was *me*? Why?"

"An anonymous tip to the Trad cops with all the artifacts left nice and neat for them to find, except the one with this supposedly incredible magic power? Come on, Avi, she knows you."

"What's that supposed to mean?" I said coldly. My blood pounding in my ears sounded like a voice whispering *Infernal* over and over again.

"Admit it. You were mad that Trads got this case instead of Maccabees. You'd want this artifact off the streets to get it verified by your own experts and lock it away if necessary. If it went into the evidence lockup at Trad HQ, you'd never get your hands on it. Not anytime soon at least. The politics involved would be a nightmare."

I relaxed. "Okay, yes, that's fair, but I didn't do any of that. Also, I'm hardly a seasoned thief. The likelihood of someone seeing me if I did attempt to take it would be pretty high."

"So what? You could make them forget you were there."

"I'm a Blue Flame," I said. "We illuminate weaknesses, we don't cleanse memories. That's Yellow Flame territory."

He laughed. "Yeah, right." He drew his brows together. "You really don't know?"

"Know what?"

"Blue Flames can wipe memories," he said.

"No, we can't."

"It's really rare, but it's possible for a Blue Flame to meld their consciousness with an actual flame, giving them fire sight. I don't know if there's a technical term, but they see what's happening via flames."

"They spy via fire?" My eyes widened. There were candles in the spa. "How does the memory loss play into it?"

"If the Blue Flame wants to extinguish the memory of the events they're watching, they snuff out their magic in a certain way. I don't have the specifics."

The wood creaked under my weight as I twisted the gold Maccabee ring on my finger, calling up every detail of the crime scene I could remember. Was Maud actually a Blue Flame and that's how she'd erased the memories?

Part of me was annoyed that I'd never known this about my magic type, but more of me was seriously pissed off that Maud got a cooler ability than me.

I sat back in my chair. Except...her yellow flame magic was a matter of public record. *Poker player*, Cherry said. Which came first? Maud hiding her real magic to become a world champion poker player or using that cover to hide her magic? For her magic to have been hidden through childhood, her mother was involved.

I gave a bitter smile. It always came back to the mother.

I straightened out a bend in the lid of the donut box. Constantine had told the truth that he wasn't part of the abduction. He wasn't shocked that I knew Maud was involved, he was stunned that she'd kidnapped Calista in the first place.

I didn't feel bad for killing the vamp bouncer though. A death for an attempted death and all that.

Okay, so Maud, a Blue Flame, lied to Quentin to secure his help to stake Calista, spied on us at the spa through the candles, and wiped Mason's, Rachel's, and Dawn's minds of the crime. For her grand finale, she dragged Calista out of the can and into the basement, where she imprisoned her to scan her retinas and fingerprints and get control of the portal leading to the Copper Hell.

It was quite the plan.

Having gotten all I could out of this meeting, I stood up. "I expect an invitation to Rukhsana's new place of business." Look at me, making plans like I had a future.

"Now that we know you weren't involved in any part of this robbery, you'll get one."

I nodded and headed for the door. "Thanks for the donut."

"Next one's on you."

I made it home, collected Darsh and Sachie, and got to the Jolly Hellhound, still unharmed. The pub was closed, but Darsh had arranged for the owner to get us into the back room. The protocol of ordering a Bitter Abyss was trumped by Maccabee authority. By which I meant Darsh's "do not fuck with me right now" attitude when the dude tried to enforce it.

Before we stepped through the portal, Darsh gathered Sachie and me into a tight circle, and placed his hand in the middle. "Count of three," he said.

"Wait." I held up a hand to stall the chant we used to kick off nights out together. "There's something I need to tell you both." In order to fill them in about Maud's unique blue flame ability, I came clean about investigating Sire's Spark to Darsh. I didn't have to, but I wanted to. "I'm sorry I lied," I said. "I didn't compromise this investigation, but I did defy your no-secrets rule, so I'll take whatever punishment you see fit."

It was a relief to confess.

"Since we're sharing," Darsh said slowly. He fiddled with the beads in his leather wrist cuff. "I used to be a regular visitor to the Copper Hell."

"Did you know Calista was the Prime involved from the start?" Sachie said.

"I suspected. Strongly. But I didn't know that staking her wouldn't kill her. I swear that was news to me."

Sach crossed her arms. "Did you have history with her?"

"No. I barely knew her. I had no personal feelings about her one way or the other."

My head was reeling. "You should never have been lead on this."

Sachie glared at me. "This isn't about you not getting to be in charge."

"That's not what I meant. Well, okay, maybe I meant it, but you kept this secret for a reason, so there was more to it than visiting the Hell. You could have compromised our case."

"I didn't though," Darsh said. "Not at any point. Nor will I."

I narrowed my eyes. "It compromised *you*. You got hurt going back there."

"More emotionally than physically. I—" He squeezed the leather cuff. "I lost someone because of that place." His gaze went distant and haunted.

"Who?" Sach spoke softly but that one word was infused with steel.

"My younger brother. Patrin." Darsh shook himself like a dog shaking off water. "And that's it for story time today."

"You shouldn't go back," I immediately said.

"If you and Sachie want to take over, go ahead. But I'm seeing this through to the end," he said.

"Because you want to do your job or because of what will happen to you if you screw up as a Maccabee?"

"Can both matter?"

Yeah, they could. I knew that better than anyone, but still I hesitated when Darsh placed his hand in the middle of our circle.

"Please," he said softly. "I need this band to stay together."

I slapped my hand over his. "So do I, you idiot."

Sachie sighed theatrically and placed her hand on top. "I was going to have a fantastic solo career."

"No, you weren't," Darsh said. "You can barely carry a tune. On three."

At his countdown we chanted, "We are fabulous!"

"We got this," I said.

"And we've got safety in numbers," Sach added. "Even Delacroix will think twice before harming three Maccabees. He wanted Calista back so he could feast on the misery that his business generated? Well, if he gets the organization up in arms over our deaths, the only misery will be his. It's not worth it."

It was a comforting thought. Too bad that when we stepped into the portal, I was the only one who stepped out.

Chapter 26

The portal was nothing more than a doorway. Whatever presence stripped me of my glamor and broke me down into my shedim form was gone. Whether it was an actual entity that lived within the rift that Maud dispensed with when she took control, or simply a magic alarm set by Calista, there was no trace of it now.

Thrilled as I was that I didn't have to start this takedown battling an invisible force to remain in my default human skin, why weren't Sachie and Darsh right behind me? Was I permitted through while they were caught up between realms, fighting for their lives? Or was it already too late for them?

My heart raced. Nothing was ever as simple as it seemed in the supernatural world. According to our timeline, Maud shouldn't be here yet, but if she hadn't prevented them from coming through, who had?

The portal here in the minuscule entryway vanished. I wrenched open the door to the main room and strode through, ready to insist to any Li'l Hellions barring my way that it was in their best interests to steer clear, and the hairs on the back of my neck stood up.

The Copper Hell was completely empty, devoid of any signs of life.

I took a few tentative steps forward, the rumble of engines that once vibrated through the space replaced by the creaking of the ship and water slapping against the narrow dark windows. A haunting silence hung over the room like a heavy curtain, and I shuddered as I peered into the night sky and dark ocean, feeling the weight of the emptiness pressing down on me.

I walked farther into the abandoned casino with only the faint echoes of my own footsteps for company. At least this time, I wore shoes. Wow. My low bar was positively subterranean.

The chandeliers were turned off, and the honey-colored lights that spread across the ceiling were now dim and flickering, casting long shadows over the brushed steel walls along with a deep sense of foreboding.

Machines that formerly filled the area with clanking pachinko balls and the clackety-clack of roulette wheels stood silent and dark, their lifeless forms like monuments.

It was as if the place was frozen in time, waiting for someone to bring it back to life, except when I swiped my finger over the green felt of a poker table, it came away dust-free, and the metal slot machine handles gleamed.

Did Delacroix know Calista was dead and close the Hell in mourning? Could he not keep everything going without a Prime managing the business? Were both things true?

So much recently had defied expectation and appearance. Had I misjudged the shedim's feelings for his missing partner? Were his complaints about handling the business while Calista was missing nothing more than a front? To shedim, emotions were things to be manipulated and exploited; Delacroix would never expose such a weakness in himself.

I hadn't believed him capable of such feeling, but right now, I wasn't sure what to think.

A waft of cigar smoke tinged the air, and I whipped around.

Delacroix stood there in his fisherman's sweater and jeans, smirking. He held a half-full crystal highball glass in one hand and a lit cigar in the other, and his salt-and-pepper hair was more windswept than usual. It reminded me of a tangled fisherman's net, like he'd stood at the prow of the yacht, eyes closed, with his face to the wind and his arms outstretched.

I almost snorted—and glanced out the window for icebergs. "Where are my friends?"

"Friends? This is a social call?" He made a big show of looking around. "Where's the person who dared kidnap Calista? If you let them get away…" Water slapped against the yacht so hard it rang through the enormous space and the entire ship rocked sideways.

I grabbed on to a poker table for balance, the leather bumper bashing against my wrist.

The only silver lining was that he didn't seem aware that Calista was dead.

"They'll be here momentarily," I said. "But I plan to arrest our suspect. You aren't dishing out payback for your business partner."

He puffed on his cigar and blew the smoke at me. "You think you can get to them first?"

I brushed my thumb over my Maccabee ring, calculating how I could physically hurt him enough to let the magic cocktail in the top compartment latch on and kill him. I didn't have an answer yet, but I wasn't leaving him alive.

"Calista." Delacroix breathed out her name.

She'd staggered out of the foyer door, wearing the same shapeless dirty brown dress as when she'd been held captive, her strawberry-blond hair sticking up every which way.

Ezra didn't kill her. The hope sent my pulse skyrocketing, but not even a Prime survived her head being torn off.

This was Maud in a stellar display of acting.

I started toward her, but Delacroix knocked me roughly aside and gathered her into an embrace.

His back was to me, so when his shoulders shook, I thought he was crying, but his laughter echoed through the casino.

Along with the sudden sizzle of flesh from his cigar on the fake vamp's cheek.

Maud screeched and stumbled back. Her glamor was smeared, dripping off her real face like drops of water.

I jumped on Delacroix's back and grabbed him in a chokehold.

Maud would pay for trying to kill me and for staking and abducting Calista, but her punishment would be determined by a court of law, not a demon.

"Off!" Delacroix accompanied his snarled command with a tentacle of water that slapped me into a pachinko machine halfway across the room.

The air was knocked from my lungs, and I crumpled in pain to the ground.

Delacroix studied Maud. He'd restrained her in a watery python hold—like he'd done to Ezra. "Why did you take Calista? Did you forfeit something you should never have bet?" he said in his gravelly voice. "Your magic? Your life? Go on. Hit me with your villain monologue. Maybe I'll be entertained enough to kill you quickly instead of, well…" He gave an almost coy smile, then slowly crushed the entire crystal glass to dust in his hand.

Ice, amber liquid, and blood spilled onto the plush moss-colored carpet, creating an almost beautiful pattern of swirls.

I pushed to my knees, gritting my teeth against the blazing throb along my side. Delacroix's first question should have been to find out where Calista was, not Maud's motive.

The promise Ezra referred to before he killed Calista. The reason why he did it. The events of last night rearranged themselves with a sickening clarity.

"You made Ezra murder Calista," I said. "Was that the price of letting him go that first night here at the Hell?"

Delacroix glanced over his shoulder at me. "Might be hope for that girl detective badge yet."

You condescending douchebag. I can't wait to annihilate you for everything you've done. I stood up. "Why kill her?"

Darsh was in favor of Calista's death because of the revenge she'd take and the harm and chaos that would ensue, but Delacroix wouldn't care about any of that.

"She let herself get caught." The shedim sneered at Maud. "By a human. I expected better from a Prime. Calista was compromised. She became worthless."

Ezra wasn't worthless. Yes, he'd been caught and tortured, admittedly by another Prime—a high-level foe—yet he'd reforged himself. Ironic, of all the things for us to have in common. He was smart, and whatever his agenda, he was pursuing his goals with a single-minded ruthlessness, while still doing his best not to hurt those closest to him.

The memory of his regret before he tore the Prime's head off made that clear, as did him simply accepting Darsh's edict that Ezra was off the team and out of the Maccabees, instead of fighting back. He'd even given Sachie an apology scarf.

Delacroix, on the other hand, had lived in a world of forfeits for so long that the only value he recognized anymore was power and strength. His was a world of winners and losers, and when Calista fell hard from her lofty perch, she became a weakness to be exterminated.

The pungent sting of brine made my eyes water.

Maud's black hair had turned crimson, and there was a dangerous glint in her eyes, which were now the exact shade of green as Cherry Bomb's.

Delacroix's face slackened in a way that would have been comical, were I not wearing the exact same expression. "You're a..." he began. The restraints he'd created fell apart into a puddle on the floor.

Half shedim, I mentally finished. I'd never seen people like me in their demon form, and my shock that Maud and I were the same was tempered by fascinated curiosity.

Maud swiped a hand armored with green frosted scales across her face as if wiping away the last of her glamor to truly reveal herself, and notched her chin up with a defiant glare.

Holy shit. She had the same frosted scales.

Delacroix narrowed his eyes. "One of my bastard brats."

My mouth fell open.

The shedim's words hung in the air like the smoke drifting off from his cigar. Time suspended, and the air was still, suffocating, and stagnant.

Delacroix was my...

I shuddered, but I'd said it myself: it always came back to the mother. I just hadn't understood how true that was.

The room was going around and around, spinning slowly at first and then picking up speed. It felt like a car that had lost its brakes and was heading toward a ditch.

"Changying Liu," Maud said.

Her voice reached me as if through a long tunnel. I white-knuckled a chair, sweating and desperately trying to regain my equilibrium. I had a half sister?

"What about her?" Delacroix didn't sound like he knew who Changying was.

Maud let out a strangled growl. "Hong Kong, twenty-eight years ago. You got her pregnant and disappeared."

Demon sperm daddy was consistent. I'd give him that much.

Delacroix bound her up again, wagging a finger at her furious expression. "Give me a minute. I meet a lot of people."

I couldn't stop staring at Maud and cataloguing our similarities in shedim form, notably the crimson hair, frosted scales, and eye color. She didn't have the extra muscle mass, but then again, her human body was slenderer than mine. She also didn't have claws, but two bony horns peeked out of her hair. They were shorter than mine.

It had to work like human genetics, didn't it? We shared these traits because Delacroix had them.

That might explain why Maud and I had Blue Flame magic; it corresponded most closely to Delacroix's shedim powers. Ordinary human thirst for money or power might account for why people visited this yacht, but the cruelty of the forfeits was where Delacroix's evil genius lay.

He didn't incite Quentin to play dodgeball. Quentin wanted that all on his own. But look at what the man was willing to bet. What Delacroix's magic made it *possible* to bet.

Maybe stepping through the portal was the demon's first insidious attack on patrons to break them down and find all the little cracks—weaknesses—where he could slip in.

Take my mother's uncharacteristic "bad girl" one-night stand. Michael was an exemplary Maccabee with a rigid moral code who happened to have a fondness for feminist lyrics involving modern ideals of love and sex. She'd had a couple casual relationships while I was growing up, but I'd also overheard her say to friends that she wasn't all that interested in it. I pressed her when I was older, asking if she'd refrained from boyfriends or having lovers because of me? My mother laughed and assured me that I'd been out of the house for years. She could do what she pleased; she simply didn't care about it.

Delacroix unearthed something Michael enjoyed and twisted it. It wasn't bad that she uncharacteristically had sex with a stranger, but that she slipped up on the birth control. Maybe my arrival didn't totally ruin her life, but it certainly negatively impacted it.

One "bastard brat" might be an accident. I studied Maud, steaming mad and waiting for Delacroix to remember her mother. Was two a pattern or a coincidence?

I had my opinions, but right now, I was more concerned with what Delacroix's abilities meant for my initial visit to this yacht. I glared at the demon.

My weakness he exploited that night wasn't my forfeits, it was the pain I'd suffered in the charade of being in debt to Ezra and not being certain how much of it was an act on my ex's part. The plan was my idea, but in the same way I'd never ordinarily agree to forfeit my power for any amount of time, had that really been my only—or wisest—course of action?

"Changying." Delacroix's confused expression cleared. He sucked on his cigar. "Right. The nut who wouldn't stop pestering Calista to see me. She's lucky she only got blacklisted."

I was lucky that I didn't have Eeyore demon as a sperm daddy, but Delacroix's true form was still a mystery that I suddenly badly wanted to unravel.

"Yeah, our lives were one stroke of luck after another," Maud said bitterly, her eyes bleak. I wondered why her voice sounded different until I saw her mouth. *She had fangs?!*

"Fun as this little reunion has been"—Delacroix freed Maud with a flick of his fingers, only to batter her between two plumes of water—"I've wasted enough time chitchatting."

I ran toward her, but a watery vine twined around my feet, tripping me.

Maud fell to the carpet, yellowish-black bruises blooming along one side of her throat under her torn collar. She ripped a metal wand from a thigh strap under her dress and pressed a button.

Flames shot out, engulfing Delacroix. He roared in pain, the stench of charred flesh filling my nostrils as his eyes shifted into toxic green beacons surrounded by fire.

Maud ran for the demon, jumping the line of fire snaking across the carpet. She raised her hand; something gold glinted.

A Maccabee ring. She was going to kill Delacroix.

I sprinted to Maud and knocked her aside before the magic in the ring could take hold.

The ring went flying.

"Stay out of this!" She grabbed me by the hair, trying to push me out of her way.

I snapped my forearms down on her elbows and broke her hold. "You can't use that ring." I started coughing from the noxious plumes of smoke fogging the air and threw an arm over my mouth and nose.

"Why?" she sneered. "I'm not good enough because I'm an infernal?"

"You didn't take the oath, you idiot. Use it and you'll die."

She wrinkled her brow. "Why do you care?"

"I'm not adding to the body count on this case." I had to yell over the crackling and snapping sounds of the growing fire.

I grabbed Maud and shackled her wrists with the magic-nulling cuffs I'd hung on my belt loop, then wiped sweaty soot off my face. "How do we get out of—"

The narrow windows imploded.

I screamed and threw a hand up against the flying shards from the shattered windows. Cold gusts of air whistled through the casino and water splashed over the frames.

Delacroix was shifting, his thick scales snuffing out the flames, yet he hadn't completely transformed from his human glamor. He was vulnerable enough that I didn't need to beat him up. My magic ring would find and latch on to his kill spot during this transformation. I could take him down for good.

I closed my fingers into a fist, but I didn't move.

Skin melted away from the shedim's frame like water, and his limbs assimilated seamlessly into his new shape. There was a majesty in his thick serpent's coil and a wild oceanic beauty to his silver scales. Ours were pale imitations of his armor, baby monsters trying to be scary.

Delacroix wasn't trying. His demon form alluded to an

ancient untamed world beyond our reach. Beyond our comprehension.

Heavy black horns curved upward off his head, his teeth were razor sharp, and crimson spikes protruded from his neck almost like a cape.

I ran a tongue over my flat human teeth and swallowed. My head was tipped practically all the way back, watching the demon grow and grow until his head brushed the top of the high ceiling and his coils pooled mere centimeters from my feet.

I'd lost my chance to use my ring. The magic would dissipate uselessly into the air now, and I didn't have the physical strength. I'd have to outwit a demon and flee.

Chapter 27

Delacroix's coils extinguished most of the fire, but small pockets of flame danced throughout the casino. We had to leave, asap, but the only time I'd exited the Hell, the shedim had thrown me out. I could take my chances in the foyer, but even if I found a portal, I had no idea where it might lead.

I was a puny human at the mercy of a lethal monster, still, a curious sense of calm descended over me.

That's called shock, Cherry scoffed, but she helped me stand tall and not cower.

Delacroix locked his gaze on Maud. His eyes gleamed with a malicious glint, and his lips curled into a sinister grin as he swayed and bobbed, prepared to strike. "You're pathetic."

He didn't care that Maud was his own flesh and blood.

He wouldn't care if he learned about me either.

There was an odd freedom in knowing that. I'd always harbored a tiny fear that if I met my father that I'd be caught in conflicted loyalties.

I jumped in front of…my sister. There was no point using the flamethrower—it wouldn't scorch the demon in this form —but I was making a stand.

A choice.

"Step aside, girlie," he hissed, his voice echoing through the chamber. "This is family business."

He had no idea.

"Yes," Maud said, struggling against the cuffs. "This is between me and him."

"Points for tenacity," I said over my shoulder to her, "but seriously. Shut. Up." I turned back to Delacroix. "This is Mac—"

Maud knocked me to the ground from behind and pulled the chain of the cuffs taut around my neck like a garotte.

"There's hope for you yet," Delacroix said.

I wormed my hand under the chain so I could breathe, then headbutted her backward.

Maud screeched.

I ducked free of the chain to find her tipping her head back and plugging her nose to stop the blood.

In my head, Cherry grinned. We liked this sibling gig.

"You cow!" she said.

"You started it."

Delacroix was watching this exchange a little too closely.

I smoothed back my hair. "As I was saying, this is Maccabee business. Now, I'm going to do exactly what I said I would: arrest our perp. Then she and I will walk out of here. You will not hurt either of us, and you will not come after us. Ever. You so much as whisper a threat in our direction and I'll whip the Maccabees into such a fervor over your destruction that there won't be any realm you can hide in."

Delacroix loomed over me, fangs out. "I could kill you," he said conversationally. "The Maccabees would never know what became of you."

"They'd find out," I said. Even if something had happened to Sachie and Darsh—I banished that thought as swiftly as it came—Ezra would burn down the world to get answers.

This certainty, or the knowledge that were our positions

reversed, I'd do the same even now, even after everything, was set aside to be dealt with at a later date.

Meantime, the same perverse urge to annoy Delacroix—the one I'd had from our first meeting, and which now made total sense—drove me to raise an eyebrow. "Open a portal back to Vancouver, you miserable moray."

"Back to the alliteration, huh?" He snorted, which was all kinds of weird coming from a giant serpent.

However, a second later, the snake was gone, replaced by the Delacroix I knew and loathed. He was totally unharmed, once more in his sweater and jeans.

Water splashed up through the glassless windows and across the carpet, dowsing the remaining flames and soaking our feet.

Delacroix fished a cigarette out of his crazy hair with nicotine-stained fingers and used it to gesture from Maud to me. "You should take lessons from this one. She wouldn't screw up killing me, would you, girlie?" He leaned closer to me. "I see it in your eyes."

Great. Dad was playing favorites. He didn't seem to know I was his kid though. He wasn't treating me any different than he ever had, nor was he giving me some knowing look, and I was pretty sure he'd have alluded to it—or openly used it to his advantage.

"The portal, Delacroix." I scooped up Maud's Maccabee ring.

The air shifted into an oval rift strung with magic mesh.

"Happy?" He picked up the discarded flamethrower and lit his cancer stick.

"I'd say it's been a delight, but I've had more pleasant encounters stepping on Lego." My fine exit leading Maud out with my head held high was wrecked slightly by my hesitation to step into the portal in case it sucked us into a dark void or the bottom of the sea or something, but I continued on with a steady gait.

"See you at Brimstone Breakfast Club, girl detective. Don't make me repeat the invite."

"What? No way." I spun around, but the portal—and Delacroix's mocking smile—vanished.

The meager back room at the Jolly Hellhound was as wondrous a sight as Oz. I'd survived this entire fucked-up investigation with my secret intact and our suspect in my custody. All I had to do was determine Sachie and Darsh were safe, and the celebration could commence.

Maud bowed her head, looking fully human once more. "You let that demon win," she said brokenly.

I thought of Quentin taking his own life, Calista murdered, and Maud and I forced to hide our entire lives. "It wasn't about him winning," I said, "it was about making sure you didn't lose." I gentled my tone. "You've lost enough."

"Yeah, right."

I nodded at one of the tables. "Sit. I have questions."

She remained standing, glaring defiantly.

"Sit," I said in a hard voice. "Or I'll make your life miserable. You had a Maccabee ring and I want to know how."

She took her chair like a petulant child. "My mother's best friend was an operative. She was badly wounded in the line of duty and I…" She grimaced. "I asked for it as a token."

I held up the ring. "You're sure you didn't steal it?"

"I'm a lot of things, but I didn't stoop to stealing from my godmother on her deathbed."

I accepted it as truth. Crappy truth, but still. "You knew it killed demons."

Maud nodded.

I sighed, wishing my assumption hadn't been confirmed. "You're a smart woman, Maud, but you were blinded by emotion, and you didn't bother to find out the risk of using it."

"It really would have killed me?"

"Yes. If someone steals one from us and uses it, they'll be

274

sorry." I pocketed her ring. "Why didn't you wipe my memory as well? You must have seen me at the crime scene with your fire sight."

"You—you know about that?"

"Yeah. I'm a hell of a detective and I hate unanswered questions."

"I thought I had, but then you showed up at the hazard table and I was scared it hadn't taken because you were onto me."

Sachie was bang on about that.

"You were right it didn't take." I'd assumed it was because I was out of range when Maud had wiped the others, but now I worried it was because of Cherry. "But I had no idea you were involved until after you tried to blow me up. Thanks for that, by the way. Such a fun experience I never wanted."

Maud slammed a hand against the table. "I wanted a normal life, but when I couldn't get that I went for revenge. Won't be getting that either." She made a snarky face at me. "Thanks for that, by the way."

I tamped down my grin.

"Now what?" she said. "I rot in prison for the rest of my life?"

"We like to put people on trial first. Let a jury condemn you to rotting in prison. It takes it off our conscience."

She huffed a laugh. "You're a bitch."

"And you're not going to jail. Why would you, when Constantine compelled you to go after Calista?"

Maud's mouth opened. Then she closed it and frowned. "No one will believe that story."

I raised my eyebrows. "Are you or are you not a champion poker player?"

She scowled. "There's a world of difference between poker and this."

"Is there?" I shrugged. "It's not like he's around to dispute the story. Was he not old enough to compel?" Vamps under two hundred hadn't grown into that ability.

Maud took the news of Constantine's death wearing the poker face that had won her multiple titles so I couldn't tell if she was upset. "He was old enough."

I spun my Maccabee ring around, thinking through the story aloud. "Constantine was in love with Calista, but he was spurned and he was angry. She'd banned Quentin and destroyed his life because of some nothing vamp she'd turned but she rejected *him*? Initially, Constantine intended to use Quentin to get close to Calista and stake her, but the man's condition quickly drove him mad, and no one would believe he masterminded this plan on his own. Constantine knew your mother had been banned so you became his next patsy." I paused, grasping for the next piece.

"I'm a world champion poker player," Maud said huffily. "Word gets out I was duped and my rep goes to shit."

"Go to jail and see how many tournaments you get to compete in. He's an old vamp, he played you. Can you sell that? Yes or no."

Maud glared at me, then her expression twisted: big pleading eyes, a downturned mouth. She wrung her hands, but not too dramatically. "I liked him," she said plaintively.

"Good start."

She narrowed her eyes. "The memory I forfeited to you when we played hazard showed me flirting with him, right?" Off my nod she continued. "I'd been seducing him for months, plying him for tidbits on Calista's whereabouts, but it works the other way too. If we were seen spending time together, people would believe it was an affair, not him coaching me on what to do."

"Perfect. Constantine used those assumptions to his advantage and never bothered to seduce you. He compelled you from the start, and he kept reinforcing it. His death freed you from it, but you were too messed up by that point to know your own mind. I got the story out of you after I rescued you from Delacroix, whom you'd gone to see…" I shot a finger in the air in triumph. "Because that was the last part of the plan. Delacroix had to see you glamored as Calista to believe this was all your idea as revenge for your mother being banned. Constantine was going to kill Calista while you went to see Delacroix. He knew that staking her would torture her. He wanted her to suffer, but he had to finish her off. Meanwhile Delacroix would finish you off." I brushed my hands together. "Nice and tidy. Except I killed Constantine, and it all went to hell. So sad."

"Delacroix can refute this."

"He could, but I doubt he'll bother. He can blab that you came after him as his kid, but it doesn't negate you being compelled in the first place. If it comes to it, feed that into the story of what Constantine knew about you." I shook my head. "Anyway, I doubt Delacroix will be leaving that ship anytime soon." Other than going to Breakfast Club. "We got away because he let us, magic alarm system or not. That won't happen again. He'll tighten security on the portal."

She held out her hand. "Can I at least have my godmother's ring back?"

"Eventually. For now, I wouldn't mention anything about it. You asked for it under false pretenses and presumed to use it, even though you aren't a Maccabee. That will be held against you, so keep your mouth shut on the matter."

Every word of that was true. Did I also plan to use all the magic in the ring? Damn skippy I did. Its weight told me that it was still full of the magic cocktail. That was four demon kills, four chances to feed Cherry. Each time I depleted my stash and had to refill my ring, I used the override codes that I'd gotten from Michael. She was totally tracking how often I reupped, even if no one else was.

"Why would you do this for me?" Maud said.

"Like I said, you've lost enough." *And I've just found you.* I'd felt so alone my entire life, the only other people like me either murder victims or criminals. Violent, evil criminals, I amended. Maud wasn't that. "I also don't believe you're a danger to anyone else."

She finally dropped her neutral expression and regarded me shrewdly. "Okay," she said simply.

She knows.

That first spurt of fear was quickly followed by relief, because there was no judgment on her face, simply understanding. Still, I was a realist. Maud might be bluffing and plan to make her suspicions public. I assured myself they *were* suspicions, because if she had a shred of proof, she'd have said something in front of Delacroix, or leveraged that information to achieve her end goal.

Well, I didn't have any good way to silence her, and protesting would only confirm it. I was putting my trust in her having been as lonely as I was, and wanting someone in this world who would see all of her, without making her hide or hate herself.

I thought that you of all people would understand wanting someone who knew your secrets, to be there for you without having to ask.

I shook Ezra's words away.

"Ready to go?" I motioned for Maud to stand up. "I'll take you to Maccabee HQ and we'll sort things out. You'll be questioned, but so long as you stick to the story, you'll be fine."

She followed me to the door. "Maybe when this is all over, we could meet up sometime."

I'd always sworn that Sachie would be the next person I came out to. She was my best friend, my ride or die.

But she wasn't a half shedim.

And she wasn't my sister.

I shrugged. "I'll think about it."

Chapter 28

The second we entered the main part of the pub, Darsh and Sachie sprung up from their barstools, both of them rigid with tension.

Sach explained that they'd bounced right out of the portal. I gave a soft "thanks" to the universe that they were safe. Professional demeanor now, all the hugs later.

Darsh raked a quick but thorough gaze over me and took Maud from my custody.

Sachie grimaced at the blood clotting Maud's nostrils and the bruise over the bridge of her nose. "Did you do that?" she asked quietly, holding me back to speak to me while Darsh escorted Maud through the empty pub. "Michael is going to freak out if you get another complaint on an arrest."

"Maud attacked first," I said and headed for the door.

The Jolly Hellhound should have been open for lunch. Darsh must have commandeered it until my safe return.

"As you're a Chinese national, but the crime was committed on Canadian soil," he informed Maud when we caught up with them outside, "we'll be petitioning to have you tried here."

This was a tricky situation, because the Maccabee presence in China was tenuous. There was a rift to the Brink outside Shanghai and obviously Eishei Kodesh among the city's millions of people, but we were allowed only a minimal setup in that city, and none in any of the others. Hong Kong was an exception, since we'd established ourselves there during the one hundred and fifty plus years of British colonialism. The Chinese government let us stay when Hong Kong reverted back to them, but this might well test our privileges.

Luckily, my story cut through all those problems. "Maud was a victim. She won't be prosecuted."

I couldn't read the look Darsh shot me and that bothered me. I followed him over to Sachie's car, trying to catch his eye, but failed.

No one asked questions until we had Maud set up in the interview room in the basement at HQ. Sachie took her statement, while Darsh ensconced me in the conference room for my debrief. This was all fairly standard, but I would much rather have had Sach question me, because I could keep my racing heart and the sweat beading on the back of my neck from her.

I stuck to the truth as much as possible, keeping Maud's half-shedim nature a secret. When I brought up Delacroix's admission that he'd forced Ezra to kill Calista, I gave free rein to all my anxiety, hoping Darsh would take Ezra as the cause of my concern.

Sachie joined us with details of her interview. Maud's experience in bluffing and knowing how much detail to give away in order to win big served her well. Our stories matched up, not to the letter, which would have been weird, but in alignment enough to be completely believable. Like me, she'd stuck to the truth as much as she could, with the compulsion being the notable falsehood.

Maud even accounted for why she lied about her magic type her entire life, saying it was so rare that her mother was scared she'd be used by people wanting to take advantage of it. It was a justified fear for people with unique magic abilities.

We'd achieved the best possible outcome, but this was only stage one.

People weren't held accountable when committing acts under magic compulsion, however, the process to determine that was indeed the case was rigorous, going through various levels of specialists. Ordinarily, Maud would have sessions with a number of Maccabee psychiatrists, and with the director herself. Since Michael wanted Calista's abduction and death kept secret, Darsh wasn't sure how this would be handled. My testimony would likely have more weight, but he went upstairs with my debrief report and the interview tape to speak to Michael.

Well, he went after I crushed him and Sachie in a hug, telling them how scared I was that they were lost to the portal. They'd been torn between fears that the same had happened to me and that I'd made it in and was on my own in the Hell.

Sachie and I grabbed food from the fridge, got some tea and snacks for Maud, since she was still being held in the interview room, and collapsed on the sofas, waiting for Darsh to return. I told my friend how terrifying yet beautiful it was to behold Delacroix in his demon form and that my presence was expected at a future Brimstone Breakfast Club.

Sachie munched on a cracker. "That's not good, Avi. It's bad enough he coerced Ezra, a Prime, to do something for him, but if the shedim compromises you?" She shook her head. "Your career will be toast. Stay far, far away from him."

Would Sachie believe her career would be comprised being too close to a half shedim like me?

"I'll do my best," I said, "but I don't want him putting a target on my back because he's feeling ignored either."

"We'll figure out a way to keep you safe. Until you can kill him anyway. Our world will be better off without him."

"Yeah." I meant that with ninety-five percent of my heart.

A solid eighty-seven percent of it. Fine, I had to sort out my conflicting feelings between wanting him dead and wanting all the answers about who I was. I had secrets and a few minor sins on my conscience—jealousy and lust—but patricide? That was a flagrant disregard of twenty percent of Moses's commandments right there. Though Delacroix was a demon, so maybe killing him would be a mitzvah.

Remember how good it felt to kill Constantine? My mental picture of Cherry Bomb waggled her eyebrows at me.

I'd killed Constantine because he'd tried to kill me, and because vamp criminals tended to be staked instead of imprisoned, but that defense rang hollow. Maud had given the orders, and I was bending over backward to protect her. The truth was, it *had* been fantastic to give in to my bloodlust.

Darsh returned. He sank onto the edge of a chair and scrubbed a hand over his face.

"Well?" I prodded.

"Michael is going to question Maud and put her through an assessment with Dr. Olsen." She was bringing in one of the Authority Council to interview Maud? My mother really wasn't trusting the information of how a Prime had been abducted to just anyone. I rubbed my chin. Dr. Olsen was notoriously thorough. She'd broken supposedly rock-solid stories before.

I had to assume this one would hold, because if it tanked, I was going down with it.

"Where's Michael doing it?" I wasn't ready to face my mother so soon after my shedim family reunion.

"She'll be down in a few minutes," Darsh said. He knotted his silky brown hair into a bun at the nape of his neck. "She was oddly sympathetic to Maud's plight."

That possibility hadn't occurred to me, but it should have. My mother hadn't been compelled, but she didn't get involved with Delacroix knowing the truth either. I shuddered, trying to cover it with a cough like I'd choked on my sandwich, but ewwwwww. That demon and my mother had sex.

"She *should* be sympathetic," Sachie said. "Like you said, Avi, Maud is a victim."

"She's a survivor," I said.

There was no reason for Michael to assume that Maud was a half shedim and shared the same demon daddy as I did, but my stomach was a knot. I'd always assumed I was a one-off, not that I had siblings. Had my mother ever wondered about that or tried to look into it? Michael had never told me the demon's name. She'd said there was no point. If she knew him as Delacroix, that name was all over my debrief and Maud's interview. Was my mother aware of who I'd been crossing paths with?

I wished that I'd pressed her on my demon father's identity growing up, because right now, I had no clue what information my mother had and what might undermine my plan to get Maud out of any charges. I couldn't count on Michael's sympathy if Maud's true nature came to light, given the hard line my mother had taken with me.

There was a more pressing hard line to deal with, however.

"What about Ezra?" I said. "Is he safe from Maccabee retribution?"

"Provided he admits to being forced to kill Calista, then yes," Darsh said.

"He probably couldn't say anything at the time," Sachie said. "A magic bond would ensure Ezra's cooperation and his silence. But who knows if he can admit to it now?"

"True." Darsh leaned back against the sofa cushions. "Though there are ways around that in how we question him. I'm not as worried about what he can and can't say as what he will and won't. He's not one for sharing."

"That's not fair," I said. "He's come clean of his own volition a bunch of times, and I'm sure if he could have admitted what was up, he would have."

"Why did Delacroix let you leave?" Darsh said out of the blue.

I flinched then scrambled for something to explain my reaction. "What, you're saying that he was going to just keep me in the Copper Hell forever? Out of spite? That's a shitty thing to wish on someone."

"I don't wish it, but this shedim placed a magic gag on Ezra, yet he let you and Maud leave in one piece and report back?" Darsh shrugged, watching me. "Odd, don't you think, puiul meu?"

"Delacroix has taken a personal interest in Avi," Sachie said. "That was evident as soon as he invited her into the demon realm."

Darsh went dangerously still. "He what?"

Sach shoved my shoulder. "You didn't tell him?"

"Not on purpose. There was a lot going on and I forgot. He brought me for threats and his creepy senior's special."

"You're forgetting to share a lot of things recently," Darsh said. "My feelings are starting to get hurt."

"Darsh—"

The elevator doors opened, and Michael strode toward us. She gave Sachie and me a brief nod. "Good job."

That was it? This was the first time she'd seen me since I'd been in an explosion. Obviously, we were at work, and she'd never hug me, but could this have been more underwhelming? Was a simple "glad you're alive" too unprofessional for her? She'd sanctioned me pretending to be dead and feeding from Ezra. A little gratitude for the commitment to my job would not be unwarranted.

I kept a tight smile on my face as my mother passed me.

She paused. Then squeezed my shoulder and continued on her way. "Now where's Ms. Liu?"

"Over here." Darsh led the director to the interview room.

Sachie slung an arm around my shoulder.

I rested my head against hers. "When Daniel broke his leg, she arranged meals for his kids that first week." Our chapter head's custodian was a single dad, and it was very considerate of Michael, but I was her kid and all I rated was a shoulder squeeze?

"She holds you to a different standard," Sach said. "She always has. You know she cares about you. She's always made sure that people are clear that you've earned everything you've achieved." She sighed. "She just goes too far the other way with how she treats you in a professional context."

"Okay, fine, but it was me and my two best friends. You guys weren't going to report her for unprofessional conduct. I wasn't asking her to rend her shirt and wail. Just take two seconds and say, 'I'm glad you're alive.'" My chest was tight, and my mouth was dry as a desert.

I needed to get away, to clear my head and think. I mumbled some excuse to Sach about taking a walk and escaped.

Outside, people went about their normal lives, grabbing coffees, pushing strollers, and doing errands. Life still went on. Millions of people coursed through this city, unaware of the evil lurking. They bought lunch, chatted at stoplights, bumped into each other coming and going from work to home and back again.

It all seemed so fragile, a weary system with a delicate balance. We worked so hard for this to stay like this. Why did things have to change?

Maybe that's why my wandering led me to the hotel where Ezra was staying.

I wasn't exactly surprised to find myself peering through the glass front doors. Ever since his return, we'd been magnets, flipping poles to push and pull each other, and I could no longer handle our dynamic. Not in light of all the many other revelations of today.

Ezra had to leave—Vancouver and my life—once and for all.

I rode the elevator up to the penthouse suite, tapping my foot to stomp out my desire to seek emotional comfort from my ex after meeting my father.

Ezra answered the door, bleary-eyed and barefoot, in jeans and a T-shirt stretched tight over his torso. It bore a stylish logo from a vamp soccer team. He leaned his forearm against the doorframe, clinking the ice cubes in the glass of blood dangling from his hand. The drink reeked of booze.

I crossed my arms, seriously unable to believe he was feeling injured and sad after blowing up our team and ruining our mission. He'd gotten exactly what he wanted. "Am I interrupting your pity party?"

He swallowed some of his cocktail. "Just trying to fall asleep."

Eishei Kodesh vamps didn't require much rest, and Ezra as a Prime required even less. When he did sleep, he dropped into it immediately and deeply, though he remained always on guard for danger. We had a bet back then about whether I could grab Ezra's arm while he slept before he woke up and caught me. I got bored after seventeen days.

I never considered it beyond a cursory "huh," but Ezra let me be around him while he slept. Granted, they were cat naps not lasting more than ten or fifteen minutes, and he'd go elsewhere to sleep when Sachie was home, but he'd permitted himself to be incredibly vulnerable around me.

As proven, he'd wake up at the tiniest noise, so there wasn't a huge danger, but still.

"Aviva." Ezra rested his head against his arm braced on the doorframe. "What did you want?"

We'd gone from being more vulnerable with each other than anyone else, to being two feral cats circling each other.

I brushed off the heaviness in my chest. "I know that

286

Delacroix made you kill Calista in order to get free and leave the Hell that night."

"Girl detective badge unlocked," he said wryly. "Is that all or did you need something else?"

I frowned, expecting surprise or anger. Once again, Sachie, Darsh, and I had learned that the invincible armor that Ezra presented to the rest of the world had some major dings and chunks torn out of it. That he was not as he appeared. But he didn't seem to care at all.

I glanced to my sides at the long hallway leading to the elevator. It was very plush and very empty. "Can I come in?"

"I'm not up to company." He shut the door.

I jammed my boot forward before he could close it all the way. "Conquering the world is a bloody, messy business that's bound to do your head in."

He took another swig. "I'm too tired for whatever cryptic shit you're alluding to."

Was indifference his new armor or was something wrong? I narrowed my eyes. "Something" being the traumatic reality of murdering the only other person like him in existence? His desire for payback notwithstanding? I motioned at his left biceps. "Your tattoo. 'I dreamed of conquering the world.'"

Ezra stared at it for a moment then laughed harshly and walked away, leaving the door open.

I followed him inside, shut the door, and leaned against the wood. "What's so funny?"

"Nothing."

I clenched my fists. "Another secret to add to all the others. You keep all your cards so close to your chest, Ezra. Trying to understand you, to connect with you is exhausting."

"Is that what you've been doing?" He fired back his drink. "Connecting? I don't think that means what you think it means."

"We discussed this years ago," I snapped. "You're no

Inigo. Also, don't make me out to be some bitch. If you have something to say, then say it."

He set his glass down with a decisive clunk. "I take back the girl detective badge comment. You're a shitty investigator."

I sucked in a breath. "I'm an excellent detective. Think what you want of me personally, but don't you dare disparage my professional abilities."

"Oh, I dare." He prowled toward me, his silent footfalls only underlining the barely leashed violence in the set of his jaw and shoulders.

Oh, hello.

Shut up, Cherry.

"You think you're so clever," Ezra said, "but you couldn't even do a proper Google search, Sherlock."

"Meaning?"

He slammed his left hand against the door, level with my ear.

I flinched and glared at him.

His lips curled into a mocking grin, and he fired off something in Spanish.

"Slower and in English?" I attempted to smack his arm away, but I didn't budge it.

Ezra folded back his shirt-sleeve. The tattoo read *cuando era niño soñaba con conquistar el mundo*.

"Fine. I missed a couple of words. What of it?"

"When I was a kid, I dreamed of conquering the world."

"Mazel tov," I said sarcastically. "Your delusions started young."

"Ahora me doy cuenta que tú eres mí mundo y me has conquistador."

"What's that? A comment on how much I suck?"

"More or less. When I was a kid, I dreamed of conquering the world, now I realize that you're my world and you have conquered me." He placed his right hand on the other side of my head, effectively trapping me. "You only got part of the quote."

I barely heard him over the rushing in my ears. Ezra had never said he loved me when we were together. I hadn't expected it in our whirlwind six-month relationship, though it had been true for me.

I stared at the dark ink against his brown skin.

Was my best-case scenario really that he'd tattooed this on himself for another woman? The idea of him loving someone else made me want to vomit, but it had been six years since our breakup, and I doubted he'd lived like a monk.

But, fuck. It was so much worse if he had loved me just as much and still walked away. He claimed he didn't care about Cherry, but if that were true, he should have stuck it out with me. There was nothing we couldn't face together, not even his father's disapproval if he found out his prince and heir was seeing an infernal. I suspected that had a lot to do with it.

You're my world and you have conquered me. I reached for his tattoo with twitching fingers to trace the ink, but instead, I made a fist and slammed it into his gut.

His grunt didn't make me feel better because I may have broken a finger on his rock-hard abs. What a dick.

"You tattooed that incredibly beautiful saying on yourself as a cautionary tale? Asshole!" I punched him again. This time in the biceps, which were no less hard, but my hand was still mostly numb from my previous attempt at grievous bodily harm, so it didn't hurt. Not physically anyway.

He caught my hand. "Beautiful?"

"Objectively, yes," I said through gritted teeth, trying and failing to pull free.

His eyes crinkled at the corners, and he rocked back on his heels. "Want to know when I got it?"

"Nope."

"Right after our reunion in Michael's office on the last case."

This immortal vampire wanted a piece of me on his skin forever? I went still. Swallowing suddenly became very difficult.

"The second you saw me, you went right for my throat," he continued. "Metaphorically speaking."

"It was my consolation prize. I meant to go for your balls. Literally speaking."

"I know." His amusement vanished. "It wasn't a cautionary tale, and it wasn't penance. It was a realization, six years and a breakup too late, that for all my dreams of power, I'd been irrevocably and forever conquered."

Every fiber of my being quivered under the weight of his words, threatening to unravel me at the seams. The room seemed smaller, suffocatingly intimate, as though his admission had erected impenetrable walls around us.

I ducked under his arm and stomped deeper into the room. "Am I supposed to melt at that declaration?"

"A mild swoon might be nice." He stood there, his eyes soft, and his hands spread wide, with a soft grin tugging at his lips and that damn tattoo taunting me.

Fury rose hot and tight inside me. It wasn't penance? Well, it should be. I sauntered toward him. "I don't want a realization. I want you to taste regret like ash on your lips and to burn all the color from your world." I rose onto tiptoe and whispered in his ear, relishing his shiver. "Conquering you isn't enough, Ezra. I want to ruin you."

Chapter 29

Ezra's nostrils flared. "Then do it."

Lust pooled in my stomach, and my nipples strained against my sweater. I brushed them against his muscled chest, and he hissed.

His fangs scraped over my neck, and I arched into him, remembering the heady intoxication of drinking from him. His body had gone tense when my lips first touched his skin, each sound he'd made when I'd tasted his blood catalogued in my brain forever.

What would happen if he drank from me now? I shivered. This was the most dangerous thing I could possibly do, and I wanted to run headlong into it. Drinking from me wouldn't bond us, but still. Ezra was the last living Prime, my ex, and the one guy I shouldn't be left in the same room with. I knew all that, but none of it mattered. I wanted his teeth on my neck, to be closer than close to him, and damn the cost.

I swayed toward him, drawn by some heady magnetism.

"Aviva, no." Ezra's voice was ragged, and with effort, his fangs left my neck. "Not like this."

"You don't get to decide. You don't get to control this game. *I* conquered you, remember?"

"Still…" He rubbed a hand over the back of his neck. "I've never. Not with anyone."

"Not with me, that's for sure. You were so careful with me. So sweet," I taunted. "Ironic that you held yourself back only to break me anyway." I let my eyes flash green. "But I'm not so fragile, am I, Cardoso?"

I sucked on the hollow of his neck, licking the light, salty sweat, and then I bit down. It was with teeth, not fangs, and I didn't break the skin, but he reversed our positions with a growl. My back smacked against the wallpaper so hard, a painting crashed to the carpet.

Ezra rocked against me, his hard cock pressed against my thigh. "A lot of talk, Fleischer. I know you well enough to know you only do that when you're scared."

Well, I was a smart human being throwing caution to the wind to play some fucked-up sexcapade with her ex, so it's not like he was wrong. However, I was not one to back down from a challenge I'd started. I pulled my sweater off, leaving me in the magnificence of my lace push-up bra. "Maybe I want you to beg for it."

His lips ghosted across mine. "You'll be waiting a long time, sweetheart."

I popped the front clasp and dangled the bra off my finger before dropping it to the floor.

Ezra palmed my breasts. "Nice," he said, "but not worth begging for."

Why? Because they wouldn't rate in the boob pantheon you'd seen as Prime Playboy? My jaw hard, I undid the top button on my jeans and slid the zipper down halfway.

His gaze sharpened, tracking my hand as I ran it along my bare stomach and slid one finger under the elastic of my bikini briefs.

"Shall I continue?" I said.

He shrugged, but there was a tightness in his shoulders. "I don't get to decide. Your game, remember?"

"True, but you never could resist joining in when I played by myself." That last word came out in a moan as I fingered myself, already soaking wet.

A muscle ticked in his jaw.

I slid my finger in and out achingly slowly, my lips parting on a sigh.

Ezra caught my hand and sucked the finger into his mouth.

Fizzy bubbles exploded in my blood.

His eyes flashed almost pure silver, and his mouth crashed down on mine. He kissed me like I was his favorite memory. His lips tasted of booze and a faint tang of blood that snapped any last civilized impulse.

I slashed his shirt off with one swipe of my claws, then scraped the sharp tips along his biceps.

His response was to press more firmly against me, his kiss turning demanding and hungry.

My claws melted back into fingers that I raked tenderly through his curls. I was finding it hard to ignore things I hadn't felt in years, like being cherished by that one special person. A feeling that I could tuck away to draw strength from on a bad day like a talisman.

This kiss was restoring pieces that had fallen out of me so long ago, I'd assumed them lost forever, now slotting them back into place.

I stiffened, pushing Ezra until the backs of his knees hit the love seat. I shucked out of the rest of my clothes and bent over the top of the couch. "Fuck me."

Ezra flipped me over with one hand, like I weighed nothing. "If you're going to ruin me," he said, "have the decency to look in my eyes."

"Why? Worried I'll forget who's behind me?" I patted his cheek. "Aww, sugar."

"Worried I'll forget who's in front of me," he shot back.

I stilled. It was just for a split second: a cold dash of fear that I wasn't holding the reins, much as I wanted to believe otherwise. I immediately masked it with a cocky sneer, but Ezra had clocked it.

"Aviva." He brushed the back of his hand across my jaw.

I smacked it away and wrapped a leg around his waist. "My rules."

His expression hardened. "My mistake."

His next kiss wasn't combustible passion, it was a methodical grinding down of my defenses, like water carving a canyon through perennial cliffs. He threw all his weight into that embrace. All his attention. It was slow and thorough, his tongue tangling with mine. The hairs of his short-cropped beard tickled my skin, but it wasn't unpleasant.

That same liquid lightning sensation as when I'd drank from him snaked through me like a lazy river, except it didn't come from his blood. It was the taste of his lips on mine and the feel of his naked chest under my hands as I relearned the planes of his body.

The relief of getting to touch him this way again was almost painful.

My chest was heaving when I came up for air. "Condom. Now."

"Bedroom. Now." He picked me up and sprinted from the room before placing me carefully on his mattress, not unlike how he'd cradled me when I was wrapped in the burn blanket. Like he was scared I'd break.

The sheets were cool under my back, and the room smelled like him. I sat up, watching Ezra disrobe and grab a foil package from a drawer. A Prime could get a human pregnant, and we'd always been careful in that regard.

I studiously did not think about why he had one handy.

He tore it open, and I took the condom from him, desperate to roll it over his cock and feel how badly he wanted me.

Ezra watched me through slitted lids, his lashes a dark sweep against his skin.

He tensed when I wrapped my fist around him. He was hot and hard, and my insides were going rubbery with need.

I rolled the condom down and lay back on my elbows, watching him with a hooded stare.

He sucked his bottom lip between his teeth, fisting himself a couple of times. "I'm going to take you spreading your legs wide as enthusiastic consent."

"Don't jump ahead of yourself. You haven't earned enthusiastic." I rubbed my clit, grinding my hips in invitation.

He yanked my legs toward him, resting my feet on his shoulders. "I will."

"Have at it." My words ended on a breathy sigh as he sank inside me, that final missing piece snapping into place. It wasn't that he completed me, it was that I hadn't let myself be fully present with any other lover since him. Except, as I lay here, naked with him inside me, I didn't feel vulnerable. I didn't feel powerful either.

I was simply happy.

Neither of us moved, because this game had gotten suddenly and sensationally real. Ezra returned the dopey grin I was flashing him with a kiss to the side of my foot. He was filling me up from within and holding me down to keep me from floating away.

Ezra and I weren't easy together. Not anymore. I wouldn't be giving him a young woman's heart on a cushion. Let him in and I'd be handing him the keys to my kingdom, along with a map of all the structural vulnerabilities and trusting a ruthless vampire not to exploit them.

Again.

But what if he didn't? What if he paired ruthlessness with a devotion that lit up all those dark, neglected corners of my fortress?

My smile faded. This brief encounter was supposed to be

me making him regret walking away six years ago, not making sure he didn't do it again.

Still inside me, he slowly rolled his hips. "Now, this I'd consider begging for." He pursed his lips. "I mean, I'd say please."

I couldn't help it. I laughed.

He joined in, but his eyes darkened and he bit his fingers into my hips. "Naked, laughing, and under me. You have no idea how long I dreamed about being here again."

"Since I fed off you?"

He gave me a crooked grin. "Sure."

I didn't want confessions, damn it. Why didn't I appreciate secrets when I had them? This didn't change anything; it just made my heart hurt. "Don't get used to it." I slapped his bare hip. "Move already."

Ezra slammed against me, the movement rough and delicious, pinning me in place with one hand and running the other along my leg.

"That. More."

"That sounds suspiciously like begging, sweetheart." There was no heat to his words but there was to his kiss.

I wrapped my legs around his waist to take him deeper inside me, that tight coil heating to the point of becoming stardust scattered across the universe of my closed lids. I cried out his name when I came, my orgasm hitting me harder than it ever had.

Ezra followed with a hoarse shout.

I blinked my eyes open.

"Enthusiasm unlocked," he pronounced, his voice still a little breathy.

I shrugged. "Eh, I've had better."

"I haven't," he said seriously.

I wriggled backward to disengage. Oh no. I'd done what I came for, ticked that box, solved the problem of my attraction to Ezra. I wasn't supposed to unlock a much, much bigger problem. "You don't get to say that. That's not what this is."

"Make me take it back," he mocked.

I kept silent, not wanting to fight. Five minutes. I'd give myself that long to enjoy this, then I'd go. Walk away first exactly like I said I would.

Ezra got out of bed, and I bolted up, thinking I was about to be denied my chance at closure, but he strode naked into the living room.

He wasn't running off, just getting water or something. I closed my eyes, flexing my fingers and toes and enjoying the delicious ache in my body. Four minutes.

"Here." He dropped a light bundle on me. "Thought you might like this."

I opened my eyes to a puddle of crimson on my chest.

He'd knitted me a sweater in the exact same shade as my shedim hair. It was thigh length, with long sleeves that had those thumb holes in them to pull the fabric over my hands and keep them warm. *All* of it would keep me warm because it was the snuggliest garment I'd ever seen. Wearing it would be like being in a constant hug.

I brushed my cheek against it. Bunny fur was abrasive steel pads compared to whatever he'd used.

The light caught the threads, revealing that it wasn't one solid color. There was an ocean of crimson, folds that drew the light into dark depths and cuffs that glinted with sparkly accents.

It was the most beautiful thing I'd ever seen, and Ezra had made it for me.

He watched me practically hugging it, his eyes dancing, and a soft smile tugging at his lips.

I dropped the sweater like it was on fire.

Ezra flinched. He opened his mouth, but I was already bolting from the bedroom to retrieve my clothes.

I pulled them on with sharp, frustrated movements. This

was supposed to be hit it and quit it. Fuck Ezra's brains out and go. He could have knit me a scarf, an impersonal pair of gloves, something basic. Not something so beautiful that reflected a part of me that I'd shown to only him.

"What did I do wrong?" He came into the living room in jeans, a T-shirt slung over his shoulder, holding the sweater.

"Nothing. It's lovely." I mustered up a polite smile, but I also looked away so I didn't snatch it out of his hands. "Lovely" didn't come close to describing it. I wanted to come home after a hard day and slip into it, reveling in Ezra's thoughtfulness and care, but I was here to close a door, not keep one open. Accepting the gift and leaving was too cold-blooded.

Even for me.

"I have to go," I said.

"Why?"

"Because." I yanked on the thin hoodie I'd come here wearing. Backward. I muttered a curse and straightened it out. "This was supposed to be goodbye."

"A fuck for the road," he said icily.

He didn't get to be a willing participant and then play hurt. Anger flashed through me, making my hands tremble as I zipped up my jeans. "Well, you didn't stick around the Maccabees long enough to get a retirement watch, so I figured I'd give you a parting gift," I said nastily. "Killing Calista saved you a resignation letter, remember?" I jammed my feet into my boots and stuffed my socks in my pockets. "We both know you were never sticking around. You'd be reassigned. This was fun, and now we have a good final memory of each other. Better than our last parting, right?"

Ezra tossed the sweater on the sofa. Eyes glinting danger-ously, he was like a carving by Michelangelo. Untouchable perfection but as cold as marble.

He didn't get to retreat into some emotional fortress. Not

when I'd said I was here to ruin him. Not when he'd told me to.

Finish this, Cherry whispered.

I jerked my chin at his tattoo. "Consider yourself well and truly conquered, baby."

"Don't confuse being conquered with being compliant. I'm a Maccabee, too, remember?"

Maccabees were operatives, but we took our name from the resistance fighters who scored a major military victory over the powerful Antioch IV.

Had Ezra just declared his intention to fight for me?

"No," I said. "You *were* one. And you do not get to decide that the past six years don't matter." I'd fought hard to free myself from the heartbreak he'd left scattered like buried mines, which detonated without warning for years. "And I'm not some territory you get to lay siege to. You chose to be conquered, but you'll never decide that for—" I screeched and jumped backward.

A portal swirled open not five feet away from me. One strung with magic mesh.

"Wh-why is a door to the Copper Hell opening here?" I said, inching backward.

He shot it an annoyed glance and shrugged into his T-shirt. "It doesn't matter."

"*Doesn't matter?!* I sure as hell think it does!" I glanced from the portal to Ezra and then back again. "What did you do?"

He yanked on his leather hunting jacket. "So quick to assume I'm at fault."

"You're not freaking out, so yeah, Ezra, I think you did something. I demand to know what it is."

"You're not in any position to demand a thing." Ezra buttoned the jacket up from waist to chin.

"Tell me," I snarled.

He shrugged tightly. "Why do you think Delacroix let a Maccabee leave his yacht alive?"

"He wanted me to find Calista." I shook my head at him like that was obvious.

"Right." Ezra laughed mirthlessly. "He's a shedim, Aviva. You decided that was the full story, instead of only one chapter in it, because it suited you."

The portal had grown, crowding me back against the wall. There was a tension, an insistency to its pulsing, like a telephone that wouldn't stop ringing.

"Killing Calista was the price of your freedom. It wasn't a condition for me to remain alive." I paused. "Was it?"

"No. Killing Calista was the only way Delacroix would let me go free that night."

An eerie yowl emanated from the portal, sending shivers down my spine.

Ezra swore in Spanish. "Hold your horses," he muttered, rooting under the sofa and pulling out shoes.

Was I losing my mind? My head? Ezra wasn't handing me over to Delacroix, was he? The demon could have killed me when I faced him with Maud—why let me go? Had Delacroix decided Ezra was my ultimate weakness and he hoped to inflict the pain of yet another betrayal on me?

"Are you delivering me to him?" I said.

Ezra shot me such a look of contempt that it dissolved my fear.

I threw my hands up in the air. "Then if I'm not being offered to the sea demon, why are you going back?" My stomach twisted. "Did you martyr yourself for me? Strike some deal with Delacroix to let me remain safe?"

Ezra crouched down, focusing on his shoelaces like they were a complex math problem that required all his attention to solve.

"You traded your life for mine," I breathed.

"Ah, mi cielo." He stood up, eyes alight. "If I'm dead, how will I lay siege?"

I ground my teeth together at the term of endearment.

The first night we met, we stayed up talking and wandering around the city. Dawn found us sitting on the seawall at Stanley Park watching the sun. Ezra shared the Spanish word for "sky," and how he was so thankful he could still see the sky by day, unlike Trad vamps. That it was a precious gift he'd never take for granted.

He called me "mi cielo" for the first time less than a week later.

"Then what is happening here?" I had to yell over the portal's deafening growl.

Ezra stretched his arms out wide. "Meet Delacroix's new co-owner."

My mouth fell open, my emotions a tangled snarl. "You're the Lord of the Copper Hell?" I said contemptuously.

"You make it sound like I'm an escapee from Riverdance." He shoved his phone in his jacket pocket. "But yes. Consider it a mitzvah. I'm filling a power vacuum before things get ugly."

"Ezra, don't." I edged around the portal to stand face-to-face with him. "The Maccabees will let you back in if you tell them Delacroix forced you to kill Calista. Whatever reason you had for joining, don't sacrifice it for me. I can take care of myself. We'll deal with Delacroix after."

Ezra stepped between me and the portal. "I didn't sacrifice shit for you. Not everything is about you, Aviva. I didn't get the results I desired from the Maccabees."

Hadn't he joined to instigate his playboy cover story and fortify his defenses? That still felt true, but nothing about Ezra was easy. Why have one agenda when he could have three?

"What results?" I said.

"This is a better way to reach my goals." He flashed me a cocky smile. "Though I can't lay siege if you're dead either."

I wasn't his goal. Well, not the one he carried over from being a Maccabee to running the Copper Hell. I swallowed a frustrated scream and grabbed his arms. "You can't do this."

"I can do whatever I please." The Crimson Prince met and held my gaze relentlessly.

My grip on him tightened. If he left, if he became a party to my father's brand of pain and misery, I'd lose Ezra.

Or he'd lose himself.

"It's one thing for you to leave the Maccabees," I said urgently, "but do this and you draw a line between the two of us that there's no coming back from. We'll be enemies."

"You proclaimed me your personal nemesis first with that Count von Cardoso crap. You're so determined to make me your villain." Ezra broke free of my grip with a mocking salute. "Careful what you wish for."

He stepped through the magic mesh and was gone.

Once again, Ezra had walked out of my life in a shocking exit, but this time I was left standing. Confused and angry, but unbroken.

Delacroix's motivations, everything that had happened with Ezra since this case began, including tonight—I was certain I'd seen all of it clearly. I'd survived the Copper Hell, caught our suspect, and fucked Ezra out of my system. I'd triumphed with the winning hand.

Except all this time, I hadn't been playing cards or rolling dice. I'd been watching a shell game where the cup had finally been lifted, revealing nothing but air.

I picked up the sweater he'd made me, almost like it was a feral cat, and feeling only slightly foolish, I sniffed it. It still smelled like him. I slipped it over my head, sighing at the feeling of being inside a pillow that tumbled over me.

Ezra and I were definitely enemies now.

But we were far from done.

Chapter 30

I stared blankly out the window of the Uber on the ride home, wondering how I'd missed so much: the meaning of the tattoo, Maud's motives. Never had so much *not* been as it appeared. I prided myself on my ability to illuminate, not only physical weakness, but clarity in a situation, yet I'd had some pretty freaking huge blinders on when it came to things close to me.

I rubbed a hand over my chin. Did I have blinders on about anything else? Not bad things necessarily. Sachie believed that love was easy with the right person. She'd meant romantic love, but what about love for your best friend? Was my fear of losing her or scaring her off if I told her about Cherry blinding me to the possibility that she'd be okay with it?

It was worth thinking about.

My only other consolation was that I wasn't the only one who'd missed some crucial details. Delacroix hadn't seen Maud, his daughter, hiding in plain sight all this time and waiting to take him down.

He didn't see us either, Cherry whispered. *I can't wait to jump out and say boo.*

Yeah, that would be fun, but this was not about us. Maud

hadn't bothered to learn that using the ring could have killed her. She'd have been better off chucking a rock at him.

Or a heavy crystal. My chuckle died, my thoughts snapping to Sire's Spark.

Rukhsana and Jordy assumed I had it. Yes, I'd want a dangerous artifact removed from play, and I'd also gift wrap the other artifacts for the Trad cops to deal with.

They'd thankfully missed any deeper motivation in their conclusion.

But I could take their same hypothesis of a tireless defender of justice and pair it to a secret agenda. One also involving half shedim and a Maccabee with enough power and influence to make the things she wanted happen without question.

My mother was a complicated woman.

Once the artifacts were stolen, these different criminal factions were caught up in accusations and assaults, and the Trad cops were running around chasing their tails, she saw an opportunity and took it.

Michael knew the fences in town. She could easily have tracked this one down and stolen the artifact from him. I tapped a finger against my lip. She was a Yellow Flame, but she couldn't wipe people's memories. That didn't matter though. We had a Maccabee on staff who could. One who was fiercely devoted to my mother. Michael could have had that woman retrieve Sire's Spark, made sure the other artifacts got to the Trads, handled any witnesses, and not gotten her own hands dirty.

I changed my end destination to Mom's condo, intending to go in guns blazing. I let myself in, flipping on lights and calling her name, but the place was silent. I pulled out my phone to call her, but when I hit the home button to turn the screen on, my open text chain with her lit up.

I stared at the heart emoji she'd sent after my alleged death. Was it a sign of guilt, not connection? After all, she was more of a Maccabee than any of us. I'd never mistake her conquering her situation, i.e. having a half-demon child she'd trained to keep her real nature secret, for compliance—an acquiescence or resignation in having an infernal as a daughter.

Shoving the phone in my back pocket, I headed into her office and moved the painting of an Icelandic sky away from the safe. Michael kept her will in it, and she'd trusted me with the code years ago.

I almost laughed at myself as I punched the numbers in. Suppose she did steal Sire's Spark, she wouldn't hide it here. It was too obvious.

You mean hiding in plain sight? Cherry pointed out.

The safe door swung open.

I didn't immediately look inside, because once I did, there was no going back. I sat with the hope that I was wrong, then I took a deep breath and pulled the door wider.

My heart sank.

Cautiously, I reached for Sire's Spark, stopping short of making contact. I didn't feel any magic, but that didn't mean anything in terms of whether it had power or not. However, it was safer this way, because that meant any magic in it had to be activated. The items that emitted a vibration were the ones you had to beware of. They could mess you up with the brush of a fingertip.

In spite of my better judgment, I hefted the octagonal crystal, the rough artifact filling my palm. I closed my hand around it and sliced it through the air, its soft pink color catching the light.

I must have come up with a dozen explanations for why my mother had done this, but only one made sense.

My mother was tangled up in this mess involving the dead half shedim, and their missing blood. Had she shut me down from investigating further because she was trying to protect me? Stop me from jeopardizing her own search? Or keep me from learning how deep her disgust for infernals went?

I glanced at a photo of Mom and me at my graduation ceremony from Maccababy to level one operative. She had tried to talk me out of joining the organization a million times, but that photo caught me tapping my brand-new Maccabee ring to hers, like we were superheroes about to unleash our joint powers. She'd rolled her eyes but she'd laughed, and that's when the shutter clicked.

It was one of my favorite memories of the two of us.

Part of me longed to walk away before I learned something that irrevocably tainted that memory, but it was already too late. I shot the photo one last rueful glance, then placed Sire's Spark back in the safe, careful to leave it like I'd found it.

I shut the safe door with a quiet click. It seemed my mother and I were both keeping secrets.

But as I'd said earlier, I was an excellent fucking detective.

THANK you for reading DEMON ON DECK.

If you enjoyed this book and want to be first in the know about bonus content, reveals, and exclusive giveaways, become a Wilde One by joining my newsletter: http://www.deborah wilde.com/subscribe

You'll immediately receive short stories set in my various worlds and available FREE only to my newsletter subscribers.

Aviva's next adventure will be **BETTER THE DEMON YOU KNOW (Bedeviled #3)**

Evil has a scent: lemon.

It was supposed to be a routine drug bust. Arrest some magic jerks and move on, but then a fellow operative is murdered, and Aviva is thrust into a perilous black ops mission to disprove corruption charges.

Meanwhile, her half-sister is being blackmailed for being

an infernal, and as Avi struggles to protect her, she's set on a collision course with the one person she hoped to never meet.

And just when she thought things couldn't get any crazier, her ex drops a bomb about second chances.

Aviva must navigate a minefield of love, betrayal, and powerful Maccabees gunning for her, to expose her enemies—and keep her secrets hidden. But hey, running for your life is good cardio, right?

Pre-order it now!

Acknowledgments

Thank you to the usual suspects who make my books and my world a better place: my editor, Dr. Alex Yuschik, my husband, and the world's best kid.

About the Author

Deborah Wilde is a global wanderer and hopeless romantic. After twelve years as a screenwriter, she was also a total cynic with a broken edit button, so, she jumped ship, started writing funny, sexy, urban fantasy, and never looked back.

She loves writing smart, flawed, wisecracking women who can solve a mystery, kick supernatural butt, banter with hot men, and still make time for their best female friend, because those were the women she grew up around and admired. Granted, her grandmother never had to kill a demon at her weekly friend lunches, but Deborah is pretty sure she could have.

"Magic, sparks, and snark!"

www.deborahwilde.com

Made in the USA
Coppell, TX
24 March 2024